When She Walked on White Lake

Originally published as A Multitude of Mercies

Fay Harvey

Gotham Books

30 N Gould St.
Ste. 20820, Sheridan, WY 82801
https://gothambooksinc.com/

Phone: 1 (307) 464-7800

© 2024 *Fay Harvey*. All rights reserved.

No part of this book may be reproduced, stored in a retrieval system, or transmitted by any means without the written permission of the author.

Published by Gotham Books (September 13, 2024)

ISBN: 979-8-88775-831-2 (H)
ISBN: 979-8-88775-829-9 (P)
ISBN: 979-8-88775-830-5 (E)

Because of the dynamic nature of the Internet, any web addresses or links contained in this book may have changed since publication and may no longer be valid.

The views expressed in this work are solely those of the author and do not necessarily reflect the views of the publisher, and the publisher hereby disclaims any responsibility for them.

"This Editor's Choice Book of the year award winner is a beautiful tale of one sister's fear, despair, hope, and love for another... A story with wide audience appeal, it is poignantly touching while at the same time revealing in the laugh out loud antics that help keep her and her relations from falling into self-pity."

—Victoria Sutherland, publisher of Foreword Magazine 2005

"Superb and stunning... a page-turning onslaught that will result in you burning dinner and holding your bladder until the very last possible moment. Ms. Harvey (name changed) doesn't do this through trickery or thriller-esque manhandling. She does it the old fashioned way—through great writing."

—Independent review from the blog, Girl on Demand

"Be aware that if you read this book, you will be alternately laughing, crying, and marveling at the unexpected gems of wisdom found throughout."

—Judith Lamontagne, freelance editor and retired English professor at Cal Poly Tech

"A Multitude of Mercies is moving and touching, tender and poignant. It is a story of love and acceptance... ruthless in its honesty. She writes with empathy and care, lovingly wrapping Laura's story around the family who never gave up on her. You will cry buckets of tears, but you will also laugh and cheer, rage and weep and wonder about the unfairness of it all and be inspired by this family's unrelenting faith.

(This book) is a touching reminder that at the heart of doing the best we can, it is our loving kindness and compassion for those who are suffering which makes the difference."

—Susan Brown at Pacific Book Review Star

Table of Contents

Prologue ix
Chapter One 1
Chapter Two 22
Chapter Three 26
Chapter Four 40
Chapter Five 52
Chapter Six 65
Chapter Seven 71
Chapter Eight 82
Chapter Nine 89
Chapter Ten 98
Chapter Eleven 108
Chapter Twelve 122
Chapter Thirteen 136
Chapter Fourteen 147
Chapter Fifteen 164
Chapter Sixteen 171
Chapter Seventeen 187
Chapter Eighteen 197
Chapter Nineteen 213
Chapter Twenty 219
Chapter Twenty-One 229
Chapter Twenty-Two 241
Chapter Twenty-Three 249
Chapter Twenty-Four 260
Chapter Twenty-Five 268

Chapter Twenty-Six 282
Chapter Twenty Seven 295
Chapter Twenty Eight 303
Chapter Twenty-Nine 314
Chapter Thirty 320
Chapter Thirty-One 326
Chapter Thirty Two 330

I remember thinking back to what I had been doing the day my sister, Leah, left her body—where I was at 11:30 in the morning. I hadn't felt a thing. I was standing in my kitchen making fondant flowers for a wedding cake to be delivered that weekend. She had died without my even knowing.

I wish I could say I paused, or that I felt a sudden loss, or sense of peace, or understanding. I should have felt something to mark the immense change that was taking place in my life. I should have felt her death. The bonds of sisterhood, though stretched thin over thousands of miles, should have proved strong enough for me to feel the slack at the other end when she let go.

She died on April 16, 2003 around 11:30 in the morning, but I didn't know it until about 9:30 that night. I'd come home from a church meeting, wearing a pair of shoes I'd bought because they seemed like something she would wear. As I came in the door, I immediately noticed a shocked look on my husband's face. He spoke three anguished words that still cause me physical pain to recall.

"Leah died today."

When I learned of her death, I had just finished chapter fifteen of a book we both agreed I should write, and for a while, I lost its direction along with her. But in finishing it, I have found her again. I discovered that she never really left me. I believe she stood over my shoulder as I finished it because I have felt her with me. We are bound together again in the pages of this book.

I do believe in God. I also believe he took a strong interest in Leah's life, and that he took her to him as a loving father would, to say, "It is enough. Come home."

This book is for Leah Ann Harvey, graduate of the University of Nevada, Reno, honor roll student, who struggled for seven long years in the clutches of schizophrenia.

It is also dedicated to those who were fortunate enough to know her.

Prologue

"Are you coming or not?" Laura demanded as she stood bent between two wires of the fence.

I stood hesitantly, staring at the faded, rusty "No Trespassing" sign. "I don't think we should go in there. Mama's gonna kill us if she finds out."

Mama told us never to go out there. She was afraid of the alkali and warned us never to go out onto the dry lake, where there was a large concentration of it in the white dirt. Alkali is poison in large amounts. It's the kind of poison that burns from the inside out, not sudden, like acid, but slow, festering 'til it made that old lake deader than a mud puddle. No fish, no boats. It was too shallow for that, when it held water, and too treacherous to swim in. The lake killed two little girls a long time ago.

They went to swim in it when their Mama wasn't home. One got stuck, mired down in the mud and her sister drowned trying to save her. The lake claimed them both. No one went out there anymore, not even when it was dried up, like it was now. I stood right where I was.

Laura shrugged, rolled her eyes, and squeezed her way onto the alkali flat, leaving the taut wires vibrating behind her. She didn't look back to see if I was coming. Though she was four years younger than I, she was twice as brave, or ornery, depending on how you looked at it. Sometimes I wasn't sure if she was really all that brave, or if she just did things to make me look bad in comparison. See, I'm doing it. I'm no chicken.

"I'll stay here and watch for the cops," I called after her.

She shrugged, but didn't hesitate. She headed straight for the small lump of fur that we'd been watching for several minutes. We'd been walking along the highway when we heard the screech of brakes and a sickening thud. Yelping pitifully, the dog got up and limped onto the alkali basin—the dry lake bed—before he collapsed.

I watched as Laura bent over its still form. "Be careful! It might bite you!" I called.

Ignoring me, she got down on her knees and stroked its back. Even from a distance I could see its body quiver at her touch. It growled.

"Come and help me, will ya?" she hollered over her shoulder. "He's hurt pretty bad."

I squeezed awkwardly between the wires of the fence and ran to her side.

The black dog was bleeding badly. It was obvious it would soon be dead.

"Laura, just leave it."

"We have to do something!" As she spoke she reached again toward the dog, who growled menacingly.

"It probably has rabies, Laura. Don't touch it!" I scolded, pulling her away.

"It's not his fault if he does. Poor thing. What should we do?"

I sighed in exasperation. There was nothing we could do as far as I could see. I liked animals as much as the next person, but I knew I didn't have that soft place in my heart for them that Laura had.

"Let's go home," I said. We were late already and Mama had decided to see if she could go off her medication again. She'd been very short with us lately. The last thing we needed to do was get on her bad side. Mama without her Prozac scared me more than just about anything.

The dog put his head down and panted. His eyes rolled back into his head. I could see it was dying—anybody could see that. I pulled at Laura's sleeve.

"You go on home if you want. I'm staying here." she said, kneeling again at its side. She put a hand across his back, but he was too weak now to protest. "Poor boy! Do you have a name? What shall I name you? Buddy? That's a good name. Poor Buddy," she cooed softly.

Buddy's breathing became shallow. His muscles twitched. Bright red blood matted his fur in grotesque clumps and spilled onto the hardened clay bottom of the dry lake, his final bitter resting place. I looked away.

Laura was quiet when we finally walked home, past the pump jacks that never ceased to plumb the depths of the alkali laden dirt for oil. Laura stopped to stare at them as they bobbed slowly, silhouetted against a blaze of orange sky. Sudden tears ran in dark pink streaks down her freckled face, cleaning the dust from her cheeks as they fell. She picked up a rock and threw it at the pumps. "You don't care!" she hollered. "You never stop, do you? I hate you! Big, stupid, good for nothing rigs!"

The rock fell pitifully short and skidded to a stop, raising a tiny ghost of dust. I looked over at her as we walked back to the road and saw that she was still crying as she tried to brush off the white dust that clung to her jeans. She was crying over a dead dog, a dog she had named Buddy only minutes before he died. But then, Laura was like that. I didn't always understand her. I felt like I might cry too as we walked, but I wasn't sure why. I didn't feel all that sad for the dog, but Laura made me sad that day because it was the first time I ever wondered what made her different from the rest of us.

Chapter One

"There's a difference 'tween being sick in your body and being sick in your head," Grandma explained to Mama as they sat on the porch. "You tell someone you've got a cold, they say they hope you get better. You tell someone you've got diabetes, they feel sorry for you. You tell someone you're a schizophrenic with serious paranoid tendencies, they scoot their chair further away." She studied her stitches, then continued, "What can they say anyway? Sorry you're crazy? They can't say, 'Oh, it's been goin' around. Had that myself last week.' They don't tell you about their aunt Verna. The one they all suspected lost her marbles when she started setting out the fine china for her cats and took up smoking a pipe and singing "Swing Low" 'stead of saying her prayers at supper. Aunt Verna's the one people just don't talk about to outsiders. Sure they send a pie once in a while, or a card, or come in just for a second, leaving the kids in the car to make sure the visit will be short."

Grandma sighed and rocked quietly, her fingers flying with her knitting.

"I know it," said Mama. "The question I wonder about is this, when do you tell someone you're not right in your head? Do they need to know?"

Grandma sighed and shook her head.

"I just don't know what I should do." Mama continued. "How long should she date a man before the family starts pressuring her to 'tell him now, before your heart gets broke again,' or 'tell him straight out so he knows what he's getting into, or 'don't tell him nothin' 'til he gives you a ring.' Uncle Theo seems to think Laura's freckledy face and pecan pie ought to be enough to keep any man."

Mama shook her head and was quiet for a time as they rocked together before she spoke again. "Everybody has an opinion about what Laura should do. For Pete's sake, all I want for her is to be happy." Her voice was choked with sadness. "I've thought about that one a good long time and, bless her heart, I don't see how we're gonna get her married."

I was doing the dishes inside the house and could hear them through the open window. Mama and Grandma had come over to help with Thanksgiving since I was pregnant again.

The entire house had smelled of both nutmeg and sage. There were the proverbial too many cooks in the kitchen as my mother, my grandmother, Aunt Helen and I twisted and turned and bumped about in the kitchen in the final rush to get everything out to the table. I didn't make things any easier, seeing as how I was almost as big as a house, but I refused to sit on the couch as Helen suggested several times. This was my kitchen, after all.

It was my first time hosting Thanksgiving at my house for the family and I was determined to have everything perfect. And it was, all but the green Jell-o that had refused to come out of the mold. The turkey was done to perfection, the skin crispy and golden. It had been a good crust day for me when it came to the pies. Perfect crust only happened for me just once in a while and I was thrilled that today had been one of those rare occasions.

We added all three leaves to the table and used every chair in the house to set around it. Sam the dog lay beneath it with his head on his paws, his brown eyes hopeful.

Uncle Theo's blue eyes beamed as he took in the bounty and Grandma Alice swatted his hand away as he reached into the fruit salad to steal a strawberry.

I stood in the doorway of the kitchen, feeling nostalgic over the whole thing as everyone gathered around the table and began to take their seats. Everyone was there except for Laura, who had decided to spend the holiday with her boyfriend's folks.

The table looked beautiful like that, piled high with food. I sighed contentedly. I'd pulled it off. That's when the phone rang and Daddy, who was closest to it, picked it up.

"Now who'd call at a time like this?" Aunt Helen wondered out loud as she eyed the phone impatiently.

'This is George Harris," he replied to the receiver. Daddy's face looked grave as he listened. The entire room suddenly went quiet as everyone watched him stand there, his knuckles white as he clutched the phone.

"Alright," he said quietly, almost secretively. "I'll be there as soon as I can." There was a pause, then he said, "Yes, I'm leaving right now."

He hung up the phone and put on his jacket. "Dora, would you come in here a minute?" He asked Mama.

"George, what is it?"

He took her into the kitchen. I followed them.

"It's Laura," he said. "She's sick again. I'm going to go get her."

"Oh no!" Mama whispered. "Where is she?"

"She's in Greentree, there at the clinic." As he spoke he headed for the door.

"Try to get everyone cleared out, Nan, before we get back. I'll take the long way."

"I will, Daddy," I said.

I looked to Mama, whose eyes were so sad. "What are we going to do?" I asked.

"We're gonna sit down and have some dinner," she said, squaring her shoulders as she headed back out to the dining room. Everyone tried to look like they hadn't been straining to listen. Mama paused, her strength wavering for just a moment.

To say there was an awkward silence would be an understatement, but it was short lived as Theo said impatiently, "Well, are we gonna eat this food, or what?"

Mama smiled at him appreciatively. "Yes!" she said almost too cheerfully.

"Yes, let's do. Will you bless it, Theo?"

I'd actually never heard him pray before, but he was game. He cleared his throat before bowing his white head. "Lord, bless this food—if it ain't too much trouble. Bless the turkey so it won't be dry, bless the dressing so it won't be soggy, bless me that I can remember to save room for the pie…and bless Laura, who couldn't be with us. Amen."

There were a few chuckles around the table and Helen glared at him. "Disgraceful," I heard her whisper under her breath as she reached for the potatoes.

For Mama and me, it was probably the longest dinner of our lives. I tried to look cheerful. Mama managed it better than I did. All I could think about was that Laura was sick again, and sick didn't mean she had a cold.

I was there when it first happened—when she first got sick and was touched by God. Some would say she was touched by demons. I just tell it like I see it.

It was seven years ago, just after I miscarried my first baby. I was called down to the clinic again less than a week later. Something was wrong with Laura.

I got myself out of bed and walked out into February—my thoughts more chilling than the unusual breeze that managed to make even Texas feel cold. I was half froze before I got there, and scared half to death.

My mind whirled. What did the nurse mean? What was wrong with Laura? My mind snapped to attention with the touch of the cold door handle. I looked up and saw Clance, Laura's fiancé, standing in the waiting area. He squinted at me, creasing his tanned face as he repositioned his black Stetson over perfectly greased hair.

"She's possessed!" he said in a loud whisper. "Said she's got evil spirits in her. Won't let me touch her."

He stood behind me, arms folded, as Regina, the head nurse, approached. Her overwhelming perfume choked out any breathable air in the hallway.

"Oh, you're here!" she said, sounding relieved. "Yeah, where is she?"

"Now wait a minute, Honey," she said, putting her hand on my shoulder and leading me down the hallway past the front desk. "She's had a severe psychotic break. It will be scary for you, and since I know you were just in here last week..." she faltered.

"I'm alright," I assured her. "Been bleeding just a little bit now." As I spoke, I put my hand over my belly, then caught myself and had to swallow the lump that came to my throat. A baby had been in there only a week ago, and now it was gone.

We stopped before a closed door.

She nodded her sympathy. "That's good...that's good. You'll be back to normal in no time." She creased her thick lipstick covered lips in what must have been a smile.

Normal? How could I ever feel normal knowing something had actually died inside me? And knowing that something had taken Laura? I took a deep breath and started to open the door.

Regina reached out and stopped me. She looked into my eyes, her brow wrinkled. "Now, Laura isn't herself and I'm telling you that before you go in there."

She shook her head in dismay, her large brown eyes oozing sympathy. "Sure wish we could've got hold of your husband first."

Why did everyone think I was so fragile? "I said I'm OK. Harold's working late this evening. He said I shouldn't expect him 'til eight."

Regina reached for the knob, then turned and spoke over my shoulder.

"Now Clance," she said irritably, waving him back. "I told you she doesn't want to see you. No sense getting Laura more upset. Go on and sit in the waiting room."

Clance jerked around and stalked back down the short hallway, clenching his fists. "Wedding's in two weeks, damn it! What am I supposed to do? Those stupid invites she sent cost eighty-five dollars!" he shouted over his shoulder.

I never liked him, and even now, after all this time, I wish I would have just told Laura so.

The hair stood up on my neck as Regina opened the door. Laura sat on the torn white paper that covered the examination table with her back against the wall, her feet stuck out in front of her. The laces of her untied loafers were a jumbled mess. I barely recognized her as she sat there clenching her hands together in a tight ball on her lap. Laura's whole body seemed stiff and statue-like. Her face was all red and blotchy, her eyes wide open, her mouth devoid of color. Her dark, curly hair was all mussed up and in her face.

I could see right away that she wasn't herself. She was arguing with the doctor, her chin jutting defiantly. Normally Laura was a little shy with strangers, meek and soft spoken.

"Fine," she was saying, "you call it what you want, but I'm possessed, I know it. Let 'em in myself last night when I was reading the Bible."

She turned at the sound of the door and saw me. "Oh Nan, you're here! It's about time. I can't get anyone here to listen to me. No, don't touch me. It's not safe."

I pulled back and stared at her. She stared right back, her eyes boring into mine. "Laura's with us now," she whispered mischievously.

"What are you talking about?"

"They wanted to come in and I let them. I was praying as hard as I could so I would know if God wanted me to marry Clance or not, and they came—the lost spirits. We came."

Laura stared at me for at least a minute, a challenging look in her dark blue eyes. "You don't believe me either." She began furiously tearing at the paper on which she sat, never taking her eyes off me.

I felt sick. I couldn't believe any of it. This couldn't be happening.

"I just don't understand what's happening yet, that's all." I said meekly.

"They don't like Clance," she said. "Don't let him in again."

"I won't. Are you OK?"

She stopped tearing and finally looked away as she sat back against the wall.

"No."

The doctor, I can't remember his name now, said she needed to go to the mental health facility in the Falls—almost fifty miles away. "The sooner the better," he urged. "We don't have the facilities to take care of mental patients."

"But she says she's possessed. Shouldn't we get the pastor in here?" I asked him.

"I don't think she's possessed. She's just been under too much stress with finals and planning her wedding. She's had a psychotic break." As he spoke he drew a picture of an old fashioned water tower, the kind that empty into passing trains. "Here's how much stress a person is supposed to take," and he drew a line across the well. "Here's what happens when there's too much. It's just got to tip and spill. That's what's happened. It will take quite a while for her to get back to normal—if she does."

There was that phrase again—back to normal.

The doctor continued, "I explained all this to her fiancé out there, but he seems to like the idea of her being possessed a little better. I'd suggest you keep him away from her for a while. Do you have a car?"

"Harold and I just have the truck and he's using it to haul today. Clance is the only one I know who isn't working in the middle of the day."

"Well, I guess that'll be OK. Just keep her as quiet as possible. She's not dangerous," he reassured me.

I walked back to the waiting room where Clance was dozing with his dusty black Stetson pulled over his face.

"Hey Clance? Can you give us a ride into The Falls?" I asked.

His head jerked up. He looked at me warily a minute, then his eyes narrowed.

"What?"

"Can you give us a ride? The doctor says Laura can't stay here and that they can help her up in the Falls." I hated having to ask him for anything.

"Aw, she'll be alright. She's just been on a diet again. I told her myself she better start eating something other than salad. It ain't healthy." He scratched his armpit. "We'll stop by the Seven Eleven on the way to your place and get her one of them jumbo hotdogs. Get some meat in her, you know. Maybe call the pastor over to exorcize her just in case. She'll perk up."

I wanted to slap him. I clenched my teeth.

"No, Clance. She's really sick and I'm afraid. We've got to take her in."

He yawned, exposing several silver teeth, then scratched his elbow. He sighed impatiently. "Alright. 'Bout out of gas though. Got any money?"

"We can stop by my place on the way. I've got some there."

"Okay then, let's hit it." He got up, fishing his keys out of his pants. "I'll wait out in the truck."

The drive there was awful. We stopped by my apartment and I grabbed my laundry money and packed some of her things into a duffel bag, my hands shaking as I did so. I handed the only money I had to Clance before hopping up into his truck.

At the gas station he bought some gas and a large bag of M&Ms, the kind you pour into a big bowl for parties. He didn't give me my change but instead tore open the bag and perched it up between his legs. He sat and ate every one of them as he drove, his right arm along the back of the seat. He steered with his knee each time he reached in for more. Laura sat between us, staring straight ahead. His fingers kept brushing against my shoulder as he stroked her arm. I felt sick.

"Take your arm off her!" I wanted to scream, but I kept quiet and looked out the window as the chalky white dry lake rolled by. I watched the ghost of a dust devil dance across the clay a few moments before it disappeared. I stole a glance at Laura. She'd been watching it too.

Laura didn't talk much, but when she did, she used her own name as if she were talking about someone else.

"Laura is a good girl," she said, smiling. "Laura didn't want any of this to happen, but it did." She laughed. "Bet Clance didn't want any of this to happen." She said, her voice suddenly ugly.

I could tell she didn't like him touching her. She moved her feet back and forth rhythmically as we drove, like a cornered cat flicks its tail.

Finally, we pulled up to a large brick building with a white sign out front that read "Pleasant Hills Mental Health Center."

I took Laura's hand and pulled her to the reception desk. "Um, hi. My name is Nancy Parley and this is Laura…the doctor called you…um we're here. I…don't know…well, are you going to check her or something?"

She pushed a button and a nurse came and took Laura's hand. "Don't touch me," Laura said, jerking back her hand.

"Laura, she's going to help you. Please go with her," I urged.

Laura stared at me a moment. "You aren't leaving me here are you?"

"No, I'll be right here 'til you get back, okay?"

Laura stared at me a moment before turning to follow the nurse.

"Can I use your phone?" I asked the receptionist. My hand shook as I dialed.

I called Harold. "Honey, something's happened," I said even before hello.

"What is it?" he asked in sudden concern. "Are you okay?"

"I'm fine, but Laura…well, something is wrong with her. I don't even know how to say it. It's like she's…crazy or something."

Harold was quiet on the other end of the line.

"I'm here at Pleasant Hills Mental Institute with her. I guess we're gonna check her in."

"Whoa, slow down, Honey. You're where?"

"I'm at that place off the highway in The Falls, the mental health hospital.

Clance drove us here, but I don't want to ride home with him by myself. Can you come pick me up?"

"I'll get off as soon as I can. Are you alright, Honey?" he asked.

"I think so, I'm just worried about her. I'm a little scared."

"I'll tell Chet I need to leave right now, then. Hang on, Baby."

"OK, I love you."

"Be there in a bit."

I came back to the waiting area and sat two seats away from Clance. "You don't have to stay. Harold will be here in a couple of hours."

"Nah, don't have nothin' else to do. How's old Harold? Haven't seen him in a while."

"He's good. Chet likes him."

"That's saying something! Chet doesn't like anybody. I'm working at the dairy now, so he can shove it, for all I care.

I knew there was no love lost there. Clance had worked exactly two days for

Chet's Lumber before getting fired.

Clance was as mean as a starved, stray dog. Sometimes I wondered if that was why Laura let him into her life in the first place. Some dogs, though, are beyond help, and will steal all they can from you 'til eventually you have to kick them out the door and throw a rock after them to make your point. But Laura would never do that, not even if the dog bit her. I was glad when he got up and walked to the other end of the room to turn up the TV.

Finally, they brought Laura back out to us.

The nurse who held her arm was an older, tired looking woman. She motioned me over to the desk and looked at me out of large watery eyes. "We will admit her if you'll sign this." She held out a stack of papers. "Does she have insurance?"

"I think so. She's staying with me so she could go to school, but I think she's still covered under my Dad. He lives in Arizona."

"Write his number down then," and she indicated one of the lines on the form.

I looked down at the papers. "Laura, do you want to stay here?" I could hear my voice shaking a little as I asked.

"They said they could help me, so I guess I better."

"Okay then, here we go," and, just like that, I signed her up as incapable of being able to take care of herself due to mental illness.

"When can she leave?" I asked as I handed the papers back.

"Probably not for at least two weeks, maybe more. It depends. We need to get her medicated. She's delusional and paranoid. She's showing signs of acute schizophrenia."

Laura had gone to get a drink from the fountain. I was glad she hadn't heard.

I felt like the floor had just dropped out from under me. Schizophrenic people were crazy.

I sat down before my knees buckled. Schizophrenia? I recalled a stupid poem

I'd once heard and laughed at. It played incessantly in my thoughts there in that hospital full of crazy people.

Roses are red,

Violets are blue,

I'm schizophrenic,

And so am I.

I squeezed my eyes shut, willing the lines of the poem to stop pounding mockingly through my mind.

"When are they going to let her out of here?" Clance asked as he sauntered up to me after the nurse left. He sat down right next to me, and looked down my shirt. 'Too bad you and Laura aren't a little more . . . alike," he said huskily, leering at me with his brown eyes. Laura's chest was flat as a board.

I clutched my shirt closed, blushing with anger. "Stop it!" I hissed. It wasn't the first time he mentioned his preference to my chest. I scooted further away.

"She might be here for two weeks, maybe more." I sighed.

"Two weeks!" Clance blurted. "The wedding is in two weeks!" He stood up and stomped to the door, pulling it open with every ounce of attitude he had. He let it go as he walked through it with an exaggerated gesture and loud exasperated sigh. "Be back tomorrow." he said without looking around.

I went to Laura then and hugged her. She started to shake as I stroked her hair gently. "It's going to be alright." I promised her.

"I love Clance." she said, as if trying to convince herself. "He's going to leave me, isn't he? I hope I don't miss the wedding."

I swallowed hard and walked with her as the nurse guided us to her room. The felt quiet, gloomy. The gray curtains and splotchy green wallpaper muted what light struggled to get in. There were two beds, draped in matching gray blankets, a table, a chair, and a bathroom. The tile floor was hard. The whole room felt hard. I didn't know then how hard it would be on Laura—this room, and other rooms like it.

Laura's bright pink shirt looked riotous amidst the gloom as she sat slumped over on the gray bed.

We cried together after the nurse left. "I'm scared, Nan," she sobbed, looking to me for comfort.

Laura, who had been fearless…

She was still Laura, I reminded myself. She wasn't crazy. I knew they were wrong.

"Are you feeling any better?" I asked after a while, unsure of what to say. She had stopped crying and was watching her feet as she moved them back and forth.

"Better than what?" she asked.

I stared at her a moment.

"Better than you?" she continued. "How could I feel better than you? You've got everything, Nan. Little Miss Perfect. Little Miss Pretty." Her eyes bored into mine. "I'm glad you lost the baby." Her voice was cold, mean.

I sat there stunned. She watched me as if to see my reaction to what she had said. I put my face into my hands, my mind spinning.

She put her hand on my back. "There, I hurt your precious feelings, didn't I?" she asked innocently. "Shut up!" she suddenly screamed, putting her hands over her ears. She squeezed her eyes shut, as if in agony.

"Shut up! It was them! I didn't say those things, Nan! I didn't say that!" She burst into new tears.

I walked out of the room and paced the hall for at least ten minutes before coming back into the room. I felt I needed to explain to her why I'd checked her in.

"Laura," I began, unsure. "You're going to stay here a while 'til they figure out what's wrong with you. I just want to make sure you're okay with that," I said as I sat down next to her again.

"Oh, I'm just dandy. Perfect. Real perfect." She watched her shoelaces drag on the floor as she swung her legs.

We sat silently for a while. It tried not to stare at her. She didn't have schizophrenia. I was sure of it. She understood the situation and was afraid too. Laura often hid her fear with anger. I looked up and saw that she was staring at me.

"You're going to be fine," I assured her.

"Pretty Nancy, always so pretty," Laura said, suddenly smiling up at me. "I want to grow up to be like you. I know you're right, you always are. I'll be just fine."

I started to cry again, I couldn't help it. Never had I felt so inadequate.

She threw her arms around me. "Don't worry Nancy, you're going to be fine, too. I won't let anything happen to you." As she said so, she kissed my cheek, something she'd never done before.

The belligerence had left her and she reminded me of an innocent little kid as we sat together. She clutched my arm the whole time, as though she was afraid

I'd leave. Harold came a while later. I was relieved to get out of there. I hadn't been scared, I'd been terrified.

I cried the whole drive home. Harold reached out and held my hand, letting it go to shift gears, then taking my hand again. "She's in good hands, Nan. Don't feel bad for leaving her there."

I wished that was what I had been thinking about, but it wasn't. I miscarried on Valentine's Day…and now this…I was worried for Laura, but instead dwelt on another thought that intruded itself: what if this happens to me? I didn't know much about schizophrenia then and the word loomed like an enormous storm cloud in my brain.

When I got home I called my Dad and told him. To this day I don't know how I managed to form the words into a coherent sentence that told him his daughter had gone crazy. There was utter silence on his end.

"Daddy, maybe you should leave that part out about her being possessed when you tell all this to Mama."

He was quiet for a moment, then said, "Yeah, you may be right. I'll take some of my vacation days off and drive up there as soon as I can. Are you alright, Big Sister?"

"I'm doing OK, just a little shook up."

"I love you, Honey. Be there soon as I can."

"OK," I said as my throat tightened again. "Love you too."

The next day was Saturday and Harold drove us out to see Laura again. When we got to her room, Clance was already there, whispering into her ear as she sat on his lap. "We're going to get married," she said as we walked in.

"Soon as you get better, Babe," he said as he patted her left cheek.

Harold glared at him. "How about you get your hand off her backside? You know she doesn't know what you're doing."

"Just tryin' to cheer her up, that's all." he said sulkily. "I oughta git anyway. Next milkin's at eight." He bent and quickly kissed Laura before standing.

A nurse approached us then, and held out a clipboard for me to sign to approve more meds.

"This one's an anti-psychotic, and the other is so she can sleep. She's been up all night," she explained.

"Is she getting better yet?" Clance asked, almost in irritation.

"Well, no. Schizophrenia is very difficult. Sometimes we have to try several meds before we find one that works. It isn't easy to medicate at first, and even then, often the medication stops working after a while. She could be in here for several more weeks."

Clance glared at me, then stepped back. "She's Schitzo? Nice." He swung the door violently as he left. I had the urge to throw a rock at him.

"I don't like him," Harold said under his breath to me.

"Same here," I whispered back. "No wonder she didn't want him near her.

Now she's so drugged up she doesn't know what she wants."

A few days later my dad arrived. I heard him pull up and looked out our apartment window. There he was, strong as ever. I was relieved as I watched him unstrap his helmet before swinging his leg over the seat of his Harley. He stretched a moment to work out the kinks of a long ride. He'd lost a little more hair—was almost bald. He unzipped his leather jacket and folded it carefully before placing it in one of his saddlebags.

He didn't bother rubbing the dust off the gas tank and chrome pipes like he usually did. Instead he headed straight for my door. I felt saved by my wonderful, quiet, daddy.

Other people didn't understand him. There were some who called him downright unapproachable. My friends seemed nervous around him, and when he'd crack a joke and be funny like he always was with just us, they couldn't believe it. They didn't know Daddy.

When I took him in to Pleasant Hills I wasn't prepared for it—to see him cry, I mean. When we walked into Laura's room, she ran to him and hugged him. On that day she was acting like a little kid again, just kind of sweet. The nurse told me that they had to heavily sedate her because she'd been running around waving a Bible at people and poking them with it. She'd bothered one man in particular almost incessantly.

As I watched my dad hug her, tears flowed down both of his cheeks, losing themselves in his beard.

"How's my girl?" he asked in a husky voice.

That was when Laura began hurting us, I realized. She made my big strong daddy cry.

"Well, looks like I've gone crazy, Pop." He squeezed her tightly as he chuckled.

My dad always understood her better than the rest of us did. Laura always sort of had her own way. Sometimes I was jealous, like right then when he hugged her so tenderly and didn't let go right away—like he always did with me. He hugged her for a long time.

"Hey Nan, want to get a drink with me?" she asked after a while. We'd been sitting there, none of us knowing what to say.

I went out into the hall, leaving my dad alone and waited as she stooped over the fountain. As I waited for her, a woman in a pink robe came up behind me, and asked "Are you the gatekeeper?" She was petting an imaginary dog. "He's so thirsty," she explained to me.

Laura turned around and glared at the woman. "Get away from my sister!"

She hissed as she grabbed my arm and steered me away from her. Over her shoulder she yelled, "You're a nut, lady!" As we walked away Laura whispered confidentially, "Some of these people are totally psycho. It's actually kind of funny though."

"Except him." she said as we rounded a corner. "I'm scared of him."

He was a thin, graying old man in a green bathrobe. He wore large glasses that made his eyes look huge. "He's one of them. He's Psycho Joe. He's crazy. Hurry, let's go back to my room."

We came back to my dad just as he was getting up off his knees beside her bed. Tears came to my eyes as my daddy got up and flicked a tear from his cheek.

Laura watched him a minute, then said, "Let me say one." She got down on her knees beside him and propped her arms up on the bed. With the simple trust and innocence of a child she prayed, "God, please help me get better in time for the wedding. In Jesus' name, Amen."

As we drove home, Daddy said, "I've never felt so strongly before that God was listening to someone. I know he heard that."

I'd felt it too.

The next day when we came, the nurse said they'd had to sedate her again because she kept trying to take her clothes off. We went into her room and she smiled at us, but wouldn't talk. She didn't talk the whole time we were there, and when we took her to the cafeteria, she pointed at the things she wanted, then didn't eat them anyway.

She pulled me into the bathroom with her after we left the cafeteria. It was like she was afraid to do anything by herself. As she sat on the toilet she finally spoke. "They're trying to poison me."

"No they're not. You need to eat something, Laura." I could see her jeans were getting very loose.

She stared at me a while, then started to cry. "You don't believe me. Nobody does."

That was all she had to say that day. Wouldn't even talk to Daddy.

As my dad and I drove back to my small apartment I looked over at him and saw he was crying quietly again as he drove.

"I'm going home tomorrow, Nantucket. I'll go crazy too if I have to sit here doing this every day. I have to get back to work. I need to get back to your Ma."

He was quiet for a while longer, his cheeks glistening in the glare of headlights. "I think it's my fault," he said quietly. "I kept telling her she could do it, to stay in school. I kept telling her she'd be fine. She called last week and said she was getting stressed out, and I gave her a pep talk instead of listening. I reminded her of the time old coach Barton tried to talk her outta takin' honors History in high school cause he was planning on failing her. He said she wasn't cut out for his class. She sure shouldered up that time. Got an A." Daddy said the last part thickly as new tears emerged.

Seemed to me then that parents tried to blame everything on themselves.

Mama even said once that maybe Laura got sick because she nursed her longer than me. She'd been suffering from depression at the time.

Dad was quiet the rest of the way home and left in the morning. He squeezed my shoulder as he went. "I'm sorry you have to be in charge of all this, Nan. I have to get back or I might lose my job. I'll send Mama as soon as we can."

Three days later I saw Clance at the gas station with Sue Downy. She was in his truck tucked under his arm as the gas pumped.

He jumped out guiltily when he saw me. He quickly threw away the cigarette that had been hanging precariously out the side of his mouth. I never knew he smoked, and I doubted Laura did either. She was allergic to cigarette smoke.

"Hiya Nan! Got myself a date!" and he indicated yellow haired Sue. We all knew she wasn't really blonde. "How's Laura?" he asked with a smirk. I could hear Sue giggling inside the truck. "Tell her I said Hi."

You know, I'll always wonder what God had in his mind when he took Laura's, but sometimes I think it was the nicest thing he ever did. I know he'd heard her prayer, and he gave her the only answer a loving father would. Laura didn't love Clance. She was afraid of him. I don't believe she ever would've backed down in time for the wedding. She was stubborn and loyal. God just sort of reached down and canceled it for her. He said no.

I still see Clance every now and then with Sue. They've got three of the ugliest kids I ever saw. Mean too, just like their dad.

It took several months to get her back into the swing of things that first time after they sent her home with Mama. After a long break, she went back to school and almost finished a semester before she got sick again and had to go home and start over.

In some ways it was worse than the first time because we all thought the doctors were wrong. We figured it was just one of those things and that she was fine now. What do they know? They didn't know Laura like we did.

Then she got sick again, and it took longer to get her out of it that time. In fact, it hit my Mama so hard she up and had a nervous breakdown herself and they hauled her off to Pleasant Hills right along with Laura.

About that time I seriously started to get afraid for myself and my baby. That was around seven years ago, and I'd just had a beautiful, fat little girl with the biggest blue eyes. I tried not to, but every once in a while I'd wonder if I was going to "lose it," too. And then I'd look at my new sweet Josie and I'd get to scaring myself to death, wondering what would happen if I got sick. I didn't want to see Laura at all the second time she went crazy.

It's easier to stay away from people who make you feel uncomfortable, or that make you sad all the time. I didn't like pain.

A few years ago a lady at church lost her boy in a car accident. I didn't know her that well, but felt like I ought to offer my condolences or something. But as I sat in our pew, twirling my five year old Benny's hair, I thought about what it must be like to lose a son. I chickened out. I couldn't stand to be close to that much pain, even if it wasn't mine. I regret that now, now that I know a little about what it is to hurt. It's like Grandma says—pain's just part of the deal, and it's dealt out in a way that we can handle if we put our trust in God to get us through it.

Laura was stronger than me. I sure didn't want to try to shoulder her load.

It seemed to me that sometimes her recovery was worse than her sickness. We all do things in our dreams that we would never do in real life. Problem with

Laura was, sometimes she couldn't tell the difference. They'd finally pull her out of it and get her medication straight, but there was always a stout and ragged wave of humiliation in it's wake. She'd go into a severe depression once she started remembering. She lost more than one friend in her nightmares and woke to find them gone for good. Sometimes I thought it might have been easier for her if she just stayed crazy.

Chapter Two

My dishwater had gone cold. I sighed as I watched my mama out there on the porch.

Thanksgiving wasn't all that thankful this year. Mama and Grandma sat out there planning what to do and what they were going to tell Michael, Laura's new boyfriend. He wasn't in on our little family secret yet. Laura seemed very normal when she was medicated right. Truth is, I didn't like Michael much either. Laura had merely taken in another ungrateful stray. I didn't see that he needed to know anything.

I told Mama to let me do the dishes after supper so I could warm up my hands. They're always cold when I get upset. What I really wanted was some time to think. I was mad, furious even, and ashamed of myself.

Thanksgiving was ruined.

I was due any day now. I had yet to bring a child into this world without the cloak of worry that hung over my head, knowing Laura was in the mental hospital again, and me wondering if I was going crazy or just hormonal. I wasn't sleeping well either. I always got pregnant all the way around, not just out front. Plus, my bladder was shrinking. Seemed like the two pitiful drops I took all the trouble of coming down the hall for were all I could hold. The floor boards started creaking before I was eight months along, and I could see a low spot wearing its way into the linoleum that led down the hall into the bathroom. I needed Mama just to pull me off the couch when Harold wasn't home. Now she would be spending all her time with Laura. I knew it was selfish to be angry, but somehow I couldn't help it.

I was rinsing the last of the silverware when I heard Aunt Helen join them. She'd finished putting cling wrap on all the leftovers and tucking them neatly into the fridge. She trudged out onto the deck, the oak beams trembling beneath her.

"I overheard about Laura," she said as she settled her ample bottom into a flimsy lawn chair. I peeked out and saw her backside. Little square pink paisley bulges squished out between the canvas weave of the chair as she sat. "Ain't it a shame, though?"

Aunt Helen had a knack for stating the obvious. No one paid much attention to her.

"Funny thing is, I always figured if one of them was to lose it, it would've been

Nancy," Helen observed, tucking her unnaturally red hair behind an ear.

"Shush, Helen! Nan's right inside there doing the dishes!" Mama whispered severely. They all turned around and stole a glance through the window. I kept my head down and hummed loudly as I ran the water.

"Well, I mean," she whispered loudly, "Nancy was always the emotional one.

She's so scatterbrained. Laura takes after her daddy. But Nancy…" It occurred to her a bit late that to say I took after Mama wouldn't exactly be polite after she'd already dug that hole. "Well, it's a shame anyway." Her chair creaked beneath her as she shifted her weight.

Aunt Helen was the kind of woman who would never go crazy. There was no room in her tight little mind for any kind of nonsense. Her house was the most orderly I'd ever seen. She was always coming over to my place and picking up things. I even caught her peeking behind my shower curtain once and clicking her tongue. "Would you look at that," she'd said under her breath. I had left the night before's washcloth in the tub basin, and a few bath toys were strewn about.

Funny how stuff like that never bothered me personally, but she had a way of making me ashamed of myself once I'd been caught in the least degree of slothfulness.

"What are you all going to tell that nice boy, Michael?" she asked then, filling the tense silence.

"Well, Helen, we were gettin' to that. Fact is, I didn't think he was all that nice myself," said Mama.

"Well beggars can't be choosers, now can they? You want to know my opinion…" No one did, but we knew we'd get it. "I don't think Laura's ever going to get married."

The silence that ensued was tense. I could hear a fly throwing itself against the window. I was clutching a fork and looked down to see that my knuckles had gone white. A fork could be a dangerous weapon in the right hands. I had the urge to run out onto the porch and poke one of her little pink paisley bulges just to see if she'd pop. She had enough hot air in her to fuel a blimp. I walked out onto the porch.

"Your front's wet, Honey," Helen said when she saw me. "Well, I've been doing the dishes." I said as I sat down.

"I never get my dress wet when I do the dishes. That's what aprons are for."

I could see Grandma rolling her eyes. She always got quiet and suddenly deaf around Helen. Helen was Harold's aunt, actually, and Grandma never could stand her. Grandma's mouth was set in a grim line as she furiously cast her stitches.

"Now Nancy," Helen continued, "I noticed you had crumbs in your silverware drawer again. Saw 'em when I was going in for the gravy spoon this evening.

If you just shut your drawers all the way before you wipe the counter down, it will solve that problem. I know it don't really matter with just us, but if you were ever to have a formal dinner or something, you might get embarrassed."

"Helen," said my Grandma. "Be sweet and get me a glass of ice water. I'm parched sittin' out here."

Helen got up quickly, smoothing her dress and whisked herself off to the kitchen. She returned in a few minutes.

"Found an empty ice tray in your freezer!" she teased and wagged a reprimanding finger in my direction.

"Here you go, Alice," she shouted. She always talked to Grandma as if she were deaf.

It seemed like Grandma had suddenly developed the shakes as she reached for that glass. Just as she got hold of it, her fingers slipped and the glass tipped. Water splashed all down the front of Helen's dress.

"Oh, bless your heart, Alice," she said in a loud, high voice, thinly veiling her irritation as she jumped backwards in shock. "I guess I let go before you had hold of it. Shall I get you another one?"

"No, I'm fine now," Grandma said.

"Front's wet, Helen," said Mama.

Chapter Three

No one seemed to want to leave. Sometimes it's hard to get moving after a

Thanksgiving dinner, but no one really ate that much, except Helen.

I'd planned for days to get the dinner just right. It was the first time everyone was going to be out to my house instead of Mama's, and I was determined to do it right. Some of Harold's folks even came over. I was so proud to open the door to everyone. I'd lit candles and set out the good plates . . . and then the phone rang.

Thanksgiving dinner tasted about as good as unsalted oatmeal to me after that. Josie wasn't much of an eater anyway, and Benny still had a bit of flu, so he didn't eat much either. Harold's family didn't like my way of cooking. They never trusted anything that came from my oven. Even if it was good, they wouldn't have admitted it. They all watched me, too. They figured Harold had married into bad blood. Laura wasn't a secret to them anymore either.

Grandma couldn't eat much besides the mashed potatoes anyway, and Mama didn't eat a thing. I know because I watched her. I'd made her secret pineapple pie and couldn't wait to get her seal of approval. I could see, though, by the way her head shook just a little bit as she sat there, that she was thinking of Laura, unaware of the food before her.

Uncle Theo was kind enough to try the pie, and winked at me. He was my favorite relative, next to Grandma. He was actually my great uncle, Grandma's brother. He moved in with Grandma after Grandpa died to take care of her. He had a quick wit and a ridiculous sense of humor that always made me smile. But on that day, I felt like I couldn't, not for real anyway. I'd been walking around with a smile that felt like it had been pasted to my face.

Thanksgiving felt more like a funeral feast, and everyone just stuck around, not to offer condolences, though some did. I think they mostly stayed out of curiosity. After seven years of having a schizophrenic in the family, word had gotten around, at least among the aunts and uncles. It made me mad that they just sat around waiting, hours after the table was cleared, and hours after I quit playing hostess. I was sure Harold's family stuck around to see just what exactly he'd married into.

I knew it was too much to ask for anyone to leave during the Cowboys game. I'd have been strung up to the nearest tree for heresy. The game finally ended and no one moved.

I even turned on the vacuum, but all anybody did was lift their legs as they sat there watching reruns of Gilligan's Island. One of the stations was having a marathon. No one wanted to miss the show that would likely be acted out live in my own living room when Daddy got back with Laura. Pleasant Hills said they couldn't admit her 'til morning since their staff was shorthanded.

Mama was lying down in my bed, but I knew she wasn't asleep. I knew she was crying and didn't want anyone to know it. Mama couldn't even cry these days without someone asking her if she was taking her medicine. Feminine emotion of any kind in our family had a way of making people shush each other. It was a sleeping dragon to the men, and they tiptoed around it the best they could, or offered some way to fix it–to turn it off. "Take a pill, Honey."

Harold went to get the spare room ready. Most of the time it was my sewing room, but since Laura was coming, he had to make sure it was safe. He needed to move all the sharp things into the hall closet. We just never knew how Laura would be. Sometimes she wouldn't talk at all. Other times she swore like a truck driver. Once she flipped off the pastor and told him to go to hell when he tried and failed to cast out her demons. And sometimes, she'd tell you over and over how much she loved you, and would follow you around like a puppy with a silly grin on her face.

I loved Laura and couldn't stand for any more talk about her. I just knew Helen was itching to get some started. Even though I knew I was more angry at Laura than anybody else that day, I couldn't stand having everyone see her when she couldn't help what she did or said.

It would have been easier to take her to Mama's place, but their condo was small, and Mama was afraid Laura might get out onto the balcony and hurt herself.

So, it was up to me to get them all out before Laura got to my place, and I wasn't sure I was up to it. Helen's husband, Lars was snoring loudly on the recliner. His comb-over flopped to one side, six inches long and his bald head glistened with sweat.

Helen had just returned from the kitchen again, and was halfway into her third helping of pumpkin pie. "Did you use cloves in this?" she asked, crinkling her nose.

"It's gettin' kind of late," I said I don't know how many times. Nobody paid any attention. I even put the kids' pajamas on and started reading to them right there in front of everybody.

"You all should go on home." I finally urged, but Helen wouldn't hear of leaving me with "all that mess" to clean. She'd already dusted every square inch of the place twice. Lars kept snoring, and it never did seem like I talked loud enough to get any of Harold's family to hear me. I stomped into the kitchen.

"Hey little Miss Purty," Theo said from behind me, tugging my hair. "Looks like we got a full house for the homecoming, eh?"

"Wanna yell "fire" for me?" I asked.

"I got a better idea," he said, and his eyes twinkled.

He reached into his green polyester pants pocket and took out two tiny capsules. "Benny left these on my seat out in the car. Thought it would be funny, I guess. Glad I went outside to have a smoke and didn't sit down. Saw 'em sitting there on the seat. That Benny sure is a character. All boy." Theo chuckled.

I couldn't help it. A smile started crossing my face.

"What do you say, Nantucket?"

I already knew how hard it was to get the smell of just one stink bomb out of the carpet. I'd been there, done that, bought the T-shirt and even sent a few post cards. But two?

"So, what'll it be, Little Miss Nasty or Little Miss Purty today?" he asked.

I was tempted. I was sorely tempted…Theo always did bring some sort of ridiculous humor into the worst possible situations. He'd been a prankster his whole life, and I wouldn't have been surprised if I found out Benny had gotten those terrible bombs from him in the first place.

"Can you put 'em in a jar or something? I want the smell gone as soon as they're gone."

"I knew you was my Little Miss Nasty ever since the first time I set eyes on you! Purtiest baby I ever saw, but you had my sense of humor, I could see that right off." He gave my hair another playful tug. "Miss Nasty, I'm liable to pull your hair out directly!" His eyes gleamed as I rubbed my head. "I got it all planned out. Helen was just saying how you should dust your fans more often.

She's sittin' there with one blowing right on her. Got her dress wet." He winked.

"Now," he continued, "Where's that old Sam dog?"

Sam was part Basset hound and part Akita. Funniest looking dog I ever saw.

He was Laura's. She picked him up at the animal shelter, and we kept him at our place since her landlord didn't allow pets. He had a giant head, shaped like an

Akita's, only all the markings were that of the hound, and he even had long, dragging brown ears. He had a long body, too long really and a curly cue tail, like an

Akita's, all fluffy and soft. His front legs were only about six inches long, and his back legs were a bit longer, always making him look like he was crouching. His uneven legs were supported by giant Akita feet, and he always got gassy after cleaning up under the table. That's where I found him taking a nap. I brought him out back to Uncle Theo.

"Now Nan, you go tell Helen you've got a fancy to dust that fan and bring it out here. Come on Sam boy."

Helen had already dusted the fan. I figured she would have. "Well, I'll just tighten it a little so it won't wobble like that. I'll bring it right back." I told her as

I hauled it away.

I brought it out to Theo. "What are you going to do with it?"

He just smiled at me. "You take that hound for a walk. Get him all hyper. He always comes crashing through the place after a walk, wanting to lick everybody.

Be back in about ten minutes."

I walked along the dry lake. There was a road that twisted along its shore and led up to Chuck's Circle C, the gas station and mini mart. I had quite a job keeping that dog in line. Here I was, big as a house, with that dog pulling me along.

He was so strong–must've been his low center of gravity or something. I didn't know then, that I'd be glad of that ridiculous dog's strength later. It was like God designed him specifically for pulling, and for Laura to have him.

A few cows grazed along the edge of the lakeshore and tossed their heads up to watch us pass, casually flipping their tails at flies. As I walked, a stream of quail raced across the road in a perfect line. Sam barked and tried to chase them. It was all I could do to hold him back as he plodded on before me, his lolling tongue almost dragging on the pavement. The sun was on its way down, making the dry lakebed look like dull gold.

It was what I liked to call a once-in-a-while lake, but really it was no more than an alkali basin that sometimes had some water in it. After the spring rain it would be full to overflowing with water, depending on the amount of rain we got. At its fullest, it would span 2 ¡ miles across and about a mile wide. It was absolutely gorgeous to watch the edge of a sunset out the kitchen window and see it reflected in the deceptively clear water. But when you sneaked through all the

"No Trespassing" signs and stood at the edge of the lake, it was no more interesting than a giant mud puddle. During a particularly dry summer, sometimes it would be all dried up before July melted into August. The alkali basin would then start to blister and crack, forming an enormous, intricate jigsaw puzzle.

On one moonlit night when I was a kid, my dad suggested that we go for a walk after Mama had gone to sleep. Though we were a little scared, Laura and I followed behind him, sliding through the fencing wires, pretending not to see all of the signs prohibiting our presence. My dad always seemed to feel he had more right to that lake than whoever put up those signs. He'd been coming here for years before it belonged to anybody, before the oil pumps came and made White Lake a viable town. It was more a settlement of hermits and desert dwellers then, and those who'd got off the highway to somewhere and forgot how to get back on.

In 1963 he rode his first motorcycle across it. His mother, my Grandma Harris, once boasted that she had sped across it at 80 miles an hour on a 650 BSA. Grandma and Grandpa Harris were dead now, buried in the cemetery with Grandma Alice's husband Samuel, my other grandpa, the one I could hardly remember.

My dad shared these stories as we walked across its surface, the ground below us crunching pleasantly. Occasionally we saw coyotes skittering off into the distance and watched them 'til they blended too well with the shadows.

Daddy told us how he'd come out there with some friends one time in an old pickup truck. He was driving and had two guys in the cab with him. Once they got going pretty good across the lakebed, my dad put it in neutral and he and the guy sitting at the other window got out and climbed into the back, leaving the middle man a little bewildered. After a bit, he braved up, let go of the wheel, and climbed back there with them to enjoy the ride. That was the beauty of a dry lake. It just went on forever with nothing to worry about or crash into.

Finally, we reached the point we'd come for on that walk so long ago. Daddy stopped and looked around. I followed his example and we all stood quietly, turning slowly in a circle. All around, as far as the eye could see, was emptiness. Nothing but an expanse of cracked clay softly glowing in the subtle moonlight that went on forever. Above us, a full moon shone amongst the bright stars. It felt like we were standing on one moon and gazing off into space at another. I'll never forget that feeling, standing there on that lakebed with my dad, pondering the immensity of the universe.

That was before Daddy lost his job and had to move with Mama. They took

Laura with them to Arizona, to a job offer he couldn't refuse, where he worked 'til he was able to retire. When she graduated from high school, Laura moved back with Harold and me to go to school. That was before any of us gave a thought to schizophrenia. Once Daddy retired, he and Mama came back and bought a small little condo on the other side of the lake. I guess we had alkali in our blood, seeing as how we kept coming back to live beside a lifeless expanse of poisoned water. We just accepted it as it was. You can't make that kind of a lake into something it's not. Those little girls' tiny headstones in the cemetery were proof of that.

I could feel my little baby getting restless. She had some toes up into my ribs and it hurt. I guessed it had been long enough, so I headed back.

From where I walked, I had a nice view of our suffering little town. I say suffering because it was. White Lake, Texas was a bad idea to start with. It was just foolish to plan a town around a lake as poisonous as ours was. The alkali wasn't just in the lake, it had filtered its way down into the soil, making things difficult to grow. You had to be patient in White Lake for things to turn out, and you had to water all the time. Nothing but weeds grew by accident. You had to bring in outside soil, and mix it in with the alkali laden dirt to give it a better balance, and you had to be careful what you planted.

White Lake, like most towns, had several sides to it. There was my side of the lake, the side you started out on because that was all you could afford, and you just tried not to notice the pump jacks and the dilapidated houses with the eclectic yard collections of old rusted-out cars, and the thorny weeds that sprung up almost everywhere.

Those of us who lived in my neighborhood, butted up against the lake, counted ourselves lucky that at least we didn't live in the trailer park, the darkest and dingiest side of White Lake.

And then there was "The Heights". The rich side, though the only height involved, in my opinion, was in the way those people over there held up their noses. Calling it The Heights was just wishful thinking, as White Lake was flat as a pancake. Sometimes I wondered why rich people would pick our town to live in anyway, but mostly the rich folks just started out on my side, and through some luck came into money. Then they just moved to the other side, away from the oil pumps that lined their leather wallets, so they could show the rest of us.

Nicer homes had been springing up all around us. My little neighborhood, older than the rest, began to look shabby in comparison, even to me. The county even re-routed the main highway away from my neighborhood so no one would have to see it. They planned it in such a way that it curved around the other side of the lake, and past the lovely houses, so people passing through would think

White Lake was something other than it really was.

White Lake's only purpose was to house those who worked in oil: the laborers, the rich folks, and those who lived here to do the other necessary things that make a town work, like running the gas station, the Supersaver, the lumber yard, the funeral home. And so White Lake limped along.

Theo was waiting outside the door when I got back. "You go on inside, and act natural. Give me that dog. I'm going to turn him into a skunk. This other bomb is for the fan."

I went inside and sat down. I was so tired I didn't care what happened next. A few minutes later Sam came galloping into the house. He smelled awful, like I knew he would. He jumped up onto one relative after another, licking them in the face. Lars was so startled he looped out on the recliner. The whole thing tipped over backward as he snorted awake. His feet stuck straight up in the air as Sam enthusiastically licked him in the mouth.

"Hell, Nancy!" he sputtered. "Get this horse off me!"

Helen went to help, but Sam reared up, clawing her dress and trying his best to lick her in the face and just about bowled her over, too. By now everyone was up and holding their nose.

Harold came running in from the back, saw what Sam was doing and stood in front of Grandma to protect her from the onslaught. "What's that dog been in now?" he hollered, looking at me.

I shrugged, trying my best to look bewildered. "Maybe he's just gassy again."

Harold took him by the collar then and dragged him out, his shirt pulled up over his nose. "Go on out, you old stinker!" he hollered, kicking Sam along.

Sam yelped and went out. His feelings were hurt. He skulked off to his dog house and slumped down, resting his jowls on his enormous paws and sighed.

"Nancy, where's that fan? Bring it in here quick!" ordered Helen.

"Oh, right. Good idea!" I went out back to get it. Theo was there, on his way in. He had the fan held away from him as he walked.

"Step back now, Girlie. This thing's not exactly pleasant to get too close to, if you know what I mean."

I laughed out loud and gulped a little too much of that foul air. I pulled my shirt up over my nose and followed behind him.

"Set it up in the middle of the room!" ordered Helen. "Make sure you put it to oscillate."

Theo did as he was told, then went outside. I followed him and the two of us laughed so hard we both had tears streaming down our faces.

"That shore was a good one, Miss Nasty! Uncle Theo's fan polish, eh?" he chuckled between breaths.

We could hear the commotion inside as everyone jumped around the room arguing, their voices loud enough to hear all the way down the street. "It still stinks! What ungodly thing has that dog gotten into? Did he take a dump in here somewhere? No, aim it over here, I think Helen's going to pass out! Quit hogging the fan!"

Benny and Josie were the first to scamper outside. "Mama, I think Sam got squirted by a skunk!" wailed Josie.

Benny looked speculative. He wandered over to Uncle Theo's truck and peeked inside. He came back over to us and looked up at Theo. Theo winked and chucked him under the chin. A large grin spread over Benny's face.

It took about eight minutes for everyone to evacuate. Helen and Lars were the first to come out, followed by Harold's sisters and their husbands. His mama came next, pinching her nose. They were followed by a stream of nieces and nephews. They all got in their cars and drove off, slamming their doors shut after they got moving.

I walked back in with Theo and he took the fan out. Harold was turning over all the sofas and chairs, looking for what it was Sam had brought in.

I hugged him from behind and he turned, startled. "What in the–"

I just kissed his cheek, standing on my tippy toes, and asked, "How about we open some windows, and have a piece of pie out on the porch?"

Theo was helping Grandma to her feet, and held her under the elbow as they walked out to the truck. Grandma had lost her sense of smell a long time ago and couldn't understand what everyone was fussing about. Theo loaded her gently into his truck. "Call us if you need anything," he said and got in himself.

"Thanks Theo!" I called after him. "Good night Grandma!"

"Now you've got some explaining to do, Nantucket!" Harold said sternly.

"I asked Uncle Theo to help me get all these people out of here, and he did.

That's all."

I didn't look at him at first. I knew he wouldn't be mad, not if he called me

Nantucket, but I was a little worried he'd think our prank was in poor taste, considering the situation. Finally I looked up at him. Harold looked like he was trying hard not to smile. He was the serious type and sometimes didn't give in to laughter as easily as I did.

After a while it got a bit chilly out there on the porch. Mama came out after a bit and brought me an afghan. "The living room smells kind of funny, Nan." she said as she tucked it around me.

"Is it bad?" I asked.

"No, just a little. Was there a skunk or something?"

Mama's face was red and blotchy. She'd been crying a long time, I could tell.

She was in a quiet mood, thinking a lot, I guess. She kept looking down the road.

"Sam," was all I said and she nodded.

My brief moment of humor began to wear off as we sat and waited for Laura's arrival. The one thing I wished for was that it hadn't been a bad one. She had been surrounded by strangers this time, and I just prayed for the best.

It was a little after nine when Daddy got back with Laura. I saw them coming up the walk as I peered out from behind the curtain. Daddy's face was grim and

Laura's showed no emotion. She just looked sort of dazed. Daddy helped her take off her sweater, then pushed her down gently onto the couch.

"Not talking?" I asked.

"Nope. I gave her some sleeping pills on the way over and she took 'em without a fight. I guess we'll get her to bed and see what happens tomorrow."

"Harold's got the sewing room ready."

Harold and Daddy helped her into the room. She crawled into the extra bed and pulled the covers up, then turned over to the wall. Daddy watched her for a minute, then shut off the light and closed the door.

"What happened?" I asked after he'd sat down a while and took off his hat.

"Well, as far as I can tell, Laura drove herself to the clinic, and just sat with her hands on the wheel in the parking lot 'til somebody noticed her sitting there and asked her if she needed any help. She asked to be checked in, and that's all she said to anybody."

"Now that's strange," observed Harold. "None of Michael's folks were there?"

"No. I don't understand it either."

"Well, good," said Mama. "Maybe it's going to be better than we think."

My folks went home a little while later. I assured them that they could leave

Laura with us. Harold was so good with her. In the past he'd stayed up all night with her, never getting annoyed, just being as kind as he could.

I was a little nervous. I couldn't get the idea out of my head that maybe I'd go into labor with her here. Long after Harold and the kids went to sleep, I lay there thinking. My baby kept shivering inside me.

Finally I got up and walked into the spare room and sat down by Laura. She was sleeping on her side, facing me. She was a beautiful girl. She had long shiny dark brown, almost black hair with a natural curl to it that I never did think was very fair. Her skin was pale, just the right shade, I always thought, and she had a sprinkle of freckles across her nose and on her cheeks. Her eyes were bright blue with thick, dark lashes, and her eyebrows arched like some of the models I'd seen in Vogue.

People thought I was pretty. I'd grown up used to the idea, and just sort of accepted it and didn't give it much thought. I had dark brown hair and greenish eyes. I didn't have any freckles, and my eyebrows were sort of flat. Laura, on the other hand, was beautiful, but I don't recall too many people mentioning it. Sometimes I think I called more attention to myself because I had more of a figure. I had a big bust, and big hips, and once I had this baby, I hoped to have a sort of small waist again. Laura was flat-chested and had small hips. Her waist wasn't big at all, but it just didn't show up as much without any hips. To be honest, I would have rather looked like her.

As I sat by her, she moaned softly, and turned onto her back. "Nan?" My heart skipped a beat for a minute, then I said, "I'm here, Laura."

She turned and stared at me, then sneered. "Nan took it. Nantucket. Nan took it. Nantucket." she started to chant. She got louder. "Nan took it. Nantucket. Nan Nan Nan."

I ran out of the room. I was terrified. My heart thudded against my ribs as I ran to our bedroom. "Harold, she's up!" I said in a frantic whisper. "She's got an awful look on her face."

Harold stumbled into her room and came back just a few minutes later. "She's sleeping Nan, which is what you should be doing."

I crawled back into bed and lay there for hours. I don't know why it scared me so much. I'd never seen her like that, but later when I got honest with myself, I realized why.

I blamed myself, too. Once we got in a scuffle as kids and I punched her hard in the face. She fell back and hit her head on the bookcase. It gave her a lump that took a long time to go away. Sometimes I thought it was my fault she was sick.

Nantucket was what everyone called me. It was a nickname that just accidentally happened one day. I'd sneaked into my mama's room and got her perfume. She never would let me near it. I was about twelve or thirteen maybe and I wanted to wear some to school. I was so nervous as I tried to put some on that I dropped the bottle and it broke all over the floor. I knew I was in for it then, and as I was wiping it up, Laura came in and saw me. We didn't always get along very well when we were younger. Her eyes narrowed, and she grabbed the largest piece of the broken bottle, then she ran out to tell Mama.

"Nan took it!" she hollered. That was why I punched her.

Daddy thought that was the funniest thing, not me punching her, but the way she'd said Nan took it. He started calling me Nantucket right after that. It caught on, and I'd almost forgotten myself how I came to be Nantucket. I was grounded for two weeks after that. One for stealing the perfume, and one for punching Laura.

Chapter Four

I woke up late the next morning with a headache and my eyes were swollen. Then I remembered I'd cried just about all night, and that Laura was in the next room. Harold had gotten up some time ago. I could hear him and the kids in the kitchen.

I got up. I stopped by the spare room and saw that Laura was gone. In the kitchen, Harold was frying some eggs and bacon. Laura was on the sofa with the kids watching cartoons. She looked normal. Josie was brushing her hair and clipping all kinds of barrettes into it.

"Morning," Harold said with his back to me. "Breakfast is just about ready. I called your mama. Said she'd be over in a while."

I got out the plates and silverware and set the table. I was afraid to talk to

Laura. So far everything looked good, and I wanted to just stay inside that little bubble as long as I could.

I tried to get Harold to look at me so I could see what he was thinking– but he wouldn't, so I knew then that she wasn't alright.

Laura had a way of saying things that would startle me so much my heart would stop for a minute, then I'd wonder if it was her talking, or the schizophrenia. I could tell she'd said something to Harold– something about me, so he wouldn't look at me.

Harold went to the couch and told the kids to come to the table. I noticed he didn't invite Laura. She just stared ahead at the TV.

Breakfast was quiet, even Josie and Benny were quiet. They knew something wasn't right with their aunt Laura, but she was always kind to them, sick or not, and they couldn't understand the way some of us treated her sometimes.

I sneaked a few glances at Laura as we ate. She was looking at the ceiling. Every once in a-while she'd reach her hand up into the air as if she were trying to catch something just over her head. Laura heard voices sometimes, and I guess she could see things that weren't there, too.

I wondered what it would be like to be stuck in a dream. Laura told me once that was what it was like. All kinds of odd things happening and strange voices telling you things, and not knowing if you were ever going to wake up.

I always dreamed of tornadoes. It was never about just one either. It would always split into two or three, and there was never a way to escape. I used to be able to wake up by just wondering if I was dreaming. Lately, though, that didn't work. Then I'd be terrified that this time it was real, and I'd run from tornadoes for hours. I always woke up in a cold sweat with my heart racing when I had one of those dreams and was so relieved to find out that none of it had actually happened that it was all in my head. My heart ached for Laura.

Mama came a while later, and Laura left without a word. Mama drove her over to Pleasant Hills and got her checked in again.

When they were gone, I asked Harold what had happened. "She just got to saying things again, that's all."

"Like what?'

Harold looked irritated. "Does it matter?"

"Obviously it does, seeing as how you think it's important enough to keep from me. I've had a schizophrenic sister for a long time, you know, so I'm not as fragile as everybody thinks. I want to know what she said."

"No, you don't."

"Harold, what did she say? Tell me!" I was mad, and though I knew I was a little afraid of what she'd said, I wanted to at least know what it was.

Harold was quiet for a long time. He cleared the dishes from the table, then sent the kids outside. He almost told me, then walked over to the TV and turned it up and sat on the couch.

Sometimes I wondered if Harold worried about me right along with the rest of them. Any time I got emotional about something I had the feeling he didn't want to be anywhere near me. He always tried to downplay whatever I was upset about. He was compassionate, but wouldn't want to hear me talk about what I was feeling. It made me feel like he was a little afraid of me. He'd rather hug me when I cried than listen to the reason. It hurt me when he did that, and slowly, over time, I'd stopped talking to him about some things. I knew where he'd drawn the line by now. I got real good at crying without sobbing, so I wouldn't wake him at night.

I started to cry as I wiped down the table. I couldn't help it. I hated it when I cried. I did it all the time and got just as sick of myself as I knew he did.

Harold sighed, then said in an even voice, "She said that baby isn't mine."

I was shocked enough to quit crying on the spot. Then I was as mad as I'd ever been. I must have stood there a full two minutes before I walked over to the couch and sat down next to him. He wouldn't look at me. Suddenly I realized he wasn't sure about what she'd said. Sometimes, in the depths of her illness, Laura said things that turned out to be true. Usually they were things everyone else didn't want to think about. Laura was fearless when she was sick. Harold and I had been through some rough times, but I couldn't believe he'd ever doubt that a child I carried was his own.

I stared at him, willing him to look at me, but he wouldn't.

"I know you've been lonely, Honey, and I haven't exactly been around much," he began. "I take for granted that you'll always be there, but I know there's been times when I wasn't there for you." He looked at me then, his eyes fearful, and repentant.

"Harold, you give me your hand!" I shouted.

His chin was trembling as he did. I put it down on my belly so hard it hurt.

Little Baby felt it too and kicked back. "Feel that? That's a Parley in there! I am ashamed of Laura for saying such a thing! More than that, I'm ashamed of you for doubting me even for a minute."

Laura hurt all of us. As much as it stung, it only made me feel more sorry for her. What would it be like to not be in control of your own mind, so you'd say such hurtful things to the people who loved you the most? Sure, it hurt me that she'd even think up as big a lie as that, but I knew she'd be so ashamed of herself when she got her medication squared away that she wouldn't even be able to look at me. I'd forgiven her already.

I knew Laura was jealous of me. All she ever wanted was to be married and have a family. I had a good husband, two kids, and a mortgage payment that kept me up some nights, but I had what she wanted. I felt guilty for ever taking any of that for granted.

She got engaged to Clance when she was only 18. The one thing they had in common was that they both liked horses, and somehow, she got it in her mind that would be enough.

Michael wasn't good enough for her, either, but she kept with him, thinking he might just be her very last chance, so she didn't leave him when he said all those mean things to her. I'd heard him myself and asked her once if it bothered her. I knew it did, but she never could leave anybody. She was the sort of person who just let things happen to her. She trusted people, probably more than they deserved.

More than anything I wanted to know exactly what did happen to her this time, but Michael never called. That fact alone worried me.

Three days later I went into labor. I'd been having so many false contractions for the last few weeks that I didn't even pay any attention at first. Then my water broke and the contractions started coming fast and furious. I stood in the middle of the kitchen, trying to pull myself together. Thank goodness the kids were at school. After that first hard contraction was over, I waddled over to the phone and called Harold.

He was out to lunch. I called my folks, but they were gone. Probably over at Pleasant Hills with Laura. I tried everyone I could think of, and no one was home. I stood there, going into shock in that puddle of amniotic fluid, and my hands started to shake. It always did seem unfair to me that the doctor got paid so much when I did all the work in labor. I wanted him more than anything right then, though. I called the hospital and they told me to come in. I told them I was stuck.

"We'll send an ambulance over for you," the lady on the other end of the line said.

We were flat broke, and I knew it would be expensive to do that. "No, give me five more minutes. I want to get myself there."

The nurse sounded skeptical. "How far apart are they?"

"Well, I don't know! I been having kind of funny contractions all morning, but since my water broke, I guess about three minutes."

"Mrs. Parley, you need to get in here. I'm sending the ambulance."

Just then Aunt Helen walked in the door.

"I'm bringing myself!" I shouted and hung up.

Helen was startled, and as she walked into the kitchen, she dropped the grocery bags she was holding. First time I'd ever seen her make a mess.

"Nancy!" she shouted. "Are you alright, Honey?"

She was looking at the floor. I knew the fluid was pink, and that was bad. I'd been trying not to think about it.

For the first time in my life, I flung myself into her arms. "I need you to take me to the hospital!" I sobbed.

She sat there sputtering a minute, then pulled herself together. "Alright. You're going to be fine, Nancy. Just let me get a towel for you to sit on, and we'll hit the road."

I had three contractions while just trying to get out to the car. Seemed like we'd take just ten or twelve steps then I'd have to stop. I never was good at being in labor. My whole body shook with each contraction. I just sort of went limp in her arms and she held me tight 'til it was over.

Once we were in the car, it seemed like it took her forever to get her keys into the ignition. I realized then that I wasn't the only one who was shaking. I grabbed the keys from her and shoved the right one in just before another contraction hit.

Aunt Helen never broke the law, and she wasn't about to start that day. She did exactly 25 miles an hour. I tried to get her to speed up, but she said, "I'm not going to go any faster, Honey. You've got plenty of time. Didn't it take something like 37 hours for Josie? Just calm down. I don't want a ticket, and a crash wouldn't do either of us any good."

I had reason to believe that I was almost out of time. It was about a twenty-minute trip to the hospital since Helen was afraid of the freeway.

"Helen, if you don't go faster, you're going to have one hell of a mess to clean up in this here Cadillac." I never was one for cussing of any kind, but everyone has a limit to how nice they can be.

Well, I must've made my point. We did all of thirty-five the rest of the way. Helen gripped the wheel tightly and judging from her demeanor, you'd think we were in the Indy 500. She rolled to a stop out front and got her ample self out of the car. By then I was already up to the stairs, and I ran.

"Slow down, Nancy! For Pete's sake! We're here now, so calm down. Don't go hurting yourself!"

I stood at the front desk, panting. I was breathing so hard I couldn't even explain what I needed. The attendant couldn't see I was pregnant behind the tall desk. Just then I started into another contraction.

She jumped up and led me to a wheelchair. I was so relieved I made it. I just couldn't stand the idea of being one of those women who had a baby in a car somewhere.

Helen had caught up to me by then, panting herself. "Name, please?" the nurse asked.

I was in the middle of another contraction.

Helen took charge. "Nancy Ann Parley. Don't sit there staring at her lady, get her some help! You just wheel her off and I'll take care of the paperwork."

I was wheeled back to the emergency room where we were met by a large black intern. He looked more like a lineman for the Cowboys than a med student.

"Now let me just take a look," he said reassuringly. "My name's John. I guess

I should introduce myself before we get personal."

I'd lost my modesty a long time ago. As beautiful as it was to bring a child into the world, there was nothing modest about it. I didn't know him from Adam, but he looked pretty much like an angel to me right then, all in white in his lab coat.

"Oh my!" he almost shouted. "Get me some scissors, quick!"

I felt like a fool. I still had my nylons on. It all just happened so fast.

A nurse quickly handed him a pair. He grinned broadly as he cut a large hole in my nylons. "Now looky here!" he said. "Put your hand down there, Ma'am, and you can feel that little ol' head."

I did, my hands shaking. He steadied my hand for me, then squeezed it tight.

"Now if you've just got a couple of good pushes in you, we'll have that baby out in a jiffy. Hang on to me now, here we go!"

I pushed as hard as I could, and felt the horrible burning sting they called the ring of fire in my birthing class. The baby's head emerged. John's smile left him as he worked. "Give me another good one now, Honey! Push as hard as you can!"

His face was grim.

I gave it all I had and pushed its little body out. I opened my eyes then and looked down. The baby was blue.

She was small, and she wasn't moving. Her eyes were closed and she just lay in that big old black hand with her bottom up in the air.

John immediately began rubbing her back and chest. He worked quickly, suctioning her nose and throat once more, then slapped her bottom.

Her little cry was the last thing I heard before I lost consciousness myself.

I came around several hours later. Harold was holding my hand and rubbing my thumb. I looked up at him, and then I remembered.

"The baby, is she…"

"She's just fine. You sure had us scared, though."

"What happened?"

"You passed out, that's what," said Helen from behind him. "You sure lost a lot of blood, Honey. After you had that baby you started to hemorrhage. You looked white as a sheet. Scared me half to death. They finally got the bleeding under control, but you weren't coming around so they gave you an emergency transfusion."

My head started to spin again and I closed my eyes. "Honey!" said Harold in alarm. "Honey, are you alright?"

It felt like my eyelids weighed fifty pounds. I kept them closed as I asked, "Where is she?"

"They've got her in the nursery. She's doing fine. They just wanted to keep an eye on her. I guess you two had quite the adventure."

"Yeah, remind me to never give birth with my shoes on ever again."

Harold chuckled. "I'm just so sorry I wasn't there for you, Honey. I'm so glad

Helen came when she did. If she hadn't, I…" Harold faltered, his voice getting husky.

Helen clicked her tongue. She didn't like any show of emotion. "Just did what anybody would have done."

I found out later from Harold that she had gone back to my place after I'd been stabilized and cleaned up that awful mess and then took the kids over to

Grandma Alice's after they got home from school. It felt odd to feel a warmth toward Helen. It was a new experience for me.

"Can I see the baby?" I asked.

"I'll go tell them you've come 'round," said Helen, glad to remove herself from the awkwardness of our emotions.

A few minutes later a nurse, accompanied by Helen, pushed in a little cart with a pink card attached. It said, 'Baby Parley, female.'

I remember wondering just before I gave birth to Benny if I'd be able to love him as much as I did Josie. It seemed impossible to have enough love to put that much again into another person. That was before I met Benny.

I looked up at that tiny little girl and knew once again the experience of loving again with everything I had, and still love everyone else the same. She was crying and swinging around her tight little fists as the nurse handed her down to me.

"Were you planning to breast feed?" the nurse asked.

"Of course!" I said as that little girl grabbed hold of my nightgown.

"Now would be a good time, then. She's hungry and we can't get her to take a bottle."

I held her up to me, and she latched right on.

"Look at that! She's a pro!" said Harold in delight. "Just a little bitty thing, isn't she? What did she weigh again?"

"Six pounds, two ounces," Helen pronounced proudly, folding her arms.

I looked up at Helen and noticed she had a cotton ball taped to the inside of her left arm. I looked quickly at Harold and he shook his head slightly, so I didn't say anything 'til she left an hour later.

"That Theo's probably got the kids so wired up they're driving poor Alice crazy!" she said as she slung her purse over her shoulder. "Can I get you anything, Nancy?"

I shook my head because Little Girl was sleeping against my breast. Helen briskly walked out.

"Harold, did she give me the transfusion?" I asked as soon as the door closed behind her.

Harold didn't answer at first, then he started to smile. "I'm under oath, Nan. I can't tell a lie, so I'll just choose to keep quiet. The donor wanted to remain anonymous. Said she didn't want just anybody's blood going into her niece. Made quite a fuss over it."

It seemed odd to me that Helen and I would share the same blood type. I just couldn't imagine the two of us having anything in common.

My eyes started to get a little misty as I thought about how very little I actually knew Helen. What I did know of her, I didn't like very much–'til today.

"What are we going to name her?"

"I don't know. I thought sure it was going to be a boy." I'd never even given much thought to girl's names. I had 'Connor Jay' lined up.

It seemed like Harold was having the same thought I was. Benny and Josie weren't named after anyone in the family, and it almost seemed unfair to everyone else if we started now.

"How about Marie Helen?" I asked.

Harold looked down at Little Girl and she grimaced in her sleep. He chuckled. "No one ever likes their middle name anyway. Sounds about right to me, though. I don't think it would make a very good first name, so sticking it in the middle seems fine."

"Well alright then, Miss Marie Helen. I'll have to tell you about that middle name someday."

Just then there was a soft knock on the door.

"Come in," I said.

An enormous black man walked in and smiled at me. I had no idea who he was. He wore a dark blue sweatshirt and black jeans and had enormous hands. Then

I remembered. It was my angel, John, without his white robe.

"Come in, John!" I said excitedly. "Harold, this is John. He's the one who saved Marie and me."

He grinned and shook Harold's hand. "Thank you, John. I can't thank you enough. You did real good. Are you going into obstetrics?"

"Nope." He grinned wider. "I'm going to specialize in pediatrics. I was just on call as a substitute in the ER today. I sure got hollered at after it was over. I was supposed to inform the doctor on call for serious emergencies. I just jumped the gun a little. It's not hospital procedure to deliver babies from a wheelchair."

"Good thing you did!" I said. "No one could have handled that better than you. I'm glad you were there." I smiled up at him, then said, "Oh, this is Marie Helen." I held her up for him and he took her gently into his arms.

"Well, Miss Marie, you were sure in a big hurry to get here. Made it kind of hard on your mama!" He tickled her gently on the cheek. "How are you doing Ma'am?"

"I'm fine, just tired, and hungry. Do you know when they serve dinner around here?"

"Oh, about five thirty. You can eat any time, though. Just tell the nurse. Tell her you want a T-bone steak. You lost a lot of blood today, Ma'am." He grinned. "Make it rare!"

Harold chuckled. I could tell he liked John.

"Well, I best be getting home. I have to study and I have to sleep and I've got just five hours to do it in." He handed Marie to Harold. "Oh, I got you something Mrs. Parley."

He reached into a pocket at the side of his sweatshirt and pulled out a small package. He winked at me as he put it on the bed beside me, then left.

"Isn't he sweet!" I exclaimed as I opened the gift.

"Well, I wouldn't exactly call him sweet. He's too big for sweet. Can you imagine him as a pediatrician?" Harold's eyes sparkled with laughter.

I burst out laughing once I got the wrapping off. It was a pair of pantyhose.

Chapter Five

I started missing my kids after the second day in the hospital. They said they wouldn't release me 'til my iron and blood pressure went up. Harold brought them in a couple times to see me, but Helen was always there and shooed them out after only fifteen minutes. She wouldn't hear of either of them holding Marie. Both Benny and Josie were scowling as they left the second time.

Daddy came in during the day, usually in the afternoon. Laura was mad at him and had refused to see him the last few days, and she'd hardly let Mama out of her sight.

"How's Nantucket?" he asked as he came in the first time. "Doing good. They said my iron is up a little."

He looked a little tired as he sat down and took off his hat. He fished around in his pocket for a minute, then gave me a small box. I opened it.

Inside were two little pink bubble gum cigars. I looked up at him, smiling. "That's all they had in the gift shop that I could get with what's in my pocket," he explained.

"Thanks, Daddy! Want to chew one with me?"

"Nah. You and Harold can, or maybe give 'em to the kids."

Daddy was quiet for a while as I fed Marie. He kept looking around the room, a little embarrassed, I think.

After a while Marie went to sleep and I asked, "Want to hold her?"

"Oh, I don't want to wake her up."

"You won't. She sleeps just like her daddy."

He came up to the bed and bent down awkwardly, handling her like she was made of finely spun glass.

Just then she giggled in her sleep.

"Did you see that?" he whispered excitedly.

"She did that yesterday, too. I think the other kids laughed in their sleep when they were tiny too. Josie didn't laugh when she was awake 'til she was about five months old."

I smiled at Daddy as he caressed her cheek gently with a giant finger.

"I wonder what's so funny when they're that small."

"I don't know. I figure maybe angels are tickling them."

Daddy smiled at that. "You were just a tiny thing too. Seems to me you looked just about like this one."

I smiled at him but turned away when I saw his chin was trembling.

"Kids just grow up so dern fast. Seems like it was just yesterday I was holding you like this, Nan." He was quiet for a while as he got a better hold on his emotions, then continued, "You remember that first time Laura got sick, and she was just acting like a kid? I remember thinking, 'Well, if this is as bad as it gets, it'll be alright. It's just like I got my little girl back, that's all.' She wouldn't see me again today. She's got it in her head that it's my fault about Michael."

"What all happened anyway? Has he called?"

"No. Laura won't say much, other than that she thinks it's my fault he doesn't love her."

"Did she say that?"

"Pretty much. I still have no idea what went on that day."

"Is she getting any better yet?"

Daddy sighed and handed Marie back down to me.

"No, she isn't, Nan. This is a bad one. They can't get her to respond to any of her meds, and they've had to isolate her several times."

"What for?" I asked. I noticed my heart had begun beating faster.

"Oh, just being a bit crazy, I guess."

I was being protected from something again. Whatever it was, he wasn't going to tell me. Suddenly I realized that I didn't even want to know. Thinking of

Laura was making me anxious. The aura of giving birth to a new life faded a bit, allowing fear and darkness in just long enough to keep me up that night.

After Dad left, I kept thinking about her. I must have been up 'til at least three in the morning. When I finally did sleep, I didn't dream of tornadoes. I dreamed of being lost in a maze of splotchy green wallpapered rooms. I knew I was supposed to find something, but I couldn't remember what it was I'd lost. People in bathrobes were muttering all around me, laughing at me, and shouting directions I couldn't understand. Suddenly I got that familiar hot tingling in my breasts as my milk came in, and I knew what I'd lost. I couldn't remember where I'd put Marie and I knew it had been ages since I last fed her.

"What kind of a mother would forget to feed her own baby?" a woman in a yellow robe sneered.

I awoke and found my milk had indeed come in, and that my nightgown was wet in front. I pushed the button to call the nurse. My hands were sweating.

A young nurse came in and raised her eyebrows in question.

"My milk's come in. Could I get another nightgown, and could you bring me

Marie? I want to feed her." That last part came out on a sob.

"You just did two hours ago. Are you OK, Mrs. Parley?"

"That's right. I remember. I just want to hold her."

She stood and looked at me a minute as I wiped a tear away. "Are you in pain?" she asked, coming and putting a cool hand on my head.

"I just want to hold my baby, that's all. I'm OK."

A few minutes later she pushed Marie's cart in and gently handed her to me.

Marie woke, and started sucking her fist.

"Well, I guess she may be hungry after all," the nurse said, and walked back to her station.

Marie nursed noisily and I smiled as she smacked again and again. After a while that horrible panic leftover from the nightmare faded, and I slept peacefully after the nurse came and took Marie back to the nursery.

Mama came in the next day and stayed about an hour. She was fidgety and restless even though it was the first time she'd seen Marie. She held her, smiling, as she cooed at her, but I noticed her head shook slightly as she looked down at her. Mama started shaking after they'd given her shock treatments that last time she had a nervous breakdown over Laura. Seemed like she couldn't remember a lot of things after that, too. She usually shook when she was thinking really hard or trying to focus on something. She gave up needlepoint a long time ago, even though it was one of her favorite things to do. She figured it just wasn't worth all the blood she had to spill over it. The treatments worked, however. They got her head straight, but she just lost a bit in the process. Mama had suffered from severe depression her whole life, and chronic anxiety, PMS, and a chemical imbalance that led to the removal of her thyroid gland. Emotionally she was a mess, but she was kind and the most giving person I knew. She couldn't stand the idea of any of her kids suffering or being in any kind of danger. She had to stand by for the last seven years watching Laura suffer, get hurt, even humiliated, and there wasn't much she could do about it. Even though Mama wasn't schizo- phrenic, I know she thought it was her fault, that somehow she'd passed something on to Laura. No wonder she shook sometimes.

I thought of the way I shook in labor. I just felt so helpless 'til it was all over and they handed me a perfect little baby. I wondered if she really was perfect, or if she'd turn eighteen someday, and we'd find out she had…

My heart started racing again as I watched Mama and my baby. There was a family I'd read about in some of my research. They had five sons. The first was seventeen when he started showing the signs. The second made it to 19. The third was 21, and the fourth was actually 26. He'd been the hope of the family, and it hit him later, just when they'd thought it was safe. They didn't bother waiting on the fifth. They started him on anti-depressants before he turned 15. That story made me sick. I never told Harold about it. I was only 23 when I read it. I quit reading about schizophrenia after that.

There were times when I got angry at Mama and at Laura. I'd ask God why I was a part of this family. Seemed like sometimes my own happiness wasn't even real. I guess I just started to think of everything as being merely temporary. It didn't seem fair the way pain was dealt out in my family. My mama, my sister, Daddy, and Grandma, they'd all been through hell, and here I sat with three beautiful kids, a house, and a good husband. I figured my turn to suffer was coming, and I was always sort of flinching just in case.

I asked Mama how Laura was. She took a long time answering.

"Well, she's mad this time. Mad at just about everybody. She kicked me out today. Slammed the door in my face."

"Why was she so mad at you?"

"Because I didn't believe her. The thing is, it's just so hard to tell with her. She may be telling me the truth." Mama shuddered visibly. "I sure hope she's not."

"What did she tell you?"

"Oh, never mind, Nan. I shouldn't have brought it up."

I just didn't feel right after she left. I could actually feel my heart pounding.

Seemed like I could hear it too. I held Marie almost all day and she calmed me a bit, but not quite enough. I didn't sleep at all that night. I tossed and turned, my mind as belligerent as a toddler at bedtime. It just refused to quit. As soon as

I would finally get one fear resolved, another would push its way in. The worst fear of all was the one that hovered in my mind the whole time. It was that I was starting to lose my mind, and I didn't know how I'd be able to take care of this baby. What would Harold think of me when he came in tomorrow and saw me gone crazy? I was utterly petrified. Never had I been so afraid in my life. Even my skin tingled all over. I was in a very dark place that night and was too afraid to ring for a nurse. I didn't want anyone to know. I was humiliated by what I might do when the last threads of sanity left me. I didn't even want to see Marie. I spent all night trying to hold on to a mind that wanted to flee.

Morning came, but it was so gray and rainy it was hard to tell when exactly the sun had come up. I lay there staring at the wall. I turned on the TV. It was a commercial for anti-depressants and was listing all the side effects. I shut it off. Just then the phone rang. It was Laura.

"Hi Nan!" she said cheerfully. "How are you?" "I'm OK, I guess. Are you allowed to call me?" "No. I sneaked. How is your baby?"

"Oh, she's just beautiful," I said. My heart was pounding again.

Laura was quiet for a long time on the other end. I wondered if maybe she'd wandered off.

Finally, she spoke. "Nan, I'm pregnant. I told them I was, and they said I'm not. I know they're wrong though. I can feel it moving already. It's a girl."

I felt like my bed had been dropped from a ten-story building and I'd just landed. I hung up.

Just then Harold walked in with a bouquet of daisies, my favorite flower. I burst into tears when I saw him. He walked quickly to the bed and bent down to hug me. I sobbed and sobbed. I had no idea when I would stop.

"Honey!" He whispered in my ear. "Honey, what's the matter?"

I thought of telling him I went crazy last night, but instead I only sobbed more. It was all over now. He'd leave me and take the kids.

His family would finally be able to say "I told you so." I held him tighter as I cried.

"Is something wrong with Marie?" He looked suddenly terrified.

Just then the phone rang again. "Don't answer it!" I pleaded. He picked it up anyway. "If it's Laura, tell her I can't talk to her right now."

It was Laura. I knew by the way he looked quickly at me. He listened to her for a while, said something with his back to me, then hung up.

He turned back to me and watched me a minute. "What's all this about,

Nan?"

I waited a long time. He sat down on the bed next to me, and rubbed my hand with his thumb. He looked down at me, clearly anxious. I took a deep breath, and told him what happened. I told him about my night, about how I couldn't get my brain to stop, and how I was still so afraid.

He flinched visibly before hugging me again. "Just calm down a bit, Nan. That's all. Just take a deep breath, and calm down. There's nothing to be afraid of."

I knew he wouldn't understand. I couldn't even remember what calm felt like. "Would you send in a doctor?"

"What for? Are you hurting?"

Harold was trying not to hear what I told him. He was not willing to listen. I was hurting, but in a way he didn't want to hear about or understand. I sat back against my pillows and closed my eyes. My mind raced back to when we'd first met. He was so tall and handsome and quiet.

I was in college, majoring in art. Harold was a physics major. I passed him sometimes in the hall and noticed him, but he always walked purposely, not looking around much. I knew he'd never really seen me.

One of my abstract sculptures made it to the student display on the lower level of the art building at the end of the semester. I named it "Infinity." It was my attempt to make rock appear fluid and infinite. I was walking to class one day and saw him standing in front of it. He stared at it for a long time. I timidly walked up behind him. My name was on the card, but I knew he wouldn't know it was me.

"Interesting, huh?" I said from behind him, as if I were just another casual observer.

Harold turned quickly and saw me for the first time. I liked the look in his eyes. I got tingles all down my spine as he looked me over a minute before turning back to the statue.

"I can't tell what the hell it is," he said frankly. "This abstract stuff is a joke. I don't know who started the idea of calling junk like this art."

I was hurt but determined not to show it. "Well, why have you been looking at it so long?"

He looked at it a moment more, as if he didn't know the answer. "It's just kind of weird, I guess. It really doesn't look much like marble, even though it says here that it is. I guess I was just trying to figure it out."

"Oh," was all I said before walking away. I heard him trying to follow me, but the lobby was crowded.

"Hey!" he shouted after me, but I pretended not to hear as I stepped outside the door.

He saw me a few days later in the hall and approached me. He was sort of nervous, and finally asked me out without even looking at me. It was amazing to me that a man so large could appear so sheepish. I hadn't forgiven him yet, so I told him no and walked away.

I couldn't get him out of my mind, though. He had light brown wavy hair and the nicest, strongest hands I'd ever seen. He had a straight nose, and a small mole under one eye. His skin was tan and his eyes were a soft amber brown.

I saw Harold several more times and usually looked away before we could make eye contact. He was obviously from a wealthy family. He dressed well and had an air of quality. After a while I regretted my hasty departure, but my feelings had been hurt. I wrote him off as an unfeeling, unartistic, egotistical dud. But I couldn't forget the way he'd looked at me.

Finally, one day I felt someone grab my arm from behind. I turned and saw him. He had a sort of bewildered look in his eyes.

"Have I done something wrong?" he asked. "I haven't stopped thinking about you since I first saw you. I don't understand why you won't even let me get to know you. I've watched you a few weeks now, and I don't see you with anyone else. Why are you so cold to someone you don't even know yet?"

I felt cornered. Sometimes it's easier to go on hurting than admitting it to the person who hurt you. I felt silly. He was being so forward and open, something totally unexpected based on what I thought I knew of him.

"I'm sorry. I guess I've just been very busy. What's your name?" "Harold Parley," he said, shaking my hand. "May I ask yours?" "No."

The hurt and bewildered look returned to his eyes. He stepped back a minute and then noticed I was smiling.

"Can I buy you lunch? Bribe you a little?"

I caved. I knew I would and felt giddy. He bought me a giant submarine sandwich across the street from the campus. I never was good at eating those neatly. I was so embarrassed when I spilled some mustard down the front of my white sweater. He pulled off his jacket and buttoned it up for me. When he got to the top button he brushed the bottom of my chin with his finger.

"If I'm ever going to get this back, don't you think I ought to know who's borrowing it?" he asked.

"Number 17, the Anderson building."

He accepted this as if he enjoyed the game we were playing. Then he walked me home. He kissed my forehead before leaving. "See you around, Seventeen."

Three days went by before I heard from him. Finally, a bunch of long stem roses were delivered to my dorm room. On the card it said, "I am an "infinite" idiot. Forgive me?" Under that he wrote down his number. He must have gone to the Anderson Art building and finally figured it out. I guessed that was why he hadn't been by. Well, I was glad he felt like an idiot and let him sweat it out for a couple days before I called him. The phone rang about five times, and just as I was about to hang up, I heard his voice.

"Hello?" he said.

"Hi," I said dumbly. I couldn't think of anything else to say.

"May I ask who's calling?"

There was a long pause. I said, "Nancy."

There was an even longer pause, before he said, "Can I come over?"

I said yes and kept on saying yes right up to the altar. We were married just a few short months later.

I took him to meet my Grandpa Harris in the old folks home a few weeks before he died. Grandpa hardly ever said anything to anyone. His main goal once he'd been admitted against his will was to go back home to Oklahoma. Once he almost succeeded. After batting away several nurses, sending them sprawling, he wheeled out the front door, pushing his wheelchair forward with all his might.

Problem was, the parking lot was sloped downward, and his strong lumberjack arms weren't what they used to be. He lost control and careened down the parking lot where he landed in the ditch. He was none the worse for wear, however.

He was one of the strongest men I ever knew.

Daddy and I introduced Harold to him just after we were married. Grandpa looked at Harold a minute, and then looked away. He was quiet throughout the visit as Daddy tried to coax him into conversation. It was a bad day. He never said much of anything to anyone after Grandma died. After a while, it got uncomfortable. Just as we were about to leave, I noticed Grandpa had finally taken notice of Harold, who stood with his arm around me. He looked from me to Harold then said, "Boy, you two are sure in love."

That was the last time I saw him before he died, but I took his last words to us as a blessing on our happiness.

I realized I had been sitting quietly for a long time. I looked up, wiping new tears away and saw Harold looking down at me. I wanted more than anything to be perfect for him, to be the girl I was back then. He had no idea what he was getting into when he fell for me. I was afraid maybe he was starting to regret it.

After I'd gotten pregnant the second time, I quit school. He finished up with his Associate degree but went no further. I had Josie, despite all my fears that the first miscarriage was a bad omen. She was beautiful, perfect, and expensive. Harold had been working at the lumber yard between classes to make ends meet and had no intentions of a career in lumber. But further schooling became impossible for him as he cared for his new family. His dad disapproved of our marriage. I believe his exact words were, "Well, if you think you're man enough to get married, then you're man enough to pay your own way."

Harold didn't seem to give much thought to physics or the wonders of the universe anymore. He was too tired and sweaty after a day of hauling wood. He'd worked hard since then, though, and was now general manager at the new lumberyard in town. Money was still tight, but since then we'd managed to buy a small house and raise the kids reasonably well. I shopped second-hand stores and used coupons religiously.

I looked up at him again. I loved him so much it hurt, and I didn't want to hurt him with what I thought was happening to me.

"I'm sorry, Harold. You just didn't know what you were getting into when you fell for me."

"Well, you're past warranty, so there's not much we can do about it now."

It stung, and I looked quickly up at him. He was smiling, and that look I loved was in his eyes as he bent down and kissed me firmly on the mouth.

"I'm crazy for you, Nancy. I don't care if you're crazy for me, or just plain crazy. I'll still kiss you like this…and this…and…"

"Stop it, Harold! What if the nurse sees us?" I giggled.

"She's going to give me the "after your wife gives birth" lecture anyway. They always do."

When he left, he took the weight of the world off my shoulders. I'd felt so horrible, and so scared, and he chased it all away. He still loved me more than anything and despite everything. I just wished Laura could find the same for herself.

I talked to a doctor later about what happened to me that night, and he explained it was most likely a panic attack. I gave him a little of our family history and he said it was no wonder I got a little over-stressed. He reminded me that I had just had a baby, had enormous emotional turmoil over my family, and that my iron still wasn't quite up to what it should be.

"So, I'm okay, then?" I asked.

He was quiet a minute, studying my chart. Then he looked up. "Well, you don't sound crazy to me. However, given your family history, it wouldn't surprise me if you had generalized anxiety disorder."

My heart stopped, then raced furiously. "What does that mean?"

"Well, last night you had a panic attack."

"I know, but it was just one. Do you mean…"

"What I mean is, you had a panic attack, which is a symptom of the disorder. Given your gene pool, it's very likely. It can be medicated. Since you've chosen to breast feed, I won't give you anything right now. Many people don't require medication for it at all. If you reach a point where you have, let's say, a panic attack every day, then you'd need medication."

I was quiet as he looked at me. I didn't like the idea of having something wrong with me.

"What I would suggest is that you try to slow your life down a bit. Take a break from Laura. Maybe you shouldn't even talk to her for a while. If your in-laws bother you, don't let them in. If you're concerned about something and losing sleep over it, let me suggest a technique. I'll be right back."

He returned after a few minutes and held up a small file of index cards. "See this file? Pretend it's your brain, and all these little cards are your thoughts. Things you're worried about, things you have to do, whatever. If something is causing too much stress, you stick it in the back, like this." He pulled a card from the front and put it in the back. "This is your worry box. You just file those things away that you can't handle right now. Then later maybe you can shuffle things around a bit."

He smiled reassuringly at me and squeezed my shoulder. "Just try it. Keep in mind, people with anxiety disorder are not crazy. You're just a classic worry wart, that's all. But now that you're aware, maybe you won't worry yourself sick."

"Is that possible? If I get too stressed will I..."

"Now Nancy, that's one of those cards that needs to get put way in the back.

I'll see you again tomorrow."

I looked down at the box he'd given me. All the cards were blank. I spent the afternoon filling them up.

Chapter Six

I went home after about five days. I still felt sort of weak and tired, but I figured I might as well be tired at home, seeing as how that was free. I had no idea what the bill was going to be. I wrote that down on one of my cards and stuck it way in the back. I kept telling myself we'd be fine, that there was nothing I could do about it, and that Harold would handle it. Somehow that card just wouldn't stay put, though. I could put it in the back of the file, but it wouldn't stay in the back of my mind.

I didn't talk to Laura. I just couldn't stand the thought of talking to her. I felt like that was the one thing that would put me over the edge. When you think you might be going crazy, the last thing you want to do is hang around with crazy people—just in case it might rub off.

Putting Laura out of sight didn't necessarily put her out of mind, though. I still thought about her every day. I felt guilty for not calling her or going to see her. Most of all, I couldn't get what she'd said out of my mind.

Laura had high standards for herself. She would never in her right mind do anything that would ruin her virtue. Mama raised us that way. I just wasn't sure what state her mind had been in when she called me that morning.

Christmas was coming. The streets of White Lake were hung with lights. Ridiculous looking bells and candy canes hung precariously on the streetlamps. Like most things in White Lake, the spirit of Christmas had to be brought in and put up, and it came in the form of tacky tinsel wreaths and plastic snowmen on brownish lawns. A white Christmas was something only dreamt about in Texas.

Harold had gone out with the kids while I was at the hospital and picked out a tree. They didn't decorate it 'til I got home, though. I was always sort of picky about where I liked things put on the tree. I didn't get much chance to be artistic anymore, so I always wanted the tree to be a masterpiece.

We all decorated it the night after I got home. I sat in the chair and told the kids where to put each ornament as I handed it to them. Harold had meticulously strung all the lights perfectly and made sure the bead garland was perfectly spaced. We listened to the local radio station's Christmas broadcast since I didn't have any decent Christmas music. I always wanted to buy some every year, but the good CDs cost a fortune, and I just couldn't bring myself to spend the money. Then, after Christmas, I'd heard all the carols I could stand and didn't even buy any once they were half off.

It felt good to be home. I sat back and watched the kids as they decorated the tree. I felt calm for the first time in a while. I looked around the living room fondly. I'd painted it a light sage green with buttermilk colored trim. It was an old house. Something about this house had charmed me the first time I went through it. I loved all the old crown moldings and baseboards and hardwood floors. Harold wasn't really thrilled with it. The only thing he liked about it was the price. We looked at a few newer open concept homes, but they were all out of our price range. Harold finally gave in and we made an offer for this one. He apologized to me that night because he couldn't get me a decent house to live in. "Honey, I love that house. I liked it as soon as we walked in. I could just see myself living there," I reassured him.

He was quiet for a while. I knew it was sort of a blow to him, having been raised in The Heights. He probably never imagined he'd live in a house on the lower income side of town. He had to swallow a lot of pride to make the offer for this one.

I went on, "I've got all kinds of ideas already to spruce it up. I'm going to paint it and we can reside it someday, and I know just what will make the kitchen nicer. Harold, I'm thrilled with it."

"Aren't you afraid of ghosts?" he asked. "That house has been there forever."

"Well, as long as they're nice ghosts, I won't mind a bit. It's nice to think that somebody else has worked it in for us. Just think, Harold, fifty years ago some other young couple probably bought that house and had kids in it. And before them, somebody else. Don't you think it's kind of neat? That house has a lot of memories. I can feel it."

And it did. It already had some that we'd added to it ourselves. Some memories were obvious, like the day Benny finally learned how to write the letter A and he scribbled it all over the kitchen wall. Others just found their way into the cracks and into the gentle aging of the wood paneling.

I was so enchanted with the idea of owning my own house, I painted stripes on the dining room walls to celebrate. I'd always wanted to do that and everyone said it looked nice, except Mama. She came from generations of white walled houses, or maybe beige. Color was terrifying to her, and stripes were...let me put it this way...she called one morning and said she thought the walls were what was making my blood pressure go up with my latest pregnancy.

"Nancy, "she said, "I've been up all night thinking about it, and I'll help you repaint those walls. I'll even buy the paint. It looks like an Egyptian circus in your dining room with all that color. I just know that room is making you nervous. You have to think about impressions, Nancy, and your own mental health. Some people might think you're crazy in the head when they see those stripes! I don't know anyone with stripes on their walls. I mean it, Nancy. You repaint those walls!"

It was good to be old enough to disobey Mama. The stripes stayed.

Uncle Theo and Grandma Alice came by just after we got the Christmas decorations up.

"Oh, Nancy, that tree is just gorgeous!" exclaimed Grandma. "I don't know how you do it. Somehow your tree always ends up looking better than everybody else's. Now I'll go home and look at mine and get depressed."

"It's so nice to see you, Grandma!" I said and hugged her. "You too, Honey. How are you doing anyway?"

"I'm good. Marie gained a whole pound already."

"Well, she needs it. I never saw such a bitty little thing."

Theo came over and tugged at my hair. "I still can't get over how my Little Miss Nasty's got herself all grown up. Alice, I think we must be gettin' old!"

It seemed to me that Grandma and Uncle Theo had always been old. They'd been old longer than I'd been alive. I could barely remember Grandpa. I only had vague memories of the scent of chewing tobacco and whiskey.

I got out my eggnog and some of the cranberry bread I'd baked. I served everyone as they sat in the living room.

"For Pete's sake, Nan! Sit down and relax!" Grandma kept saying.

Benny and Josie piled onto Theo's lap. He ate both of their noses and was going for their ears when Benny said, "You didn't really eat my nose! See, I still got it!"

"Nah, but I sure am going to show you something special now. Here, Boy, pull my finger."

I knew what was coming and went back into the kitchen. Harold followed me.

"Let me get that, Nan. You go on back in there and visit." He took the plates I was holding and put them in the sink. He never said it, but I got the feeling Harold disapproved of Theo.

"Come on over here, Nancy and sit by me," Grandma beckoned. She had a small pink package next to her on the sofa. She plunked it onto my lap, then looked away while I opened it. For some reason she always got self-conscious whenever she gave me anything.

It was a beautiful pink and white afghan with matching booties and a bonnet. "How did you know I was going to have a girl? This must've taken you weeks!"

"Well, I didn't. Got a blue one just like it at home. I figure somebody's going to have a boy sometime, so I'll just hold on to it."

I thought of Laura again and was quiet for a while. The one thing I really liked about Grandma was that she didn't need anybody to talk to her. If you just wanted to sit and think then that was fine. I tried the booties on Marie and they were way too big.

"Well, babies have a way of growing up quick as anything. I still can't believe

Josie is going to be seven." I said.

Grandma startled me then with her next question. "You're not going to go see

Laura this time, are you?"

I didn't say anything.

"I was by to see her today," Grandma informed me casually. "They've started her on some new medication. Sure wish I could remember the name of it. It's just out this year. I couldn't tell the difference yet, though."

I couldn't think of much to say, so I asked about the medicine.

"Well, it's got some pretty serious side effects. The worst being that it might lower her white blood cell count. Your Daddy explained it to me. If that happens, it'll ruin her immune system," Grandma explained.

"How do they know it won't happen to Laura?"

"Well, they don't. So, they're going to take a blood sample once a week just to make sure."

Laura always hated needles, and having her blood taken. The veins in her arms were so delicate, the doctors always had a hard time even finding one. I tried the bonnet on Marie. She looked adorable in it. I held her up and kissed her nose.

Grandma put her hand on my arm, willing me to look at her. "Nancy, she's been asking for you. The way things are going, she won't be out by Christmas."

We sat quietly together for a spell, then she continued, "Some things just need doin', even if you think you can't stand it. Somehow, you've let what everyone's been saying go to your head. You're not delicate, Nancy, not by a long shot. You can stand to go visit your sister when she needs you. People have been through worse."

Grandma had, and it shamed me to think of it. It seemed to me that people were just tougher a few generations back. It's hard to accept things that you can't control. I think that was the difference between my generation and theirs. They accepted that life was long and tough and rewarding only after hard work.

I hadn't told Grandma about what happened to me in the hospital. I hadn't even told my folks. I overheard them talking once. Mama was crying about how it was just so hard to watch Laura's life. Daddy stood behind her, and took her shoulders and said, "Well now, look at Nancy. She's doing fine and standing on her own two feet. We've got a girl who is OK, too. I take my happiness in that sometimes when I get too down with what's happening to Laura."

All I had to do was be OK. I was ashamed of myself.

Chapter Seven

I called Helen to see if she could come and watch the kids for me. She sounded kind of grumpy when I asked her. She hemmed and hawed a while, then decided she better come on over. I just knew she was itching to scrub out my bathtub again. Sometimes I think she was surprised to see my kids had made it this far. If you ever wanted to hear a story about someone dying from a staph infection, or salmonella, or botulism, you just had to let her take a look in your tub or your wastebasket.

She was amazingly quiet when she came over. She just sat on the couch and put out her arms to hold Marie. I thought it was kind of odd that she never commented on Marie's middle name. Sometimes you think you're doing someone a great honor and I guess you sort of expect a certain kind of reaction. I was disappointed. She just said, "Oh, my," and that was it. I guess I just wasn't sure if I should've been thanked or not.

I drove over to Pleasant Hills by myself. I figured if I chickened out, nobody would have to know but me. I told Helen I needed to get some shopping done.

When I got to the familiar, sprawling brick building I noticed my heart started to race a little. I took the bag of salt and vinegar chips I'd brought and got out of the car. Laura and I were the only ones in the family who liked them. They were sort of sharp, and a little shocking at first, but the more we ate, the more we liked them.

I walked in the front door and up to the reception desk. No one was there at the moment. I looked around and saw no staff members in the area. I noticed the man in the green robe I'd seen before. He still wore those same enormous glasses. I figured he must be a regular, too.

"Looking for Laura?" he asked, approaching me.

"Yes. I don't even know what room she's in. Do you?"

"I certainly do, but she's not in it."

"Well, do you know where she is?"

"She sure doesn't."

"Excuse me?" I said, a little startled.

"She don't know where she is, that's what I said. Wish I didn't." With that he shoved his fists into his robe pockets.

"Do you know where you are?" I asked.

"Pleasant Hills Mental Care Center, 2347 Birch Street."

"Well, then what are you doing here?" I asked.

"I've got some friends my family doesn't like, and every time I get to talking to 'em, they send me in here."

"Well, that's odd. What's wrong with your friends?"

The man started to get agitated, and kept putting his hand in and out of his pocket. "I haven't seen 'em in this place. They said they'd come to see me, but they lied to me."

He started to cry. "They're the only friends I got, and my stupid sister is trying to take them away from me. I'm afraid maybe she told them I was crazy so they won't come see me anymore. Have you seen them?"

I was getting very uncomfortable. "I–I don't know them. What do they look like?"

He looked at me a moment, as if startled. "Well, Martha is kind of old and fat, but she's sweet. Johnny is about my age. He plays a mean game of chess. I always tell him he looks like Clint Eastwood, but he doesn't believe me. And then there's

Marie. She started coming to my place after school. She brings me paper hearts and pictures she draws. She's going to be an artist someday. She's got black hair and black eyes. She's Vietnamese. Sweetest little thing. I miss Marie the most."

"Oh, well, I'm sorry. I haven't seen them. I have a baby named Marie, though."

He beamed. "Huh, I'll have to tell her that. Does she have black hair?"

"Well, no. She's pretty much bald, actually."

He watched me a minute, not realizing he was still crying. Tears ran unheeded down his cheeks.

"I think maybe you'll see them," he said hopefully. "If you do, tell them I'll just be in here a while. Oh, and could you give this to my Marie if you see her? I promised I'd give her this."

He put a purple heart medallion into my hand and saluted me. "What's your name?" I asked.

"Well, your sister calls me Psycho Joe, but you can just call me Joe."

"I don't think you should be giving this to a stranger, Joe." I tried to give him back the medallion.

"Oh no, you're not a stranger. I've seen you lots of times. Laura says you're a very talented artist. She says you're the best sister a girl could have, and she always brags on you. Says you're beautiful on the inside, even. I can tell she trusts you, so

I will, too."

Laura had never said anything like that to me. I was touched, but grew uncomfortable with the way he looked down at me, his cheeks still wet.

Finally, a nurse arrived. She looked harassed and tired. "Joe, you trying to give away your purple heart again? Leave this poor woman alone. You're supposed to be in the movie room with everyone else."

She took the medallion from me and put it in a drawer at the reception desk before raising her eyebrows at me. I watched Joe as he was escorted by an intern down a hallway.

"Don't worry about him. He always does that. Did he ask you if you've seen his friends?"

"Well, yes, but I didn't really think…"

"He has schizophrenia and talks to people who aren't there. Every once in a while he comes back in here because he refuses to take his medicine so his sister brings him in."

"Does the medicine work?"

"Oh yeah, but then he just cries all the time so we have to put him on anti-depressants."

"So, the medicine makes his friends go away?"

She looked at me over the tops of her glasses, clearly irritated. "He doesn't have any friends."

"Then why do you medicate him? Is he dangerous? Seems like he deserves to have some friends, even if they're just in his head."

"Ma'am," she said, "That man is a veteran of the Vietnam war. Of course he's dangerous. Who knows how many kids he's killed?"

I didn't like this new nurse, Louise. She had her name on a small tag over her left breast. I'd never seen her before, and she was starting to rub me the wrong way. My daddy was a veteran of that war.

"I don't know the procedure in mental hospitals, but is it common to discuss a patient's case with a total stranger?"

She turned red in the face and her lips just sort of disappeared. "Are you here for a reason?"

Just then Laura came down the hall. "Nan?"

"Oh, that's your sister," the nurse said, as if that somehow explained everything.

Laura grabbed my arm and steered me toward her room. "I can't stand Louise," she whispered.

Her room was done in the same wallpaper. It was midday, and it looked a lot brighter than I remembered these rooms being. A plastic stained-glass type picture hung in the window. It was of a few brightly colored fish and some seaweed, colored with markers.

"Do you like that?" she asked.

"Yes, it's really pretty. Did you make it?"

"Yeah. The craft lady was in yesterday. I made one for you too."

She went to a drawer and pulled it out. It was a brightly colored butterfly.

"You just hang it in a window so the sun can come through it." She looked suddenly sheepish. "I stayed in the lines better on this one, so I was going to give it to you."

"Thank you, Laura!" I said, relieved that she seemed almost normal. I noticed she kept moving her feet back and forth as she talked, but other than that she seemed fine.

We sat in silence for a while. I didn't quite know what to say. She seemed content to just look up at the picture of fish. Then I noticed her feet were moving faster. I could tell something was on her mind as she sat next to me.

Finally, she spoke. "I called Michael yesterday. He told me not to call anymore."

I suddenly panicked. "Laura, you're not supposed to call anybody, especially not when you're in here!" I felt humiliated for her, for anything she may have said to him.

Laura put her head down. "He doesn't love me, you know. He never did."

"I know, Honey. He never even deserved you." I pulled some hair from in front of her eyes and tucked it behind an ear.

She started to cry. I waited a minute or two, then asked, "Do you want to talk about what happened?"

She looked at me suspiciously a minute. "Did Daddy send you in to talk to me?"

"No, I sneaked in here today. Helen thinks I'm going shopping." "Oh, you sneaked!" Laura seemed to like that. "Well, alright then."

She took the picture of a butterfly off my lap and walked over to the window and held it up. It cast shades of red and blue and green all over her face. She stood there under a rainbow of color in the barren gray room and told me what had happened.

Michael's family always had an enormous Thanksgiving feast up at their lodge. Aunts, uncles, cousins, friends, everyone was there. Michael brought her in, then basically deserted her in a house full of strangers. He spent most of his time with a young woman Laura had never seen before. He didn't sit by Laura at the table. Laura knew that everyone there disapproved of her, she could just feel it. Besides casual, polite small talk, no one even seemed to notice her.

I could just imagine how awful that must have been for her. She was so shy around strangers.

"I couldn't eat anything. It all tasted like somebody'd dumped Lysol in it. After a while I could tell something was different. Everyone started staring at me. At first, I couldn't understand it, then I realized I was standing on my chair at the table. I just wanted to get a better look at the chandelier. It had lots of those little crystals, the ones that make rainbows. I wanted to touch one."

I felt just sick for her. I wanted to leave, but I remembered what Grandma had said, and so I stayed to hear the rest.

"Michael noticed me then. I smiled at him, but he had such a look on his face…"

Laura started to shake gently, and she rocked back and forth on the balls of her feet. "He took me out to my car. He put me inside and started it. Then he walked away. He never did look at me the way Harold looks at you, Nan. Sometimes he looked at me in a way that made me sort of scared, like he was thinking he might…" She shuddered then and put a hand on her lower abdomen.

"Oh Nancy! I feel it again. Come over here, quick!"

I stood and wiped a tear away. She grabbed my hand and put it low down on her belly. "Feel that?"

I didn't feel a thing. I looked down at the floor as she pressed my hand in harder. "There! You had to feel that!" she squealed in sudden delight.

I didn't. In fact, Laura looked thinner. There was no bulge in her abdomen, not one big enough to support the baby she thought she felt moving inside her. I couldn't look at her. After a while she relaxed her grip on my hand. "I made you cry, Nan. Why? Aren't you happy for me? The doctors said I never could get pregnant, but see, they were wrong!"

"How long have you had this baby inside you?" I asked. She thought a minute. "What's today?"

"Tuesday."

Laura counted on her fingers like she used to do when she was a kid. "About nine days, I guess."

"Why do you say that? You've been in here the last nine days."

"Well, that's when Jake came in here."

"Who's Jake?"

"He's the father, Nan. He came and he…"

I closed my eyes. Suddenly I felt like I weighed five hundred pounds. "Is Jake a patient here?"

"No, he was visiting someone."

Laura started to get agitated. "He told me it would be OK. He said as long as

I stayed quiet…"

I couldn't stand it. I just didn't want to hear any more. I reached out and grabbed her hand. "Did you go see the nurse afterward? Did he hurt you?"

Laura was shaking terribly then, and her face had gone white. "Do you believe me, Nan? Mama and Daddy don't. They don't want to."

I didn't want to either, but I didn't want to hurt her. I didn't know what to do. Suddenly I remembered the chips I'd stuffed in my purse. "I brought you these, Laura. You go on ahead and eat some. I need to step out a minute."

I went up to the nurse's station and was met by Louise. She looked smug.

"Was there a patient here by the name of Jake in the last two weeks?" I asked, barely hiding my rage.

"I don't see how that's any of your business," she said, smiling sweetly.

"Well, I plan on making it my business. Yours, too, when I file a lawsuit for negligence against you and this whole establishment. You tell me now, lady, or so help me I'm going to hop over that desk and educate you." I didn't exactly know what that meant, but I'd heard Theo use the term before. I figured it had something to do with me pulling her hair out.

She looked suddenly afraid and backed up. "No! There's been no one by the name of Jake admitted here!"

"Anybody named Jake visit?"

"Excuse me," said a deep voice behind me. "Can I help you?"

I whirled around and saw Laura's doctor. I never could remember his name.

"Can I see the guest book, please?"

"Nancy, right?" he asked. He was looking at me very strangely, as if he'd encountered an interesting medical case. "Why don't you step into my office?"

I nodded and walked with him down a short hallway and into a tiny office.

"Sit down, Nancy. I gather Laura told you about Jake."

"Yes. Is she telling the truth?"

"We have no way of knowing that. I'm sorry. We did have to isolate her several times. She was just too forward with our male guests, and yes, our records show a man named Jake was in here early last week."

"Did he..."

"I'm not going to lie to you, Mrs. Parley. It could have happened. Our staff is inadequate to watch every patient all the time. However, I personally consider it very unlikely that what she's alluded to did take place."

"How do you know?"

"Well, for one thing, this Jake was in to see his mother, who is in here for early-onset Alzheimer's. She says he was with her the whole time."

"But she has Alzheimers! How do you know what she's saying is true?"

"Well, we don't, and that's the pickle."

"Has Laura been given a pregnancy test?"

"Yes. Two of them. Both negative. There's just no evidence to support her claim."

"None to refute it either."

He sighed. "I'm sorry."

I walked back into the room. Laura was sitting cross legged on her bed. She had placed the only unbroken chips from the bag in a semicircle on the bed in front of her. "I'm going to eat these ones last," she explained.

I sat down by her and watched her sort her chips. "Why don't you eat the good ones first, Laura?"

"I just don't like it when there's nothing but crumbs at the end, that's all.

They're too bitter."

I stayed for another half hour. Laura wanted me to sing with her so I did. She had a beautiful voice. We sang old Eagles songs.

"I sure wish I had my guitar," she said after a while. "I could bring it to you."

"Nah, somebody would steal it. Can I ask you something, Nan?"

"Sure," I said, ignoring my racing pulse.

"Did Harold ever, you know, pressure you into things you didn't…I mean…did he expect you to…"

"Are you talking about Michael, Laura?"

"I guess."

"Well, Harold is a man, Honey. Men need some direction when it comes to things like that. They'll try to feel out all the boundaries…literally. You just got to let them know where the boundaries are and stick to it. They'll respect you if you do. Harold did, once I let him know the rules. But then, when you get married, you don't need those boundaries anymore. It's like your chips there, Laura.

You save the good part for last. You give yourself to him whole, not in pieces."

She thought about that a while. She started to cry again.

"I'm not whole, Nancy. I never was. This, this thing in my head…"

"Laura, did Michael take advantage of you?"

"He said I was a baby, and just too scared to be a real woman. I wouldn't let him, though. That's why he left me."

"Thank God for that!" I said and stood up. "Laura, I want to tell you something, even though I know you're sick right now. Please try to remember this.

You are worthy of a nice man, a man who will respect you and treat you the way anybody deserves to be treated. I don't care what's wrong with you. You don't have to settle for less than that."

Laura stared at me for a long time, her eyes piercingly bright. She nodded her head slowly. "Ten Four, Nantucket."

"All right then. Are you going to share those chips with me, or just eat them all yourself?"

I went to see my folks that night. I told Daddy that I'd been by to see Laura, and that I knew what had happened. He sighed and shook his head. "I just don't know about that, Nan." He didn't believe her—didn't want to.

Mama was quiet at first, then she said, "It makes me physically ill to imagine something like that happening to her. I feel like suing that hospital."

I felt the same, though I said, "But you can't, not when she was sick at the time. How do we know if she consented or not? How do we know if it even happened at all? It seems to me like we better just leave it alone. I think it would only make things harder on her if we did something as public as that."

"Why would God let something like that happen to her?" Mama demanded. Her face was livid. "She told me when she first got in there that she saw Jesus— Jesus Christ! She said she felt so lost and alone and scared, and he came into her room one night," Mama had begun to cry. "I asked her if he said anything, and she said no, that he'd just touched her hand, and said he loved her. She said she'd never felt anything like it, and she knew that she would be safe and alright 'til she could get out. And now this…" Mama got up and wiped her nose. She walked into her room and shut the door.

I had goose bumps. It was hard to imagine Christ himself coming down out of heaven. I was raised to believe in him, and I did, but all the same, it was just hard to imagine.

"Daddy, do you believe Laura saw Jesus?"

He was quiet for a while, and chewed the corner of his mustache a minute before responding. "I don't see any harm in believing that."

Chapter Eight

I gave myself a day to catch my breath and relax a bit, then went to see Laura again. Thank goodness there was a different nurse at the desk when I came in. I asked to see Laura.

"Are you related to her?" "Yes, I'm her sister."

"Oh, well, the thing is…" she trailed off as she sorted through some papers in a file. "Here it is."

I looked over the desk and saw a paper written all over in purple crayon. It looked like a child's handwriting. On the top it read, "People I don't want to see." Below that she'd written 'High and Mighty Nan' about twenty times.

"Are you Nan?"

I gulped. "Yeah."

I turned around and left. I felt like someone had punched me in the stomach.

I found out later that Laura had attacked that nurse, Louise, and she had quit.

Laura had screamed over and over, "You were supposed to protect me!" as she tried her hardest to bludgeon the woman to death with her slipper.

Laura didn't make it home in time for Christmas. She'd gone far off the deep end. I began to hate schizophrenia as if it were my own personal antagonist. It was cruel, and mean, and it teased you. It let just enough of Laura shine through one day, just enough so you'd get your hopes up, and then it would snatch her back into its selfish claws.

The bad news came after Christmas. Daddy's insurance would only cover Laura's stay for thirty days. She'd been in there for twenty-seven and showed no improvement yet.

"What about that Clozaril they put her on? Isn't it doing any good?" I asked

Daddy.

"Well, they haven't given up on it yet. Dr. Devanson said it takes time."

"What are you going to do, Daddy?"

He sighed and threw up his hands. "I don't know." He wrung his fists.

"Damn it! I just don't know."

Mama quit going to church. She gave up on a God that could just stand by and let this happen to her daughter. Daddy went alone and sat with us in our pew. He knew that God was out there somewhere. He'd gotten to know him pretty well during his tour of duty in Vietnam. He knew God had power. So, he waited, sometimes humbly, and sometimes impatiently, for God to make things right again.

I didn't sleep much. Sometimes at night, just before I'd doze off, my heart would start racing again. Sometimes I didn't even know what I was scared of. I'd just have a horrible feeling that something awful was going to happen. I'd wonder what Laura was doing. I'd wander the house, looking in on the kids, watching Harold sleep peacefully, and be jealous. It wasn't fair that they could sleep and I had to stay up and make sure we were all safe as I stood sentinel during those endless nights. I just felt that somehow, I could protect everyone if I could see whatever it was that was coming, so I waited for it.

I wasn't very nice to the kids after missing all that sleep and I was very angry at Laura. I knew if I didn't have her for a sister, I wouldn't feel this way. I wouldn't be getting sick myself.

One night after everyone was asleep, I walked out onto the dry lakebed again. I hadn't done that for years. It was a cold night, so I kept my hands down in my pockets as I walked. There were no clouds. The lakebed was illuminated perfectly. I walked on and on, hearing only the sound of brittle clay crunching softly beneath my feet. I looked down and studied the endless broken pieces of the alkali basin. My throat felt tight as tears welled up into my eyes. I gave myself over to my sadness–my bitterness–and cried like I never had before. I was alone, and no one could hear me, so I just let it all go. In the distance I heard the solitary whine of a car on the highway.

When I got to what I believed was the center, I wiped my eyes and turned slowly in a circle. I was in the middle of emptiness. All around me was the bitter smell of alkali.

I lay down on my back and looked up at the stars, so clear and bright, and imagined I was on another planet. As I looked up at the stars I forgave Laura and all her broken pieces. Then I made her a silent promise. Never again would I let another man hurt her.

Laura came home. She wasn't better yet, but she was showing some signs of improvement. My folk's condo wasn't very big and they were crowded. Laura's apartment had been rented to someone else in the meantime, and a pile of her stuff was stashed in one corner of my garage. I went to the community college where she'd been enrolled in some classes and had her schedule for next semester canceled. Some of her mail had been forwarded to me. One was from the school. It said if she didn't show up, she would lose her spot in the crowded classes to someone else. Even after all this time, Laura was still determined to get a degree. She swallowed some pride when she enrolled in the community college instead of going up to the Falls to the university there so she could stay close to Mama and Daddy.

I felt like the right thing to do would be to offer to keep her with me, but I was afraid. I just didn't know what she'd do, and I had kids to think about. I took them over to see her and she'd scared Benny a little. Plus, Laura hadn't forgiven me yet. I wasn't sure what exactly she thought I'd done, but I had a feeling it was that I was living the life she couldn't.

I ran away from Laura again. I didn't call and I didn't go to see her. I didn't offer to help Mama. Mama always seemed to know what to do with Laura, long after Daddy had thrown up his hands. She could laugh with Laura at three in the morning when neither of them could sleep. They played silly games together that made sense only to Laura, but Mama never seemed to tire of it, and she brought Laura around when it looked like nothing would.

Mama kept me posted on her progress, and things were starting to look up. A month went by and then another. Laura responded to the Clozaril. It was a dangerous drug, regulated by the government and handled like a narcotic. It took special permission to even be on the drug. We found out real soon that we couldn't get a refill just anywhere on it. There was a ridiculous amount of rigamarole she had to go through. But it was worth it.

Over the next few months Laura found herself again. She decided to go back and try to finish school. There was always a lot of pressure on her to stay in school. We all wanted her to get that degree, and as long as she remained a student, she also remained under Daddy's insurance. No one seemed to know what we'd do when there was no longer any insurance to cover over four hundred dollars worth of meds each month.

She had her blood tested regularly, and so far it looked good. We all just held our breath. This drug could save her or kill her, but it was the best anyone could offer.

I started going over to see her and sometimes she came to see me. She just loved Marie and always wanted to hold her.

Sometimes she'd talk about her stay in Pleasant Hills, what she could remember of it. There was one thing she never talked about, and none of us ever brought it up, though I noticed Laura didn't take the sacrament at church anymore. She was punishing herself.

We found out during those months about another side effect of the drug. Laura started to gain weight. It was subtle at first, and I wasn't sure if I was just seeing things. But one day she stopped by and I knew I wasn't imagining things. Laura was getting fat. It made me sad to see her beautiful skin puffed up like that.

I invited her to go swimming with us over at the community pool one day. She and I were in the locker room changing. She wouldn't undress in front of me. She went into one of the bathroom stalls and didn't come out. Finally, I got tired of waiting and knocked on the door.

"Are you coming out?' I asked. "The kids are waiting."

She opened the door. Her face was all red and blotchy. She kept trying to pull the back of her swimsuit down, but it wouldn't stay. I could see why she was crying. I wouldn't want to come out if I looked like that either.

"I don't think I'll go with you today." she said. "I've got a paper to write anyway. I think I'll just go on home."

My heart ached clear up into my throat. Laura had been so lovely.

It seemed to me that she'd had to make some hard choices. She could be well in her mind, but only at the risk of her physical health. So far, her white blood cell count was good, but the insides of her arms looked terrible from all those needles.

I went to see her at my parents' condo that night. Laura was still upset. Mama told me she'd burned her swimsuit. I went into Mama's room and sat down by

Laura on the bed. "You just need a different suit, Laura. Let's go shopping tomorrow."

"It's just not fair!" she said then. "I get to be fat, or I get to be crazy. I don't know which is worse."

"Well, are you eating any different?"

"A little, I guess. I use the vending machines a lot at school because I just don't have enough time. It seems like I'm always so hungry."

"Well, let's make them taboo. Even if you have to get up a little earlier in the morning, you're gonna start packing a lunch. In fact, you can stop by my place.

I'll have one ready for you each morning."

She nodded.

"Anything else?" I asked.

"Well," she said, laughing nervously. "I guess I better get rid of these."

She pulled a bag of chips from her backpack and a package of powdered white donuts.

I was surprised. Laura had always been the healthy eater of the family. Sometimes she sort-of made me ashamed of myself when I'd go for seconds or offer to drive us to Dairy Queen.

"Alright," I said. "Let's get rid of these foul demons."

Laura giggled as we walked out to the trash cans.

"Do you feel like going for a walk, Nan?"

"Sure," I said. "Let's do it like those old ladies we used to laugh at. Let's swing our arms as high as we can."

We laughed together as we sped down the sidewalk, trying to outdo each other. I'm sure we looked ridiculous, but stuff like that didn't bother me anymore. Those old ladies had the right idea. Before long we were out of breath.

Laura was ahead of me.

"Come on Ethel!" she called over her shoulder to me. "Get a move on, you old biddy."

"Now wait a minute, Maude!" I laughed, trying my hardest to keep up with her. "If you had jugs like mine, you'd move a little slower, too. I'm about to give myself a black eye back here."

Laura fell over laughing right there on the sidewalk. I joined her. We sat there sprawled out, laughing our heads off for a long time. A retired couple crossed the street to get away from us. I think we scared them. They were talking quietly with their heads together. We caught one phrase of their conversation, "…crazies always come out at night."

We looked at each other and burst into new laughter. "You got that right!" I called after them.

We laughed some more, then just sat there a while with our backs leaning against each other as we caught our breath. It was a beautiful night. It was almost summer.

"Thank you, Nan," she said after a while. "You're a good sister."

I tipped my head back 'til it touched hers. "You're not so bad yourself, Maude."

Chapter Nine

Laura had more determination in one finger than I had in my whole body. Once she put her mind to something, it was going to get done. She started to eat right again, and we walked together in the evenings. It was good for me too.

It rained a lot that spring, and as we walked along the lakebed by my house, we could see it was filling up. I figured in a couple more weeks, if the rain kept up, it would look like a real lake again.

"How are things going at home?" I asked as we walked. "Well, to be honest, I can't stand it."

"Mama?" I asked.

Laura never directly said anything bad about anybody, but I thought I knew what she was thinking. Mama had a way of loving you to death. As sweet as

Mama was, it was almost unbearable as a grown woman, to be her daughter sometimes.

"I just want to be more independent," Laura sighed. "I want a job. I want my own place again. I can't get my own place 'til I get a job, and I can't get a job with

Mama always worrying over me. Daddy told me all I had to do was go to school and not worry about anything else. Do you know how much tuition costs just for a mid-semester block class? My books alone cost over a hundred dollars. I'm going to be twenty-five years old, Nan, and I want to pay my own way, but I just don't see how I can do it. Besides that, once I'm 25 Daddy's insurance won't cover me anymore."

"Well, it seems to me like you could use some money the most right now. You could get a job first and start saving."

"Yeah, but who's hiring in this lovely hole in the earth?"

"Actually, that new restaurant has a sign in the window. What's it called again?"

"You mean the truck stop off 67?"

"Yeah. I pulled in there the other day because Benny had to go. I think you could be a waitress there, seeing as how you used to work in the café."

"Well, I sure won't try to use them as a reference, though."

One of the cooks in the café was always on Laura's case. She didn't mark her tickets just the way he liked. He wanted an order of pancakes to be written as a stack, and he wanted her to use initials with steaks. It bugged him that she'd write out 'medium rare' instead of just MR.

One day he threw one of her tickets off the wheel and came storming out. "Is something wrong with your brain?" he asked. "How many times am I going to have to tell you…" That's about as far as he got. He found it was hard to keep talking with a gallon size tub of syrup oozing down all over his face.

"Well, something's obviously wrong with yours!" she'd hollered back. "What difference does it make what way I write it, as long as you can read it? People like you who waste time on stupid details are the ones who are crazy."

We found out soon afterward, that Laura's meds weren't quite right at the time.

I could tell Laura was seriously considering what I'd said. "But Mama, though."

I finally said what I thought I should've said a long time ago. "You can move in with us, Laura. Mama still won't like you working, but at least at my house you wouldn't have to hear about it all the time."

I looked over at her. We'd stopped along the fence and leaned against it as we looked into the murky water. Something in her face changed subtly.

I always wanted to say the right thing to Laura. For some reason I dreaded saying the wrong thing that might hurt her. She was a deep person and thought about things a lot, so I knew that anything I said would make her think for a while. I had waited a long time before offering my home to her, and I felt bad about it, but I was sincere now. I wondered if I'd hurt her feelings by just waiting so long.

Laura was dependent on everybody. It seemed it took all of us to watch over her sometimes. In her moments of lucidity, I knew she resented us. Or maybe it was that she resented needing us. She wanted so badly to be on her own, but it would take more time to be sure her medicine would continue to work. We all waited and watched her closely, and I knew she hated it.

"Are you sure, Nan? Have you talked this over with Harold?"

"We've talked about it a lot, actually. He's fine with it," I didn't tell her that he'd suggested it a long time ago, and I'd been against it. "And you know the kids just love you. Besides, I could use a little help in that area sometimes. Maybe

Harold and I could go on a date once in a while."

Laura was chewing her lower lip. Her chin started to tremble. "Thank you,

Nan. I promise I won't be any trouble."

If you can help it, I thought, and then felt ashamed. The question, "But what if?" wasn't asked, but it hung thickly in the air. Neither of us answered it.

I helped Laura move in the following week. She didn't have much, so we got it all done in an afternoon. We put her in the spare room, and I moved all my sewing stuff down to the basement.

"Laura's going to live with us?" asked Josie as she surveyed the mess we were creating as we tried to find a place for everything.

"Is that OK with you, Josie?" Laura asked.

Josie thought a minute, like she always did before answering questions. "I guess. Could you braid my hair for school?"

"Sure!"

Josie watched Laura unpack for a minute, her brows knit together, then said quietly, "Mommy said I shouldn't stare at you or ask you too many questions.

And she said if I see you acting funny, I'm not allowed to tell my friends about it."

My heart stopped. I felt sick and was afraid to look at Laura.

She was quiet a minute. "Sounds like good advice. I can tell you some jokes you could tell your friends, if you'd like."

"OK!" Josie squealed. "Mommy's not funny like you."

When Josie left the room, I felt I had to say something. "Laura, I didn't…"

"You did, Nan, and that's OK. You're just concerned for your kids. I understand." She folded some jeans then went on. "And concerned for me. You don't have to be ashamed of that. It's awkward for both of us. You wouldn't hurt me on purpose, Nan. I know that."

I'd said the wrong thing again. I knew I'd hurt her, but she tried her hardest over the next few days not to let me know it.

She applied for the job waiting tables at Ted's Take a Break and got hired the very next day. The turnpike there on 67 was heavily traveled by truckers and was an ideal stop for some hot coffee. Most truckers started with just the coffee, and ordered once they got a look at the menu. They stayed for a drink or dessert after they got to looking at the waitresses.

The uniform wasn't exactly flattering to Laura's figure. She had a-ways to go before she would be slim again, but she looked alright. Her face was as beautiful as ever.

She was nervous on her first day and asked me if I could stop by. She was working a late shift so it wouldn't interfere with her the morning classes she'd signed up for. After I put the kids to bed I drove over a little after nine.

As I walked across the parking lot, I heard a loud whistle, then a shout. "Hey

Babe, want to go for a ride in my rig?"

I walked faster and pulled the door open. Inside there was a long counter. The room smelled of coffee, liver and onions, and slightly of perspiration and stale leather. The latter odors emanated from the men seated at the counter, and slouching in the booths. I couldn't believe I'd suggested Laura apply here. It was new and clean, but the truckers gave it an unpleasant and unwholesome atmosphere.

I sat at the farthest end of the counter, a good three stools away from the nearest trucker. I didn't see Laura anywhere. Feeling awkward, I grabbed a menu. The man three seats down was surveying me closely.

I looked up at him nervously. He had an enormous red face and scraggly brown beard. He grinned. "Hi Darlin'! What are you sitting so far away from me for? Scared of old Bob?"

"No, I just like to maintain a lot of personal space," I said, trying to sound glib, and not like a scared little girl.

I could hear several of the men around us chuckling.

Old Bob scooted closer to me. "You don't need that much personal space,

Honey."

My heart started to race.

"Bob, get your sorry backside back out to your rig and sleep it off. You've had enough," said a man who had been down the counter a-ways. He got up and escorted Bob, who has sputtering in protest, out the door.

He returned in a few moments and sat down three stools away from me. I appreciated it.

"We're not all like that," he said, not looking at me as he sipped his coffee.

"The highway and the loneliness work into some men's blood, and turns 'em mean. Others just start out that way, and driving's the best thing for 'em, cause they're out of the way of the general public. Bob there, is one of the ones who started out mean."

This trucker was younger than most of them, I thought. It was hard to tell, though. He had an auburn colored beard and wavy red hair.

"Thank you," I said.

"Nothing to thank. Just making sure a lady is treated like she ought to be.

Some of these here highway Jacks just forget their manners sometimes."

"How long have you been driving?" I asked.

"Oh, now let me see," he said, scratching his shoulder. "Going on twelve years now, I guess."

Just then Laura stepped in from the back. She noticed me right away, and after filling some of the men's cups she came over.

"Hi Nan! I'm so glad you came in."

I watched her face. I wanted to know how she really felt about working here.

"How is it?"

"Oh, it's not bad. It was scary at first with all these men in here. At dinner time, though, some families actually came in, and it felt more like a restaurant then. So far the tipping has been real good."

The red headed trucker was holding up a menu and studying it closely. He put his empty cup out in front of him, and Laura stepped over to fill it up.

He looked up at her and smiled. "What would you recommend?" he asked, putting down the menu.

"Well, today's my first day, and the only thing I've had here so far was a club sandwich."

"Was it good?"

"Yeah."

"Alright then. Give me one of them clubs and a piece of cherry pie."

Laura caught my eye, and I knew she wanted me to wait a minute for her. She stepped back behind the swinging doors that led to the kitchen.

The red headed trucker and several others watched her appreciatively as she went.

"I sure like that freckly waitress." said one of them.

"You like 'em all, Al!" said the man sitting next to him.

"Yeah, but she's by far the prettiest one I seen in here. Got some meat on her bones too. I like 'em that way."

Several men nodded their agreement.

The red headed trucker by me was frowning. It seemed to bother him to hear the others talking like that. I started to like this pleasant man.

"What's your name?" I asked him.

"Charlie. Charlie Green."

"Not Charlie Brown?" I asked playfully.

He looked over at me and smiled. "Nope, Charlie Green. And may I ask yours?"

"Nancy Parley."

"Well, it's a pleasure to meet you Miss Parley. Is that waitress your sister? I see a resemblance."

"Yes, and it's Mrs. Parley."

"Sorry Ma'am."

"Well, I'm certainly not!" I said, smiling.

"No, I meant…well, I just didn't see your ring."

A few minutes later Laura returned with his plate. She placed it on the counter in front of him. He smiled at her again, thanked her, then dug into that sandwich like he hadn't eaten in three days.

Laura came around and sat down by me. "Are you hungry, Nan?"

"No, I ate dinner a while ago. I just thought I'd stop by and see you. How's it going? I feel a little bad for recommending this place to you. I had no idea! I got whistled at when I came in, got offered a clandestine ride, and got rescued by

Charlie there when Old Bob started invading my personal space. I can just imagine what you've been through today."

Laura rubbed her eyes a minute, then looked at me. "It's not bad, Nan. I'm getting tired. It'll take a while to get used to this shift, but the men treat me pretty good. They're not all bad. Some of these guys are really nice. There's always one to stick up for me if one of them is ornery. As long as I keep smiling, they tip really well. Besides, Ted, the owner, keeps an eye on things too. He's real nice, Nan. He even said I could wear a long sleeve shirt under this uniform. My arms, you know, aren't exactly pretty these days. I told him I was diabetic."

I watched her when she got up again to fill the coffee pot and went about refilling the men's cups. I wanted to make sure she really liked it, and wasn't just putting on a brave face. I noticed I wasn't the only one who watched her. Charlie looked up now and then, just to see if she was in the room. I always enjoyed it when others took notice of Laura, but I started having misgivings about Charlie.

I thought maybe I ought to warn her but decided to wait. She was a big girl, I reminded myself. But I'd seen that look in someone's eyes before.

Laura took a break after a while and sat with me. We shared a piece of pie.

Charlie got up and looked like he'd have said goodbye to Laura, but she was sitting with her back to him. He looked at her one more time as he pushed open the door and left.

I left a little after that. Laura would be on shift until midnight.

When I drove home it was well after ten. It was only about a ten-minute drive so I decided to go through downtown. I felt like I needed to think a little bit before going home. As I passed the pub on the corner, I noticed what looked like Helen's Cadillac. I slowed down a bit, not believing my eyes at first when I saw her supporting someone on her shoulder as they stumbled together toward her car. It was her husband, Lars. I drove by quickly before they could see me. I felt like I'd just got a peek at something that was none of my business.

I hated knowing things about people that I had no right to. It made me feel funny whenever I saw them. One of my friends confided in me once that her husband had a low sperm count, and that was why they couldn't have kids. That thought never ceased to jump to my mind and make me blush whenever I saw him after that. I thought everyone had a right to privacy, and I understood that, I think, more than most people.

Chapter Ten

I couldn't sleep after I got home, so I decided to wait up for Laura. I took out my worry box and wrote "Charlie Green" in red ink on one of the cards that was still empty. I held the card in my hand for a while, then tucked it into the back of my box. Next, I wrote "Helen and Lars at the Pub" and stashed that one in the back, too. It was like Harold always told me, there's no need to invent something to worry about, so I put Helen and Lars out of my mind. Charlie, though, was a little more stubborn. Had Laura noticed his soft brown eyes?

Close to one in the morning, Laura came in quietly. I heard the door creak open, followed by the soft sound of someone plunking down on the sofa. I walked into the living room as she was pulling off her shoes. Sam had his big head on her knee, and she was scratching his ears as he moaned his delight.

"Oh, hi Nan! Did you wait up for me?" she asked, looking surprised.
"I just couldn't sleep. How was work?"

"My feet are killing me. I'm going to have to get better shoes." As she spoke, she was rubbing the bottoms of her feet and wincing.

"I've got just the thing!" I said and hurried off to the hall closet. I dragged out the foot bath Harold's mother had sent for Christmas.

I brought it into the kitchen and filled it up with water. I set it down in front of Laura.

"I've only tried this thing once," I said, "but it was like heaven. I just never have time to sit around soaking my feet."

I plugged it in and sat by Laura on the couch, listening to the gentle gurgling of the foot bath. Laura leaned back and closed her eyes. Sam eyed the water as it bubbled. He sniffed it gingerly, growled, then settled down to watch it. Just then I heard Marie. I got up and found her crying in her crib, throwing her fists around in frustration. She was hungry. I brought her back out to the living room and sat down by Laura again as I lifted my shirt.

"Hungry?" Laura asked, watching me.

"Yep, dis little girl needs a midnight snack," I said in the voice I always used when I talked to Marie. She looked up at me with one eye as she sucked contentedly. She had a rhythm she always vocalized when she nursed. She'd suck three times, gulp, then sigh contentedly, then start sucking again. I just loved her soft little sigh with each swallow. I loved the way her soft, chubby little cheek squished up against my breast.

Laura started to laugh. "That is adorable. She sounds so funny!" Laura watched a while more, then asked, "Does it hurt?"

"No, only at first. It actually feels sort of nice. I think some women who don't breast feed their babies really miss out."

After I said that, I regretted it. Laura had retreated into herself again.

I felt awkward for a moment, then changed the subject. "I noticed a lot of the truckers there admiring you tonight."

Laura opened one eye and looked at me a minute. "I got admired more than I could stand. I hope they don't keep it up once I'm a regular there. It sort-of gave me the creeps."

"Anyone in particular there, who made you nervous?" I asked, probing.

She thought a moment. "No, not really. They all just sort of seemed the same.

You know, I always thought truck drivers all looked the same. After looking at them all day, I still think so. I can't tell one of them apart from the other. I could have sworn I served one guy twice, but maybe I was imagining it."

"What did he look like?"

"Like a truck driver."

"You know what I mean."

"Well, after you left some guy came in at about 11:30 and ordered a club sandwich and a piece of pie. Seems like he had red hair. It was weird. I got a kind of Deja vu thing about it. I served so many men today, though, that I may have just been imagining it. I must've served at least fifteen club sandwiches tonight."

"Do you remember his name?"

"No, I don't think he told me. He was very friendly, and more polite than the rest."

"Did he make you nervous too?"

"No, no he didn't. He talked for a while, then said he had to hit the road. I wrapped the sandwich up for him and put the pie in a box. I figured there wasn't much sense in asking his name since I'd never remember it anyway, plus, he could be from anywhere. I figured I probably wouldn't see him again any time soon."

I thought otherwise, but I didn't say so. I wasn't surprised he'd come in one more time after I'd left. He struck me as a nice man, and I suspected he may have been good looking under that beard. He certainly made me nervous.

After Marie finished, she still wanted to play. "Can I hold her a while?" asked Laura.

"Sure," I said. "You want to put her down for me when she falls asleep? I'm exhausted."

"No problem," said Laura. "I just love to hold this little baby."
"Alright, good night then."

I moved Charlie's name to the front of my worry box before I went to bed. There seemed to be no sense in denying that he was one of the first things I'd need to handle, and soon.

The next morning, I woke up and went to check on Marie. She usually woke up by six thirty or so to eat again, and it was seven thirty when

I woke. I went into the nursery and she wasn't in her crib. My heart stopped. I was panicked. I ran to the living room and saw Laura asleep on the couch. I checked the kid's rooms, but she wasn't there either. Harold had already left for work. I checked Laura's room and her bed wasn't even slept in. My heart was racing as I went back to the living room. I had to wake Laura. I had a horrible feeling of impending doom.

I went over to her still form and leaned over her. Then I saw Marie. She was snuggled up to Laura's chest. I put my hand on her back and felt the gentle movement of her breathing. I was so relieved I had to sit down right there on the floor and catch my breath.

I never slept with any of my babies. It was dangerous. All the parenting books said so. I was angry at Laura for being so irresponsible. I went through at least ten emotions as I sat there and watched Laura sleep with Marie. I felt sorry for her. Sometimes she couldn't help it when she fell asleep, yet I wanted to strangle her. I wanted my baby in my own arms where I felt she would be safe, and yet she seemed so at peace sleeping that way with her aunt. I wanted to cry for her, I wanted to snatch my baby out of her arms. I wanted to be OK with Laura holding my baby like that, and I wanted to tell Laura never to fall asleep with her again. As I struggled with my emotions, Marie stirred. She awoke and looked at Laura's face, her eyes crossing as she tried to focus. She put out a tiny plump hand and grabbed Laura's nose. Laura's medication made her sleep very deeply. Sometimes it seemed almost impossible to rouse her. I gently took Marie out of her arms, and back to the nursery where I sat in the old rocker Grandma Harris had promised to me when she died. I rocked 'til eight o'clock then roused the kids and got them ready for school. Laura was still asleep when I left the house.

I dropped by Grandma's house to visit after getting Josie and Benny off to school. I walked in without knocking like I always did and heard them bickering in the kitchen.

"Theodore, you get your hands off of those eggs! They won't poach right with you sticking your finger in there every two seconds."

"Alice, everybody knows you can tell a poached egg by the way it gives. You're going to ruin those eggs!"

"How long have I been making eggs?" she demanded, spatula in hand.

"Long enough to know how to tell when they're done! I'm telling you, you're overcooking them!"

Grandma turned her back on him and pushed him aside. "Mind your biscuits and quit messing with my eggs! If you don't hurry and get those done, we'll have poached eggs and no biscuits!"

Theo's biscuits were legendary in our family, and even Grandma had to concede that his were better than hers, so she let him make them.

Theo started swearing as he stirred the sticky biscuit dough. The more he kneaded them, the more he cussed. Each string of obscenities got worse as he flopped the dough over and over, as he got madder and madder. As he cut each round biscuit, he'd damn this one to hell and insult that one's mother. I watched, always entertained by their antics in the kitchen. Neither of them had seen me yet. Grandma was getting madder and madder as she listened to him profane and take the good Lord's name in vain. Finally, she threw down her spatula and grabbed the sheet of biscuits before he could stop her. She pulled open the sliding glass door and threw the biscuits out into the driveway.

"Hell, Alice, what did you do that for?" he roared.

"Ain't no one's going to eat biscuits that's been cussed over, and swore at and damned. I'll be damned if I eat even one. Shame on you!"

Just then she noticed I was standing in the doorway. Theo noticed too.

"Well, Nancy, nice of you to stop by. I'd offer you a biscuit, but your granny here just launched them out the door to the birds. It's a long story," he said as he winked at me.

"Well, the best way to keep a long story short is to don't tell it," Grandma said, pushing him out of her way. "This old man gets meaner every day. How are you Nan? Let me get a look at that pretty little girl of yours. Sit down on the davenport there and take a load off." She ushered me into the living room and took Marie from my arms.

"Oh, she's a fatty, yes she is," she cooed. "What are you feeding this kid, custard?"

It was a running joke with the family that I produced custard-style breast milk since all of my babies had no less than four donut rolls going up each thigh and their cheeks just melted into their necks in a soft pink mass.

Marie giggled as Grandma nibbled her cheeks. I could hear Theo swearing in the kitchen again and smelled the reason. There's no mistaking the smell of burning eggs. I was glad Grandma couldn't smell it, or else she'd worry that Theo was really going to have a heyday with her for forgetting about her eggs.

"Your Mama tells me Laura's staying with you. Got herself a job?"

"Yeah, she's working over at the truck stop on '67. Ted's Take a Break," I said as I recalled the name.

"Your mama is worried about her, Nan. I don't know if a truck stop is such a good idea either. Is it a nice place?"

I thought a minute before responding. "Well, it's brand new and clean, and they sure make good pie. There's a lot of truckers come through, but she says families come to eat there, too."

Grandma was studying the crocheted edge on one of the couch pillows, a habit I'd gotten used to. It meant she wanted to say something, but was choosing her words and lining them up carefully before she spoke.

"And what does Laura think of it?"

"She says the tipping is good. They gave her the late shift so it wouldn't interrupt her classes. She likes her boss."

"And the truckers?"

"Well, I guess she's learning how to handle them, and Ted keeps an eye on things. They're not all bad, Grandma. One of them in particular seemed nice. He sort of stuck up for me when…" I didn't mean to say that last part. I was kicking myself enough as it was since I suggested she apply there in the first place. I didn't need Grandma's disapproval on top of it. "Some of the men didn't talk very nice, that's all." I said lamely.

"I knew a trucker once," said Grandma. "He seemed nice. I married him."

I looked at her, but she was tracing a stain on the carpet with a slippered foot.

"Grandpa was a trucker?" I asked. I knew almost nothing about him. No one talked about him much, especially Grandma. I guessed it was too painful for her since he died. He was found beaten to death in an alley behind one of the down-town bars. That was all I knew about it. I wondered who would beat up an innocent old man, but I never brought it up. I just thought about it sometimes.

"Yeah, he was when I met him anyway," she sighed then hollered into the kitchen. "You minding those eggs, Theo?"

Just then he emerged from the kitchen with a plate of buttered toast and a glass of orange juice. "Take your pills first, Alice," he said and offered her a small glass of water and a handful of colorful pills.

"Watch this," she said to me as she tipped her head back. "I'll swallow thirteen pills all at once."

Before I knew it, she'd done it. I couldn't believe it. I had trouble with just one. "Good grief, Grandma!" was all I could say. "What are all those pills for?"

"My heart, my kidneys, my bowel movements, and who knows what all. Theo just makes sure I take 'em all, and I quit complaining and do it all at once to get it over with. Where's my eggs?" she asked, when she noticed she had only toast.

"I let a couple of 'damns' slip out while they were poaching so I chucked 'em out the window to save you the trouble."

"Oh, for Pete's sake! I don't know why I put up with you!"

'It's payback Alice, just payback. You 'bout drove me nuts when we were kids, and now, since I'm younger than you, and stronger, I'm taking my revenge, and there's nothing you can do about it 'cause you're just too old and slow."

I wasn't shocked. This was a typical conversation at Grandma's house. Theo loved Grandma Alice, and it showed in the way he gently took her arm when they walked and in the precision with which he dispensed her endless medications. And she loved him for it, but both were too old and crotchety to admit it to each other. Sometimes I think he got her riled just to keep her blood circulating.

Theo started coughing then and went into the back room. I could hear his muffled coughing through the closed door. He never liked Grandma to hear him cough. It made me a little worried, too, but he'd been doing it for years. After a while he re-emerged.

"You know, you ought to go see a doctor about that cough, Theo." she said in a withering voice.

"I don't trust 'em," he said. "You go in to see one of 'em for a sore throat and they stick their finger in your butt." He coughed gently again and said, "One of 'em tried that on me once—said he wanted to check my prostate. I said, "You want me to bend over what? And you're gonna stick your finger where?" I educated him real fast, and he tried to bill me!" He coughed again. "No more doctors."

Grandma prudently changed the subject. "How's Harold and the other kids?" "They're all fine. Benny's getting so tall I think he may pass up Josie before her next birthday."

Grandma laughed gently and clapped her bony hands together. "Oh, that

Josie is a character. I never saw two kids more competitive with each other. I bet it rankles her that he's getting so tall."

"I passed you up before I was twelve, Alice," Theo reminded her. "That Benny and Josie remind me of a couple of old crotchets I know."

Grandma nodded, chuckling. She had the most beautiful face I think I've ever seen. It was wrinkled, and worn out, but she was the most beautiful woman I knew, especially when she smiled. She was wise and kind and always said the right thing. She also never missed an opportunity to say what needed to be said.

She always smelled faintly of Oil of Olay and stale lipstick. Her white hair was always perfectly done and curled neatly. I came over once and caught Theo giving her a permanent that he'd bought at the drug store. He made me promise not to tell Harold or Benny that he knew how to set a perm. I found out later that he'd been doing it for years since she stopped going to the beauticians, claiming their rising prices were highway robbery. Theo knew how important it was for her to look nice, so he took up perming her hair. He made sure she continued to feel like the southern belle she once was, even though they usually argued about how to set the rollers the whole time he worked on her hair.

"Is that Helen giving you trouble?" she asked then.

"Well, no. She hasn't been around much. I had to scrub out my tub myself last week." I thought of the way I'd seen her last night.

"If ever there was a busybody buttinski, she's it. I honestly pity you sometimes, Nan. Harold's nice and all, but you sure got the short end of the stick when it comes to in-laws."

I almost surprised myself by sticking up for Helen and telling Grandma I had some of her blood in my veins, but I kept quiet. I didn't exactly like Helen, even now. She was a tough one to like, and it wore me out sometimes trying so hard. It was easier when I just plain didn't like her.

"Well, at least she comes over and acts like she's interested in me, which is more than I can say for the rest of them."

"I guess," Grandma conceded, but sounded unconvinced. "I'd have sent her on her way a long time ago, if I was you Nan. But I'm not. I guess you're just nicer than your old Granny. Set in my ways, I guess. I figure I've earned the right to dislike some people. I spent my whole life being nice, Nancy. And it just...well, you don't let her walk all over you, you hear?"

"Oh, I don't," I promised, but it wasn't true. Helen terrified me most of the time, and I meekly submitted to her endless advice and nit picking. I guess before Marie I just plain resented it, and then after what she'd done, I felt I owed her something. I had no idea what, but I figured I could at least act like I was listening when she spouted off about the proper way to disinfect the kitchen sink.

"Her husband, Lars is so tight he'd crawl under the gate if he could, to save the hinges." Grandma observed. "I never saw two people more nit-picky and tight-fisted. They've got all that money, and they don't share nothing but unwanted advice."

Sometimes I'd wonder about Helen. I never wondered much about Lars. He was completely uninteresting to me. But Helen got under my skin so bad sometimes, I'd wonder how she could stand herself.

Chapter Eleven

I never understood how a woman who made herself so at home in my house could make me feel so unwelcome in hers. I stopped by Helen's on the way home and knocked on her door. I knew she was home. I saw her Cadillac parked in the driveway along the perfectly manicured hedges, but no one came to the door. Just as I was about to leave, I heard movement within her house. I rang the bell again, and I heard her heavy footsteps coming toward the door. She cracked it open and peered out.

"Nancy?" she said, startled. "Is something wrong, Honey?" "No, I just thought I'd stop by."

She peered at me a minute, then shut the door to release the chain before opening it again.

I never just stopped by, and so I figured she was a little confused. "It's been ages since you've seen little Marie, so I thought maybe you'd like to sit and hold her for a bit. I've got time before the kids get off school."

"You want me to babysit?"

"Oh no! I just thought…" Well, I don't know what I'd been thinking. I was ready to leave.

Helen looked at little Marie, who was sucking her blanket. Marie pulled it out of her mouth when she saw Helen and grinned. A string of drool stretched from her mouth to the blanket, then ran down her chubby arm.

Helen winced. "I wish you would've called, Nancy. I have all kinds of things out that she might break. I'm afraid…"

"She's not even crawling yet," I said, smiling, trying my hardest not to look as awkward as I felt. Somehow, I sensed that Helen needed some company. "Besides, she's been crying in the car, and I hate to just pull over and nurse her in a parking lot or something." As I spoke, I kept asking myself why I was so determined to stay.

"Oh, alright then. Just come on in, I guess."

I guessed that would have to do. At least she didn't shut the door in my face. I felt like she had though.

"Take your shoes off and put them over there," she instructed me. Her house was a mass of white carpet, and expensively upholstered furniture. I thought what

I always did at Christmas (which was the only time she ever invited any of us over) that it was a good thing she never had any kids. You could always sort of tell when children lived in a house, and Helen's made even me, at twenty-nine years old, feel unwelcome. Every square inch of her couch was covered with embroidered pillows and cloth and porcelain dolls. There wasn't even room for a person to sit, except on the edge, and I didn't dare move any of her precious pillows. It struck me as odd that a woman who had no children would have so many dolls.

She was a collector, though, and had a few that were really worth something.

Their glass eyes stared out from behind curio cabinets throughout her house and from shelves high up on the walls. Josie had the nerve to touch one of them once, and Helen swooped down on her in a flash and yanked the doll out of her reach.

"Now Honey, these dolls aren't for playing with," she said in her sickly sweet voice to a startled Josie.

"What are they for, then?" Josie had asked innocently.

"For looking at," she said and patted Josie on the head.

Josie just stared and stared at all those dolls every time we came to Helen's.

She wanted more than anything to touch one and hold one, but she didn't dare.

"How have you been?" I asked her then.

"Let me hold that little baby," she said, reaching out her arms. "You really should put a bib on her, Nancy. She's going to ruin this pretty dress. Is she teething?"

"Yeah, she's got two on the bottom, and she's working on the top two right now."

I sat back and watched Helen with Marie. There was always a certain amount of reserve in the way she held a baby. She never nibbled her cheeks the way

Grandma did. With Helen it was a matter of business, like everything else she tried to manage. Babies were to be held just so, and that's the way she did it every time. Marie started to cry so Helen promptly began thumping her briskly on the back, trying to burp her.

"Actually," I said, trying not to grit my teeth as she thudded Marie's back, "I think she's hungry. Mind if I nurse her?"

"In here?" she asked, horrified at the thought of someone's breast not being confined beneath a respectable under wire bra at midday on her sofa. She looked desperately around the room.

"No, I'll go do it in the bathroom," I said, getting up.

"You'll do no such thing. I just meant that I thought you might be more comfortable in the back room. We're right in front of the window sitting out here.

Anyone might see you, Nancy."

Heaven forbid someone should see a mother nursing a baby, I thought as I walked into the guest bedroom that hadn't been slept in for at least ten years, probably more.

Helen closed the door behind me, and I sat alone in a gloomy room with the curtains drawn. More dolls stared out at me from the tops of the dressers. It gave me the creeps.

I made my excuses and left right after that. I had no idea why I had come over, and promised myself not to do it again. I thought I could see relief in her eyes when I left.

I still had several hours before it was time for me to pick up the kids. I stopped by to see Mama, but Daddy said she was in town doing the laundry. Mama refused to pay the laundromat prices there at their condominium complex, so she always packed it all up into the back seat of her car and went to the cheaper laundromat in town. Mama was used to the routine, but it seemed she always got herself into an argument of some sort with the other weary patrons watching endless rounds of laundry spin in the dryer. One time she'd been waiting over half an hour for a dryer. There were three down on the end that had stopped, but no one came to claim them, so she decided to unload them neatly into the wheeled baskets and then put her things in. Just as she was filling the last one, two enormous

Navajo women came in and saw what she'd done. One jerked Mama around, and asked her what she thought she was doing. Mama wasn't one to be pushed. She never was. I could just see how her eyes must have lit fiercely as she asked the women if they could read. She pointed above her to the sign which read, 'Any unclaimed laundry in the dryers may be removed by the next patron.'

"It says right there that I have the right to use this dryer."

The women backed off. Mama told me about how they'd gone to fold their things while shouting threats at her and calling her what she thought must have been bad names. "You know, I was glad my hearing isn't too good. I couldn't hear a word they said, and I think that really pissed them off."

Another time on one of Mama's laundry trips a man had seen her unloading her car and offered to help. He carried in a couple of baskets for her, and then tipped his hat and walked into the bar next door. After Mama got her stuff loaded into the machines, she couldn't find her purse. She knew she'd left it on the seat of the car while she unloaded, but it wasn't there anymore. She walked straight into the bar, past several large, stinky men and right up to the philanthropist who she knew had helped himself to her purse.

She stood in front of him as he sneered at her. "I want my purse back."
"I don't have your damn purse, lady." He said.

"Yes, you do," she said evenly.

He stood up and spread his arms, his black trench coat trailing about him.

"Search me, then, if you don't believe me."

Mama did, amidst their laughter and found nothing. I hate to think what she would've done had she been armed that day. Sometimes her courage and boldness astounded me. She was livid as she retold the story to me that night. The next morning the manager of the laundromat called and said they'd found her purse out in the bushes behind the bar, but it was empty except for her driver's license, her hairbrush, and a few maxi pads. You never wanted to cross Mama when she was on her period.

Mama hated the laundromat. I figured she could use some company. I pulled in and saw her car parked diagonally across two spaces. Mama's driving scared even the most stout-hearted. Daddy always said it took a whole legion of guardian angels to get her home in one piece when she took to the road. I'd given up worrying overmuch about her driving a long time ago, but I did everything possible to avoid being a passenger in her car if I could help it.

I went inside and found her in tears as she folded the last of her laundry. Oh brother, I thought. Here we go again.

"Hi, Mama! What's wrong?"

Mama wiped her nose. "Oh hi, Nan. Could you help me get all this out to my car?"

"Sure. Is it locked?"

"No."

I headed out with two baskets stacked on top of each other. Mama followed me out and loaded the last two baskets in the back seat.

"Are you hungry? How about I take you out to lunch?" I asked

"I'm not really in the mood, Nancy. I just want to go home."

"Get in my car, Mama," I said as I locked the doors to hers. "I'm going to take my mother out to lunch today."

Mama conceded and sat down. I handed her a Kleenex. She blew her nose loudly, then started to cry again. I noticed Mama had been crying more than usual. I had a pretty good idea that she was full swing into menopause, but I didn't dare ask. I always got mad when she'd ask me if I was on my period whenever I got upset about something.

I pulled up to the Wendy's drive through since Mama didn't want to go in with her face all blotchy. We ordered our food then I parked under an old elm tree. Her head shook slightly as she ate. After she finished her burger, she wiped her mouth with her napkin and said, "I just get so mad sometimes, Nan. I spent my whole life cleaning other people's houses and listening to nit-picky people telling me what to do. My own family does it. Everyone assumes I don't know what I'm doing, and it makes me mad. I'm not stupid, Nan."

"I know you're not, Mama. What happened? Did you fight with Daddy?" "No, though sometimes I'd like to hit him over the head with a two by four.

No, it's not your daddy, Honey."

Mama took a few sips of her soda, then told me.

"I was unloading the car, and there were only four machines left. I put some baskets in front of them, to sort of claim them, you know, and then went back out to the car for the rest. When I came back in there was a foreign, Arab-looking lady in front of my machines. She had her stuff in them and was about to put her quarters in. It was so rude! My baskets were pushed to the side. It made me mad,

Nan, and I went up to her and said, "that's my machine." She looked at me like I was something stuck to the bottom of her shoe and said in a high and mighty tone, 'Your machine?' She looked me up and down, Nan, and crinkled her nose.

She had a thick accent, and I just thought, 'How dare you talk to me like that.

I'm an American, and I've been coming to this laundromat for years.' So, I said..."

Mama trailed off. I think she was ashamed of what she'd said. She fortified herself with a couple of French fries. "I said, 'You're an asshole, Lady. Go back to where you came from.'"

Mama shook her head, repentant one minute, then belligerent the next.

"Don't look at me like that, Nan. She might have been a terrorist."

I had no idea what to say. I sipped my soda, not looking at her. I never could quite get my mama. She was the sweetest lady, with the foulest temper. Mama would not be pushed around by anybody. She loved her kids beyond reason, but she was quick with a switch when we crossed her as kids.

"I'm sorry, Nan. I shouldn't have said that, I guess. But she was just so...I don't know. I guess Jesus wouldn't have done that. I was going to pray about it, but I figured I already knew what he'd think."

Mama went off into another burst of tears. "I just don't know what's wrong with me. I guess you're embarrassed to have a mama that's so stupid sometimes. Everyone in the whole laundromat heard what I said and wouldn't look at me after that. They all left."

"Mama, everybody has the right to get mad. And I think everyone has the right to act a little crazy sometimes, too. I think you're the one who told me that. You just shouldn't make a habit of it, that's all."

Mama sighed, then chuckled as she wiped the last of her tears away. "What would the pastor think if he'd a heard me, Nan?"

"I think he would have had an apoplectic seizure to see the former chairman of the charity committee use the word 'hole' after the biblical reference to 'ass' while talking to another human being."

Mama laughed out loud then. "I love you, Nancy girl. Tell you what, let's not go back to the laundromat yet. Take me over to Kelly's Appliances. I'm going to charge me up a washing machine and a dryer. Our condo has a hookup in the closet. George just won't hear of me going into debt to get a set, but I'm just going to do it."

I agreed wholeheartedly. Mama had earned it and Daddy nodded once I told him what had happened.

He hooked them up after they were delivered less than an hour later, and we celebrated the first spin cycle with a glass of root beer. Mama was giddy. "Nancy, why don't you and Harold and the kids come over for dinner tonight?"

The kids. That's when I remembered. It was three forty-five now, and they'd been home alone for at least twenty minutes, assuming they'd decided to walk when I didn't show up out in front of their school.

I rushed out to the car, leaving Marie with Mama and sped over towards the school. Just as I was pulling up, I saw flashing lights in my rearview mirror. I pulled over and waited as the deputy took his time walking up to my window.

"Ma'am," he said in irritation, "any idea why I pulled you over?"

I had a sinking feeling I'd been speeding, but then I remembered I'd forgotten to take the car in for registration last month. I gambled on that. "Is it my registration? I've got the papers at home. I just haven't filled them out yet."

He glared at me. "Well, I could ticket you for that too, but I think I'll choose to overlook that." He leaned down, and talked slow, to make sure I'd understand.

"This here's a school zone that you're tearing through. You want to tell me why I just clocked you at 38 miles per hour, when the limit is 15 'til four o'clock?"

I didn't know what to say. I figured it wouldn't help my case to say I'd forgotten my kids, then sped through a school zone to find them. I remained silent.

"Ma'am do you have kids?"

I nodded.

"Do you like the idea of somebody speeding around while your young 'uns are trying to walk home?"

I shook my head, and despite all my efforts not to, I started to cry.

"You'd be doing a lot more crying, lady, if I had to knock on your door and tell you one of your kids was just struck by a car, now wouldn't you?" He was mad, and full of himself, and not going to give an inch. "I don't like giving out tickets, Ma'am, but I shore am going to give you one today. You ought to be ashamed of yourself. Just so you know, the fines are double in a school zone," he said in a thick drawl. "Driver's license and registration, please."

I fished through my purse 'til I found my license, and handed it to him along with the expired registration from the glove box. I wiped my eyes and tried to get hold of myself while he sauntered over to his squad car.

Just then I saw Helen walking out of the school with Benny and Josie. The school must have called her to come down and get them. I tried to scrunch down lower in my seat, but she saw me, and looked horrified. She stopped in the middle of the bus zone and gaped, then her face changed to one of smugness. She stared at me a moment more, giving me in one glance the depths of her disapproval, then headed over toward my car. I waved her away before she could come any closer. I overheard Benny ask, "Are they going to take Mama to jail?" Josie started to cry.

I was ready for any available bottomless pit to fling myself into. The officer came back to my window. "Looks like today will be your first ticket, Mrs. Parley." He leaned in on my window, giving me the full benefit of his bad breath.

"Maybe you'll think twice before putting any more children in grave danger," he said.

I'd heard enough and shocked myself with what I said. I ended up getting two tickets.

When I got home, Helen was already there with the kids. I got out of the car and overheard Benny asking her, "What's a jackass?"

I submitted meekly to Helen's ensuing lecture and was relieved when she'd said her piece. She'd gone on and on about the example I was setting and that she wondered at me sometimes and that I'd not been myself lately and that she was getting concerned for the state of my mind. Frankly, I was wondering a bit myself.

I was glad when she left.

"Did you break the law, Mama?" Josie asked once Helen had whisked her self-righteous backside out my door.

"Yes, I did, Honey. It was an accident, and I won't do it again."

Josie started to cry again, ashamed of me. She'd been taught that policemen protected us from bad guys, and it was a blow to find out her mama was one of them.

Benny reacted differently. He looked up at me in admiration. He never knew his mama had a dark side, and he found it fascinating.

I found the whole experience exhausting and went into my room to lie down and wait for Harold to come home. I had no idea what I would tell him. I knew he'd be angry about my tickets. He always said that getting a ticket was the worst kind of extravagance. You have to pay for something, and you don't get anything in return but a write up. "I might as well just throw our money right out the window as I'm driving down the road."

He'd gotten a few tickets, and was always thoroughly disgusted with himself and the entire White Lake Sheriff's department.

I started to cry as I lay there, waiting for him to get home. Suddenly the phone rang. I answered it, trying to sound normal. It was Mama, and she was practically a psychic when it came to her daughters.

"What's wrong, Honey?" she asked.

"Oh, I got a ticket today. Well, two of them, actually. I was in a school zone, so the fine is going to be double, and then I got one for the car not being registered."

"Oh, Honey, so you finally got your first speeding ticket?" she was laughing at me.

I had always promised myself I would not grow up and be like my mama. I would be in control of my emotions, I wouldn't fly off the handle and say things

I'd regret, and I'd be a safe driver. It made me mad to think I'd blown it today.

"Harold's going to kill me," I said, starting to cry again. "We're so broke right now with hospital bills and everything. I can't stand to see him tonight."

"Tell me what happened today," she said then, ready to listen.

I told her, right down to the part where I started cussing. I thought she'd be shocked, but she just chuckled. "Well, sounds like he had it coming. It's too bad saying it like it is has to be so expensive sometimes."

"Yeah."

"Well, I've got your little baby over here, Honey, and she's mighty hungry. She won't take that bottle you left me."

My heart stopped then, and I was overcome with guilt. I'd completely forgotten about Marie. It had been several hours since I last fed her at Helen's.

"Why don't you come on over now, and I'll call Harold and tell him to come to our place for dinner tonight." She was quiet for a few minutes, then said softly, "It's alright, Honey. It's just a ticket anyway. I can't even remember how many I've gotten. Did you cry? Sometimes that works, you know. Men fall to pieces when a woman cries."

"Oh, I cried, Mama. I felt awful. I mean, I could have hurt someone. I can't believe I was speeding through a school zone."

"Well, did you hurt anybody?" "No."

"Alright then. Now come on over and feed this little girl of yours."

I got up and wiped my eyes. Benny and Josie were in front of the TV. I wasn't in the mood for a dinner party, but Mama wanted to celebrate her liberation from the laundromat.

"Come on, kids, we're going to Grandma's house. Get your shoes on."

Just before we left, Mama phoned again and asked if I could stop by the store for some milk. It was well after five thirty by the time we were in the elevator going up to Mama's condo.

Daddy met us at the door and held out his arms for me. He gave me one of his giant hugs. "Following in your mother's footsteps, eh?" he asked, rubbing my back.

I didn't respond. He'd hit a nerve.

He held me out from him at arm's length and looked me in the eye.

"Your mother is a fine woman, Nancy. I wouldn't trade her for anything, tickets, and all. You remember that. You're just like your mother, and that's fine. No sense trying to swim against your own gene pool."

He stepped aside, and I was astonished at the group of people that were crowded into that small apartment.

The first person who rushed up to me was Theo. He tugged my hair like he always did. "So, you're Little Miss Nasty, after all, eh?"

I smiled. Theo always made me smile.

"I hear you got yourself a bona fide potty mouth today. The thing is, I just can't picture my little Nantucket saying that. I got to hear it myself. What do you say Nan? Let's hear it."

"Leave her alone, Theo!" said Grandma, coming to my rescue. "You better feed Marie, Honey. Come on and sit by me in your mama's room."

Grandma sat by me on the bed while I nursed a very thankful Marie. "How do you like having huge boobs?" she asked, then.

I couldn't believe her directness sometimes. I must've turned a little red.

"Oh, I didn't mean to embarrass you, Honey. I've just been flat-chested my whole life and always wondered what it was like. You do have very nice breasts,

Honey."

"Well, it got me a lot of attention in high school, and Harold doesn't seem to mind them too much."

Grandma chuckled. "Harold is a lucky man, Honey, and a good one, because he knows it. Don't you ever forget that."

When Marie had finished, we went back out to the living room. Harold was standing there, holding a bouquet of daisies and a card. Mama must have told him, I thought. He hugged me and traded Marie for his gifts. I opened the card.

"Welcome to the world the rest of us live in. Drive on, Speedy. I love my little lead-footed lady. Slow down once in a while, though, to smell the daisies. Love,

Harold."

Laura was there. "Way to go, Nan." she said as she patted my back.

I hugged her then, and we laughed together. I went to find Mama. She was giving the neighboring retired couple a tour of the insides of her new appliances.

Dinner was served out on the deck. Daddy had fired up his grill, setting wieners and hamburgers to sizzle over the flames. Mama made her fruit salad, and

Grandma had brought her famous potato salad. It was a feast.

Once we'd all filled our paper plates to the point they sagged, Theo stood up and banged his plastic spoon against his Dixie cup. "Attention, attention. I'd like to make a toast to my niece, Dora Mae Harris. Now Dora's been giving 'em hell over there at the Cyclone Laundromat for years, and now she's going to retire.

I'm sure they'll miss her over there, and won't find anything to do but read those ancient magazines since she won't be picking any more fights. I'm sure she'll be missed, but they've all been replaced by her shiny new Maytags. Let's hear it for Dora!"

We all clapped and hollered for her, but Theo didn't sit down. He cleared his throat once again to get our attention, and went on, "And there's another lady here who's setting out on a new life, and that's my Little Miss Nasty. Today she shot her perfect driving record all to hell with not one, but two driving tickets and a warning to watch her mouth when speaking to a police officer. Let's hear it for Nantucket!" Everyone cheered and clapped while I blushed.

"Whether it amounts to temporary insanity or just plain meanness, Nancy

Parley cussed today, and I'll be damned if I don't get to hear it for myself. What was it you said, again? Something about a jackass?"

I shook my head.

Theo, ever the public performer, held up a jar filled with money. I saw quite a few twenties in there. "Now Nancy, I've put a fifty-dollar bill in here my own self, and everybody here has donated to the cause. Probably enough here to cover those tickets if you'd just oblige us on this one point."

"All right then. Benny and Josie, plug your ears."

Even Harold cheered me on as I stood and tried my best to give the exact phrases I'd used with the proper inflection.

Theo whistled. "That's some fine swearing, Miss Nasty. Now go wash your dirty mouth out with soap."

Chapter Twelve

I stood terrified on the porch as gray clouds swirled in the strange sky above. I heard a distant howling as leaves rushed across the sidewalk. The tornado touched down just like I knew it would, and twisted, bent slightly sideways, toward my house. It howled fiercely as it skittered about on the ground, headed right for me. The kids were in the house, yet my legs refused to move. Somehow, I had to get myself off the porch and get the kids to safety. In the distance I saw a red barn disintegrate to nothing, obliterated from the twister's path. People ran screaming in all directions, only to be caught up in it, their shrieks stifled as they disappeared. I watched as a frozen spectator to the destruction. Suddenly, the twister divided and split in two, sister cyclones with a deadly purpose as they danced menacingly toward me.

It was really happening this time, I realized. They'd never come this close before. I could hear the shingles on the roof trembling, and I could smell the dust that spun about in the air all around me. Suddenly I was able to move and ran inside. The children were in the bathtub, all three of them. I screamed for them to get out, but they wouldn't listen. They were so slippery and wet I couldn't get hold of them. They wiggled out of my grasp. Just outside the door I heard what sounded like a locomotive and watched in frozen horror as our front porch spun off into the air. I slammed the bathroom door and crouched in front of it with my arms over my head. This was it, I thought. This is how we're all going to die...

"Nancy! Nancy! Wake up, Baby. You're having one of your dreams again."

Just as I spun off into darkness and dust, I heard Harold's voice, and felt him shaking me. I opened my eyes and saw him peering down at me in the darkness. "Oh, thank goodness!" I gasped and reached up to hug him.

He squeezed me tight, and whispered softly into my ear, "It's alright—just a dream, just a dream."

I sobbed uncontrollably for a minute, then was startled by distant thunder. "Is there a storm?"

"It passed through a few minutes ago. It's gone, Honey. Nothing to worry about. Just a spring storm, same as every year."

I wiped my eyes and felt suddenly foolish. "I'm sorry, Honey. It was so real this time. I told myself before it got bad that it was just a dream, like you told me to, but it didn't work again. I could smell the dust, Harold!"

"You have the most active imagination of anybody I know. Man, wouldn't I give something to have a dream like that. It'd be like having a movie in your own head."

"No, it's like living in a movie, and you don't know how to turn it off. It's ter- rifying, Harold. I hate those dreams."

I realized something suddenly, as I recalled the dream. Harold wasn't there. He never was.

Harold got up and went to the kitchen. He came back with a glass of water and handed it to me.

"Is Laura back yet?" I asked. "What time is it?"

"It's about one thirty. No, she hasn't come in yet. She probably had to help with inventory again."

Laura had been working there two weeks now. She seemed to like it, and was even getting to know some of the truckers who stopped by regularly on their routes.

"Are the kids all asleep?" I asked then, getting up.

"Of course. Now you better get back to bed yourself, Nantucket. Everybody's safe and snug in their beds."

"Laura's not."

"Laura is a grown woman, Nancy. She'll get here when she gets here. Now come on back to bed."

I crawled back in and snuggled up to Harold's warm body. He draped an arm over me, and caressed my arm softly 'til his hand fell gently to the pillow, and I could hear his soft snoring. He never had any trouble sleeping.

I lay awake a long time, watching out the window as the soft moonlight reflected against the giant pump jacks off in the distance, illuminating them in quick flashes as they bobbed up and down like giant dark birds sipping at a birdbath.

Just after two, I heard Sam's claws clicking as he walked across the floor toward the door. He always knew when Laura was coming. I got up and found him sitting in front of the door, wagging his tail expectantly.

Laura came in and patted Sam's head. He moaned blissfully and licked her hand. "Nancy! What are you doing up?" she asked, startled to see me.

"I had one of my dreams again and couldn't go back to sleep. Why are you home so late?"

Laura sat on the couch and took off her shoes. She twisted her ankles, rotating her feet in circles a moment, then looked up at me. "I stayed after my shift a while and just talked to somebody."

My heart raced a moment, and I asked, afraid of the answer. "Charlie?" "Who's Charlie?" she asked then.

I breathed a silent sigh of relief and went on. "He was just one of the truckers

I met that time I came over to see you at work."

"Oh, well I don't know anybody named Charlie."

"Who were you talking to?"

"Nancy, you told me you weren't going to be acting like Mama if I moved in with you. It was just somebody who wanted to talk, that's all."

I had to be satisfied with that. I didn't want her to think I was being nosy.

"Did you hear the storm?"

"Yeah, we had a lot of people pull off the highway and wait it out at the truck stop. We were so busy there for a while I thought I was going to pass out from exhaustion. I made out really good, though, as far as tips go." As she spoke, she pulled a giant wad of cash and several piles of change from the pockets of her uniform.

"How much?" I asked, amazed at her cache.

"I don't know, I haven't counted it yet. You count the change, and I'll sort out all these bills."

I counted out five dollars and fifty-eight cents as she smoothed and sorted her bills. "Good grief!" she exclaimed suddenly. "Here's a twenty!"

"Didn't you notice it when you took it from the tables?"

"No," she said, mystified. "You know what, I bet someone tipped me two dollars and accidentally put a twenty underneath a one." She fingered the bill, and turned it over as she did so, possibly looking for some clue as to who may have been so generous or so absent minded.

"Well, I guess we'll never know," I said. "Was there a red headed trucker there, by any chance? Kind of young and soft spoken?"

"Yeah, there was. He was real nice. We talked about one of my classes. I was just so put out by the price of books that I vented to him a little bit. He was very understanding about it and said I should pay for them anyhow. Gave me a pep talk about the importance of education. Sounded kind of funny coming from a truck driver, you know?"

In my mind the mystery had been solved, but I remained quiet. Apparently

Laura didn't see him as anything special.

"Why do you ask?" she asked.

"Did you think he was good looking?" I asked casually.

She looked up at me suddenly. "What are you getting at, Nan?"

"I was just wondering," I said, shrugging my shoulders.

She turned her head to the side as she tried to recall his face. "I don't know.

It's hard to tell. He had a beard and he was wearing a white Stetson. No, I don't think he was all that good looking. Too old anyway, Nan. Are you trying to imply something?"

I was satisfied, so I distracted her with "How much did you make?"

"Looks like a hundred and thirty-eight dollars! How much change is there?"

"Five dollars and fifty-eight cents. You're rich, Lady."

Laura sighed contentedly and leaned back against the couch. "You know Nan, things are looking up, wouldn't you say? I think I even lost a couple more pounds. I stay on my feet all night, and there's never much time to eat."

"Don't go starving yourself, Laura. You look just fine, you know."

She was closing her eyes, idly petting Sam's head, which was perched on her knee. "Tell me about your dream," she said, her eyes still closed. "Sometimes I think I'm pretty good at figuring them out."

"It was just another tornado one."

"You know what I think, Nan? I think you're scared to death of tornadoes."

I chuckled. "Some analysis there, genius! Of course, I'm scared of them!"

"Is it just tornadoes, Nan, or are they just the embodiment of something else?"

Her question startled me. I'd never thought about that before.

"In my psych class, we were discussing dreams one day and the professor suggested that dreams aren't always just disconnected fantasies and thoughts. Sometimes they are the brain's way of telling you what you can't stand to face when you're conscious. We haven't had a tornado touch down in this county for over five years, Nan. You've never even seen one, except on the news. What is it, really, that you're afraid to face?"

I was quiet as I sat and looked at her neat stacks of tips. "Laura, did you ever suspect there was something wrong with you, you know, before the first time you got sick?"

It was Laura's turn to be quiet. "Yes," she said, after a while. "Sometimes I'd just get weird thoughts, and I'd wonder if other people thought of stuff like that or if it was just me." She sat quiet for a while longer, then looked up at me smiling. "I used to think being crazy was the worst thing that could ever happen to me. I was so ashamed of it. Sometimes it was easier not to take my medicine. Then I didn't have to be accountable and nobody expected me to act normal. I know every square inch of Pleasant Hills now, Nan. It's nowhere near pleasant, I'll tell you that. But you know, it's familiar. You can get used to just about anything after a while, even being crazy."

"How do you feel now, with this new medication?"

"I still have a hard time waking up sometimes, but I finally feel more like myself. Some of the drugs they gave me just subdued everything and slowed me down. You know how it feels just before your ears pop? Everything seems so muffled? That's what it was like then, and with this stuff, I don't feel like that." As she spoke, she idly rubbed the insides of her left arm. She sighed. "I'm wiped out, Nan. I gotta get to bed. Goodnight."

Laura also had no trouble sleeping. I sat at the couch for a long time, watching the storm move away from us. Occasionally I'd see lightning illuminate the dark clouds. I thought of Charlie. I had to do something about it, but I just didn't know what. He was a nice man and I could see he genuinely cared for Laura. The last thing Laura needed right now was another heartbreak. At least Clance and

Michael hadn't been worth keeping. I wasn't sorry to see either one of them abandon Laura. I was only concerned for her feelings. I couldn't stand the thought of what an abandonment would be like if she really loved the man.

Obviously, Laura didn't love him; she hardly seemed to notice him. But he hadn't put himself forward yet, and I knew he would. I think somehow he sensed he had to approach her carefully, and I knew he was waiting for his chance.

The next morning was clear and bright. I loved the smell of a morning after rain. The lake was almost full, but it looked brown and ugly. Storms always stirred up the alkali in it, just like they had a way of stirring up the undersides of my family, the parts we would have liked to have left settled at the bottom.

Laura didn't have any classes 'til the afternoon. It was her day to have her blood drawn, and she asked me to go with her. After we dropped off the kids, we drove over to the clinic. I waited in the uncomfortable chairs littered about the waiting room and flipped through the Golf Digest that seemed to be the only thing that was ever available to read. I'd already read all the pamphlets on breast cancer, colon cancer, prostate cancer, and the one about shaken baby syndrome. I wondered what on earth was taking so long.

Finally, Laura emerged from the hallway, wiping her eyes. She was crying.

I stood up. "What's wrong, Laura?" I asked anxiously, putting my arm around her. She shrugged off my arm. She never liked being touched very much.

"That idiot in there has no idea what he's doing. I told him where to put the needle and he acted like he just knew everything and wouldn't listen. Why do I always get the ones that are in training? You'd think they'd offer me something better since I'm a regular."

Laura held the inside of her left arm, wincing, then went on, "He must've stuck me ten times, I'm not kidding. Then, after about the eighth time of missing a vein, he started to dig the needle around a bit once he had it under my skin."

I shuddered. Just thinking of it gave me chills.

"Then, he finally got it in the right place, and the blood filled up the first tube.

He snapped the second one on then, and it just wouldn't fill up. He sat there watching it and flicking it and getting mad. When I noticed that my elbow was getting wet, I looked down and saw that my arm was in a pool of blood! He hadn't snapped the tube on right, and my blood was just squirting out the side, and running all over the table."

It was my turn to wince. "Then," she continued, "He jumped back, like he was afraid of me. He fumbled around, afraid to touch my blood like he'd get some kind of disease. He finally found something to wipe it up, but he put on a second pair of gloves before he did that. Then he wiped up my blood like he would wipe a stranger's butt." She wiped her eyes then and tried to get hold of herself.

I noticed Laura looked pale. "Are you alright? I think maybe you better sit down a minute."

I led her to a chair and pushed her gently down into it. "Hold Marie. I'll be right back," I said, settling Marie in her lap and walked over to the reception desk. "Excuse me," I said to the receptionist. She was typing and ignored me while she finished what she was doing, then looked up.

"Can I help you?" she asked sweetly.

"Yes, you can. I want to see the intern who took Laura Harris's blood just now."

"May I ask why?"

"Because he's an idiot and he owes her an apology, and I'm not leaving here 'til she gets it." The nurse eyed me distastefully a minute. "Ma'am, I can't do that," she said in a thick drawl. "You see, sometimes a draw just doesn't go smoothly, and we're not responsible for…"

"Oh yes you are!" I said, raising my voice. I surprised myself, and enjoying my anger I went on, "When I file a complaint against this clinic, and the shoddy procedures I've witnessed on more than one occasion, you just might be out of a job. I've got a list of infractions here in my purse. It goes on and on. Every time I come in here, I see things that I know aren't right. Now you get me that intern, or I go up to the hospital administrator in the Falls and ask if it's OK to spill someone's blood all over the floor, and sit there making hamburger out of the insides of a patient's arm."

Several patients in the waiting area looked over at us. One woman got up and left.

She looked at me a minute out of milky blue eyes, then leaned over and pushed a button. The telephone rang and she turned her back to me while she answered it.

A few minutes later a dark-haired young man walked down the hall. He looked smug. "Can I help you?" he asked, raising his thick eyebrows.

"Yes, you can. You can walk over to my sister and tell her you're sorry. You ought to be ashamed of yourself. Despite what you do, I'm still filing a complaint. Maybe you should practice sticking your own arm 'til you get it right."

He looked at me a moment, then glanced over at Laura. He shrugged and walked over to her. "Ma'am? I'm sorry about that. It was an accident. In the future…"

"In the future," I cut in, "you'll step aside and let someone else do her draw. You won't touch her again."

He stepped back, nodded his head quickly once, and walked back down the hall.

The others in the waiting room watched him go, memorizing his face so they could remember who he was. They wouldn't want him drawing their blood either.

"You didn't have to do that, Nan. That was so embarrassing."

"I'm sorry if it embarrassed you. I was hoping to embarrass him a little."

"Do you really have a list in your purse?"

"Sure do. Diapers, ketchup, carrots, and, oh, how about some ice cream?" I said as Laura stood.

"No, Nan. Fattening, remember?"

"You earned it, girl. We'll go for a long walk afterward." After we went shopping, I took her out to Baskin Robbins. Laura and I sat at a little wrought iron table on the deck out behind the ice cream shop.

"Geez, Nan. I feel like Lady Astor butt sittin' out here. This ice cream cost a fortune! You could've gotten a whole gallon for what you just spent on these little cups." Laura ate it slowly. "Sure is good, though. Can I give some to Marie?"

Marie sat gurgling to herself in her stroller as we ate. I hadn't given her any dairy foods yet. It made me uncomfortable. "I'd rather you didn't, Laura. She hasn't had anything like that yet. I just breast feed her still."

"Do you really think just a little bite of ice-cream will hurt her?" I sighed. "No, you'll probably make her day. Go ahead."

Marie scrunched up her face at the initial shock of cold, then her face suddenly changed. She grinned and squealed, reaching up toward Laura's cup. Laura looked to me and I shook my head. Marie started to cry.

"Oh, no! I've created a monster!" Laura laughed.

"That you did. Now she's had some ice cream she's going to demand it whenever she sees the rest of us eating it." I was a little irritated.

"Sorry, Nan," said Laura, sounding completely unrepentant. "Maybe you could just put some ice packs on your boobs before you feed her."

"Now you're going to have to make it up to me," I laughed, "You have tomorrow night off, right?"

"Yeah," she said, hesitating.

"Well, I can't even remember the last time Harold and I went out. Would you mind watching the kids while we catch a movie and some dinner?"

Laura didn't respond.

"Do you have plans?" I asked, a little surprised.

"I have a date, Nan."

My heart stopped, and before I could stop myself, I asked, "Do you think that's a good idea? Who is it?"

Laura's lips drew tight, and she turned away from me. "It's one of the guys I met at work."

"A trucker?"

"No, the cook. His name is Jim."

I remembered the cook. He was handsome and he knew it. He could have been Clance's half-brother, he reminded me of him so much. I didn't like the way he and the bus boys looked at Laura as she filled the coffee. I didn't know what it was they said as they snickered behind the pickup window, but I had a pretty good idea.

"Laura, don't take this the wrong way..." I started, but she cut me off.

"It's fine, Nancy. I'll just call it off. I told you I'd help out with the kids when

I moved in."

I felt a little sick to my stomach and didn't want the rest of my ice cream. I'd done it again. I didn't feel like there was anything I could do to make whatever had just happened between us go away. I got up and threw out the rest of my ice cream. Laura did the same. It was a long and quiet drive home.

The following night was a Friday and I got myself all dolled up. My mascara had gone bad since the last time I'd used it. It made me sad to think it had been that long since I'd done anything to make myself up. I wondered if that bothered

Harold. I decided I wanted to look my best, so I went into Laura's room.

"Can I borrow some mascara?" I asked her as she lay there on the bed with a book.

"Go ahead."

"Thanks." I grabbed her purse and started rummaging through it. "I can't find it anywhere. Is it in here?"

Laura got up slowly and pulled open a dresser drawer. "Here." she said, handing it to me, then she lay back down and started to read again, ignoring me.

I leaned over her dresser and looked into the mirror as I brushed my eyelashes with short strokes.

I could see Laura slouched on her bed in the mirror. Sam was curled up at her feet. She was really mad at me, I could tell. I had no idea how to fix it, and then I got a little angry myself. All I wanted was for her to be happy, but I was afraid for her, too. I doubted this Clozaril was a miracle drug. Besides, she had only been on it a few months. Laura just didn't need a man in her life right now, and I just couldn't understand why she didn't see that. Sometimes it seemed like she tried to hurt herself.

"How do I look?" I asked, turning once in front of her.

Nothing moved but her eyes as she looked up at me. "Fine, except your lipstick is crooked."

I scrutinized my lips in the mirror and wiped one side. "Okay then, Harold will be here any minute. I got some videos from the library the kids can watch, and I figured you could just make some macaroni and cheese for dinner. The kids love that. You can call Mama if anything happens. Don't let them stay up too late, and make sure Benny flushes the toilet when he's done."

"Okay, Okay. Just go, Nan."

I walked out into the living room and sat on the sofa as I waited for Harold. I felt like my evening had already been ruined. Laura had a way of doing that. I hated feeling guilty for just wanting to go out and enjoy myself.

When Harold and I got home, it was after midnight. The house was quiet. I checked on each of the kids and they were sound asleep. Laura dozed on the sofa. I shook her shoulder gently. "Laura, why don't you go lay down in your room and sleep?" I whispered.

She roused and asked if we had a good time.

"The movie was terrible, but we liked dinner. Thank you, Laura."

She nodded, then went sleepily to her room and shut the door.

"Is she okay?" Harold asked, watching her. "Seems like she's been a little off since yesterday."

"She's just mad at me. Let's go to bed."

I lay there long after Harold started to snore. I knew some people who hated snoring, but Harold had a way of doing it that was somehow soothing. I listened to its gentle rhythm, willing myself to go to sleep, but despite my efforts, my heart started to race, and I felt the familiar terror I always did at the onset of a panic attack. Since I got out of the hospital, it seemed that any time I got myself worked up over anything, it would lead to a panic attack that night. I tried to relax, and just ride it out like the doctor had told me to. One good thing about being diagnosed with generalized anxiety disorder was that when I did have a panic attack, I at least understood what was happening. However, I always wondered if this one really was a panic attack or if maybe this time it would go further. I snuggled up close to Harold and held him tight. I tried to think only about his snoring. It was then I realized the rhythm of it had been broken by a different sound. I thought maybe Harold was wheezing at first, but when I rolled over, I realized the sound was coming from down the hall, from Laura's room.

I swung my legs over the side of the bed and poked my feet into a pair of slippers. I walked softly down the hall with my head cocked, listening. It was a very soft but terrifying sound, and I was a little afraid to open her door. I stood out in the hall for a moment, the hairs on my neck standing on end, then opened the door.

Laura sat cross legged on her bed with her guitar on her lap. She idly rubbed her finger over one of the strings, making a raspy, mournful sound. She didn't look up. She seemed almost in a trance until I noticed a tear drop from her chin as she bent over the guitar. Slowly her fingers started to move over the strings, softly at first. She strummed a song I'd never heard before, and it made me sad.

Her fingers flew across the strings as she poured out her soul in a lilting rhythm that reminded me of something, but I couldn't remember what. Without realizing it, I had begun to cry with her.

The song ended abruptly. She put the guitar aside and lay down, pulling a pillow over her head to stifle her sobs. I closed the door again quietly. I had witnessed something again, that I wished I hadn't.

Chapter Thirteen

It was late Tuesday night as I sat idly fumbling through the cards in my worry box. It was dumb to think this box would solve anything, would somehow organize my mind and file away all my problems in an orderly fashion. Obviously that doctor didn't worry too much, or else he'd realize what a dumb idea this box was. I shoved it under my bed.

Laura hadn't talked to me much since the night of our date. Harold mentioned he'd like to do it again sometime, but I told him we should wait 'til maybe Mama was available to babysit. I felt I had no right to ask Laura again.

Harold lay snoring next to me. The kids had gone to bed hours ago. I got up, dressed again, and grabbed my purse as I headed out the door. It was a breezy warm night, the air tinged with the pungent smell of sagebrush and alkali salt. I sat on the cold vinyl seat of our old Buick and fired up the engine, then backed carefully out of the driveway. A full moon shivered on the water's surface as I wound my way along the road that led up to Highway 67.

I drove back behind the restaurant to the large parking spaces where the truckers sometimes stayed the night. I wondered which one was Charlie's, if he was here tonight. Just then I saw him walking in his usual confident manner towards a large rig. It had a green cab, and a white trailer out behind. A giant metallic medallion advertised "Green's Trucking Co." on the door.

"Well then," I thought to myself. "At least now I can see him coming."

I was glad he was leaving for the night, but had to admit that I admired him for having his own rig.

I pulled the car around to the front again and parked. I walked inside the brightly lit restaurant. Several men sat about, some dozing over coffee, others arguing why the cost of fuel had suddenly gone sky high.

I saw Laura then, talking to Ted as she wiped down the counter. Ted seemed nice. He was one of those people who smiled and chuckled even when he was mad about something. I admired him in a lot of ways.

Laura saw me then and excused herself. "What's the matter, Nan? Can't sleep again?"

"Oh, I was just laying there thinking how good a wedge of that cherry pie would be, and before I knew it, I was in the car on the way here."

Ted beamed. He let the cooks do the rest, but the pies were his. "Sit down there, Laura. Seems like you're due for a break. I'll get the pie. Ala mode, you want it? Calories don't count after midnight."

I nodded, then turned to Laura. "Seems kind of dead in here this late," I said idly.

"Yeah. Not a whole lot to do sometimes, so I just wipe things down."

Jim watched us from behind the pickup window. He winked at me when I looked up. I gave him what I hoped was a cold stare before turning back to Laura.

"Well, I knew you were pulling a late one tonight, so I figured I'd come and keep you company."

Just then, the brass bells on the door tinkled, announcing somebody's entrance. I looked up and saw Charlie heading toward us. I smiled at him despite myself.

"Well, hi Mrs. Parley! Mind if I sit here? I haven't seen a friendly face in days.

I just got off a run that seemed like it would never end. I'm so tuckered out, I forgot my wallet when I first came in, so I had to go back out to my rig. Man, I'm tired."

"You're Charlie!" Laura said then. "Nancy's told me all about you."

I blushed and was a little angry. Laura hadn't forgiven me yet, and so she set about giving me one of those little jabs she was so good at.

"Is that so?" he said, smiling.

"I got an A on my psych test last week," Laura told him proudly.

"Good girl," he said.

"Doesn't it seem odd that we've been talking all this time and we never even knew each other's names?" Laura asked. "Here you've been acting like my guidance counselor or something all this time."

"I see you two are acquainted," I cut in, but neither of them heard me.

Laura ignored me on purpose. Charlie was too busy smiling at Laura. "I've got my test in the back. I can show it to you," Laura said, suddenly uncomfortable with his smile and the look in his eyes. She escaped into the storeroom for several minutes while I dug into my pie, not sure of what to say. I noticed Jim leaned over and whispered something to her as she passed.

"Your sister looks a little pale tonight. Everything OK?" Charlie asked me then.

I hadn't noticed she looked pale, but when she came back out I could see he was right. She was pale and looked tired.

She handed him the test, and he looked it over a little too carefully and whistled. It was only a bubble sheet. "Fine job." he said as Laura handed him a menu. He set it aside. "What's good tonight?"

"Well, there's still some beef tips over noodles left. Jim's already scraping down the grill, so he doesn't want to cook anything." I looked over her shoulder to Jim, who eyed Charlie with keen dislike.

Charlie looked over at Jim and gave him a measuring glance. "Is that so? Said that himself, did he? Hey Ted," he called over his shoulder. "Any problem with my ordering a steak well done?"

Ted came over and pointed to a very large sign on the front door that read,

'Sorry, all out of steaks tonight.'

"Otherwise it's not a problem," Ted said apologetically.

Charlie got quiet all of a sudden as that stubborn streak died visibly in his face.

"Oh, I didn't see that. Sidetracked by this pretty waitress," he said smiling too broadly. He picked up the menu and studied it a long time before setting it down, and saying. "I'll take those tips, I guess."

Laura brought out his meal shortly thereafter and started to sweep the floors.

Charlie and I watched the TV and chatted idly as we ate. Jim whistled as he closed up the kitchen for the night.

"We have some breaking news to report," a brunette woman with a square face suddenly cut into our program. "Route 67, south of Greentree was the site of a horrible accident only moments ago. Police are actively searching for survivors among the seven-car pile-up caused by a large semi that jack-knifed across three lanes of the highway. It is unknown at this time what caused the semi to lose control. The driver has been rushed to the hospital in critical condition." As she spoke the camera panned out, revealing what looked to be a war zone. "The fire you can see behind me, is the semi which caught fire. It was carrying a load of chemicals as yet unidentified. Police and rescue personnel are moving quickly to remove drivers who may be trapped in their vehicles."

Jim came around from the kitchen, wiping his hands on his apron to watch. "Oh, Man! I hope it blows up, that would be awesome!" He whistled as he watched, his eyes lit up like a kid about to see some fireworks.

Ted looked at him in disgust. "Don't you have a grill to scrub?" Jim sulked back into the kitchen.

We watched for a while as the camera panned over the crumpled vehicles and men struggling to make things right again as they pulled people from cars, towed cars away, and put out fires. It was the worst kind of disaster, brought on by a split second that would have lifelong repercussions for the families involved. It made me sick to think I'd been on that road probably just minutes before all of this happened. Harold wouldn't have known I was even gone and would never understand what I was doing out on the highway so late at night. I ached to go back home and just hold him again. Suddenly my thoughts were interrupted by Charlie's voice.

"Do you ever think about how much trust there has to be on the road? I mean, there's just this little dotted line separating us from disaster. Nothing's stopping anybody from crossing it. We just drive along at seventy miles an hour, hoping the other driver isn't crazy or drunk, or falling asleep. Sometimes I think, "Man, all I have to do is swerve over, and they'd be dead." Lucky for them, I'm in my right mind."

I looked quickly over at him. I'd had that thought before, too, and was relieved I wasn't the only one who had morbid thoughts like that once in a while. But what he said disturbed me, too.

"Yeah. Kind of scary the way anything could happen at any time, isn't it?" I said offhandedly. "Ted, could you change the channel?" I asked. I'd seen more than enough.

"I appreciate the way you've been encouraging Laura with her classes," I said, changing the subject. "It's been hard for her, but she's determined to get a degree."

I looked over my shoulder, but Laura must have gone back into the kitchen. "What's her major, exactly?"

"Psychology and Family Science."

"Huh." he said thoughtfully. "Wonder why she'd want to go studying crazy people and their dysfunctional families. Seems kind of depressing, don't it?"

I didn't respond. He had no idea he was hurting me with what he said, and I was determined not to show it. "Seems to me like driving a truck all day would be depressing. I don't know how anybody can do it."

It was Charlie's turn to be slow in responding. "Well, I guess it is sometimes. Somebody's got to do it, though. People need their Pepsi Cola and corn chips. Might as well be me bringing it to 'em," he said, a twinge of bitterness tainting his cheerful voice.

The look in Charlie's eyes made me sort of sad. I sensed there was more to him all of a sudden. He wasn't telling me something, and I realized I hardly knew him as I watched him quietly eat the rest of his food.

"Do you get lonely on the road, Charlie? I've always thought that truck drivers were sort of loners, keeping out of the way except when they're hogging the road," I added, embarrassed that I'd asked him such a personal question.

"You can be lonely anywhere, Mrs. Parley."

I looked through the pickup window and saw Laura putting away the ketchup, and thought of the way I'd seen her playing her guitar the other night.

"Yeah, I guess so."

"You asked me a personal question. Now I'll ask you one, if you don't mind."

He hesitated, then continued. "That little waitress in there is lonely, isn't she?"

"Charlie," I paused as he looked at me intently. "Laura doesn't need any complications or distractions. She's only a semester away from graduating."

I looked up into his eyes and saw them harden. "I understand that, Mrs. Parley." He said slowly as he got up. He tipped his hat to me as he walked toward the door and jerked it open, then paused. "Is she alright?"

I looked up at him but couldn't find an answer, and he walked out while I struggled to open my mouth.

I went through downtown on the way home to avoid the highway since I figured it would be blocked. The colorful neon signs blurred through my tears as I drove along. I felt for Charlie, I really did. He was the nicest man I'd come across since Harold, and yet I'd warned him off. I had to protect Laura. I promised myself I would do that for her since everyone else just seemed to stand aside and let things happen to her. I never told her what a creep I thought Clance was. I never said anything when she let Michael treat her so bad, and since she'd been out of Pleasant Hills, I was determined not to stand by and watch her hurt herself again, or hurt someone else. It made perfect sense to just leave off dating altogether. I'd begun to think Helen was right after all. She probably wouldn't get married; it was too much to ask of anybody, and yet I hated myself as I drove home.

When I got there the house was quiet. No one knew I'd been gone, and I was thankful no one, especially Harold, knew what I had done.

The next day Helen came over. There was a sale over at K-mart and she was one of those who couldn't stand to let a good sale go to waste, so she not only stocked up for herself, but stocked up for everyone she could think of, then asked for a check to cover it. I really didn't want 24 rolls of paper towels and a giant bucket of laundry soap I couldn't even lift, but I didn't tell her so as she sent Lars to the trunk of her car to get it.

"So, how much was it?" I asked, my pen poised over my checkbook. "I spent 34 dollars total, counting the socks I got for Benny."

Benny sat and scowled as he clutched a package of miniature argyle socks. "These are dumb socks!" he finally said when Helen had gone out to the car for another load.

"I know, Honey. We'll take them back later."

Josie came out of her bedroom wearing the flannel pajamas Helen had gotten for just $4.95. They were dark blue boy's thermals, but Helen figured since they were her size she wouldn't mind a bit. "They're hot and scratchy," she complained, wiggling irritably.

"Hush up, Sweetie. Helen might hear you. You don't have to wear them, especially since it's June. Take them off and go play with your brother." I looked over at Benny. "Benny, stop poking the package! I can't return it all full of holes.

Give me that stick and get on outside!"

I heard chuckling behind me and turned to see Theo standing in the doorway holding a large package of paper towels. "I just thought I'd stop by and see if I could finagle my way into a dinner invite, and Helen put me to work. You figuring on sopping up that alkali mud puddle out there with all these here towels?"

"K-mart had a sale," I explained.

He grinned, "I see. Well," he went on as he put down the towels, "I'm about starved, and I had a feeling you'd be cooking up some of your chili since I know you want to win the cook off at the church social barbecue this Saturday."

Theo was right. That was exactly what I was serving for dinner. In fact, I'd served it in different variations for the last three nights, and the kids were sick of it. Harold never seemed to notice what I put on the table; he just cleaned his plate and told me it was a good dinner.

I realized then why Helen had stopped by. She was spying on me. She did it every year, trying to figure out what exactly it was I put in my chili. She never admitted she liked it, but I could tell she was jealous of the honorable mention I'd gotten last year.

So, I set four more places at my table. Theo went out to his small pickup and helped Grandma up the steps. I noticed she looked a little more tired than she used to, and her skin was pasty.

"How are you, Grandma?" I asked.

"Oh, fair to middlin' I guess. I'm old, Nan, so I don't exactly feel good anymore. Sometimes I wish I'd just kick off."

I hated it when Grandma said that. She'd been doing it a lot lately. It never sounded like she felt sorry for herself, just that she was tired, and looked forward to the eternal rest we all heard so much about in church.

"You got another ten in you at least," said Theo as he helped her get settled onto the recliner. "You're just too stubborn to die yet, no matter what you say."

Grandma swatted him. "Go protect Nan from that woman," she said under her breath as Helen reappeared with flushed cheeks. She set down another economy size package of paper towels.

I chuckled. "Well thank you, Helen. We were just about to eat. Why don't you and Lars join us?"

"Oh, I couldn't possibly intrude, Honey. I was just stopping by with a few things."

"Then why the hell didn't you let us stop to eat on the way over?" demanded

Lars.

"Oh hush. I guess we could stay for a bite. Lars is hungry, but I probably will just have some water or maybe a salad. I don't want to put you to any trouble," she said as she settled herself down at the table. "Is that your chili I smell?"

After Helen's second helping of chili, which she scrutinized with every bite, she asked, "Where's Laura? Is she working today?"

I didn't answer, so Harold did for me. "No, she's on a date with the cook over there at the truck stop. She won't be home 'til sometime after midnight."

"How is she doing? Looked pretty skinny last I saw her. She's hasn't gotten anorexic or anything has she? I saw something about that on TV. It said some people just go all wrong in their head when they're trying to lose weight, and start starving themselves. And you know, Laura's not exactly…well, you ought to keep an eye on her, Nancy. I don't think she should even be dating either. Good heavens! What on earth is that girl thinking? She's got no right to just string some boy along and not tell him what's wrong with her."

Theo cleared his throat. "I saw the biggest pile of horse shit I've ever come across out behind Ned's barn today."

Helen choked on her water. "Theodore, what on earth has that got to do with anything? And at the table too? Such language!" she shrieked.

"Something just put me in mind of it. Calm your anus down." Theo shoveled a large spoonful of chili into his mouth as he looked squarely at Helen. "What? That's the proper word, ain't it? Nancy, pass me more of that chili. Makes me fart."

Helen and Lars left soon after that. She and Theo never could be in the same room for any length of time. Theo made sure of that.

I waited up for Laura long after everyone else had gone to bed. Harold had stopped me when I tried to talk Laura out of her date. All I did was ask where they were going, and Harold cut in and said, "You go on, and have a good time, Laura. Nancy, will you come in here a minute?"

I could tell from his tone he wasn't going to budge, so I listened to him and went into the kitchen with him as Laura got herself ready. I didn't want to hear what he was going to say to me. Instead of talking, he just took me into his arms, pressing my face into his chest so I couldn't say anything and held me tight 'til he heard the door close behind Laura.

"You can't stop her, Nan. She deserves to live her life, too. And if he does anything to hurt her, I'll kill him myself. Now, quit worrying. That little punk she's going out with won't last. She'll tire of him."

"But Harold, she never breaks up with anybody. She just goes along with them 'til…"

"Nancy, she'll be fine. She's smarter than you give her credit for."

That stung. I never doubted Laura's intelligence, just her judgment. "Well, I know why she's going out with that loser. He looks good in a pair of jeans, he's paid her a few compliments, and he's safe as far as her heart goes. She knows she won't fall for him. It's like she's just given up on finding somebody decent because she figures no one will give her a chance once they know."

"What is your problem, Nan? Don't you think Laura deserves to be happy, that she doesn't just have to settle for a second-rate life? It sounds to me like you don't believe anyone would give her a chance, so you're just going to keep her safe from every man that comes her way, whether he's decent or not. Don't tell me you agree with Helen. I thought you were better than that, Nan."

Tears welled up in my eyes. "I don't agree with Helen, Honey," I said, fumbling to defend myself. "It's just that I think she should wait. Don't you see? We don't even know if this drug is going to work! It's only been a few months! And she needs to graduate! Damn it, Harold, she's been in school for the last seven years trying to get that done! It's been harder for her than anybody!"

Harold took me into his arms again. "I know you love Laura, Honey, but don't you think it's time you quit being her big sister and tried being her friend?"

He squeezed my arm and walked out the back door.

He was ashamed of me, and I was ashamed of me. I sat up for hours waiting for Laura to get back home.

Chapter Fourteen

The following day, I needed to see Daddy. He had married my mama, and had dealt with her bouts of depression, anxiety, and even craziness; yet I knew he loved her more than any other woman and was proud of her. I wondered what he'd say.

Mama was out to lunch with Laura. I hadn't been invited so I headed over to

Daddy's to see what he was up to.

I knocked on his door and found him watching a motorcycle race on TV.

"Well, hi, Nantucket!" He said, opening the door wide to let me in. "Haven't seen you in a while. What's Big Sister been up to?"

I hugged him and let him hold Marie while I brought in a tub of my leftover chili.

I stared at the race a minute, then shook my head.

"Those boys are crazy, aren't they?" he said. "Man, I thought I was going fast way back when. Maybe it just looks faster to me 'cause I'm getting so old!"

"You're not old, Daddy!"

"Well, not as old as some, but definitely slowing down."

Daddy had more hair on his face than on his head. He had a large graying beard and a receding hairline that left only a few hairs on top, and a small ring of hair around the base of his head. When he realized he was going bald years ago, he just shaved all his hair off. My daddy wasn't one to hide anything, and the idea of the comb-over made him ill. "If I'm gonna be bald," he said, "I might as well do it right."

"Are you and Mama going to the picnic on Saturday?" I asked.

"I'm sure planning on being there, but your mama is being difficult, if you know what I mean. It's been so long since she's gone to church, she just feels sort of uncomfortable. Shame too, since her chili took second place last year, and I tell you what, she's improved it! I can't wait to try this here," he said, indicating the tub I'd set on the table. "Is Laura going to enter her pecan pie this year?"

Laura had entered her pie once and got first place. She was the only one of us, besides Theo and his salsa, to get a first-place ribbon in our family. Theo took first place every year, so it had sort of lost importance since everyone just expected it.

"I don't know. I haven't actually talked to her about it. I haven't really talked to her about much of anything, Daddy."

"Is that so? You girls fighting again?"

"Not exactly, just not talking a whole lot. Laura's real good at ignoring people when she's mad at them, you know."

Daddy looked thoughtful. "I remember you two girls used to fight something fierce. Laura would come after you, swinging her arms like a windmill, and you'd just run for cover."

I laughed, remembering. "Yeah, that windmill technique was hard to defend against, so I usually just ran. That girl had a mean streak in her then. She wouldn't take anything from anybody." I got quiet then, remembering all that

Laura had let happen to her since. I sighed. "She's dating one of the cooks over there at the truck stop."

"Is that so? Do you like him?"

"No."

Daddy thought for a while, bouncing Marie on his knee. "I didn't figure you would."

"What is that supposed to mean?"

"That you're a good judge of character. I've seen him."

I always liked getting a compliment from Daddy. "Thanks," I said beaming.

"So, what's troubling my Nantucket? You've got a face that don't hide much, you know."

"Well, there's this trucker over there that really likes Laura, and I like him,

Daddy. He's real nice, but I sort of discouraged him a little. I think he's perfect for her, but I just thought he should wait—at least 'til she graduates. I mean, we still aren't sure about this Clozaril, and she's so close to graduating this time.

Everything looks so good, you know?"

Daddy was quiet.

I got uncomfortable with his silence. I started to feel small and guilty. "Can I ask you a personal question, Daddy?"

"I'll reserve the right not to answer if it has anything to do with anything I smoked when Johnson was in office."

I smiled, but then got serious. "Did Mama tell you about her problems before you got married?"

Daddy looked thoughtful as he picked up Marie's toy she'd thrown. "Yes, she did. I loved her already, Nan. She told me she'd been in the hospital once for a nervous breakdown when she was nineteen. She told me she had a chemical imbalance, and that she suffered from depression. I admit I was shocked at first, but when it came right down to it, I just didn't care. I figured all that wouldn't matter. Besides, after what she'd been through growing up, it seemed only natural to be a little mixed up."

"What had she been through, Daddy?"

"You'll have to ask your mother that sometime, Nan."

I was intrigued, but more interested in the next question I wanted to ask.

"And what about now, Daddy? Does it matter?"

He breathed quietly for a time, blowing air slowly out of his mouth, slightly puffing his cheeks. "Well, it's different than I thought it would be. I thought it was all behind her."

"When Mama broke down that time Laura was sick, nobody told me much about Mama. What was it like for you Daddy, to see your wife acting crazy?"

Daddy was quiet a minute. "I came home from work one day. Think it was

January." He rubbed his beard in thought. "Yes, January 'cause it was just freezing out. I had to wear a jacket to ride my bike. I came in the door and the whole house was dark, though your mom's car was in the driveway. It was freezing inside. I started calling for her and finally found her hunched down in a corner by the bookshelf, shivering miserably. I tried to help her up, but believe it or not, that little woman knocked me over. She wasn't making any kind of sense, kept saying they were coming for her. I asked who and she said I was one of them. She grabbed a bookend and said I better not come near her or she'd use it."

I searched his face, trying to probe his thoughts while he continued.

"I believed her. She always did have an ornery side to her, so I told her I'd call the police. Glad I did. It took three of them, plus myself, to get her into the car.

I've never been so black and blue in my life. As they drove away, she kept screaming for me, said I was letting the bad guys take her. 'George! Don't let them take me!' she kept hollering."

Daddy's chin had begun to tremble as he rubbed his forehead.

"It was hard. She was afraid of me after that, when I came to see her. Didn't want me anywhere near her. Kept flinching any time I moved, like she thought

I'd hit her. It was hard," he said again. "It hurt me that she thought I'd do anyyhing to harm her. She was absolutely out of her mind if she could think I'd ever hurt her on purpose. There's been times in our marriage where I hurt her without meaning to. I know I should have tried harder to be more romantic, but I'm just a dud sometimes I guess." He looked ruefully up at me before continuing. "After the shock treatments they sent her home, but she still wasn't quite right for a while. She was so afraid of everything, and meanwhile Laura was still at Pleasant Hills, and they wouldn't let your mama see her. Then Dora started practically worshiping me. She was so thankful for everything I did for her. She said thank you to me about twenty times a day. It was like she was thanking me just for sticking around or something. She told me how wonderful I was all the time and how much she appreciated me. It got to the point where it became exasperating." Daddy smiled then. "She perked up, though, and started thinking I was a jerk most of the time. Then I knew she was getting better."

I smiled. Mama was always nagging Daddy about things, and lecturing him when he wanted to relax and just watch TV. She got upset when he'd take off on his motorcycle for long rides. She'd walk around muttering about how he never wanted to spend any time with her, then I'd find her in the bedroom kneeling and praying that he'd get home safe. She was always afraid either his Harley or the highway would claim him, and he wouldn't come home, but she wouldn't let him sell it when they came on hard times once he got fired. She insisted that he keep it. She loved him and he loved her. It was a sweet and complicated relationship they had.

"Daddy, would you still have married her if you knew then what you know now?"

Daddy looked at me with an odd, questioning expression in his eyes before he answered.

"Absolutely. I've never come across a better woman. She's not perfect, but she was always perfect for me. Besides, she makes things interesting for a boring old stick in the mud like myself."

"Sounds like Mama talking."

"I think I was quoting her exactly on that one."

Picnic day came and I rushed around that morning trying to get the kids ready. They were bouncing off the walls with excitement. Harold held Marie while I searched the whole house for Benny's shoes. He never had any idea where he'd put them.

I felt like my head was going to explode. "Think, Benny. You came in the house, and you took them off, remember?"

He thought a minute. "Yep, I must've cuz I ain't wearin' 'em now."

"Aren't wearing them, Benny," I corrected him. Sometimes I thought my kids would drive me crazy one day. "Now, Benny, Honey," I said, trying to sound sweet instead of furious, "they have to be somewhere, right? Now I want you to find them, or you just can't go."

Benny pulled what I called the limp baby technique. He'd been doing it since he was a tiny little thing. His limbs turned to jelly and he slumped to the floor, whining as giant tears welled up in his eyes.

"Crying is not going to find your shoes, Benny! Get up now, or you're not going to go at all!"

Benny kicked his legs in all directions as he rolled over onto his stomach, still crying.

I could feel a scream welling up in the back of my throat. Why did children have to be so unreasonable? I'm sure my blood pressure was skyrocketing.

"Benny, get up off the floor, or so help me, I'll—"

Harold squeezed my shoulder from behind. "Honey, you go on ahead with

Marie. I put your chili in the car. Just take Marie and go. I'll get the other two ready."

I took a deep breath and carried Marie out to the car.

I got behind the wheel and pulled out of the driveway. I noticed the lake looked like a mud puddle again, usually a good sign a storm was coming. The air seemed awful hot and sticky that morning. Once I was on the road, Marie started to cry and kept it up 'til I pulled up to the park where our church always held it's annual picnic. I was at my wit's end.

I squinted into the crowd of people, hoping to find a familiar face. I saw

Helen. I carried Marie over to her and asked, "Could you hold her while I get my chili out of the car?"

"No such thing!" she said. "Lars! Go on and get Nancy's chili out of the car for her!" She looked to me then. "That's way too heavy for you to be carrying, Honey." I sat down at a picnic table with Marie on my lap.

Lars walked to my car, opened the door, and slowly lifted out the giant pot of chili, grunting as he did so. He had a bad back. I felt awful for him as he struggled with it, teetering this way and that, beads of sweat forming on his brow. Just as he almost got to the table, he tripped over a sprinkler fixture, and I saw the whole scene played out in slow motion. First his eyebrows raised, then he leaned this way and that, trying to correct himself. But then gravity took over and he fell slowly forward. The lid of the pot flew forward first, followed by a chunky, steaming brown streak of chili. He hit the ground, still holding the pan as it tipped, and a river of my precious chili oozed out onto the grass.

I realized I wasn't breathing when my cheeks started to tingle, so I took a deep breath, then covered my eyes with my hands. Helen was shouting as she strode over to Lars, who was struggling to get up.

Suddenly Theo was there, giving Lars a hand. But before Lars got up, he struggled again with the pan as if still trying to save my chili, but he turned it upside down in his confusion, and the last of it dripped out onto the grass.

Well, that was that, I thought. So much for all my hard work. I knew it was silly, but tears started to well up in my eyes. I was furious. All that chili sitting there steaming on the grass made me feel sick. I wanted to slap him and Helen both. Helen was eyeing my pile of chili with a strange expression. It was like she was struggling within herself over how to feel about it. Her own pot sat gleaming on the red gingham covered chili table. She looked horrified, but somewhat satisfied at the same time. It would be less competition for her.

She came over to me then and put her hand on my arm. "Oh Honey, I am so sorry."

I suspected for a brief moment that this whole horrid scene had been a plot against me, but I realized I was being petty. "It's just chili, anyway," I said. "Is Lars all right?"

Theo stood before my pile of chili shaking his head. "Dern!" He said. "If it weren't for you," he said to the pastor, who had rushed to his side, "I'd start cussin' up a storm! That there is a goldern shame!"

He squatted down then, inspecting the wasted chili. Suddenly he got up and went over to one of the tables and brought back a spoon. He shoveled a giant spoonful off the top and poked it into his mouth. He closed his eyes and was quiet for a while as he chewed. He grunted softly in pleasure. "That's some fine chili, Miss Purty."

Theo had been one of the chili judges for years. He passed out some spoons to the other old men who acted as judges, and they reluctantly shoveled up mounds of it and put it hesitantly into their mouths. No one wanted to cross Theo. One of them spat out a small piece of bark. They all bobbed their heads in a huddle as Helen sputtered.

"Well, I never!" she protested. "Eating it right off the ground! Good heavens! You all are gonna get sick!"

They ignored her, scrawling a few notes down on their score pad.

"God made dirt, and dirt don't taste all that bad in a good batch of chili," Theo said then. "Maybe you should stir some dirt into yours, Helen. Give that bland pot of muck you brought some character."

The pastor put his hand on Theo's arm. Theo looked at him belligerently a moment, then softened. "I'm sorry, Helen. I shouldn't have said that. I'll disqualify myself as a judge this year so it's fair."

Helen looked smug. Lars looked embarrassed and kind of silly all covered in chili.

"Come on Lars," Theo said then. "I'll give you a ride home in my pickup so you don't have to spoil your caddy. We'll be right back! I heard a rumor that Laura's entering her pie again this year, and I for one have fifty dollars that says it's mine!"

Every year they auctioned off the pies and the proceeds went to the church. Lars nodded and they headed off together. I noticed he was limping slightly.

Laura arrived soon after the fiasco, just as a bunch of glittering blue flies discovered my chili. She was holding a pie with one hand, and Jim with the other. I was beginning to think I'd made a huge mistake in warning Charlie off and leaving Laura to date this jerk. I shook my head.

"Another one, eh?" Grandma asked, coming to stand beside me. I nodded. "Same as the others."

Grandma looked thoughtful as she squinted at Laura. "She takes after me, choosing the rotten apple for herself, and letting the good ones go to everyone else."

I didn't exactly understand what she meant, but Laura saw us before I could ask her about it.

Jim was the first to speak when they approached. "Hi, Nancy! Hi, Grandma!" It made me mad that he called her "Grandma." He had no right.

"Hi, there, boy," was all Grandma said.

"Whoa, what happened here?" Jim asked, narrowly avoiding the pile of chili in the grass.

"That's my chili," I said.

"Oh no Nan! I swear that was your best yet! I sneaked a taste at home when you weren't looking. Dang, how'd you do that?" asked Laura.

"Lars did that," said Grandma. "I'm not saying he did it on purpose, but I am saying that Helen told him to carry it when she knows he has a bad back."

Laura glared at Helen who stood chatting with the other chili contributors around the table. "Sabotage, eh?"

"Well, I'm just saying…" said Grandma before hobbling off to greet one of her old cronies.

"Where's the pie table?" Laura asked. "I baked this last night at work. Ted kept trying to get a taste, but I told him he'd have to come to the picnic and buy it if he wanted it. Have you seen him?"

"No," I said, looking around.

"I didn't figure he'd come. I was just wondering."

"I hope he doesn't," said Jim. "I get enough of him at work."

"I like Ted." I said.

"You don't work for him," he replied before following Laura to the pie table.

Laura looked tired, and I could see she still looked a little pale. I figured she was probably working too hard, what with school besides. I decided I'd talk to her about it.

Harold arrived shortly after that. Benny and Josie came running out of the car and headed straight for the playground.

Harold was sorry when he heard about my chili. "Are you alright?" he asked, rubbing my back.

"Well, I can't be sure, but I may still be in the running anyway. Theo made all the other judges take a scoop off the top and taste it. They scored it and everything."

Harold threw his head back and laughed. "You know, he's not so bad." He said, still chuckling.

I always wondered what it was about Theo that bothered Harold so much. He was never rude to Theo, but I noticed they were hardly ever more than polite to each other. Harold was an excellent judge of character, and the only thing I had to concede that was wrong with Theo was his occasional bouts of bad language.

He was crude sometimes, but that was just his way. Maybe he reminded Harold a little that he hadn't married into what his mother referred to as "quality."

I sat at a table while Harold went to join the horseshoe competition. I watched

Benny and Josie as they played on the swings and slides. Benny was beaming, getting dirtier by the minute. Suddenly he slid down the slide before Josie could get out of his way, and he crashed into her at the bottom. I sat up straight, worried one of them may have been hurt, but relaxed when I saw them untangle themselves. Benny jumped up immediately and went to the swings. Josie was scowling at a soiled spot on her shorts. She detested being dirty and looked like maybe her day had now been spoiled. I saw her holler something at her brother, who ignored her. There never were two more different kids.

I watched them for quite a while. Josie forgot her dirty shorts after a bit, and quit sulking. Benny begged her to push him on the merry go round, and they walked over to it together. He sat down and I just barely heard her say, "Now hold on tight, Benny."

He wrapped his chubby arms and legs around one of the poles and looked at her expectantly.

She ran around and around 'til she wore herself out as Benny squealed in delight. Marie sat dozing on my lap, her chubby cheeks looking fresh and rosy. I loved my kids.

I watched Laura for a while. She and Jim had sat down at a table together and were sipping sodas. I couldn't hear what they said to each other. Meanwhile I could hear the shouts that followed the thuds and clangs at the horseshoe pits. I noticed Daddy was there, standing to the side as Harold threw, giving him a few pointers.

The judges stood around the pie table, taking a tiny bite of each one, then rolling it around in their mouths slowly. I watched closely as one of them scooped into what I thought was Laura's pie. His eyebrows shot up and he nudged the man next to him, pointing down at the pie. I smiled.

It was getting hotter by the minute. Way off in the distance I could see a few innocent white clouds forming. If there would just be a breeze, it wouldn't be quite so hot and humid, but the air remained thick and heavy.

I looked back to Laura and could see that she was suffering in the heat. She was wearing shorts, but she had on her usual long sleeve shirt to cover her arms. She looked nauseated. I got up and walked over to her.

"Mind if I sit here?" I asked as I approached them.

"Go ahead!" Laura said, smiling up at me. "Aw, look! She fell asleep! Can I hold her for a while, Nan?"

I was relieved to not have to hold Marie for a while and gladly handed her over.

Laura got up and went to sit in the shade, leaving me to talk to Jim. We had nothing to talk about, and he soon got up to watch the horseshoe competition.

Theo returned. After seeing to Grandma as she sat in the shade and giving her a fan, he came to sit by me.

He squinted up at the clouds that were now massing on the horizon. "She'll be thundering in the thicket 'fore too long. I hope they hurry and get that pie auction on. It's hotter'n hell's bathtub out here. I need to get your grandma home soon."

"Did you get Lars all cleaned up?"

"Yeah. Just between you and me, Nan, I don't think he's all right. He stayed home, and as I was leaving, I could hear him popping open a beer. Now I don't see much wrong with that on a hot day like this, but I see him at the bar just about every night lately."

"And you would know he is at the bar because..." I prodded, smiling. "Because I never drink in front of your grandma. Haven't in over twenty years now, not since I moved in with her. A man needs his shot of whiskey sometimes, but that's all I ever take is just a shot, Nan. Sometimes I wish I could drink to forget a few things, but I promised myself I wouldn't ever do that." He looked at me pointedly. "Lars has to be escorted out regularly."

Just then the pastor stood on one of the tables, put his fingers to his lips, and whistled sharply. It took a while for everyone to settle down, but when they did, he spoke loudly enough for everyone to hear.

"Looks like we got a storm heading our way folks, so we're going to get this thing underway." He cleared his throat. "First of all, Theo won the salsa contest." Everyone said a halfhearted "Yay." Theo's salsa sat alone at the salsa table this year. No one else bothered to enter any.

"Next, the chili results. Envelope, please." He said, as the one of the judges handed it to him.

"Honorable mention goes to...Helen Trudeux!"

Helen stood, her face glistening in sweat as she plodded her way through the tables to the pastor and accepted her white ribbon. She thanked him and looked relieved to sit down again. I caught her eye and smiled at her. She nodded at me.

"Are they really gonna judge my chili?" I whispered to Theo.

"They already did, remember?" He said with his eyes gleaming.

The pastor's voice boomed out over the din of comments that followed Helen's award. "Third place goes to...Eunice Blake. Where are you Eunice? There she is!"

Eunice was a tiny woman, nowhere close to being five feet tall. She never spoke above a whisper. She had a sweet, wrinkly face, and I'd thought for years that she had a crush on Theo.

"Now there's a large woman," Theo said blandly as she walked with her cane up to the table.

"I think she's sweet, Theo. You should ask her out sometime."

"I did once. Wouldn't let me kiss her. I gave up on her after that."

"When was this?"

"Now let me see," he said, scratching his chest as he leaned back. "Gotta be about seventy years ago. We were in the fifth grade together."

I laughed. "Well, maybe she's not so shy now." The pastor's voice called for our attention again. "Second-place goes

to...Nancy Parley!"

I stood and walked to his table, a little shocked. "Now Nancy's chili won't be available for the potluck after the auction," he said amidst a few chuckles from the surrounding tables. "Her chili never made it to the judging table, but we tasted a little off the top, see, and it was just about heaven, even with a few blades of grass mixed in."

He handed me my award and I sat down quickly. I knew I was blushing.

"First place this year goes to...Dora Mae Harris?" He said it like it surprised him. "Are you here, Dora?" he asked, somewhat shocked.

My daddy stood. "Couldn't make it, but I talked her into making a pot for me, and I entered it on her behalf." Daddy walked forward and accepted her award. I wished Mama had been there.

"Now, on to the pies. Honorable mention goes to..."

I listened as each of the contestants got their prizes, white knuckling the table when he got to first place.

"First place goes to...Laura Harris for her absolutely delicious pecan pie!

Come on up here, Laura!"

Laura stood, handing Marie to Grandma and walked slowly up to his table.

She smiled shyly as he pinned on her blue ribbon. She turned to take a bow like the others had done, but suddenly her face froze. She went quickly back to sit by

Grandma.

I looked to where her eyes had been and saw why. Clance was standing under a tree at the edge of the playground. Jim stood next to him and they appeared to have been talking for a while. Clance, the dog that he was, was trying to steal from Laura again. Fortunately, the way I saw it, Jim wasn't worth keeping.

Jim turned and looked at Laura as she sat in the shade, then looked back to

Clance, who nodded slowly. Jim kicked his boots into the dirt a couple times, then walked away with Clance. Apparently, they were friends. It shouldn't have surprised me. It was like Grandma always said, "frogs and toads, and slugs and bugs."

Laura looked like she was going to be sick.

I got up and went to sit with her as the pie auction began. I put my hand on her arm, and she pulled it away. I sighed and looked around me at all the people bidding on the pies. Sometimes the auctions became quite heated. Just then a pie went for forty dollars. Several more went for about twenty-five dollars.

Suddenly Grandma sat up. "Here goes, Honey! They've got yours up!" she said to Laura. Laura looked up. She made an effort to look cheerful.

"And here's that famous blue-ribbon pecan pie! What can I get for this pie? Starting at ten…over there at 15…25 over here. Theo, sit down please so I can see the other bidders."

Theo sat and cupped his hands around his mouth. "Thirty-five!"

Suddenly I heard a familiar voice shout, "Forty!" I looked up and saw Charlie standing next to Ted at the back of the group.

Theo jerked around and scowled at him. "Forty-five!"

"Fifty!" he bid, grinning.

"Sixty!" Theo shouted, looking ruffled.

"Seventy-five!" Charlie bid next.

There was a hum of chatter in the air as the bidding went higher. The highest a pie had ever gone for was 80 dollars, and that was back in '85 for old Mrs. Butler's raspberry lemon meringue. She died about ten years ago, taking her secret recipe with her.

Theo stomped his foot, and poked his hand into his pocket, drawing out his wallet.

"Going once…" the pastor said gleefully.

"Hold on there!" Theo grumbled. "I gotta check my assets. Just hold on a dern minute!"

"Seventy-nine, and, let me see" he said, fishing in his other pocket, "fifty-five cents!"

Theo waved his money in the air. Charlie was laughing. I looked at Laura. She seemed stunned and was staring at Charlie.

"Going once…going twice…"

Ted whispered something to Charlie, and Charlie piped in, "Ninety-five dollars!"

The congregation of picnickers gasped.

Theo looked enraged, but then he suddenly smiled as he regarded Charlie. "Be my guest." he said then.

"Sold to…excuse me sir, I don't know your name."

"Charlie Green."

"Sold to Charlie Green!" the pastor announced proudly as the first raindrops started to fall.

While Charlie went to claim his pie, Theo came over to us. "If he tastes it,

Laura, you're gonna have yourself a beau!"

Laura blushed fiercely then as Charlie headed toward us, shielding his prize with his body.

Theo jumped up. "He'll need a fork!" he said as he rushed to get him one. Grandma was giggling. Her laughter sounded like tiny bells. I always loved it when she laughed like that. I hadn't heard it in a while.

While the folks from church scurried around to collect their things before the deluge hit, Charlie sat down by us, followed by Ted.

"Remember, Charlie," he said, "Twenty dollars-worth of that pie is mine!"

"Come on, Honey!" said Harold, rushing up to me with a kid on each hand.

"Let's go! Get Marie! This is looking up to be a bad one!"

"Tarnation!" Theo grumbled. "You can't properly enjoy that pie in the rain,

Boy. Come on to Nancy's house! Follow me!"

Ted and Charlie shrugged their shoulders and followed Theo as he lead

Grandma as quickly as he could to the parking lot.

Laura looked about desperately for Jim, but she knew he was already gone.

She followed me to my car.

It began to hail as the dark clouds churned above.

Chapter Fifteen

Harold headed to his pickup with Benny and Josie as I got into my Buick and strapped Marie into her car seat. Laura sat down in the passenger side, still looking somewhat dazed. Outside on the parking lot, hail stones bounced around like popcorn.

I saw Theo easing Grandma into his truck, then watched as he turned to the adjoining vehicle to help little Eunice. He put his back to the hail, shielding her as she settled into the backseat of her daughter's car. Ted pulled up behind Theo and waited for him to pull out. I could only make out Charlie's chest in the passenger side. Theo got into his pickup then and pulled out, waving his arm out his window, beckoning them to follow.

I got behind them, and looked around for Harold's truck, but it wasn't in the parking lot anymore. He must have headed out already.

As I drove, I kept hunching down in my seat so I could see the sky above through the windshield. The hail let up, replaced by a driving rain. The ominous dark clouds seemed to be churning directly above our car. I clutched the wheel tightly, trying to remain calm.

"Did you see that?" Laura asked suddenly, pointing out her window.
"What?" I asked, my heart racing.

"Lightning."

Almost immediately we heard the report of rolling thunder. It rattled the windows. My palms started to sweat. I thought of all my nightmares, and realized that once again, Harold was not with me. I tried to brush the thought aside, but it quickly crept back into my mind. He had the kids with him. I realized suddenly in a horrible, paralyzing state of fear that I was going to have a panic attack right there on the road. I wanted more than anything to just get home.

"Slow down, Nan!" Laura warned. "You're going way too fast for this storm! Nan!"

Suddenly a tree branch skidded across the road in front of us.

My hands were shaking as I pulled off to the side of the road, stomping heavily on the brakes 'til the car screeched to a stop. Marie was crying.

Suddenly Laura yanked open my door and shoved me over into her vacant seat. "Put your seatbelt on." she ordered. "Nancy!" Laura slapped me then, and I came out of it. I put on my belt, then put my hands over my face as another wave of thunder rolled right over the top of the car. "Geez, Nan! You're acting like a baby! It's just a storm. Pull yourself together. You're scaring Marie!"

Marie had grown frantic. I took several deep breaths as Laura got us back onto the highway.

"Rock-a-bye baby, in the treetop…" Laura began to sing softly in her beautiful voice. "When the wind blows…"

"Sing something else," I said irritably.

"Hush little baby don't say a word, Mama's gonna buy you a mockingbird. If that mockingbird don't sing…"

I sat back then and began to relax. Marie calmed down, and cooed softly as

Laura sang. I felt safe with Laura behind the wheel. I watched the rivers of raindrops roll upward on the windshield between the rhythmic strokes of the wipers.

I always thought it was interesting the way they seemed to defy gravity. One little stream of water in particular intrigued me. It kept trying to make it to the top of the windshield. Once it almost made it, only to be flattened again by the wipers.

"I'm sorry about all that, Laura. Good thing at least one of us can keep a level head in a storm," I said.

Laura continued to sing until we pulled into the driveway of our home. Sam was in the yard, barking frantically. Charlie was already there and opened Laura's door for her, offering his hand. Laura took it.

Out behind the house I could see the lake was running over, dimpling as new raindrops crashed into it.

Harold was there when I walked in the house. He had turned the TV on to hear the weather report. I went to him and hugged him, relieved he was home. I then turned to our guests and asked them to make themselves at home. Charlie sat on the couch and Ted took a chair. Grandma sat on her favorite chair and held her arms out for Marie. Laura had gone to her room and shut the door. I handed Marie to Grandma, then went to the kitchen to find Theo. He had commandeered the pie.

"Theo, do you have permission to cut that pie?"

"Nancy girl, you just step aside and let me work. This here's important and I want it done right. Go out to the garage and get some of that vanilla ice cream from your freezer."

When I got back, he was still poised over the pie, trying to decide at which angle to cut it.

"Hell," he finally said, and cut it in half, then again and again. As he divvied out the pieces I noticed the one he handed me to give to Charlie was the smallest one.

"Now Theo, he's the one who bought it. Don't you think he should get the biggest piece, especially since he was nice enough to share it with us?"

Theo looked at me like my brain had gone askew. "For a smart girl, sometimes you strike me as kind of thick, Miss Purty. Of course, I gave him the smallest piece. That there's called strategy. Make him yearn for more, see?" He winked at me. "Watch you don't put too much ice cream on there, don't want to drown it.

It's gotta have just the right proportions. Now quit. That's enough."

I sat down after everyone had their plates of pie and ice cream. I bit into my piece and chewed it slowly, enjoying everything about it. I looked to Charlie to see how he was enjoying his pie, but he hadn't touched it. As everyone else was grunting in delight, Charlie watched

Laura's closed door. I got up and went down the hall to her door and knocked softly.

Laura opened it slowly and let me in. I looked at her closely, to see if she had been crying, but her eyes seemed dry. "I saw him too." I said.

Laura didn't look at me. She stood with one hand on her guitar. "He's gone, I,guess."I was quiet.

"I guess you feel like you were right all along about him," she said.

"I feel like I was right about you, Laura. You deserve better than that. Jim isn't worth one sad thought. He wasn't right for you." I watched her downturned face to see how she took what I'd said. She didn't seem mad or offended, so I continued after a moment's hesitation, "There's a man sitting right in my living room waiting for you to come out, and I won't have anyone being rude to a guest in my house." I tried to sound light and playful, but I realized I just managed to sound wistful. "Give this one a chance, Laura. I think it would be alright." I prayed silently that it would be.

She raised her beautiful blue eyes to mine then. I could see she was afraid. I put my hand on her arm, and she didn't pull away. I could see tears forming in her eyes. "I don't know if I could stand it, Nan, if it didn't turn out. I've actually been avoiding him lately. He's so nice, Nan. Maybe he doesn't deserve to have to…"

"Laura, he'd be lucky to have you." I reached over and hugged her.

She wiped her eyes and said, "Alright, if you say so. I don't know about that beard, though."

I pulled back smiling, trying to hide my own anxiety and ignored her inference that the responsibility of her actions rested on my shoulders.

"How do I look?" she asked, turning to the mirror.

"Irresistible."

"Alright then." She squared her shoulders before walking out the door.

Charlie looked up and smiled as Laura walked into the living room. He motioned for her to sit on the couch by him. I sat down again and lit into my pie, finishing it off.

As Charlie ate his pie, he talked to Laura. She seemed shy as I watched them interact. I had to admit it was a little odd to have Charlie sitting right there in my living room. I equated him with the truck stop and the smell of coffee and stale leather seats, and here he was in my house, looking right at home. He ended his pie by licking his fork, looking a little sadly at his empty plate.

"Good, aint it?" Theo chimed in. He had been watching them as well.

"I think it was just about the best thing I ever ate." He replied as Laura blushed.

Harold motioned for us to be quiet as he turned up the weather channel.

"They've upgraded to a tornado warning now. It was just a watch before." He got up and stood in front of the window, watching the lake as the clouds rolled above it. Just then we all saw lightning dash across the sky.

The weatherman's voice cut in, "I repeat, the National Weather Advisory has issued a tornado warning. Remain indoors and take cover if possible. We are also under a continued thunderstorm advisory 'til 5:35 P.M."

"Well folks, I guess we'd all better head to the basement if you don't mind. I don't like the looks of this." Harold said.

"Yippee!" Benny chimed. He always loved our dashes to the basement and ran down ahead of us.

We all settled on folding chairs in the basement. Harold brought down a lantern just in case. I got up and ran some water into the washing machine, then turned it off once it was full.

Ted looked at me questioningly.

"I always fill it up for these warnings. Just in case you know. We may be stuck down here a while, and I figure a little extra water might come in handy."

Harold helped Grandma onto an old chair I'd retired from my living room. I looked around but didn't see Theo anywhere. Just then I heard him clomping down the stairs and looked up to see he'd gone after Laura's guitar. "I figured we might could use some entertainment since we're all squashed together down here.

Sort of pass the time, see?" he said as he handed the guitar to Laura.

Laura didn't look thrilled with the idea of performing for everyone. There was an awkward moment before Grandma said, "I'd like to hear that one about the wind. We can all sing along. What's it called?"

I realized what song she meant. "Oh, Seminole Wind?" I asked.

Grandma pointed her finger. "That's it. Seems appropriate." We could all hear the wind as it picked up outside.

Laura sat and tuned her instrument a moment, then her fingers began to move softly over the strings. I could tell she was nervous.

"I'll accompany you," Theo said then, "but I'm going to want to sit in your spot there, Charlie." As he spoke, he took his harmonica out of his pocket.

I felt a little embarrassed at what Ted and Charlie would think of our impromptu concert, but I noticed they both seemed eager to hear it. Charlie moved to a different chair, almost opposite Laura, so he'd have to look right at her. More of Theo's strategy, I suspected.

Laura played the song along with Theo's harmonica, but she didn't sing with the rest of us. Grandma and I were the only ones who sang 'til Josie chimed in on the parts she knew. We sounded pretty pathetic, but we all clapped for ourselves when the song was over.

"Now play the pretty one," Grandma requested, nodding to Theo.

"Which one?" Laura asked.

"That one you wrote back when you were in high school. I've always liked it."

I could tell Laura was uncomfortable. It was a very personal song.

"Play it!" chimed in Theo. "Your Granny's not getting any younger."

I looked to Charlie and saw that he had grown uncomfortable too. He didn't like seeing Laura cornered, but I could also see that he wanted to hear it. He tugged at his beard and didn't look at her, sparing her at least that discomfort.

'If you want, I'll sing it, Laura. I think I remember the words." I said, hoping to help her a little.

"You don't sing it like Laura does." Theo said matter-of-factly.

Harold stepped in. "You don't have to sing it if you don't want to, Laura, but we'd all love to hear it. If you don't, I guess I'll have to sing something, and then everybody might up and run out into that storm."

We all chuckled. I looked appreciatively at him as Laura tentatively began to strike a few chords. Something about the set of her mouth made me think she was trying not to cry. I almost couldn't stand it. Theo looked concerned but hopeful. We waited patiently as she started over once, then sat back as she began to sing, very softly at first.

Grandma closed her eyes and smiled. Josie looked at Laura with worshipful eyes. Even Benny grew still as her soft voice echoed against the cement walls and floor of the basement. Marie dozed on my lap. Ted smiled, enjoying himself. Harold came to stand behind me, putting his hands on my shoulders affectionately. Theo beamed, and Charlie...Charlie had been ambushed. Theo saw to it that he didn't even have a chance, and as I watched his face while she sang, I could see he'd been taken captive already

Chapter Sixteen

It had been a week since the storm. There was no tornado, only a series of micro-bursts that felled a few trees. Charlie left and had been gone for several days on a long haul. I noticed a change in Laura while he was gone. Laura had always been sort of quiet, but now her times of quiet as she'd sit looking out of a window seemed hopeful, no longer despondent or bitter.

I came to wake her that morning, as she had been unable to get herself up lately. Sometimes the medicine made it hard for her to wake up, but I also sensed she hadn't been sleeping well, and thought I knew the reason.

I looked down at her. Every muscle in her face was relaxed, even her mouth. It was hard to imagine that schizophrenia lurked somewhere inside her. I realized then that I hadn't thought of Laura as just my sister for a long time. I always thought of her now in relation to her problems. I felt sorry about that.

I shook her gently. "Laura, Laura wake up."

Her eyebrows knit together, then relaxed, and she rolled over.

"Laura, time to get up. You're gonna miss your class."

I shook her again. She remained limp against her pillows. I grew alarmed.

"Laura! Laura! Can you get up?" I yelled frantically.

"Geez, Nan!" she gasped, sitting up irritably and throwing off her covers.

I was relieved, but when I looked at her, I couldn't hide my concern. Her face was so pale, and her eyes had gray circles under them.

"What?" she asked irritably.

"You look a little pale," I said, trying not to show too much concern. "Maybe you should just go back to sleep."

"What time is it?" she asked, squinting at her clock. "Oh no! Why didn't you wake me up?"

"I did!"

Laura rolled out of bed onto the floor and crawled to her dresser. Halfway there she sat in the middle of the floor and closed her eyes.

"What is it?" I asked.

"I'm just a little dizzy. I think I got up too quick."

I started to squat down by her, but she stopped me. "I'd like a little privacy,

Nan. I'm going to be naked here in a minute, and I'd rather not have an audience."

I smiled. "Alright. What do you want for breakfast? You're running late, so let me get it for you."

"Toast."

"Is that all?"

"Yes, but you can put it on a plate if it would make you feel better."

Laura got in her car and pulled out of the driveway, eating her toast as she went. She only had to finish out the semester, and she'd have her bachelor's degree. I shook my head. She had a lot of perseverance, I had to give her that. She was as stubborn as Mama.

I hadn't finished school. I had been spoiled growing up. I was always the best artist in class. All my teachers beamed over me, patted my back, told me I had a gift, and never taught me a blessed thing. They all assumed my natural talent included things like an understanding of color theory, the concepts of design, and an understanding of proportion. I found out soon enough when I got to college that I was seriously lacking in the basics that everyone else already knew. I wasn't at the top of my class, but at the bottom. I remember one day in particular while in my oils class. We were painting a still life of some bread, fruit, wine, grapes– the usual. I was painting the bread and wanted a lighter shade of brown, so I mixed Van Dyke brown with some white and started putting it up on the canvas. The professor came up behind me and yanked my brush out of my hand.

"Why in the name of DaVinci are you putting that horrid color on your canvas?" He sighed in exasperation as he impatiently rummaged through my paints. He found what he was looking for and squirted a glob of thalo yellow-green on my palette, and a glob of light cadmium red next to it and rubbed the two together with my brush. I was amazed at the lovely golden-brown hue that emerged as the two unlikely colors swirled together. "Like that!" he said emphatically, using large confident strokes as he roughed in the bread.

I was forced to stand and watch as he called the other students in the room to stand around and watch him paint. It was lovely when he was done, but it wasn't mine. It became a lesson to the others about what not to do and about how important it was to have even a basic understanding of color. I bit my bottom lip throughout the lesson and walked back to my apartment where I cried for at least an hour, mixing shades of golden brown over and over 'til I ran out of paint.

Fortunately, it wasn't all bad for me in school. I discovered I could sculpt and was once again near the top of my class. I'd never sculpted anything before but found I could handle clay. I didn't get much chance to sculpt once I left school to raise a family, though. I admired Laura for sticking to it.

I tried my hardest not to worry about her, but I knew something wasn't right. I called the clinic where she'd had her blood drawn the day before.

"Yes," I said when the receptionist answered. "I'd like to know the results of a blood test taken yesterday on Laura Harris."

"Am I speaking with Laura?" she asked.

"No, this is Nancy Parley. I am her sister. Check your list. I'm on it for information release."

"Hold please," she said, and I listened to endless elevator music while she checked.

She returned to the line. "OK, it's a good thing you called. Her results are just in, and we'd like to have her come in for another draw."

"What is it?" I asked as my heart started to race.

"Ma'am, we don't release information over the phone to anyone but the client. Besides, it's just a basic re-check to make sure our information is accurate. If you could tell her to come in this afternoon, we'd appreciate it."

I hung up and felt sick. I was tempted to get in the car and hunt her down on campus, but I had to get my kids ready for school.

When they were finally out the door, I grabbed my purse and opened the door to leave, nearly crashing into Helen on the doorstep.

"Oh, you were leaving?" she asked, looking almost despondent. She clutched her purse tightly, looking almost childlike. It stopped me in my tracks. I invited her in and stepped back inside.

She wasn't her usual self. For one thing, I noticed her hair hadn't been set, and for two, she didn't comment on the children's toys being strung out all over the living room.

"Hi, Nancy," she said as she plunked down on the couch. "How's little Marie?"

I handed Marie over to her and watched as Helen held her awkwardly. "Is everything all right?" I asked.

"Oh, of course. Everything is just fine. I just thought I'd stop over. I wanted to congratulate you on your chili. I'm so sorry about all that, but it turned out all right, I guess. Sometimes Lars is just…" She stopped and bounced Marie. "He didn't happen to stop by here last night did he?" she asked, as if the question was completely normal.

I looked at her a moment in surprise, then answered, "No, was he supposed to?"

"No, not exactly. I just thought he might've." "Why?"

Helen looked for a moment like a deer caught in the headlights. "Oh, well I told him to, I had something for you, but I guess he forgot." she said hurriedly. "I best be going. I have some errands. There's a sale over at the SuperSaver. Do you want me to pick up anything? Clorox products are all half off today."

I got the impression she was babbling.

Something was wrong, and she was going to try to scrub it clean, like she always did. I had a picture of her disinfecting her entire house while Lars was gone.

"Helen, is Lars OK?"

"Oh, I'm sure he's fine. He just forgot to come home." As she spoke, she broke down and cried. Her whole body shook. I realized then I'd never seen her cry before and was glad I'd managed to avoid it for the first twenty-nine years of my life. It was pitiful and violent at the same time.

I put my hand on her shoulder, and gently removed Marie from her tight grasp. "Helen, are you telling me you don't know where he is?"

She sniffed. I handed her a Kleenex and she did a thorough job of blowing her nose.

"Well, of course I know where he is. He's at work, I'm sure." She straightened her shoulders, recollecting herself. "I guess I'm just tired. I don't know why I'm making such a fuss. Good grief, Nancy, I don't know what came over me. I've got to get going. You know, you really ought to put a bib on that baby. I can see she's got stains all over that little outfit I got for her. What kind of detergent do you use?"

I just stared at her.

"Never mind. I'll just pick some up for you. I know the kinds that are the best.

See you later, now, Honey," she said as she strode out the door.

I waited 'til she'd pulled out of my driveway before I once again tried to leave, but the phone rang. I answered it, hoping it would be Laura.

It was Grandma. I'd forgotten all about meeting her and Mama for brunch.

I called the school after I promised Grandma I'd be right there and left a message for Laura to call me as soon as possible.

I got in the car with Marie and drove to Grandma's, and parked behind Mama's car.

Theo was outside hoeing his garden. He had an unbelievable green thumb. I'd given up on a garden a long time ago, blaming the alkali in the soil, but his tomatoes and peppers were legendary in the neighborhood.

"Mornin' Nantucket! Lookit here!" he said, holding up a giant zucchini.

"I don't know how you do it, Theo," I said as I walked into the house.

Mama and Grandma were sitting at the table, sipping hot tea. "There's our girls!" Grandma beamed. "We can't have a four-generation brunch with just two of us."

It had been Grandma's idea. She called in Theo to take some pictures and we all posed together around a smiling Marie. I didn't know then it would be the very last picture taken of Grandma.

"Where's our biscuits?" Grandma demanded cheerfully as Theo went into the kitchen.

"I'm gettin' your dern biscuits! Just keep your shirt on, Alice."

Theo returned, placing a plate of hot steaming biscuits before us, a plate of fruit salad, and an egg casserole.

"Mmmmm!" Mama said, smelling the biscuits. "What's your secret, Theo?"

"I'll leave it for you in my will before I kick off," he said, smiling mysteriously.

He bowed with a flourish, then stepped out, saying over his shoulder, "Let me know if you ladies need anything."

"Oh, shoo!" said Grandma, flipping her hand after him.

I put Marie in Grandma's ancient highchair and gave her a piece of biscuit.

"I used to keep your mama in that chair, Honey." she said, softly. "I never thought I'd live to see a great grandchild sitting in it. I guess that makes me an old woman. My own little girl is a grandma." Suddenly tears welled up in her eyes, but she quickly wiped them away and smiled. "Well, this old woman is hungry. Pass that casserole over, Nan, Honey."

Mama and I were silent as we ate 'til Grandma said, "Now don't go letting me spoil your food. Pay no mind to me; I just got a little caught off guard. Us old ladies just get to crying sometimes. Pass that casserole over, will you Nan?"

Mama and I looked at each other. Grandma already had some on her plate. She had always been sharp as a tack, and it concerned me that she'd forgotten that she'd already put some on her plate only a minute ago.

"Helen stopped by this morning," I said, desperate to fill the uncomfortable silence as Grandma discovered she'd already put some on her plate. "She was acting really weird."

Grandma put down the casserole dish. "I've always thought that woman was a little weird." Grandma clasped her hands together, lost in thought a moment. "Reminds me of something. It was a while back, when I was a little girl, and my job was to take care of the chickens. I had one little 'ole banty hen. Bittiest little thing, but full of spite, I tell you. She didn't blend well with the other chickens, and she kind of took to herself. There was a large walnut tree out the back a-ways, and she started settin' underneath it.

"I figured she'd gotten herself a nest of eggs, and since she was my only banty, I left her there to set on 'em. The other hens would come clucking by, and she'd puff up her neck feathers, and set to clucking so loud she usually scared even the biggest ones off. She was proud of that little old nest she had started, and she wasn't about to let anyone near it.

"I got to thinking after a while that she'd been settin' long enough, so I went out to check. She hollered and screeched and flapped her wings, and 'bout had a fit. But when I got her off, I just couldn't believe my eyes. There weren't any eggs at all, Nancy. She was settin' there all that time on nothing but a little ole pile of walnuts!"

Grandma chuckled as she remembered. "That little banty never forgave me, either. Wouldn't let me near her after that. I think she got it in her head that those were really her eggs."

Grandma ran her fingers through her thin hair as she thought a minute. "See, I told you that story, because it's always reminded me of something. When I think of that little hen, I think of Helen. She's just a perched up high on her own little nest of walnuts, just a clucking away. No matter how long she sits there, it aint going to make any difference one way or the other. "See, laying an egg hurts; I'm sure of it, based on the fuss those hens put up just before it plops down all warm and slimy into their nests. Helen is afraid to do it for real. Nothing that woman does will ever make a difference unless she's willing to get real and face that life isn't neat and tidy at all.

"What is it Theo always says?" Grandma put her fingers to her mouth as she tried to remember. "I got it: Some people's minds are like concrete, thoroughly mixed up and permanently set."

Grandma sighed sadly. "I guess I'm not really one to judge. It's easy to figure out other people's problems. I sat on my own nest once and just kept settin'. Took Theo to pry me off."

Mama put her hand on Grandma's shoulder. "You did your best, Mama. It's all anybody can do."

"Hell," Grandma said. "I didn't know any other way back then. If it wasn't for Theo, I might've…well, never mind. Here I go rambling on again. Pass me that casserole, Nan."

I left Grandma's feeling sad. She was a wonderful woman, and I was going to miss her when she was gone. I had a feeling it was going to be soon. She was ninety-two.

I got home and called the school, only to find that the message had never been delivered to Laura. I was tempted to try to find her myself, but Marie was napping so I called over at Ted's Take a Break and left a message with him.

"When is she due to start tonight?" I asked.

"Oh, she'll be in at about four thirty or so. Is something the matter?" Ted asked.

"Oh, no. Just tell her she needs to give me a call once she gets in, if that's alright."

"No problem," he said.

"Hey, is Charlie back yet?" I asked.

"Just pulled in last night. I didn't hardly recognize him. That boy shaved his beard! He looks like he's just a kid! I tell you what, that beard made him look at least ten years older. Just between you and me, I think I know why he did it. Something to do with a guitar and a piece of pecan pie."

I could see him winking as he talked. I chuckled. "I think you may be right.

Keep an eye on him, for me Ted. Make sure he treats her right."

"Will do, but I don't think you need to worry, Nancy."

I spent the rest of the day trying to get the house into some semblance of order. I peeled band-aids off the walls and chiseled some petrified play dough out of the carpet. It never ceased to amaze me how quickly my kids could mess the place up. It was absolutely frustrating.

The kids came home, and after a snack, ran out to play with the other kids in the neighborhood. It was a little after five thirty when the phone rang. I expected it to be Laura, but I was surprised to hear Ted's voice on the line.

"Nancy? We've had kind of a situation here. Charlie's bringing Laura home in her car."

My heart stopped. "What happened?"

"Well, as far as I can tell, Jim said something to Laura that got her upset. I noticed she looked sort of pale when she came in. Looked tired, poor kid. Anyway, he got her sort of riled, and she passed out cold right there behind the bar.

Don't worry, she seems fine now, but I sent her home. Charlie offered to drive her."

I was stunned and terrified. That Clozaril she was on had always made me a little nervous, and I didn't even want to think about what this meant.

"Nancy?" Ted asked, and I realized I'd been quiet for a while.

"Oh, sorry, Ted. I was just a little shocked. You said she's alright though?"

"Now that's part of the reason I called. I need a straight answer from you, if you don't mind. I just fired Jim, but I had a long talk with him first."

"What did he say?"

"Frankly, I don't give a damn about what he said, but I need to know if this will in any way affect her job here. I mean, is there anything I need to know about how to deal with this?"

Bless his heart. I knew I liked him for a reason. "Ted, when she's medicated like she is now, there's no problem. She's on a new drug now called Clozaril that seems to be working. To be honest, that's why I called. See, it's kind of a dangerous drug. It might destroy her immune system. The clinic called today because they wanted to run some more tests."

Ted was quiet on the other line a minute. "You mean, this drug might make her sick?"

It was my turn to be quiet. "Yeah."

"Tell you what. Let her take the rest of the week off. Poor kid didn't look like she was feeling too good. Tell her to come back when she's ready."

"Does Charlie know?" I asked then, apprehensive.

"I didn't see any reason to tell him. He walked in after it was all over."

"Thank you, Ted."

I don't think he fully understood what I meant about the drug destroying her immune system.

I felt utterly helpless as I waited for her to get home.

Fortunately, I didn't have to wait long. Laura came in only a few minutes later, looking flushed and embarrassed.

"Where's Charlie?" I asked.

"I told him to take my car back. I figured I could get a ride in to the diner tomorrow."

"You could've invited him in, Laura."

Laura looked angry. "I just don't feel like having company right now, okay?"

She was in one of her unapproachable moods. I noticed then that she wasn't wearing her long sleeve shirt she usually wore under her uniform. She only wore a tank top.

"What happened to your shirt?"

Laura put her hands over her face and sat rubbing her eyes a minute. "I got coffee all over it when I fell. Charlie took it off, I guess, or maybe Ted."

"How long were you out for?"

"I don't know."

"What did Jim say to you that got you so upset?"

Laura pulled her legs up to her chest as she sat back into the couch. "I don't want to talk about it right now, Nan."

"How do you feel?"

Laura sighed irritably. "Tired and a little weak. I just forgot to eat lunch today, that's all."

I remembered the clinic then. "Laura, the clinic wants you to come in for another draw."

"I just went to those bloodsuckers yesterday."

"I know, but they want to run some more tests."

Laura sat very still for a while. "Did they say why?"

"No, they wouldn't tell me anything. We'll go in tomorrow morning."

Laura started to get up and go to her room.

"Wait, Laura. Let me get you something to eat. You must be starved."

Laura turned and went to sit at the table, putting her head down on her arms as she waited.

"I hear Charlie cut off his beard," I said, trying to lighten the mood as I made her a plate.

"Yeah, I didn't even recognize him at first. He looks so different without it!"

"Well I wish you would've let him in for just a minute. Now I'm dying to see what he looks like, too."

Laura barely touched her food.

I drove her in to the clinic the next day. She disappeared down the hallway, following a nurse. I was so anxious I could hardly stand it.

Finally, she emerged, smiling.

"So, what's the news?" I asked, hopeful.

"I'm anemic!" she pronounced proudly.

"Anemic? So, what does that mean?"

"It means my iron is low, that's all. That's all, Nan!"

I was so relieved I stood up and hugged her and was surprised as she hugged me back. "I need to take some iron pills and eat a little more protein they said."

"Let's start right now then. What are you in the mood for?"

"I guess I could use a hamburger. I can't even remember the last time I ate one. Want to go to Wendy's?"

"Tell you what, let's go to the truck stop. I bet Ted can make a mean burger."

Laura stopped. "I don't know if I want to go there."

"Ted knows, Laura, and he's fine with it. Besides, he fired Jim last night."

"Oh, well in that case, let's go! Every time I serve one of those burgers it about drives me crazy, they smell so good. I haven't eaten one yet. I bet they must have about a million calories."

"Which is just what the doctor ordered," I reminded her. "Plus, you need to get your car back."

We drove over to the diner. Ted was surprised to see us. The diner was crowded, but he found us a booth that was vacant.

"What'll it be, ladies?" he asked, pen poised.

"Two of those giant burgers." I said. "And some fries."

Ted beamed as he wrote it down. "How are you, Laura?" he asked then.

"Fine, just a little anemic. I need some protein."

"Well, you come to the right place!"

As he walked into the back, I surveyed the room, hoping to see Charlie, but he wasn't there. I was disappointed.

After we ate, I walked Laura to her car, which was parked in the back. On the seat was a bouquet of wildflowers tied with a piece of twine. A few of them had begun to wilt in the heat. There was no note. I doubted two dozen red roses could have brought such a glow into her face as she bent over them and sniffed.

"Oh Laura, I'm jealous. That is just about the sweetest thing."

She sat down then with them in her lap and smiled up at me. A tear escaped her eye and she quickly flicked it away as she started the car.

I felt full of hope and joy as I drove home following her taillights, wondering what she was thinking. I remembered the sweetness of falling in love with

Harold, and I thought I shared in what she must be feeling.

Two days later he called.

"Mrs. Parley? Hi, this is Charlie. I got your number from Ted. I hope you don't mind."

"Oh, no. That's just fine. How are you?"

"I'm alright. Would you mind if I talked to Laura a minute?"

I didn't mind at all and I wanted to make sure Charlie understood that.

"That is just fine, Charlie. I know you care for her."

"Yes, I do. How is she doing?"

"Oh, she's fine. Just a little anemic, but I've been feeding her more protein than she can stand. Maybe you could take her out for a steak. Hold on, I'll get her for you."

I left the room as she talked to him.

The next evening, I got home from the park with the kids to find that he had been by to pick her up. I was disappointed I'd missed him. I wanted so badly to be able to see Charlie. I had been imagining what he looked like for three days now, so I waited up for Laura.

"Are you coming to bed any time soon?" Harold came in and asked, sitting next to me on the couch as I sat peering through the blinds.

I sighed and smiled at him. "I just want to see what he looks like without that beard. I promised Laura I'd leave her alone about how things went with him, but

I just want one little peek, that's all."

"I put the kids to bed, Honey, and I was hoping you'd join me in our room to sort of take advantage of the situation." He put his hand to his ear. "Hear that?"

"Hear what?"

"Exactly. They're sound asleep. Come on, Honey," he said, caressing my arm.

"In a minute."

Harold got up and walked into our room. I felt a small twinge of guilt for ignoring him, but I was dying to see what Charlie looked like. I wanted to know if I had been right about his looks. I knew it was none of my business, but I also wondered if he'd kiss her.

After a while I saw headlights pull into the driveway. It was a dark blue pickup truck. I wondered then where exactly Charlie lived. Probably not far if he had his truck with him. They parked out there in the driveway for a long time. I wondered what they were talking about.

Finally, I saw his door open and he stepped out. For a moment I thought

Laura had tricked me and gone out with someone else, but when I looked a little closer, I could see the soft auburn glint of his red hair reflecting the porch light.

My heart sank. He was brutally handsome, and for a moment I was afraid for

Laura. He wore a nicer shirt than I was used to seeing him in, and his hair was cut a little shorter. He wore a white Stetson. He had what I'd call a firm jaw line, but it was softened by his mouth, which I could see was his weakness, and wondered if that was why he covered it with his beard and mustache. The set of his mouth gave away his feelings, like Laura's did. He looked wistful as he walked around to her side and opened her door. She stepped down, taking his offered hand. He didn't let go and held her hand 'til they'd walked to the porch. I sensed he was a little unsure and worried about something. Laura looked beautiful with her shiny dark hair all curled about her face.

They talked for a moment. She smiled at him as he tipped his hat and stepped down the porch steps and walked toward his truck. I was a little disappointed and could see she was, too. She watched him go, then turned toward the door. I turned away, pulling my fingers from the blinds and sighed. I wasn't sure if I was glad he hadn't kissed her or not.

Just then I heard his voice as Laura's key jiggled in the door. I peeked out again.

"Laura?" he said, walking up to her, his mouth set. "Laura, I can't help it."

He stepped back up onto the porch and stood before her. She was looking down at her feet and he gently tipped up her face with both hands and kissed her softly. After a moment he pulled away to see her reaction. I couldn't see her face, but he could, and he bent quickly to kiss her again.

I felt guilty for spying. I got up and left them alone.

My heart was beating so fast, I had to sit down right away when I got to our bedroom. I almost got teary-eyed as the vision of the two of them on my porch kept playing itself out in my mind. I was so happy for Laura and pushed all other emotions aside.

I snuggled up to Harold, but he'd already gone to sleep. It was a long time before I heard Laura come in.

Chapter Seventeen

I called Helen the next morning. I was standing there doing my dishes when I thought of her and wondered if she'd found her husband yet.

"Hello?" a sleepy voice growled on the other end of the line.

"Lars?" I asked.

"Yeah, who's this?"

"This is Nancy. Can I talk to Helen?"

"Hang on," he replied rudely. I could just see him hollering over his shoulder as he called, "Helen, phone!"

I heard Helen's voice in the background. "What?"

"Phone!" he hollered.

"Well, you don't have to yell. Who is it?"

"It's Nancy!"

"Who?"

"Just get on the damn phone, Helen." I heard him sigh in exasperation.

I never did like Lars. He struck me as sort of empty. He wasn't even interesting, and showed little interest in anything. Some people you could just sort of feel who they were, sort of get an inkling of what they were thinking. Lars was as profound as a cardboard box. I'd often wondered why Helen had married him. It was obvious to me why he'd married her. She cooked and cleaned for him.

"Hello?" she asked expectantly.

Suddenly I realized I needed a good reason for calling, and since Lars was obviously home, I was momentarily at a loss.

"Uh, hi, Helen. How are you?"

"Who is this?"

"This is Nancy. I was just calling to...um, invite you over to lunch tomorrow...um, you know, if you're not busy."

There was a long silence. I could tell I'd caught her off guard.

"Well now, let me think," she stalled. "I have some errands to run in the morning, and an appointment for a permanent in the afternoon..."

"It was just a thought. I don't expect you to change any plans or anything."

"Now wait a minute, Honey. Just let me think a minute. My perm's not 'til two, so I guess I could make it alright. What time were you thinking of?"

"Oh, eleven thirty, I guess. That should give you plenty of time."

"Okay then, should I bring anything?" "Just yourself. I'll make us up some sandwiches or something. Nothing fancy."

"Well, I'll see you then, Honey." She said dutifully.

I got the feeling she was trying to suppress her excitement. I'd never invited just her over before. I didn't think she liked me much, and I never liked her much in return. It sort-of made me feel good to think I'd made her so happy. But

I felt guilty too, since I was mostly just curious about how she'd managed to lose

Lars last night and wasn't particularly looking forward to entertaining her.

The following day Helen arrived at eleven thirty on the dot with two grocery bags. She wore a blue dress that buttoned down the front. A few areas around her mid-section looked a little too tightly confined. I suspected she'd put on a girdle just to come over for lunch.

"I stopped by the Deli at the Supersaver and just picked up a few things." She explained, setting down the bulging plastic bags. A wonderful smell permeated the air above them.

True to my word, I'd only made a couple of sandwiches and felt almost ashamed as she began unloading her offering. It figured she'd try to outdo me.

However, as she began setting out the various plastic containers of tortellini salad, orange glazed chicken, Jello, and potato salad, she started to look doubtful. She took out a bag of potato wedges, and hesitated before setting them down as she took in the panorama of food already on the table. "I guess I overdid it," she said shyly before finally setting down the wedges, rearranging everything on the table to make room for them. "I guess you think I'm a pig."

"Of course not. It all looks wonderful."

"I just wasn't sure what all you'd like, and I admit I was shopping a little hungry. Where's the sandwiches you made? I'm sure they're delicious." Helen sounded nervous.

"I'm going to pretend those sandwiches don't exist." "Now Honey, I like sandwiches too."

"I don't," I said, grabbing a potato wedge. "I'll pack them for Harold's lunch tomorrow. Oh my! Is that a cheesecake?"

Helen beamed, sure of herself once again. "Do you like it that way, with cherries on top?"

"Is there any other way?"

I couldn't help wondering if anyone had ever invited Helen over for a private lunch before.

"Where's that little baby?" she asked.

"Oh she's taking a nap. Good thing too. She's been grumpy. I think she's teething again."

We chatted idly for a while as we ate. When the food started to disappear, so did our conversation. There were a few awkward pauses, filled with a last minute mouthful of food or a stifled yawn. Finally, Helen decided to appease my curiosity.

"I guess you're wondering why I came over yesterday looking for Lars."

"Well, I was a little worried about you."

"Oh, it was nothing. I was just overreacting. I forgot he told me he'd be out late with work. I imagine he just nodded off there at the office."

That was believable. Lars was one of those who seemed to nod off wherever he was. I didn't believe her, though, and the way she tugged at a button on her blouse told me she didn't believe it either.

"Well, it's no wonder you were worried. I mean, I'd freak out if Harold didn't show up some night for dinner."

"I wasn't freaking out, Nancy. Honestly, the way you put things. Makes me sound like some crazed…" She stopped abruptly and looked up.

Laura had just walked into the kitchen.

"I didn't mean that. I mean, when I said crazed, I was just…well, after all it's just a word, you know. I didn't mean anything by it."

It was physically painful to be sitting next to Helen right then. I wanted to scream at her, but Laura simply nodded and went to the living room, returning with her nose poked into a dictionary. She looked thoughtful a minute before saying in her most innocent voice, "Crazed: to become mentally deranged or obsessed; insane. Or, if you like this one better, it also says here that it means to become covered with fine cracks. Which 'crazed' were you referring to? Did you mean to "crack up" or "finely crack up?"

While Helen sputtered, I cracked up.

After a moment, Helen seemed to realize the awkward moment had passed and she chuckled softly. "I think you're making fun of me."

"I guess I was," Laura said, putting down the dictionary and plopping herself down into a chair, helping herself to some of Helen's bounty. "Me, I guess I'm just cracked up. Finely cracked up sounds kind of nicer, though, don't you think?" Laura stood then, putting the dictionary on her head and waltzed around the room, balancing it carefully. "Finely cracked up, exquisitely cracked up, La de dah..." she sang in a haughty alto, waving her arms gracefully.

Helen eyed her dubiously. She never understood Laura's sense of humor. Laura grabbed a few more potato wedges before waltzing out of the room. "Is she alright?" Helen whispered. "Has she been taking her medicine?"

Laura always got a kick out of making fun of Helen, who always sputtered and became confused. Helen never could figure out how to act around Laura.

"Helen, I'm telling you this as a friend: You need to lighten up. We are allowed to use the word "crazy" around here, you know."

Helen sat back then and chewed a carrot stick thoughtfully. "You know, my mama used to tell me that I needed to lighten up. She said I was thiry eight before I was thirteen."

I smiled. I could just picture a chubby, scolding thirteen-year-old with perfectly set hair and the kind of glasses Helen always wore that accentuated her sagging cheeks.

"How old are you, Helen, if I may ask?" "Don't tell a soul, Missy, but I'm fifty-nine."

I doubted she needed to swear me to secrecy on that one. I would have guessed at least sixty-five.

"Well, you certainly don't look your age, then!" I said smiling.

"You know, my hairdresser tells me that. He's always saying I should try a different color," she said, running her fingers through her hair, then looking down at her watch.

I didn't want her to leave yet. I wanted to get to the bottom of the Lars mystery, but I was unsure how to go about it.

"You know, Helen, I'd love to hear about how you and Lars met."

"Why?"

"Oh, you could say I'm just a glutton for romance. Come on, spill," I coaxed.

"Well, it wasn't what you'd call romantic, I guess. He just waltzed onto my porch where I was sipping some lemonade and asked me to marry him."

"I think you skipped a bit there, Helen."

"Oh, alright," she sighed. "He was head over ears in love with my best friend, Sissy. She dated him for a while but married a young officer and moved to Dalhart. She still writes me sometimes. She's been divorced three times since. I never could understand that girl. She used to spend half a day scrubbing out her oven because she never bothered to line it with foil. Some people just aren't sensible. Anyway, she broke his heart."

Helen idly chewed another carrot as she remembered. "Lars wasn't exactly good looking, but he had a good head on his shoulders. I felt sorry for him. I could tell he was miserable, so one time I saw him in church looking pretty pathetic, and I told him if he ever needed anything he could just ask. It looked like his suit hadn't been pressed for days and his hat was dusty. So, I took to bringing him over casseroles and pressing his clothes for him. He never seemed to notice one way or the other, but I couldn't stand the sight of him when he was so unkept. A man like him needed to dress well in order for people to take notice of him.

"Then one day he just asked me to marry him, like I said. I said yes because I could tell he needed looking after."

"Did you love him?"

"Goodness, you are a glutton for romance! I'm sorry, Honey, but I don't believe I did. He made it clear from the start that all he wanted out of our marriage was a partnership."

"And you were OK with that?"

"Of course! I was pushing thirty, and I could see that marriage would be to my advantage. I was never pretty like Harold's mama. Besides,

I could see he'd be wealthy someday. No sense being an old maid when a perfectly good man offers for you."

"But didn't that seem sort of…" I was at a loss for words.

"It seemed perfectly fine." Helen said forcefully.

"But, after a while…" I was searching for the romance in this. It just didn't seem right for there not to be a sparkle of some sort. "After a while, you grew to love each other?"

"I've grown used to having him around, if that's what you mean. I guess you could call that love. After all, we've been together for over thirty years. Not too many people could say that."

I could see the only sparkle in her life was a freshly scrubbed commode. As she sat there, perched on her seat and defensive, I got a distinct vision of Grandma's little banty hen perched on her walnuts. For the first time in my life, I felt sorry for Helen.

"And you never wanted any kids?" As soon as I asked, I regretted it. I hated the way things just slipped out of my mouth sometimes.

"Oh, I knew he didn't," was all she said.

I remembered the dolls all over her house. Strangely enough, a lump formed in my throat as I thought of those perfect little dolls all in rows on her shelves.

I remembered, too, what Theo had told me, and I remembered seeing her escorting Lars out of the bar.

Before I thought twice about it, I asked, "Helen, do you think maybe Lars got drunk last night? Maybe he fell asleep in his car or something."

Helen's eyes narrowed. "What makes you ask that?" she demanded.

"Well, I saw you helping him to your car once, and I just thought maybe…"

"Listen, I don't have to sit here and listen to you accusing my husband of being a drunk, okay?" She fumed.

"Helen, I'm sorry. I just thought maybe he could get some help or some????????????????? thing."

"He doesn't need help! He's fine! For Pete's sake, Nancy! What is this, some kind of intervention? Is that why you invited me over?"

I felt sick. Like Helen, it seemed I had a knack for saying the wrong thing.

"No, I just thought it would be nice to have you over for lunch!"

Helen stared at me for a long time, then reached for her purse. Her demeanor softened a bit, and she looked undecided before saying, "He just drinks once in a while. It's not like he's drinking all the time. I mean, he goes to work. He still runs the business." She opened her purse, peered into it, then snapped it shut again. I noticed her lip was quivering. "He's nicer to me when he drinks a little,

Nancy. It's like he sees me as a woman once he's had a couple." I put my hand on her shoulder. For a moment I thought she would soften her stance, maybe even lean on me, but then she stiffened. "I guess you just wouldn't understand that.

I'm going to be late for my appointment. Thanks for lunch."

As I watched her pull out of my driveway in her nice Cadillac, I realized that I never really knew Helen 'til today. I did a whole batch of dishes while I thought about what she said. Then I scrubbed out my toilet, lined my oven with foil, and mopped my kitchen floor. When I finished the floor, I stood back and watched it sparkle a few moments before it dried to a dull yellow.

Laura came back in after a while. "Is Helen rubbing off on you or something?

Did she scold you about the proper way to scrub a floor? Geez, this place hasn't been this clean since I can't even remember."

"I was just visualizing something."

"What do you mean?"

"I was trying to get some satisfaction out of a clean and organized kitchen." Laura looked at me for a moment, a question in her eyes.

"Well, I was just wondering what it must be like to get your kicks out of cleaning all the time."

"That's just sad, Nan. Helen isn't any kind of role model for you."

"I know, I just felt a little sorry for her today, that's all."

"There's just no sense feeling sorry for her, Nan. I'm sure she'd be offended anyway, if she knew you did. She is just perfect, remember? She makes a point of pointing that out often enough."

I sighed and shook my head. "You're right. I just feel a little depressed since she left."

Laura walked up to me then and put her hand on my shoulder, mimicking

Mama's look of concern. "Nancy, Honey, are you on your period?"

I laughed and pushed her away. Mama always associated any kind of emotion as being tied to the female cycle. As much as she hated having anyone doubt the validity of her own emotions, she was always quick to mention to us girls that maybe it was all just hormones after all.

I wanted to change the subject. "How are things going with Charlie?"

Laura leaned back against the counter and folded her arms. "Pretty good. I like him."

"Well, I like him too, but I'm not dating him. Tell me something romantic.

Helen's idea of romance gave me indigestion."

"Should Helen and romance be used in the same sentence? Maybe that's what's got you sick to your stomach."

"Now Laura, be nice. After all, "crazed" is just a word and she didn't mean anything by it."

Laura laughed. "She just makes it way too easy."

"Well, anyway, tell me about Charlie."

Laura hesitated before getting a mischievous gleam in her eyes. "He's a good kisser."

I blushed, remembering the two of them on the porch.

"And..."

"And I like him."

Obviously, she wasn't planning on being forthcoming, so I changed my tactics.

"Are you two going out again any time soon?"

"He left yesterday for another haul. He'll be back on Tuesday."

"Do you miss him?"

"It's only been a day since he left!"

"I know, but do you miss him?" "Yep."

"Alright then. Ask him over for supper when he gets back. You better make another pie."

"Or maybe I should just use the rolling pin to thank him over the head. Then

I could drag him home with me and keep him."

I swatted at her with a dish towel.

Chapter Eighteen

Mama called and asked about how things were with Laura. I told her things were going fine.

"Has she told him yet?" Mama wanted to know. "Mama, she just barely started dating him."

"I know. I guess I'm just a little worried about her."

"I know. Me too, but I'm just not going to think about it this time. Charlie's real nice. I have a good feeling about this…I think."

"How is she doing in school?"

"Passing tests right and left. I think she has a 4.0 so far this semester. Not a bad note to graduate on, eh?"

Mama chuckled. "Bless her heart. I have no idea where that girl gets it from."

"From you, Mama."

Mama sighed. "Thank you, Nantucket. So, when am I going to get to meet this boy?"

"Well, I talked Laura into inviting him over for supper on Wednesday. Why don't you and Daddy come too? I've got two more leaves I can put in the table."

"Do you think Laura will mind?"

"I don't see how it's her place to mind. It is my table, after all. I don't see anything wrong with you and Daddy coming. Honestly, though, Laura has been real happy lately. Hardly moody at all, if you know what I mean."

"Well, alright then. When's dinner?"

"Oh, about six-thirty, I guess."

"Do you want me to bring anything?"

"Now don't you worry about it."

"I'll just whip up a little something."

"No dessert, though. Laura's going to make another pie."

"Oh, I see," Mama said knowingly. "I'll see you both then. Hug those grandkids for me."

Instead of hugging them I gave Benny and Josie a time out for fighting. Sometimes I just couldn't stand the sight of my own kids, especially when they were fighting. I absolutely hated having to be a referee all the time. After a while, though, when I let them out of their rooms, they went straight outside and played together. I couldn't get over how cute they were.

Marie had become completely mobile and was crawling all over the place.

Thank goodness for Laura's old dog, Sam, who followed her around dutifully and barked whenever she was in any kind of danger. I checked on her and found her sprawled out on the living room floor, completely asleep with Sam snoozing next to her. I was putting her down into her crib when the doorbell rang.

Before I could answer it, Grandma walked in, followed by Theo. She was swatting his arm away as she attempted to make her way into my living room.

"You want to fall on your face again that's your business, I guess," he said testily.

Grandma paused, took a few wobbly steps on her own, then leaned on him once again.

"Grandma, did something happen?" I asked in concern.

"Why don't you ask Theo?" she snapped.

Theo saw that she was safely deposited into her favorite chair before answering.

"Now, see, I was trying to fix the lawnmower, and I had to take it apart…"

"Oh, pooh!" interjected Grandma. "He had who knows what all scattered from hell to breakfast!"

"Now see here, Alice, you're exaggerating. Nancy, I had just a few parts on the sidewalk there when Alice decides to go skipping along in her house dress."

I chuckled at the thought of Grandma skipping. "So then what happened?"

"Gravity, that's what!" said Theo.

"No, it wasn't gravity. It was a lawn mower motor."

"You fell?" I asked, astonished.

"Plumb near cracked the sidewalk," Theo said dryly.

For once I didn't think Theo was being very funny. "Oh Grandma, you fell down?"

"Of course I fell down!"

"Did you go to the hospital?"

"Stubborn girl wouldn't let me take her, so now she's limping."

"Oh Grandma! You really should go in to see somebody!"

"For a little old scrape on my knee? Why don't I just take a picture of it and send the doctor a hundred and fifty dollars along with it?"

"Let me have a look," I said, rolling up her slacks.

Her knee was slightly swollen. When I unrolled the neat bandage, there was a large scrape about the size of a quarter across the top of her knee. I breathed a sigh of relief.

"Does it hurt?" I asked.

"Like hell." Grandma seemed almost proud.

I looked over at Theo as I rolled her pants back down. He looked a little sick as he averted his face from her wound. I could tell in just one glance that it had scared him to death.

"Well, it looks like he did a good job on it," I said, trying to make Theo feel better. "Theo takes good care of you, Grandma!"

Grandma was silent for a while before responding. "Yes, he does. I just wish he wasn't so dern handy with a lawnmower when a lady's trying to water her gladiolas."

"Well then, I wish she wasn't so dern handy with her gladiolas when a man's trying to fix a lawnmower."

"Well, alright then," I said, trying to end the dispute. Suddenly I had an idea.

"Hey, what are you two doing this Wednesday night?"

Mama arrived an hour early and was in grand spirits as she whisked herself into my kitchen. She had her hair done up and wore a broach with her navy-blue dress. I was barefoot, wearing a T-shirt and a pair of cutoff jean shorts.

"Honestly, Honey," she said when she took in my duds. "You are going to change, aren't you?"

It was hot, and I was just fine with what I had on. It wasn't like I was serving creme brulee or anything fancy.

Laura was dressed pretty much the same way, and Mama instantly took exception to her outfit in particular.

"Laura Harris! You aren't wearing that to dinner!"

Mama went down the hall to Laura's room and began taking a hasty perusal of

Laura's closet. I could hear her mumbling under her breath.

"You'd think they'd actually want to look nice, for goodness sake. I never can get either one of them to have any kind of fashion sense! And just plain courtesy!

You don't dress like a slob when you have someone over for dinner! Land sakes alive, it's just in one ear and out the other–oh, what's this?"

Mama had discovered the dress she'd given to Laura. It still had the tags on it. It was pale blue with a frilly skirt. It actually was quite pretty, but not the usual thing Laura would wear.

"Perfect! This will be absolutely perfect! And with your blue eyes too! Come on now Laura, put it on."

I saw Laura's white knuckles as she clutched the doorway. For a moment I thought we were in for a stand-off, but suddenly Laura consented.

As Mama left the room, she shouted from the hall, "And wear some lipstick!"

I shut the door behind her. "You are going to wear it, aren't you, Laura?"

"Sure, why not. If I don't, you know what Mama is going to be like during dinner, don't you?"

"Oh yes, apologizing for the appearance of her daughters and for the stripes on

the wall in my dining room. I better go get something on too, then."

"And put some lipstick on, will you?" Laura mumbled from the depths of all those blue frills as they slid over her head.

I put on a cotton summer dress and wore sandals. I went into Laura's room then to borrow some nail polish. I wanted to paint my toenails.

I came in and found Laura sitting on her bed in her bra and underwear with the dress slung over one arm.

"What's the matter?" I asked.

"I can't wear this."

"Well, why not?"

"It's got no sleeves."

"Oh, I see what you mean," I said, noticing the insides of her arms. They were just a little red, not too bad looking.

"I might as well tell him and be done with it. It's like I can't even be totally happy anyway. I'm always wondering if I should tell him and when. I almost feel like I'm tricking him or something. I've got this dark secret and I just picture the look on his face when he finds out, and then I get sick to my stomach. But, I can't ever tell him, Nan."

"Do you want me to tell him?"

"No!"

"Well, what needs to be done then?"

"I guess I could just tell him not to call anymore. Then I'd have to quit my job, I guess."

"No, that sounds like a whole lot of nonsense. Let me see those arms," I said reaching out and gently turned one so I could inspect it. "It's not bad, Laura. I doubt he'd even notice. I think you're making a mountain out of a mole hill."

Laura started to cry. "Well, I feel like I'm trying to pass off a mountain as a mole hill. I'm not exactly the catch of the century, you know. Why did you invite everyone over anyway? It's hard enough without you and everyone else plotting against him, and I'm the one who's going to have to tell him. Does anyone care what I think? Or maybe you just don't believe I can think all by myself. Get out and leave me alone."

I never could stand to see her cry. I reached out and hugged her to me, even though she tried to pull away. "Now hush, Honey. You're going to mess up your make up. It's going to be alright. Now just put that dress back on. I've got a nice shirt that might do just the thing. I'll be right back."

I returned and found her wearing the dress but still wiping at her eyes. "Try this on." I said, handing it to her. It was a very sheer light pink summer shirt complete with buttons and long sleeves.

She put it on, leaving it open, and turned to the mirror. Pink was her favorite color, and in suited her well. It looked very pretty and made the dress seem a little more casual, which I thought was more appropriate anyway. "There," I said. "It's perfect."

Just then there was a knock on the door. Grandma peeked her head in. "Can I come in?"

"Sure," I said, and began brushing Laura's hair.

"Oh, my, what pretty girls!" she exclaimed as she limped in with the aid of a cane.

Laura's expression was anything but pretty as she reached up and grabbed the brush away. "I can brush my own hair, you know."

"I'm sorry," I said. "I guess I'm just so used to doing Josie's that I didn't even think."

Grandma sat on the bed. "I guess you feel a little on the spot, now, don't you,

Honey? What with all of us here and all."

Laura bowed her head and sniffed.

Grandma gently put a hand under her chin and raised her face. "Feeling a little like a show horse? Fine duds and everyone holding their breath to see how you perform?"

Laura nodded.

"Well, Honey, you just be yourself. That's what Charlie likes. Don't worry about anything else today, or tomorrow either. Things have a way of working themselves out if you just let 'em be. Just be nice to him and date him as you've been doing, and your mind will clear. You'll know what to do when the time comes. I know for sure the good Lord has a soft spot in His heart for you. Let Him see to it."

Laura nodded again, then wiped her eyes. "Nancy, will you do my make-up again? I like the way you do it."

Laura was offering me an olive branch. I gratefully accepted it.

Grandma took the brush and stroked it gently through Laura's hair. "Don't you dare smile now," she teased.

After I'd finished Laura's make up, Grandma shooed me from the room.

"Don't you have some dinner to cook or something? Laura and I have some talking to do."

I'll always remember Grandma standing over Laura brushing her hair. It was a sweet, quiet moment that I had to witness from a distance. I wasn't in the club that day.

I went to the kitchen and found Mama in charge of my kitchen. She and

Daddy were tossing a salad and Theo was slicing a cantaloupe. Daddy was talking.

"Yeah, it expired about a month ago, and I didn't even give it a thought 'til the DMV called. Hell on earth, that's what that place is. I stood in line must've been an hour, only to have some snoot tell me I had to fill out a few more lines before she could see me, and she wouldn't even wait two minutes for me to finish right there. So, I went to the side and finished it up and tried to be next in line.

She informed me that cutting was not tolerated at the Department of Motor

Vehicles and sent me to the back of the line again."

Theo whistled. "They're always making me get my vision checked. They don't think an old man can see, but I darn near got that chart memorized anyway. Do you think they train 'em to be rude? I don't believe I ever come across a pleasant person who worked at that DMV my whole life. It's like they know they have your life in their hands. I mean, you have to drive, and they get the say so."

"Oh, it gets worse. So then, when I get to the front, the only available window is with this broad again. I walk up and hand her my papers. I don't say anything as she shuffles through them. Then she spots something on my papers and literally smirks before she says, 'Sir, it says here you've got brown hair. We need our records to be accurate. Now I can put either gray or bald. Which do you want?'"

Theo stood up then, indignant. "What did you say?"

"I said she could put orange or purple, for all I give a damn. 'Just put whatever the hell you want on there,' I said."

Theo looked satisfied.

Dad continued, "So, anyway, she got offended at that and said she refused to deal with anyone who didn't treat her with respect and sent me on my way. I'm going to try again next week."

That meant Mama had driven them over. No wonder Daddy looked a little ruffled. That was enough to scare even the stout hearted. Mama, to this day, still insists she's a good driver. However, despite the fact that she scared us all half to death, she never crashed. Her guardian angels were always busy.

Theo put a hand on Daddy's shoulder. "I'll keep you in my prayers. A whole week, huh?"

Daddy glanced quickly over his shoulder and saw that Mama had gone into the dining room. "Can I get a ride home with you?"

Charlie arrived right on time. Laura was still in her room with Grandma.

"Hi there, Son. Nice to meet you. Charlie, right?" Daddy said, extending a hand in greeting.

Charlie took it. "Yes, sir. Nice to meet you, too."

Charlie wore a light blue denim collared shirt and blue jeans. He looked as handsome as I'd ever seen him. He took off his white Stetson when he saw

Mama.

Mama came in then, wiping her hands on her apron. She stuck out her hand.

"Well, it's so good to finally meet you. We've heard so much about you. My, but you are a handsome one, aren't you?"

Charlie blushed. "Thank you, Mrs. Harris."

"Call me Dora Mae." Mama looked at him a moment longer, still holding his hand.

"George, why don't you and Theo take Charlie into the living room there and make yourselves comfortable? I'll call you when dinner's ready."

Mama was most definitely in charge. I guess I didn't really mind that she'd taken over as hostess. This dinner, I could tell, meant a lot to her, and she was nervous. She probably forgot altogether that this wasn't her house.

Charlie looked around a bit, then followed them. I could tell he was a little nervous too, especially with no Laura in sight.

I went back to her room and knocked lightly before peeking in. Grandma was squeezing Laura's hand. "Now you remember that," she said before getting up.

Laura's face had changed. She looked peaceful and happy again. Grandma was a wonderful woman.

"Charlie's here," I announced.

I loved the way Charlie's face instantly lit up when he saw her. He also seemed relieved. Theo and Daddy could be a bit frightening to the un-initiated. Harold was out in the backyard working the grill with the kids scampering in the yard.

Laura sat down by him on the sofa, and he immediately took her hand. She leaned into him.

"I don't guess you like her all that much," Theo teased.

Charlie smiled and kissed Laura's forehead, then looked a little embarrassed.

"Now don't be shy, Boy. These two girls here are about the most kissable I ever come across. Ain't I right, George? Help yourself!"

Charlie laughed while Laura blushed.

"Supper's ready!" Mama announced.

We all gathered around the table. Daddy said a blessing on the food, and blessed those seated around our table. "Lord, bless the hands that prepared it and those who will partake of it this day at our table. And please bless…" Daddy struggled a moment, as if unsure how to ask for the blessing we all wanted for

Laura. I peeked up and saw her biting her lip, her eyes squeezed shut. "Bless us with many more opportunities to gather together as a family. Bless us with courage and happiness and good health. Amen."

Grandma dabbed at her eyes as she said "Amen."

I always loved to hear Daddy pray. I looked up and saw that Charlie had been touched. Daddy had included him in our family. A lump had come to my throat,

I wasn't sure why. Of course, I knew God wanted to bless us all, but I wondered if his plans for us were once again different than what we'd prayed for.

As we all started into the food, Mama started into Charlie. "So, tell us about yourself. You're a trucker? That must be exciting! I admit I'm scared to death of those semis on the freeway, though. Once I had one on either side of me, and I thought for sure they were going to suck me in."

"Oh, no, ma'am. They were doing you a favor. See, when you get one on either side of you like that it sort-of pulls you along. You don't even hardly need the gas pedal."

"Is that right? Well, I guess I'm just a big chicken then. So, do you like those big old trucks? I admit, I've never even been inside of one. You be careful, now. I don't believe I want Laura driving in one."

Mama's drawl always got a little thicker when she was nervous.

"Do truck drivers make a lot of money? I guess you must be rich." Benny observed innocently.

"Hey Benny, want me to pee on your plate?" Laura asked.

Mama's eyes just about bulged out of her head and she choked on her water.

Laura just sat there, innocent as anything, with a large spoonful of peas hovering over his plate.

Benny grinned. "Sure!"

"Pea on mine while you're going," said Theo, winking at her as he passed his plate.

I glanced at Charlie, who seemed to be enjoying himself immensely.

Sure enough, Laura had managed to shock Mama into silence for the remainder of the dinner. She kept shooting disapproving glances in Laura's direction, which Laura ignored.

Daddy was quiet as usual, but friendly. Harold and Charlie seemed to do most of the talking.

Grandma paid most of her attention to Josie as they carried on their own quiet conversation at the far end of the table.

I was busy trying to feed Marie.

Laura seemed a little quiet after the pea incident, but she smiled a lot. Occasionally she'd whisper something to Charlie, and he'd smile. To me, Charlie seemed a little worried about something. Several times I caught him glancing at the insides of her arms, which were just barely covered by the sheer sleeves of my shirt. I couldn't see anything, but then I remembered the incident at work when she'd come home in a tank top. I hadn't even given it a thought then.

I watched Charlie for the rest of the dinner, but he seemed determined to have a good time even though he had a strange set to his mouth when he wasn't eating or talking. I noticed he spent a lot of time scrutinizing each of us. I remembered, too, his concern for Laura when he asked if she was OK. I didn't even have an appetite when it came to Laura's pie, which turned out to be a Dutch apple.

Laura didn't like being pressured into anything.

After the pie, which was a little dry, we all just sort of sat around. A while later, Sam groaned. He was standing in front of the door. He looked over his shoulder at us, then groaned again.

"Looks like the dog wants out," Harold observed, getting up.

"I'll take him," Laura volunteered. "He needs a walk."

Charlie stood with her and together they headed out the door with Sam wagging his tail happily as Laura reached for his leash.

Mama and I tackled the dishes while Grandma held Marie. As I scrubbed away I had a clear view out the window of the two of them walking along the lake. I realized suddenly in a moment of despair that the water was receding. It had crept back a good ten feet, what with the recent heat wave. All around the murky water, forming a white noose, the bald alkali basin gleamed. I shuddered.

"Got a chill?" Mama asked.

"Just this hot water," I said, adding a little cold to it, even though it was barely lukewarm by now.

Mama eyed me a moment as she dried the silverware, then bent to peer out the window and watched them.

"He sure seems nice enough," she observed. "Storm's coming. See that?" she said, pointing. "They're gonna get soaked if they don't turn around."

"Looks like rain!" I said, feeling strangely relieved. The waters would be replenished, and the alkali would be covered up for a while longer at least.

I watched as Laura took Sam off his leash and he splashed around at the lake's edge while Laura and Charlie stood on the shore. He put his arm around her.

"Nancy! Nancy, what are you doing?" Mama suddenly asked in exasperation.

I'd been closing my eyes, praying silently for them, and looked down to see I was vigorously scrubbing the dish soap bottle. "Oh," I said, startled. "It was a little sticky."

Sure enough, not ten minutes later, it started to rain. I watched as Laura ran with Charlie, Sam bounding ahead.

By the time they got back, they were soaked. Laura's dress clung to her provocatively. I noticed Charlie trying his hardest not to stare at her as they came down the walk toward the porch. Before they reached the door, he stopped, still holding her hand and pulled her to him, kissing her passionately, almost desperately out in the rain. No sooner had they walked in the door, though, the rain stopped, and the clouds moved past us. It seemed hotter than before.

Laura went to her room to change, and I offered Charlie some of Harold's clothes to put on. He seemed a little awkward but at Harold's insistence he followed me down the hall to our room.

I handed him a shirt and a pair of Levi's. He took them, but seemed undecided.

"They should fit," I assured him.

"Nancy," he said quietly.

"What is it?"

"Maybe it's none of my business, but I saw Laura's arms awhile back when she passed out at work. She was all sweaty and not making a whole lot of sense at first when she came to. I figured she must be awful hot with that long sleeve shirt she always wears. She spilled some coffee on herself, so I unbuttoned it just a little at the top to give her some air. I could see she had a shirt on underneath, so I just took the outer one off. It seemed to help. I hope you don't think I'm some kind of pervert."

"No, of course not. Sounds like you did the right thing." I couldn't think of anything else to say.

"Well," he said. "It's none of my business, excepting that I care for her, but don't you think you should get her some help? I haven't dared say anything to her about it yet."

"What do you mean?"

"I know what it means to have all those needle marks on the insides of a person's arm."

"You do?" I asked, my heart racing.

"Nancy, my brother died from a heroine overdose. He showed all the same signs. Losing weight, looking pale and tired all the time…I just can't stand to think she's going to ruin her life." He ran a hand recklessly through his hair. "I care for her. I don't hold it against her, but I want to get her some help. I can't hardly imagine now what I'd do without her, and I know where a habit like that leads." He sounded desperate.

I stared blankly at him for several moments. I had no idea how to respond.

Finally, I said, "Charlie, I understand your concern, but I can assure you she's not on any drugs, not the illegal kind anyway. Good grief!"

Charlie's brow straightened. "Nancy, I'm not condemning anybody here. I just want to make sure she gets some treatment before it's too late. Do you really think you would know if she was on drugs? I didn't even know my brother was

'til it was too late. Besides, I can tell you're always worried about her. You even tried to get rid of me. I know you know something is wrong."

"Charlie," I said, beginning to sound defensive, "Believe me, I'd know. I also know why her arms look like that. You've got it all wrong. Laura's never even smoked a cigarette in her whole life, let alone a joint, or a…a…"

Charlie looked as embarrassed as anyone could. I put my hand on his arm. I spoke to relieve his anxiety before I thought of what Laura's would be. "I appreciate what you were trying to do. Laura has some health issues. She…she has to have regular blood tests done."

"Why?" I panicked. This wasn't the way it was supposed to come out. I wasn't supposed to be the one. Laura's happiness stood on the line. I didn't know what to do. My heart was racing. As he waited for my answer, I remembered my promise to Laura while sprawled out prone that night on that crazed bitter clay. For the first time in my life I looked another human being in the eye and told a bald-faced lie. "She's diabetic."

Chapter Nineteen

"You said what?" Laura demanded.

Everyone had gone home, and Harold was putting the kids to bed.

I fidgeted, uncomfortable under her horrified stare. "Well, I didn't see how it was my place to tell him about you. He thought you were on drugs! I was just trying to protect you!"

"So now we're lying to him?"

Tears sprung into my eyes. "I didn't mean to! I accidentally said something about you needing your blood drawn all the time. I was trying to make him see you weren't shooting up! He saw your arms that day! He knows something is wrong. I was just trying to give you more time to sort things out." I reached out and tucked a strand of hair behind her ear. "Laura, he was so sweet about it. He didn't even mind if you were on drugs, he just wanted to see you get some help.

He loves you, Honey!"

Laura's face was dark, her freckles stood out angrily. "Oh, so I'll just say, guess what? I'm not on drugs. I'm not diabetic. Surprise! I'm just a schizophrenic!"

She shoved my hand away.

"Oh, God!" she cried. She then lay on her side and covered her head with her pillow.

I'd never in my life heard her take the Lord's name in vain. At first, I was shocked, but as I watched her shoulders shake in silent sobs, I understood it wasn't in vain. It was a desperate plea to the Almighty.

I sat there and watched her cry for a while, then I got up silently and shut her door. I went to find Harold. I needed more than anything to be wrapped tightly in his arms, to know he still loved me, that at least I hadn't screwed up his life.

I found him in our bed reading. I crawled in blindly beside him. He instantly put the book down and looked at me. "What's wrong, Honey?"

New tears came to my eyes, and for a while I couldn't talk. He put his arm around me and waited 'til I was ready. It took me a long time.

"What is it?" he asked, cupping my face with his other hand. "I think I did something awful to Laura."

"What did you do?"

"I lied to Charlie. I told him she was diabetic when he asked about her arms."

"What the hell did you do that for?" he demanded, holding me out in front of him.

"He thought she was on drugs."

Harold looked stunned for a moment then rubbed the stubble on his face.

"Good grief!"

"I know, I know. It blindsided me too. I didn't know what to say. I just didn't think it was my place to tell him the truth."

"I don't think it was your place to tell him anything. You could have just said he needed to talk to Laura about it."

My heart sank. Harold was accusing me too. Suddenly the warmth of his body as he lay next to me became repulsive. I felt like my whole body was prickling with self-hatred and disgust. I couldn't stand to have him touching me. He was right. He was always right, and now he thought I'd blown it, too. It stung. I sat there a moment more, cringing under his gaze. I got up and walked out of the room. He didn't even call after me.

I grabbed a light jacket and put my sandals back on. I wasn't even sure where I was going when I headed out the door. Sam groaned after me, and I could hear him complaining after I shut the door in his face. I wanted to walk slowly, and not be dragged along by an overexcited hound dog.

I walked toward the lake. I always walked toward the lake. It occurred to me as

I reached the edge that I had never walked into it when it was full. I'd never even dipped a toe in. I'd always had a foreboding, an aversion to it. I thought of that poor little girl, trying to save her drowning sister, and how the lake had claimed them both. I shivered.

But Daddy said once he'd waded clear out to the middle, and it had only reached his waist. I gazed at the moon shivering on its rippling surface. I took off my sandals and walked slowly toward its gently lapping edge. The water was dirty, the color of pale mud.

I lifted my dress and waded in slowly 'til the water was up to my knees. The soft, slimy bottom squished between my toes. I dared go no further. The bottom felt treacherous and menacing. For a moment I panicked, slipping and sliding, almost falling, and then I found my footing again. I took a deep breath.

I stood there a long time, letting the lukewarm water lap gently against my legs. I wasn't sure exactly when I'd started gauging Laura's life by the depth of these murky and unreliable waters, but one thing I felt certain of on that hot night, was that they were definitely receding. Steam rose in pale mists just above the surface. There wasn't a whole lot of time, a whole lot of happiness left for Laura.

I looked up at the stars and understood Mama's anger with God. It wasn't fair.

Grandma always said that it took special people to have disabilities. She believed we agreed to it ahead of time, before we were born. "Some people's lives are shorter because their test is harder. Some people live a long time and don't do anything worthwhile, and some take a whole lifetime to do things right. I guess that's why I've been around so long and my life's been so hard. I haven't gotten it right yet." She never believed God could be cruel. That night I wasn't so sure.

Finally, I walked out of the water, leaving my bare footprints in the damp clay that had been submerged only days before. It never took long once it started to dry up. There was no outlet to the lake, and no inlet, only the chance that it might rain. And when it did, the water just sat there trapped in the heat 'til it was all gone.

When I got home, Harold was waiting for me at the door. He was fully dressed. I instantly grew alarmed at the look on his face, and the sight of Helen sitting there in Grandma's chair.

"What's going on?"

"Nancy, we need to go down to the hospital. Helen's going to watch the kids."

"Where's Lars?" I asked, not that it mattered to me at the time.

"Oh, he's been out this evening. I left him a note," said Helen. "Go on now.

I've got things covered around here."

"Where's Laura?" I suddenly gasped.

"She's gone out. I don't know where she is. Just get in the car, Honey. I'll explain on the way. I don't think we have much time."

I felt sick as we walked in the automatic doors of the emergency room. I barely even heard Harold as he asked at the reception desk, then steered me in the direction of the trauma unit.

Then I saw him. He had a bandage around his head and a large bandage on his hand. He looked awful. I ran up to him.

"Theo! Are you alright?" He barely seemed to see me. His eyes were all swollen as tears gushed unheeded down his cheeks.

"Where's Grandma?" I demanded.

He looked over his shoulder and I saw a still form lying in a bed behind him.

A doctor and a nurse stood over her. I rushed to her side.

She lay very still with her eyes closed. Her head, too, was bandaged. Her body seemed limp.

"Grandma?"

Her eyes fluttered open. "Is that my Nancy?" she said almost in a whisper.

I reached down and took her hand. "Yes, it's me."

"Oh, my sweet girl. Bless your heart. Whatever are you going to do without your wise old Grandma?"

My knees collapsed and I knelt beside her bed. "Don't say that! You're gonna be fine. You're one tough old lady!"

"Not this time, Sweetie. I can't even see you. It won't be long now. They tell me I'm bleeding on the inside." She closed her eyes for a moment before she spoke again. "Listen, Laura loves you. She told me so. She's just not always good at showing it. Sisters will always love…and forgive…sisters."

It never occurred to me until later that somehow Grandma knew. She knew the way Mama always knew when something was wrong or troubling one of her children.

"Take care of Theo for me. He couldn't save me this time. I know he'll take it hard. Bless his heart, that stubborn old fool. He loved me more than anything, I think. He gave up a lot to take care of me. Such a good brother to me. It's nice to be loved, isn't it, Honey? That's what makes it so hard when you have to go."

I put my head down and began to cry.

"Now that's enough of that!" she scolded in her soft, weakening voice. "I'm old. I always said I'd rather be hit by a truck than end up in one of them nursing homes." She put a hand on my head. "Nancy, Honey, listen now. It was always your job in this family to be the strong one, the one that was OK, the one that would be just fine. I know that's a lot of pressure on you, but that's the way God designed this family. There has to be strength to counteract the weakness and the sickness. You can handle more than you know. You can handle losing your

Grandma. I know you can. You need to be there for Laura and for your mama. It's my fault, you know, the way your mama is."

I squeezed her hand, but she hadn't the strength to squeeze back. "Where's the kids?" she asked then.

"Helen is watching them."

Grandma sighed softly then opened her eyes again. "Tell her it isn't worth it."

I thought maybe Grandma's mind was slipping. "What?"

"Tell her it isn't worth it," she whispered again. "Where's Theo?"

"I'm here," he said, turning around.

"Go away, Nancy girl. We need to be alone a minute."

Theo came to her side, bending over her as she whispered in his ear. He nodded, and leaned down to hug her.

"Oh, my family…" Grandma sighed, in a moment of regret. "Stay with them…" she prayed softly before closing her eyes. For a moment she patted

Theo's head as it lay on her chest then her hand fell softly to the bed.

The doctor came and tried to get him to lift his head off of her, but she wasn't breathing anymore anyway.

Mama arrived a few minutes later. I understood, as I watched her face contort into tortured expressions of grief and anger, what it was to love someone and to hurt because of that love. Mama didn't get to see her own mother go. She arrived after they'd pulled a blanket over her face and got no chance for a proper goodbye.

Chapter Twenty

It had been a hit and run. From what I understood of that terrible night, the other driver had swerved into their lane. Theo tried to avoid the collision by swerving to the left, but the passenger side was struck. The other driver continued down the road. Witnesses said it was a dark colored sedan, but no one had seen the plates.

When we got home, Helen was dozing on the couch, holding Marie. She looked up when we walked in. "Oh, Honey. I'm so sorry."

I reached out for Marie. Holding a baby had always been a comfort to me and

I stood in need of comfort that night.

Harold told Laura. I couldn't stand to do it. Laura didn't come out of her room for breakfast.

As I stood frying some bacon and rolling biscuits, I realized I was starved. I always thought people in the depths of sorrow wouldn't notice something as trite as hunger, but like I said, I was starved, and nothing sounded better than a southern breakfast. I was a little ashamed of myself and wondered if I was insensitive. I was glad to see that Harold ate heartily. Theo, who had slept on the couch, just pushed the food around on his plate.

After breakfast Helen stopped by, armed with at least seven bags of groceries.

She just walked right in and started putting it all away. Once she did that, she headed back out to her car and brought in several Tupperware containers and two casserole dishes.

"Now let me know if you need anything else," she said, tucking the last dish into the fridge. "This may not be the right time to ask, but has anyone made any kind of funeral arrangements?"

"I don't think so," I said.

Theo looked at her sharply. "We can handle that."

"Just let me do this one thing for you. I know how much you all loved Alice. I know she never liked me much, but I'd like to help. I can call the funeral home and the cemetery if you'd like, just so you won't have to worry about it."

"I said we can handle that. Keep your nose in your own business. No one asked you." Theo said, standing.

Helen was shocked, and so was I. I walked her out to her car. I could see that

Theo had hurt her deeply, so I wanted to make her feel better. I could tell she'd been up all night cooking for us, bless her heart.

I didn't like the idea of seeing to burial plots and caskets. It made me shudder.

"Helen, go on ahead. It will be alright, I think. Theo's just a little out of it this morning. His head is hurting him, I can tell. He got twenty-seven stitches and his truck was totaled. I know he didn't mean it."

Helen seemed relieved. There was a desperation in her eyes, something that touched me deeply. She wanted so much to help.

"Well, alright. Do you think gladiolas would be a good flower? I know she loved her glads."

"That should be fine. Thank you so much, Helen. Just do whatever you think will be nice."

Mama wasn't happy with me either when I told her Helen was seeing to things. "Good grief, Nancy! What the hell business of hers is it, anyway?"

I gave up. It seemed I couldn't do anything right, so I just stepped out of it. I'd let them battle it out. Not only was Laura not speaking to me, but Mama wasn't either. Theo barely seemed to notice me. Harold and the kids were my only comfort, but even then, I couldn't get the tone of his voice out of my head when he heard what I'd said to Charlie.

We found out from the florist, the funeral director, and the cemetery that all the expenses had been paid. They all said the same thing. A woman had come in and paid for it up front. She didn't leave her name. It wasn't the kind of gift you could say no to, so Mama and Theo let up. Helen got her way. She never came to the funeral, though.

The funeral took place a week later and Mama refused to go. I couldn't believe she didn't want to see her own mother finally laid to rest beside Grandpa.

As we prepared to leave for the church, I stepped back inside my house to talk to Mama one more time.

"Mama, I appreciate you staying here with the kids. I know they're a little young for a funeral, but don't you think you should go? I know you haven't felt comfortable coming to church, but this is different."

"You go on. I'm telling you, I'm staying here."

I never could understand my mama. It just didn't seem right for her not to attend her own mother's funeral.

As I stood at the casket during the family viewing before the services began I started to cry again. I felt guilty that I wasn't as sorry for Grandma as I was for myself. Harold stood next to me, putting his arm around me, but it just felt like a lifeless weight on my shoulders.

Charlie came. He sat off to the side with his arm around Laura. I could see that she, too, took no comfort from his touch, and he seemed a little bewildered at her coldness.

When it was time for the services to begin, I sat down by Theo, who had his head bowed and his eyes closed. I tried to think of something to say that would comfort him.

"Well, at least she's with Grandpa now." I said, squeezing his arm.

Theo jerked, then glared at me a minute. "The hell she is!" he hissed and walked out of the chapel. I had no idea what I'd said to offend him, so I got up and followed him out the door.

I went out back behind the chapel and walked into the graveyard, a mass of crooked headstones at the front that got newer and straighter toward the back.

Theo was standing at Grandpa's plain headstone. On the left side of the stone it read: Samuel Luke Johnson, born 1908, died 1973. The right side was blank, held for the spouse. Beside it was the hole that had been dug for Grandma Alice.

Theo didn't seem to notice me as I walked up behind him. His shoulders slumped as he wiped his nose every now and then on his sleeve. "I'll be damned before she lies down next to you," he muttered under his breath and spat a long stream of tobacco across the headstone and walked away. He went to his old pickup truck and took out a shovel. He brought it back out to the grave site and began filling it in.

I was horrified. "Theo, what are you doing?" I asked, pulling back on his elbow.

"She ain't goin' to lie by that man ever again. I promised her that." He jerked his arm away from me and continued to throw large piles of dirt into the hole.

I felt sick. Theo had lost his mind. I sat down in the shade of an elm tree and tried to gather my thoughts as I watched him work.

A few moments later, Mama came walking slowly toward the grave using a small shovel as a walking stick. She wore her black dress and was veiled under an ancient black velvet hat. She watched Theo for a minute, her face pale and emotionless. "I left the kids at the neighbors," she explained before she flung off her hat and joined him, hurriedly filling in the hole.

"Don't just stand there, Nancy!" Mama pleaded over her shoulder. "Help us!" I joined them, totally confused. I pushed piles of the dark moist dirt into the hole with my bare hands. My mind reeled. Everyone was going insane, and I was somehow caught up in the undertow.

Mama sobbed as she worked, Theo was silent and coldly efficient.

"Did you get it squared away?" Theo asked her after a while.

"Yep. It's the one out that-a-way, under that elm at the back. See the shady spot? I called yesterday, and it's ready."

I looked over my shoulder to where she pointed. It was a lovely spot with a fringe of poppies that swayed in the breeze. I squinted and saw a large rectangular hole excavated there, too.

I looked at my mama and Theo, completely confused. "You're going to bury Grandma way over there?"

"Yes. She picked the spot herself. She planted those poppies last summer."

Mama answered.

"But don't you think it's going to look funny when the procession comes out of the chapel and we pass right by Grandpa's grave?"

"That's why we've got to fill it in," grunted Theo as he wheezed from the exertion. "The pastor knows about our little plan. It's OK, Nan. We've just got to make it look like a mistake. If it weren't for Helen sticking her nose in things this wouldn't have been such a cussed nuisance."

The grave was almost half full and I began to sweat as I worked. I knew that before long the service would end, and the procession would come outside for the dedication of the grave.

"Well," said Theo, standing back from the hole which was now only about three feet deep. I guess that's enough. They aren't going to get any coffin in that."

I could hear singing coming from inside the church. It wafted along the waves of heat toward us, sounding muffled.

I once was lost, but now am found; Was blind, but now I see. I heard the last amen as the congregation ended the final prayer. Theo and Mama waited without saying a word. A large bumblebee inspected some faded plastic flowers poked into the ground in front of

Grandpa's grave. She bobbed back and forth between the flowers droning deeply before landing. It was a lazy sound as the bee approached. She was sure to find sweet nectar inside. She approached in confidence 'til she landed on one heavy plastic petal. She crawled around a bit, inspecting a flower with no sweetness, then moved on to the next and the next, bumping against them 'til she finally gave up and headed over to the poppies Grandma had planted at the far end of the cemetery.

Mama was watching it, too. She wiped a tear from her eye with a dirty hand and stood up. She squeezed Theo's shoulder gently then walked back toward the parking lot.

It was thought strange among the mourners that the cemetery had forgotten to finish digging Grandma Alice's grave. The grave-side dedication had a false and merely ornamental ring to it as the Pastor hurried his way through the final prayer then led the congregation to their cars, where they drove off to my house to be served endless plates of goodies as they sat and talked of Grandma and rising gas prices. The casket was brought back inside the church.

Theo came up to me in my living room and tugged once again at my hair. "Nancy, I'm going to take your mama for a drive and thought you might like to come."

We went back to the cemetery as the sun was beginning to set. It was quiet and peaceful and beginning to cool off a bit as we drove past the field of pump jacks. They bobbed up and down silently, endlessly plumbing the poisoned ground for black gold, oblivious to everything but their task. Mama held my hand as we drove and wiped her tears away with her other hand. Theo drove, staring straight ahead.

We were met at the grave by the pastor and watched as her casket was lowered slowly into the dark, cool hole. There was a gentle crunch as it came to rest on the bottom. My eyes filled with tears. Grandma had always said she liked the sound of dirt crunching under new shoes when she walked. Grandma had very rarely gotten new shoes.

"Theodore, would you like to say a few words?" the pastor asked.

He nodded and cleared his throat. He stood for a long time in silence. His shoulders shook for a minute then he straightened up.

"She was a good sister to me. I tried to be a good brother to her. I hope she puts in a good word for me on the other side, seeing as how I'm not likely to get there on my own merit. That's it. Goodbye, Alice."

He turned and walked off into the trees that surrounded the cemetery. Despite all of the day's confusion, I felt at peace as I stood by this unmarked grave. A breeze picked up then, and I almost thought I could smell Oil of Olay and stale lipstick lingering in the air about us.

The pastor bowed his head then and prayed. "Lord, we dedicate this grave unto thee as a resting place for Alice Dee Johnson 'til she may rise again in the great day of our Lord. May she rest in peace 'til then. Lord, we also ask a blessing of comfort upon this family. Help them to remember that those who are alive in Christ are never lost. Help them in their trial to know you are watching over them and blessing those that mourn. They shall be comforted. Amen."

Mama thanked the pastor then she came toward me. She put her arm around me and walked me into the trees where Theo had gone.

"Mama, what's going on? Why don't you want Grandma to be buried with Grandpa? I mean, he was her husband and your daddy."

Mama shook her head slowly. "He was my father, Nancy, not my daddy. Not ever my daddy. He was her husband only in the barest sense of the word."

Mama wiped a tear away and continued. "He was as mean as they come,

Nancy. He beat her. He made her feel like she was nothing. He called her horrible names. He tried to beat me, Nancy. Mama always tried to shield me, taking the blows herself. She loved him long after he took away all her pride and her selfworth and her ability to have more children. I was her first. She miscarried twice after me because of severe beatings, and then she was barren. The doctors had to take out her entire uterus after the second miscarriage."

I shuddered and felt cold. I felt like a rock had settled in the pit of my stomach.

"When I met your daddy, Nancy, I left her. I ran away from that house like it was on fire and I never went back when I knew he was there. I tried to get her to leave him but I knew she wouldn't. He'd threatened to kill her if she did. I don't think she cared so much about that, but I think he probably used me as a threat to her. So, she stayed with him to protect me from whatever evil he'd promised to do to me if she wasn't around. But despite everything, I know she stayed because she loved him, too. She loved him before he started drinking, and she kept that memory, held on to it, hoping the man she married would come back and conquer the beast he became when he took to the bottle. I know it wounded her that he chose to drink instead of choosing her and the normal life they might have had together. He was always so sorry once he was sober, Nan. Always so sorry, always so full of drowned promises. So sorry that I don't think he could stand who he was, and he drank to forget."

"That's why Theo hated him so much," I said then, beginning to understand. "Did he know what was going on back then?"

"He suspected, I'm sure, but Mama never told him anything. One day he stopped by to see her. She didn't want to let him in, but he came in anyway and saw her face, all bruised and swollen. She was over sixty then, Nancy, and still living in hell.

"Theo waited for him to come home. He waited out in his truck so Mama wouldn't know. When Samuel got home, Theo came inside and found him hitting Mama. Theo bashed him over the head with a baseball bat. Samuel fell to the floor, unconscious. Theo was so consumed with rage that he jumped onto his still body and pummeled him with his fists over and over 'til Mama finally had enough strength to pull him off. But by then, he was dead.

"Theo was going to turn himself in. He felt terrible about it, but Mama couldn't stand the idea of losing them both so she helped him drag the body out to his truck, and they left him behind his favorite bar and took his wallet. She refused to see anyone but Theo 'til her face had healed.

"The police tried for a while to find the murderer, but the case got cold after only a few weeks. No one missed Samuel enough to put any more effort into it."

"I just don't understand why no one ever told me," I said, bewildered.

"Well, it's not exactly the kind of thing you tell people, Nan. It was Grandma's wish and it was for Theo's protection. I'm not saying what he did was right, but I didn't shed any tears on Samuel's behalf either. Sometimes I think of it as a brutal act of kindness. He saved your Grandma from something she hadn't the strength to save herself from, and it saved Samuel from killing Grandma, which he'd been doing slowly for over thirty years. It was only a matter of time before he just hit her too hard. It was ugly and shameful, but so is life sometimes.

My only regret was that Theo had to shoulder the responsibility all this time."

"How long have you known about all this, Mama?" I asked.

"Oh, since the night it happened. I told the police during the investigation that Theo had been at our house for dinner that night. He needed an alibi and I was happy to give him one."

"Does Daddy know?"

"No, Nancy, he doesn't. Just Theo and me—and now you."

I thought of Theo off wandering in the trees alone and began to understand him a little better. He'd always made me laugh. He was quick to find the humor in things, but he was wise in ways I didn't always understand. I realized now that he'd always been a little sad, that he was compensating for something, and that he was always kind. Even when he'd cleared out the house last Thanksgiving, it wasn't just a joke, but kindness on his part, to save Laura from any kind of humiliation later. He had always understood Laura. I remembered then some- thing he'd said to me once.

"We're all just a few chemicals away from insanity at any time, Nancy. There's all kinds of crazy. Laura's just has a name and a medication for it. The rest of us just have to do the best we can."

When I got home, I stood at the window facing the lake and watched as dust devils danced across its ever-widening ring of alkali like shiftless pale ghosts.

Chapter Twenty-One

For the next few days Laura came and went—going to school, going to work, and not saying a word to me. I almost never saw her. Graduation was fast approaching. I asked Laura who she'd like to invite, but she didn't really seem to care one way or the other. So, I put my mind to that. I felt I'd go crazy if I couldn't do something. It seemed to me that my family was tearing itself apart.

I was still prickly around Harold, who had long since become exasperated with me and had given up trying to figure out what my problem was. There were times I thought I wanted him to come and just hug me, to tell me it was alright, that it was no big deal, but he didn't. It hurt. Sometimes I figured it was my fault. I wasn't exactly making it easy for him. But I was ashamed of myself, and shame is a hard emotion to let others in on. So, I had to deal with it on my own. I needed Grandma's wisdom. I missed her almost more than I could stand.

Charlie called several times, but Laura was never home. He saw her only when she was at work, and I had no idea how she was treating him there. When Laura chose, she could be as cold as ice.

He called the night before her graduation. "Hi Charlie," I said, trying to sound light. "Is Laura there?"

"No, I'm sorry, she's not. She's gone shopping or something. I don't know. She's graduating tomorrow night."

"She didn't even tell me," he said, sounding hurt.

"I'm sorry, but I know she'd want you there. It's on the quad there at the college at five o'clock."

"What happened, Nancy?" he said, in a voice that sounded tired and bewildered, and sad.

I was silent. I was terrified of making things worse.

"I know she's grieving about your grandma and I've tried to be there for her but…she doesn't want me anymore."

"No! Charlie, she does! She wants you more than anything, it's just…"

"She doesn't want to be with a man who can't read," he said, finishing my sentence.

I was stunned. "What do you mean you can't read?"

"I mean I can't READ!" he almost yelled, his voice cracking. "I'm just a bum who drives a truck!"

Suddenly I understood. I remembered the way he'd never even ordered from the menu there at Ted's, though he always made a point of studying it.

"Oh no, Charlie! I know it's not that!" I said, my heart nearly breaking for him.

"I was going to tell her, but I know she figured it out. She's too smart not to."

"Oh Charlie, bless your heart, Honey…I don't think she'd hold that against you. She might be more understanding than you think. Everybody has secrets and things they're not proud of."

It seemed to me then as we shared silence on the phone for a while, that

Grandma's death had seemed to reveal everyone's secrets, like the tide going out, leaving only a barren beach and jagged rocks filled with dark caves.

"Charlie, I want you to come to her graduation. You be there, you hear?"

"Alright," he said, his voice sounding strangely muffled.

I drove over to Theo's, bringing a few things. I knew he wasn't eating well and

I wanted to make sure he did.

I felt strange around him since learning what happened with Grandpa. I didn't know what to say. I was afraid of saying the wrong thing. I tried to treat him like I always did, but something had changed in me, and I knew I wasn't hiding it well. What he had done was just awful, unthinkable, and yet he'd saved

Grandma. Since the day of the funeral we had lost something. He could feel it, too, I was sure of it.

I walked in and found him seated at the table staring at a pair of glasses. They were Grandma's reading glasses that she'd set down atop a newspaper. I'd noticed them before, the first time I came over after Grandma was gone. It struck me then how recently they'd been laid down, how it looked like she'd just gone to the next room and was coming right back. The glasses had not been moved. They had an almost enchanting quality to them now, like they were under a spell that no one dared break. I reached down and started to shift the paper to the side so I could sit and have a clear space in front of me.

Theo's hand shot out and stopped me. "Don't touch that!"

I jumped, then sat down quickly. "I'm sorry."

"Just don't touch that," he said again, raising his eyes to mine for a brief moment. "Leave 'em be."

Since the accident, Helen had been amazingly scarce. After all she'd done, she went into hiding. She didn't answer her phone and she never answered her door, but I knew she was home. Her Cadillac was always in the driveway. I noticed I never saw Lars' car. Maybe he'd had it taken to the shop. Something about her behavior bothered me. It just wasn't like Helen to see a mess and not try to dig in, and our family was a mess.

That night I went into Laura's room without knocking. I didn't want her to tell me I couldn't come in. She had her graduation robes on.

"Well, you sure look nice. You know, I was thinking about it. You're the first one of us to even graduate college! Just think, Laura! Isn't that something? Grandma would be so proud!" I said, trying to break through her layer of ice.

She was quiet as she tried on her cap.

"Charlie called again. I invited him to graduation. I guess you forgot to."

"I didn't forget. I just didn't invite him," she finally said.

The air in her room seemed suddenly suffocating. I got a little angry at her.

"Well, why the hell not?"

"Don't try to understand me, Nan. There is no possible way you could ever understand me. You have no idea what it's like! You and your perfect little marriage and perfect little kids! Don't you dare try to see what I see. You don't know anything about my life!"

I knew she wanted me to leave, but I could be just as stubborn as she could. "I know that. I know I have no idea what it is to be you. But there's things you don't know, too. You can't see what you have! You're hiding behind what you think you know, and sometimes, I swear, Laura, you're as blind as a bat!"

Her shoulders stiffened. "Get out."

"This is my house. I can stay in this room if I want to."

Laura made a few quick strides for the door. I headed her off.

"Nancy, I swear I'll hit you if you don't get out of my way."

"Laura, I swear I'll hit you right back if you try."

Laura looked for a moment like she actually would hit me. I flinched.

She went to sit on her bed with her back to me.

I sat down behind her. "Listen, I had a professor once who taught the basic drawing class. He spent what seemed like forever teaching us endless rules and never even let us draw a thing. I was just itching to draw, but he said something I never forgot. He said we weren't allowed to draw what we see. He said we had to draw what we know, and that's why he kept lecturing us. It didn't make much sense. Then before he let us put a mark on our paper, one day he gave us a final rule that we all wrote down in our sketch books: Draw what you know, not what you see, until you understand what you're seeing, and then you can draw it."

Laura turned to look at me. "Like that works for me. Half the stuff I see turns out not to be there at all."

"But you know what you know. You always know, Laura, even when you're sick."

Laura started to cry. "Well, I don't know what to do about Charlie, and I can't see it either."

"Laura, he can't read," I said then, trying to get her to understand his feelings.

"He thinks you're holding that against him."

"I know."

"What do you mean you know?"

"I know he can't read. I've known for a long time."

Laura's insight amazed me sometimes. "Well, why didn't you tell me?"

"Because he never told me, either. I didn't think it was my place."

"And you don't care?"

"Of course not!"

"Well, what makes you think he's gonna care so much about your schizophrenia?"

"That's totally different!"

I sighed. I guess it was. "Well, he's going to be there."

Laura didn't say anything, so I left her alone.

It was hot the evening of commencement. Fortunately, Mama and Daddy had arrived early and saved us some seats. Theo sat with them.

We all sat and sweated, the whole crowd a-flutter with stiff white programs waving about as people fanned themselves. I hardly listened to the speeches. I was too busy trying to keep the kids still. I didn't see Charlie anywhere, but it was a large crowd. I watched Laura. Her face was stony as she sat up there, not the way I'd pictured her face would look on her triumphant day. She'd made the Dean's list and was graduating with honors, something unheard of, as far I knew, for a schizophrenic. It was the one thing she never let her sickness take away from her. She fought for it a long time. It made me sad to think she'd given up on other things—like Charlie.

Tears streamed down my face as her name was called. She stood and walked across the stage, taking her diploma case. The actual diplomas were sent later. She smiled as she shook hands with the officiator then sat down again. She looked so beautiful...and fragile. I hoped Charlie was watching somewhere. I hoped he'd fight for her and not turn his back on her.

Daddy didn't wait for Laura to find us after the ceremony. He fairly leapt into the crowds of blue robes and picked her up off her feet and twirled her around. "That's my girl!" he said, hugging her to him. "I'm so proud I think I'll bust!"

Laura smiled for him and for me and for the rest of us standing there, but there wasn't enough happiness in her eyes for a moment as glorious as this truly was. Laura's quiet attitude soon quieted the rest of us, and we sighed as we headed back to our cars.

As we all walked to the parking lot, I kept looking over my shoulders. Laura walked quickly. I knew she didn't dare look for him. I knew deep down she wanted him to be there but was too afraid to look around and find that he wasn't.

He was waiting for us at my car. Laura saw him first and stopped. He just stared at her and she stared back. "Congratulations," he finally said quietly.

"Thanks," she mumbled.

"Can I give you a ride home?"

Laura was biting her lip. Suddenly she rushed to him and kissed him. It wasn't a happy kiss, though. It had the finality of goodbye in it, and when she pulled back, he leaned in for more. "I just can't, Charlie, OK? I love you, but I just can't. You deserve better." With that she sat down in the backseat of my car and locked the door.

Mama and Daddy, who had walked more slowly with Theo, arrived at our car just then. "Well now, isn't this nice?" Mama beamed. "Who else feels like celebrating?"

Charlie remained standing where he was. His whole body seemed limp. I watched him out the rearview mirror as we drove away. He just stood there, looking so alone, 'til we turned, and I couldn't see him anymore.

Helen finally called when we got home. She sounded odd, like she'd been crying.

"Nancy? I didn't know who else to call. You're my only friend, really."

"What is it?" I asked, a little stunned.

"I just can't do this by myself. Can you come over?" She sounded desperate. "It's not really a good time," I said, glancing at Laura's closed door.

"Please, Nancy."

When I pulled into her driveway, I noticed her hedges weren't as neat as they usually were. Lars usually kept them trimmed just so, but their clean sharp lines had grown fuzzy. I knocked on the door. No one answered so I went in. Her house was a mess. Dolls were strewn everywhere like someone had purposely tried to dash their little porcelain faces in.

I grew alarmed. I went from room to room 'til finally I heard a faint voice coming from the garage. "In here, Nancy."

I opened the door in her kitchen that led to the garage. It was dark. I could hardly see a thing.

"Shut the door. Don't turn the lights on," she said.

"Why are you sitting here in the dark?"

"Because I didn't want to see it. I just want to cut it down and I can't do it by myself."

"What are you talking about?"

I peered into the darkness, waiting for my eyes to adjust. Helen sat cross legged on the floor, something I'd never seen her do. She was holding a pair of garden shears.

Something swung slowly above her. I didn't want to look up. Suddenly I knew what it was.

"I can't let them find him like this. Please help me cut him down. I can't even work these things, what with my arthritis."

I noticed then that she was leaning against Lars' car. Its front bumper was crushed on one side.

Helen watched me as I took in what all of this meant.

"I'm so sorry. I'm so sorry, Honey. He didn't mean it. I know he didn't.

Please, just help me cut him down."

"No."

"But, Nancy! We can't just leave him here like this! Please!" she begged, tears streaming down her face.

"No, I'm not going to help you clean this mess up. It's not my job and it's not yours. You can't scrub this one clean, Helen! You have to leave him there so the police can file a report."

"Oh, Nancy..."

"Get up and come inside, Helen. Come on." I walked into the gloom, despite my aversion to Lars' still body hanging above her. I took her hand and yanked her to her feet. "Come inside. I'm calling the police."

Helen sobbed on her sofa while I got on the phone and dialed 911. "I'd like to report a suicide," I said, my voice shaking.

I gave them the directions and in moments we heard the sirens. I sat with

Helen on her couch and held her hands while the police began the investigation.

One officer sat down beside us taking notes. "Was there a fight?" he asked gently, indicating all the dolls strewn about.

Helen looked terrified. I squeezed her hand. "You need to answer their questions," I urged.

"No, not really. He'd been drinking a little—well, a lot I guess. He didn't mean it! He didn't mean it!" she shrieked.

"No, of course not," the officer urged. "Did he do this?" he asked, once again indicating the disaster in her living room.

"Yes. He said they were all watching him and it made him crazy. He smashed every last one of them and then went out to the garage."

"And did you follow him?"

"No."

"What did you do?"

"Well, I was trying to clean it up."

"How long was he in the garage?"

"I don't know, but I was afraid to go out there. He wasn't himself."

"Can you give me a guess?"

"What does it matter?" I interrupted. "Long enough to hang himself! Why don't you leave her alone?" I could see Helen was near hysteria.

"Alright. You don't have to answer any more questions if you don't want to," he said, trying to sound sympathetic. "Do you have a place to stay? You can't stay here tonight until we've finished."

"She'll stay with me," I announced. "Can we leave now?"

I was in a state of shock as I slowly drove her home. I was glad I felt so numb. I couldn't even put two thoughts together. Helen had quieted too. She no longer sobbed. But she had her purse straps wrapped so tightly in her fists they'd gone white.

I made her a bed on the sofa and asked her if she needed anything. "No, go on. I'm so sorry, Nan."

I couldn't answer her. I had too many emotions pummeling my mind. Speech was no longer possible.

I don't believe I slept a wink that night and neither did Laura. I could hear her guitar going for hours, on and off, as she picked it up and strummed, then put it down again. Sometimes I heard her wandering aimlessly throughout the house, Sam's claws making a clicking sound on the floors as he followed her. Off and on, I heard a strange moaning coming from the living room. Helen, too, went without sleep. After a while I reached under my bed and pulled out my worry box. I pulled out the card in the very back, the one with Lars' and Helen's names on it. Then I pulled out all the others—Charlie's, Laura's, Grandma's—and laid them all in front of me on my pillow before I finally broke down and cried, burying my face against them and my pillow.

Harold woke then and nestled his body up against mine. "Honey, don't cry like that. You're gonna make yourself sick." He pleaded.

"I can cry if I want to."

He sat up and looked at me closely. "OK then, cry, but I'm going to hold you this time 'til you're done."

I sobbed for hours. I let every emotion I could think of navigate through my body and my mind. I think maybe Harold thought I was losing my mind as he rubbed my arms and kissed my forehead. Several times he asked me what was wrong, but I decided to wait 'til morning to tell him why Helen was sleeping on our couch.

The following morning Harold stood at the table, as stunned as I felt yesterday. "You mean Lars was the one driving?" he demanded.

Theo had come over too and stood behind him. Helen sat with her face in her hands.

"Well, why in hell didn't you turn him in?" Harold asked. Helen didn't respond. She just sat there covering her face.

"Helen, that was against the law! Haven't you heard of a thing called obstruction of justice? Helen, look at me!" he hollered.

"Leave her alone," Theo said quietly. "No one here is in a place to judge."

"I can't believe you!" Harold fumed. "Grandma died because of that drunk, and you're just going to sit there?"

"Yes, I am. None of this is Helen's fault," he said, coming around the table and putting a hand on her shoulder. She flinched.

"Well, where's Lars, then?"

None of us attended Lars' funeral a week later, and I don't believe Helen expected any of us to. Helen came back over when it was done and went to sit out on the porch. She'd been staying with us ever since it happened. She couldn't bring herself to go home yet and face the mess that needed cleaning.

"Where's Laura?" she asked when I went out to join her.

"I don't know. She left this morning for a walk. She should be back sometime soon though."

"I can't believe she finally graduated. I never once thought she'd do it. Every time she'd relapse I'd think to myself, "Now see, she just can't. I always thought she'd give up." Helen sighed. "That girl simply amazes me. Can I see her diploma?"

"Well, she hasn't actually gotten it yet, but she has a real nice case with a dummy certificate in it. I can show you that." I said, getting up.

I went into Laura's room. It was a mess, but I didn't give it too much thought at the time. I wasn't exactly a neat freak myself. I couldn't see the blue case anywhere. I pulled open a few drawers and rummaged through them 'til I heard something rattle.

I pulled the folded shirts away from it and saw, buried in her drawer, a full bottle of Clozaril, her anti-psychotic. Laura had always kept her meds on top of her dresser and was meticulous in taking them. But when I turned the bottle, I could see it had been filled over two weeks ago. Yet it was still full.

Chapter Twenty-Two

I ran back outside. I looked as far as I could see down the road, but I didn't spot her anywhere. The air was thick and hot, ominous. At first, I thought it was just me, but I looked over at Helen, who was watching a bank of dark clouds mass to the west. She was fanning herself furiously.

"What is it, Nancy?" she called. "Something wrong?"

I ran out into the backyard to see if she'd been walking along the lake, or at least what was left of it. I saw no one.

I came back to the front of the house.

"Nancy, you come inside, now. There's a storm coming!" Helen demanded.

"I can't find Laura!"

Helen stood, putting a hand on her brow, squinting down the road. "I think that's her right there! What's all the fuss?"

I whipped around and saw Sam pulling her along. They were just two tiny figures shimmering in the heat waves that resonated through the air. I couldn't make out her face as she ambled slowly along the road. As she got closer, I could see she was weaving, moving side to side along the white line at the side of the road.

I was terrified as I watched her approach. I didn't know where her mind would be.

Helen stood beside me as we waited for Laura. She called out, "Laura! Come on now, hurry up. I don't like the looks of these clouds!"

Laura kept on in her lazy pace, weaving. When she finally approached us, she said, "Nan's afraid of tornadoes. I bet you are, too. I'm not afraid."

Helen looked at me, then back at Laura. "Are you feeling alright? It's awful hot and muggy out here. Maybe you should come in and lie down."

As she spoke, I watched Laura's feet shuffling back and forth in tiny steps. She looked up accusingly at Helen. "Maybe you should shut up! You wanted him to kill Grandma. You told him to, just like you want to kill Sam. Stay away from us!"

"What on earth are you talking about?" Helen demanded.

I grabbed Helen's arm and pulled her back a pace, then stepped forward to

Laura, who was biting her lip.

"Laura," I whispered, "Why don't you take Sam inside where he'll be safe?"

"You're right, Nan. You're always right. Inside, Sam." Laura headed for the front door, then turned again to Helen, "I'm watching you. You stay away from my dog!"

Helen's face was twisted in total shock. "How could she say that?" she gasped.

"How could she say I wanted him to do it? Why on earth would I want to kill her dog?"

I held out the full prescription bottle of medicine, and Helen put a hand to her mouth. "Oh, Lord have mercy!"

When Laura was losing her mind, there was always a strange paranoia and anger, usually involving a delusion. She'd get an idea in her head and hang on to it. You just couldn't convince her that what "they" were telling her wasn't true.

When we came in the house, Laura was mixing a pitcher of Kool-Aid. The T was blaring and she was talking to herself. She was mumbling and I couldn't make out what she was saying over the noise. I didn't know what to do.

The hair stood up on my neck as I watched her endlessly stirring the red liquid. Helen came in and Laura looked up. "You don't get any," was all she said before looking down again to stir.

Suddenly the television screeched as a red bar rolled across the bottom of the screen. The sound cut out for a moment, then a voice read the words that rolled by. "Be advised, a tornado warning is in effect for Dane County, Dodge, and lower Sonora County. No tornadoes have yet been spotted, but the rotation of the clouds could produce one at any time. Take cover immediately. Get to a basement or innermost room away from any windows."

"Where's the kids?" I said, turning around. "Helen, where's the kids?" I shrieked.

"Calm down, Nantucket, it's just a storm." Laura said, almost laughing.

Helen bolted into the kids' room and found them playing video games. "Here they are! Come on kids! Down to the basement! Nancy, where's the baby?"

I ran down the hall to Marie's crib, but it was empty. I couldn't for the life of me remember where I'd put her. "Marie! Marie! Where are you, Baby?" I shrieked.

"I know where she is," Laura said. "I'll show you. I had to hide her from

Helen."

An almost physical weight engulfed my whole body, shrouding me in a horrible sense of doom.

"Where did you put her, Laura?" I screamed.

Laura put a finger to her mouth secretively as she went down to the basement to the laundry room. I felt sick. I realized then that it had been quite a while since

I'd seen Marie and it seemed like the last one holding her had been Laura. How could I forget my baby?

I was sobbing as I yanked open the dryer door. I felt around frantically, moving around the warm laundry. I was terrified.

"Don't be dumb, Nan. You think I'm crazy or something? I wouldn't put her in the dryer!" Laura said, sounding hurt. "I wouldn't do that!" She stared at me a moment, then her eyes got hard. "You thought I would do that!"

"No, I didn't! I didn't Laura. Just tell me where she is!"

Laura bent down and pulled a blanket off a laundry basket in the corner.

Underneath it, Marie was sleeping peacefully.

My knees buckled. "Oh, thank God! Thank God!"

Laura was staring at me.

I couldn't look at her. She walked back up the stairs and into the kitchen, then started for the front door.

"No!" Helen said, taking her arm. "You can't go out there. A storm is coming!"

Laura jerked her arm back, walked to the kitchen counter, and began stirring the Kool-Aid again. She slowly lifted the spoon and watched it drip onto the floor. "I can do whatever I want," she said quietly. She then lifted the pitcher of juice over her head and dumped it all over herself. It poured down over her like blood, soaking her hair and dripping into her eyes. She ran outside before I could stop her.

I scrambled to follow her, trying to hand Marie to Helen, but she wouldn't take her. "Get to the basement! Now! I'll get her!" Helen shouted.

"But you won't be able to catch her!"

"No, but my Cadillac can. Get down there! I'll be right back."

I took a final look out the window before I went down.

"Mommy, is there a tornado?" a small voice asked from the bottom of the stairs. Benny looked white as a ghost as Josie stood holding his hand. She looked just as scared.

"I don't know, Baby. We just need to stay down here."

"Where's Daddy?" Josie asked, her lip quivering. "I want Daddy."

I wanted him, too, more than anything as I sat there clutching Marie. But he'd gone to work—out in a lumber yard—with nails, 2X4s, and all kinds of dangerous things once they were airborne. The whole room seemed to spin. I felt dizzy. It was all just too much, too much for me to handle on my own. I didn't want to think, but I couldn't push out the thought that Harold was never there in my dreams, just before our house spun off into a whirlwind.

I could hear the wind picking up, and when I stood on tiptoe to look out the thick, small basement window, I could see hail bouncing around on the grass.

"I'm scared, Mommy!" Josie screamed as the wind picked up.

"Me too, Honey, me too! Just sit down here by me. Come on, Benny!"

We sat huddled together on the basement floor. I held Marie in my lap and wrapped my arms around the other two, holding them close. Rain started pouring down in sheets, mixing with the hail.

"Can we sing a song?" Benny asked. "At church, the Sunday school teacher said if we're scared, we should sing."

"What would you like to sing?" I asked, knowing I must keep the children calm.

"Mommy, is our house built on a rock?" he asked then.

I didn't know if it was or not, but I knew what he meant. "Yes, Honey! It's strong. This house has been here a long time!"

"I know what I want to sing then," he said, then started the words to a song so old, I remembered it from when I was little.

"The wise man built his house upon the rock,

The wise man built his house upon the rock,

The wise man built his house upon the rock,

And the rains came tumbling down." Josie joined in then, her voice a little shaky at first.

"The rains came down and the floods came up,

The rains came down and the floods came up,

The rains came down and the floods came up,

And the house on the rock stood still."

The wind was screaming in fury. It sounded like the end of the world. I heard something clatter up against the house. I joined them in singing as loud as I could to try to drown out the noise.

"The foolish man built his house upon the sand,

The foolish man built his house upon the sand,

The foolish man built his house upon the sand, and the rains came tumbling down.

The rains came down and the floods came up,

The rains came down and the floods came up,

The rains came down and the floods came up," I stopped, unable to go on, but the kids continued,

"and the house on the sand washed away!"

"Let's sing something else," I said, then started into another song,

"Jesus loves me, this I know, For the Bible tells me so…"

Suddenly the basement door swung open with a bang. I looked up and saw Helen clutching Laura tightly. Laura appeared dazed. Helen's head was bleeding slightly. "I've got her! I've got her! Help me get her down!" she screamed.

I put Marie in Josie's lap and ran up to help. Laura was drenched and slippery, her skin caked in a filmy mud that was tinged pink from the Kool-Aid.

"She was at the lake! She was trying to walk out into it!" Helen yelled. "She was trying to drown herself!"

Laura had gone almost completely catatonic. She was just staring straight ahead, and her body had gone limp. Helen and I stumbled together down the stairs, holding her between us.

We got her settled at the bottom and leaned her back against the wall. I went to my knees in front of her.

"Laura! Laura! Talk to me!" I begged.

Laura just stared straight ahead, her eyes fixated in what Daddy called a thousand yard stare. Her hair was matted to her face in chunky brown clumps.

Helen sat down beside me and wheezed. "I can't get my breath! I just can't get my breath," she wheezed. "I couldn't hardly pull her out. It was so slippery I didn't think I could do it, but then Sam was there, barking to raise the dead, dragging his leash. I tied it around her hand and that old dog pulled her out. Her dog pulled her out!"

Suddenly I heard barking and scratching at the door. I ran up the stairs and threw the door open for Sam. He bounded down the stairs, barking furiously. From where I stood in the basement doorway, I could see out the kitchen window. I froze. There it was, trembling and twisting, black as night, thundering its way across the alkali. As it picked up the light-colored clay and water, the twister changed colors, turning a ghastly white. I couldn't move. I couldn't think. I could only stare at it. For a moment, I thought I was dreaming. I hoped I was dreaming, but I knew, finally, that it was really happening this time.

"Mommy!" Benny yelled. "Mommy, my ears hurt! My ears are hurting!"

The sudden change in air pressure, I'd heard, could damage a person's ears. I ran down the stairs, slamming the door shut behind me. I put my hands over his ears.

"Shhhh! It's going to be alright! Hush now. Just let 'em pop, don't fight it.

Just let 'em pop and they'll feel better."

Marie was screaming, Josie clung to me and Benny sat with his hands over his ears. Helen was still gasping for breath and Laura stared straight ahead. All I could do was pray. Somehow, some way in all this chaos, I hoped God could hear me.

Somewhere I've heard it said that a tornado was the wrath and fury, the very finger of God. I wasn't so sure. I'd always been so afraid of tornadoes, always dreaded them, was haunted by them. To me, a tornado was the ultimate destruction, the ultimate fear materialized in a twisting, elusive column of wind. It fed on chaos. It was chaos bundled up in a tight cone of fury. As I watched, it came like a predator, hunting for discord. It sniffed out the trail of disaster made by our family and headed right for us.

I feel differently about tornadoes now. No one can stop or change the course of a twister but God, and God did that day. It turned away, and headed in another direction, following a different trail. It descended down into Helen's beautiful house built in the sand, and washed it clean, clean off the ground.

Chapter Twenty-Three

It was so quiet when it was all over. It was eerie, such absolute silence on the heels of Nature's fury. We sat huddled together on the basement floor long after the storm had passed. After a few minutes of absolute silence, I slowly lifted my head.

"Benny, how's your ears?" I asked.

He took his hands away and rubbed them. "OK, I guess. They don't hurt anymore."

"Josie, you okay, Honey?"

Josie simply nodded, then asked, "Is it over?"

"Let me go peek out. Stay here."

I climbed the stairs one more time, still holding Marie, and pushed the door open slowly. Our house was still standing, and the dark sky was beginning to clear.

I came back down. "It's alright. Everybody can come up now. Our house is still here!"

Helen still sat next to Laura. Both of them were covered in filmy white clay that was beginning to dry. They looked disfigured in the dim basement light.

"Helen, you okay?" I asked

"I'm alright, I guess," she said, dabbing at the blood drying on the side of her face.

And then I looked at Laura. "Laura? Laura!"

I shook her gently, but she didn't respond. "Helen, can you help me get her up?"

"I feel like I can't hardly move. I'm plumb wore out."

"Well, I'll stay down here with her for a bit. Go on up and take a shower if you like. Put a movie on for the kids, will you?"

Helen got up slowly. "If I can just make it upstairs and lay down, seems like I'd sleep for a week." She took inventory of herself, once standing. "Good grief, I look like I've wallowed in a mud hole."

"You did."

"Yes, I guess I did. Remind me never to do that again. I'm going to go wash all this off. I feel positively slimy. This alkali is bad for your skin, you know."

"Before you do, could you bring the phone down here? I want to try and call Harold and my folks."

A few minutes later she called down the stairs. "Line's dead, Honey. I'm sure they're alright."

I stayed down there in the basement and waited. Several times I tried to rouse

Laura, but she wasn't responding. She sat there as stiff and still as a statue. She'd gone and hidden deep inside herself this time, and I was afraid I might never find her again. She even looked different. Her eyes were vacant and her body rigid. I couldn't leave her alone down there, so I stayed by her as I heard the water running upstairs and the kids scampering about. Then I heard something I'd been listening for, the sound of the front door opening.

"Please, God," I prayed. "Let it be Harold. Let him be alright."

"Nan?" I heard a beloved gruff voice call. "Nantucket?"

"Grandpa!" I heard Benny shriek. "Grandpa! There was a tornado! Did you see it?"

"Yes, I sure did. Everyone here alright? Where's your mama?"

"I'm down here!" I called.

It was so comforting to watch my dad's large feet coming down those basement steps toward me. I felt saved.

"Nancy, what are you still doing down here?"

"Laura's sick again, Daddy. I can't move her by myself."

Daddy's face fell as he descended the last step. Deep concern furrowed his scraggly brows, and his lips were tight beneath his beard. He squatted in front of her. "Laura? Laura, Honey, it's Daddy. Laura, I need you to listen to me." He held her chin, turning her face from side to side. She didn't respond. He turned to me. "What happened? How long has she been like this?"

"I found her medicine in her drawer. She hasn't taken it in over a week, I think. She's lost it again, Daddy. She ran out into the storm and tried to drown herself in the lake."

Daddy sat down. "You pulled her out? By yourself?"

"No, Helen did, or she tried to. Sam was the one who finally got her out. Helen wasn't strong enough."

Daddy reached down and patted Sam's head. "Good old dog, Sam. Good boy."

"Daddy," I said quietly. "Do you think she was trying to kill herself?"

He leaned back, his head against the wall. "I don't know. I don't think she'd do that."

By then Mama had begun descending the stairs. "What's going on down here?"

No one liked to be the one to tell Mama that something had gone wrong again with Laura. She always took it so hard. We were silent as she walked toward us, her face in shock.

"What happened, Laura? Why are you covered in mud?" she demanded.

Laura didn't move.

"Oh," she said, sitting down, comprehension evident in her tired voice.

We all sat for a minute or two, catching our breath and our thoughts. It was always the same feeling. The same sense of helplessness and bewilderment. The same anger and confusion. The same painful regret that went along with Laura's illness. No matter how many times we'd seen her lose her mind, it was always bitter and painful to have to see it again. To have to look right at her and know that she wasn't really there, that her mind was going to be gone for a time, and that the girl left behind never acted like Laura. What we had was the girl we all dreaded, the girl who would shove Laura aside and do and say things that Laura would pay for later in bouts of depression and regret. Schizophrenia didn't steal from you just once. It did it over and over again.

Finally, I spoke. "Let's get her upstairs so we can wash her off, at least."

Daddy was a big man. He scooped Laura's still form easily into his arms and started up the stairs, leaving a trail of milky water and mud as it dripped from her body.

Daddy placed her gently on the toilet seat in the bathroom then stepped out as

Mama and I got her undressed. Normally, Laura was always so modest. She never liked anyone to see her undressed, and I felt awkward with her just staring straight ahead like that. "Laura, we're going to wash you off. We have to get these muddy clothes off, OK? It's going to be alright. We're just going to give you a bath."

Mama and I lowered her gently into the tub basin and turned on the water, running it first over her head and through her hair. The clay fell away in clumps and ran in pale rivulets down her body.

"Hold her head up," Mama cautioned me. "Don't get it in her eyes, Nan. Be careful."

"I'm trying, Mama. She's kinda heavy!" "Move then and let me hold her."

"I've got it, Mama. It's not exactly easy."

Mama took the shower head from me and began rinsing Laura. Her head shook a little as she did it, and I sat back and watched as Mama bathed her as if she were an innocent child.

Mama broke down silently weeping as she guided the water gently over Laura.

"Oh, baby girl, be patient with us. We're trying, Honey. We'll get all this off.

We'll take care of you."

We shampooed her hair and conditioned it with Laura's favorite lavender scented stuff. Mama kept sniffling and reaching over to wipe her nose with toilet paper.

"She's going to be alright," she kept saying, but Laura's expression never changed. She only blinked slowly when I accidentally got a little water in her eyes.

Helen knocked on the door. "Need any help?" she asked.

"No, no we're fine," I said.

Helen stood there a moment. I heard the floor creak as she walked slowly away. There was nothing she could do, nothing any of us could do.

Mama dried her off while I went and got her something to wear. I picked something pink, her favorite color.

"Laura, I've got your pink shirt here, and these shorts you like. Why don't we put them on?"

Laura sat slumped against the wall, wrapped in a towel.

"I think we should call the doctor," Mama said then, "I've never seen her quite like this."

"The phone's dead," I reminded her as I slipped the shirt over Laura's wet hair.

Suddenly I remembered Harold. Where was he? My heart pounded painfully in my chest. I couldn't breathe. I was instantly sick with worry. He would have been here by now if he was alright. He would have come straight home to see how we were.

I shook my head, trying to clear it. I could feel uncontrollable panic creeping through my body, making my skin prickle.

"Nancy, are you alright?" Mama asked, pausing while dressing Laura.

"Oh, Mama. What about Harold? Why isn't he here?"

"Because he had to go to work today, same as any other day." "I know, but he's never here when it happens."

"What do you mean?"

"In all my tornado dreams, he's never here. He's never here!" I said, my voice shaking with panic. "Mama! I can't lose my husband. I can't do it! I can't bear it!

Mama, what am I going to do?"

Mama reached for my hand and held it firmly in hers. "You're going to calm down, that's what. Do you think you're psychic, or something, just because of a dream? Nancy, that's absolutely silly. Everyone here in Texas has a tornado dream now and again. It doesn't mean a thing. I've dreamed for years that all my teeth are falling out, and I've still got even my wisdoms. Don't put any store by silly dreams, Nancy."

There was in her tone, a hint of Grandma's voice. I found it calming. I took a deep breath. "I guess you're right. No sense inventing something to worry about."

"Especially when you already have enough," she said, stroking Laura's hair.

She sighed. "Bless her heart, she tries so hard. She's worked so hard...harder than anybody should have to."

Mama's voice sounded suddenly bitter. Her head started to shake as she sat for a moment wiping her eyes, and stroking Laura's face. She looked upward angrily toward heaven and shouted, "Leave her alone, will you? It's enough! She's just a little girl! She's my little girl and I say it's enough!"

"Mama!" I said, shocked. "Don't talk to God like that!"

"I'll talk to him however I please. He does what he pleases with my little girl!

What's the point of all this? Why her? I am just sick and tired of it…just sick and tired, You hear me?" she said again, shaking her fist at the ceiling.

"Mama, God didn't make her sick this time. She quit taking her medicine."

Mama looked at me belligerently a moment. "What do you mean?"

"I found her medicine bottle in her dresser. It was still full. She hasn't been taking it."

Mama's face grew livid. "You were supposed to be watching her!" she shouted.

"Why didn't you make sure she was taking it? Oh, I knew this was a mistake! I told her you had too much to handle, what with the kids! I told her! And you should have known to watch her better!"

"I was, Mama. I was watching her all the time! I made her mad at me, I watched her so much. I tried, Mama! I just didn't know!"

"Well, why would she stop taking it? She knows what would happen!"

Mama and I were standing over Laura, yelling at each other, when suddenly we heard loud knocking on the door. It was Daddy.

"What?" we both yelled.

Daddy opened the door. He came in and took me under one arm and Mama under the other. "It's nobody's fault. Just knock it off, both of you. I could hear you clear down the hall. The kids can hear you, too. Now, let's keep the crazy women in this house to a minimum, alright?" He gave us both a squeeze, then squatted to lift Laura to her feet. Mama glared at him and followed him into the living room.

He placed Laura gently on the sofa and sent the kids out of the room. Both

Benny and Josie stood, staring wide eyed at Laura. "Go on out now," he said gently but firmly. "Laura needs some time to herself, that's all."

Helen came in then, holding Marie. "I think she's hungry, Nancy. I just can't do a thing with her."

I realized then that Marie had been screaming, probably for the last half hour.

It had been real, a contributing factor to the tension in the house. I reached for her and cooed softly. She sounded terrified. I sat down by Laura and opened my shirt. Marie latched on, still sobbing, and began to suck, her little body shaking with each silent sob. "There now, baby girl. It's alright. Mama's here. You're fine, just fine. Shhhh…"

Marie held her little fists up against my breast and I felt them slowly relax as she nursed. "Poor little girl…yes, poor little girl. It's alright now, Mama's gotcha." I cooed. She sighed. Then, with a final lingering whimper she continued to nurse. I wiped away the tears that remained in a little pool at the side of her nose. "Scary day for such a little girl, isn't it?" I asked her gently.

"Scary day for everybody," Helen commented, watching Laura. "I guess I better drive over and check on Theo. I suppose you're all gonna want to stay here."

"Yes, thank you, Helen." I said. "Could you check on Harold too?"

As Helen left, I could see we were in for it. Mama had that all too familiar look in her eyes. "What did you mean by that?" she demanded.

"Mean by what?" Daddy asked wearily.

"About the crazy women!" she hollered, stomping her foot.

"Dora, don't pick a fight with me right now. I'm just plumb wore out. I didn't mean anything by it."

"You did! You said we were crazy!"

"I did not say you were crazy. I just said…"

"You said 'let's keep the crazy women in this house down to a minimum,'" she said, imitating his voice, though she changed its meaning by the way she said it.

Daddy sat down on the sofa and wearily put his head in his hands. "Do you really want to fight with me today, Dora?"

"No, I don't want to fight! I just want to know why you would say something like that, and in front of Laura! Sometimes you just don't think! She can still hear you, you know. Try being a little sensitive! I don't like the way you make it sound like it's your weary lot in life to live with a bunch of crazy women."

Mama was getting herself all worked up. I could see it coming. Her head was shaking worse, and she was starting to pace. This one was going to be a doozie, I could tell.

"And try being a little sensitive to me! I don't like you inferring that I'm crazy. I'm tired of everyone thinking I'm going crazy. No one here thinks I can keep my own mind!"

I'd heard enough. It was more uncomfortable than I could stand. The problem was, I was on shaky ground as to how to put an end to the confrontation. I couldn't let Mama think I was on Daddy's side or I'd be her next target, but I didn't want Daddy to think I shared Mama's sentiments. It had always been very important to me to try to think rationally like he always did.

"Mama, stop it, please. I can't stand it. Let's just let it go."

Mama glared at me a moment and started to say something when the front door opened. I'd never been more relieved in my life. Harold stood framed in the doorway covered in dust. "Everybody alright?" he asked.

"Oh, Honey! Thank goodness you're home! I was so worried!" I said, wishing

I could jump up and hug him. "Come over here and hug me!" I demanded, tears of relief streaming down my face.

Harold sat down next to me and put his arms around me, bending to kiss

Marie on the nose. "Everybody's safe?" he asked.

"We're all OK. I saw it, Harold. I saw the tornado coming straight for the house."

"When the sirens went off in town, I could tell it was the real thing. I've never seen clouds like that. I mean, they literally growled."

I shuddered. "I can't believe it. I just can't believe it. It was coming right for us when I ran to the basement the last time. I thought sure we were all gonna…"

"Hey, it's over, Honey. I'm just glad everyone's alright. I got home as fast as I could, but we lost a lot of inventory out in the yard. I had to stay and sort a few things out. I tried to call but the phone was dead, so I drove over. The roads are a mess! Took me forever to get here."

"Tell me about it! I've been worried sick about you this whole time!"

"I'm sorry. Thank goodness everyone is OK," he said, relaxing into the couch.

There was a long awkward silence. It took Harold a few moments to feel it. "What?" he asked, unclasping his hands from behind his head.

Instinctively he looked at Laura, who sat across from him, and realized something was wrong. He stared at her blank face for a moment, then looked to me.

"She's been like that for a couple hours now. I found her medicine in her room. Looks like she hasn't been taking it."

"Oh, no," he sighed. "Poor kid. Have you called anyone yet?" "Can't, the phone's dead."

Harold looked at Daddy and Mama, who had been forced into a temporary truce by his presence. "Do you have her medicine with you? Why don't we see if we can get her to take some."

Mama left the room to get a glass of water while Daddy retrieved her medicine from the basement where I'd left it.

Daddy tipped back her head and put a pill as far back into her mouth as he could. Mama tipped a little water into her mouth. Laura coughed, nearly choking, but she swallowed the pill. Mama wiped her mouth, then laid her head down, adjusting the cushions around her. Laura continued to stare straight ahead in her prone position. "Just take a rest, Honey, just relax," Mama coaxed soothingly.

Laura blinked, then slowly closed her eyes.

Just before the phones were back online, Theo walked in the door, followed by Helen. Helen looked dazed. Her face was ashen. Theo guided her to the couch like I'd seen him do endless times with Grandma. "Sit there, old girl, and catch your breath."

I walked over and hugged Theo. "Glad to see you're alright. What's wrong with Helen?"

He steered me into another room, then said in a whisper. "Her house is gone, and I mean completely. It's like it was never there."

Chapter Twenty-Four

"I think we should pray," I suggested.

Everyone in the family sat idly about, no one doing anything in particular.

Mama paced. Daddy sat with his head in his hands. Theo was in the kitchen sharpening knives, not that they needed it. Helen wept quietly in a corner chair.

The children were in their room playing video games, and Laura was lying down in her room.

"Daddy, will you say a prayer for us?" I asked.

He was silent a moment, rubbing his beard. "I guess I could."

He sounded utterly exhausted and almost unwilling. Finally, he straightened up and bowed his head, clutching his hands in his lap. He cleared his throat before getting down from the couch onto his knees. I knelt down beside him and closed my eyes. I could hear Helen's knees popping and Theo's soft cough. We had all joined him on our knees, all but Mama, whose feet I could still see, standing over by the bookcase.

Daddy's voice was muffled as he began, "Our Father in Heaven, we are thankful this day to be safe. We are thankful for our family members, and for our homes, and for our lives. Father, at this time we'd like to ask a special blessing on

Laura. Father, help her. Help her to find herself, help her to respond to her medication, help her to come back to us. We understand, Father, that thy will must be done, but we humbly ask this favor today. Please, bless her with comfort and healing. And bless us with understanding and patience. In Jesus' name, Amen."

I felt a great sense of peace after that. It was almost tangible in the room.

I had a full house that night. Mama wanted to stay with Laura and slept on the floor beside her bed. Theo slept on a cot in Benny's room, and Helen was on the couch. Daddy decided to go on home sometime after midnight.

I couldn't sleep. I wandered the house, checked on Laura and the kids, and let

Sam out to do his business. I thought of Charlie. I wondered where he was.

I picked up the phone and dialed the number to Ted's Take a Break. It rang quite a few times before anyone picked it up.

"Hello?" a friendly voice finally said.

"Hi Ted, this is Nancy. Is everything alright over there? How did you guys weather that storm today?"

"Oh, we're alright. Not too much damage done here. How about you?"

"Well, my house is still standing."

"Hey, that's a good thing, right? Why do you sound so down? Did you lose any trees? A lot of people lost their trees. It's a shame, too. Takes 'em forever to grow in this poor excuse we have for soil around here."

"No, no, my trees are fine." I just sat there for a while, not knowing what to say. "Was Laura scheduled to come in tonight?"

"Yes, she was, but I'll understand if she can't make it. Not a whole lot of people here anyway."

"Is Charlie there?"

"I think he is. He's had his rig out back for several days now. I told him I ain't running a damn hotel out there, but he's a nice fella, so I'm letting it slide."

"Ted, do you happen to have a piece of cherry pie?"

"As a matter of fact, I do. Has your name on it even. Come on over and keep me company. I could always use a pretty face seated at one of my tables. What with Charlie moping around here, I get myself darn near depressed."

I looked in on the kids before I left and peeked into Laura's room. She appeared to be sleeping peacefully. Mama had fallen asleep on the floor with a book. I kissed Harold's forehead just before I left.

It was a chilly night like we hadn't had in a long time. All that hot and stifling air had been blown away and what was left seemed fresher, somehow cleaner. The town looked horrible, though. Trees were down all over the place, and as I drove along, peering into windows, and gazing at people still at work in their yards, I felt so sad. It was such a disaster. One minute you're in your house, and the next thing you know the world threatens to come down around your ears. And here was everyone scrambling to pick up the pieces, the thousands of broken pieces left behind once the storm had passed. Nothing was private. Odds and ends from people's lives were strewn all over the street. I saw toys, clothing, underwear, everything. It was all just out there for everyone to see. That tornado invaded everyone's privacy, digging up even the deepest secrets. I drove by all of it sadly as I set out to reveal the last of Laura's privacy.

I pulled into Ted's and parked out front. There were no other cars. The place was pretty much deserted.

Charlie looked up from the counter as the bells jingled on the door. He looked awful, like he hadn't slept in a week.

"Nancy! Everything alright? I've been meaning to call but the lines were dead. Then I thought maybe it was too late."

"Oh, that's alright. We're all OK. That old house of mine is still standing. We're all OK, but Laura won't be coming in for a while."

I could see that he desperately wanted to know about Laura. We had been a little cruel to him, I realized. No one had explained anything, and meanwhile, he had to nurse a broken heart in total confusion.

"Is she alright?" he asked, his eyes intense.

"Well, that's what I came over to talk to you about."

Just then Ted came in from the back. "Nancy Parley! You are a sight for sore eyes! Let me get you that pie. See if you can't cheer up this old lump while you're at it," he said, indicating Charlie. "I haven't seen a smile on this kid in days!"

Charlie seemed embarrassed. He turned from me and sipped his coffee for a moment. "So, what did you come to tell me that Laura can't tell me herself?" he asked bitterly.

The front door jingled. That storm had dug up another spot of ugliness, another thing better left under a rock. I turned to see Jim saunter in the door. He was the last person on earth I wanted to have in the room with Charlie and me right then. He saw me, smiled broadly, and walked over.

"Well, hi there, Nancy! How's that little sister of yours?"

He walked over to us and sat down right by me. I could smell whiskey on his breath, and his eyes were aflame with it. "I hear she's just a little crazy! My buddy,

Clance was telling me how close he came to marrying that girl! Man, did he luck out in the nick of time."

Just then Ted returned with my pie. His eyes grew hard when he saw Jim. "I thought I told you never to come in here again. Get out before I throw you out."

"I know my rights!" He said in a slurred voice. "I can sit here if I want to. This here's a public place!"

Charlie had spun around at the mention of Laura and was glaring at Jim menacingly. "What's that you said?"

"Oh, that's right. Forgot you were dating her." he smirked. "Tell you what, I ain't going to say anything. I can keep a secret just as good as her sister, here. I never liked you. Serves you right to get stuck with her." As he spoke, he weaved drunkenly on the stool, then his eyes got cruel. "You know, I bet having a lady who's a little on the wild side might actually be kinda nice, if you know what I mean. Maybe I should of stuck it out a while." As he spoke, he made a crude gesture with his hands.

Charlie's reaction was instantaneous. He grabbed Jim by the front of his shirt and lifted him bodily onto the counter. "You shut your dirty mouth, or I'm gonna plug it with my fist!"

Charlie spoke quietly, but there was unchained violence in his voice.

Jim chuckled. "Oh, you gonna hit me, Trucker Boy? You gonna hit me? I'm doing you a favor! I'm telling you what nobody else will. None of my business if you want to shack up with some lunatic. She should be good for a couple of times, at least. You'll have to let me know. I always wondered what she'd be like, you know, horizontally."

Jim's nose was instantly crushed from the impact. Blood spattered onto the floor. He flew backwards off the counter and into the serving area behind it, shattering a stack of clean coffee cups.

Before I could blink Charlie was atop the counter and jumping down onto

Jim, who lay writhing on the floor, holding his nose as blood spewed freely from it.

"Charlie! Charlie, stop it! Stop!" I screamed, afraid he'd kill him. "Ted! Help me get him off!"

Ted had dropped the pie on the counter and rushed behind it. "Charlie! Charlie! It ain't worth it. Get off of him or I'm gonna bash this stool over your head!" Charlie had Jim pinned to the floor, one of his thick hands around Jim's neck. Jim writhed in agony, clutching at Charlie's strong hand. He made horrible gurgling sounds as he tried to draw breath. He began to turn blue.

"Charlie, let him go," I begged quietly. "Charlie, I'll explain everything if you'll just let him go. I'll take you to her."

Charlie's grip relaxed, and Jim gasped loudly for breath. Ted, who hadn't been kidding about the stool, set it down slowly. "Come on, Charlie, let him go. I'll call the police. As long as you end it here, I'll just say you were helping me deal with an unruly customer. If you stop here, it will be alright. If you don't let go, it's going to be more trouble than you want. Let it go, Charlie."

Charlie let him go and stood up. His face looked awful. I'd never seen murder in a man's eyes before and it startled me. He glared at me. "Let's talk. Out in my truck, not here."

He didn't wait for me to respond and nearly kicked the door down as he went out. I was a little afraid of him. I'd never seen him like this, and I wasn't sure what to say. My heart was pounding against my ribs as I got to the door of his large green rig. He sat in the driver's seat and pushed the passenger door open. It took me a few tries to figure out how to get inside, but I found my footing and climbed awkwardly in. He stared straight ahead, breathing heavily. His mouth was set in a firm, unbending line.

I stared at him for a minute, trying to decide what to say. "Charlie, I'm sorry I didn't tell you before. I lied to you. I thought I was doing Laura a favor. It wasn't meant to hurt you in any way. I hope you understand that. I feel like you're part of my family, and I want more than anything for you and Laura to be happy. Laura loves you, Charlie, I know she does, but…"

Charlie still stared straight ahead. I tried to continue, but he interrupted me. "What was he talking about? What's so wrong with Laura?"

I took a deep breath. I had to get it right this time. I had to say what would clean up all this mess. I wanted him to love her anyway. I wanted him not to care, but deep down I knew this was probably the last time any of us would ever see Charlie. Schizophrenia was too big an obstacle. No one could look it straight in the face and willingly take it on, unless they were crazy, and Charlie struck me as a reasonable man.

"Charlie, seven years ago, I was called down to the clinic. Laura was there, and she…she wasn't herself. She acted so strange, so unlike herself. It was terrifying. She was engaged to some jerk named Clance. I know she didn't want to marry him, but she was afraid of him, see? He was mean, and Laura never had much self-esteem. She wasn't going to back out. I knew she wasn't, and I'd been praying for her, trying to get God to stop her . . . and he did."

Charlie was looking at me now, his eyes boring into my face.

"He took her mind, Charlie. She was diagnosed with schizophrenia." There,

I'd said the word.

Charlie just stared at me.

"She's been battling it for the last seven years, and it's been hard for her. She's lost almost all her friends. No one knows how to act around her. Even some of my own family avoid her."

Charlie had an odd expression on his face. I wanted more than anything to know what he was thinking as he sat staring at me.

"She's had to work so hard, Charlie. She graduated from college! I mean, that's something, isn't it? She's never given up, not once, except…" I paused, taking a deep breath, "except when she realized she had to tell you. She couldn't stand the thought of losing you, Charlie. You're the best thing that ever happened to her. I hope you know that. She gave up on you, Charlie. She didn't want you to have to take all that on. She did it because she loves you." I realized then that I'd begun to cry and wiped the tears away that had been streaming down my cheeks. "She didn't want you to have to decide, and it was too much for her to decide, so she gave up, Charlie. About a week ago she quit taking her medicine . . . and now she's sick."

I realized then that Charlie was crying as well. It just about tore my heart out to see that wonderful man cry. It was one thing for a woman to cry, and another altogether to see a man do it. I couldn't stand it. "I'm so sorry, Charlie. I didn't mean for things to end up like this."

He wiped at his eyes. "What do you mean she's sick?" "I mean she's lost her mind again. She's not herself."

I watched him as he digested what I'd said. Suddenly I felt very unwelcome in his truck. "Listen, I know I've dropped a bomb on you and I'm sorry. I understand, really, I do. So will Laura. I'm sorry I didn't tell you sooner. I better go. It's late."

I let myself out of his truck. He didn't move to help or stop me. He just sat there in his rig, high off the road, clutching his steering wheel tightly with both hands.

When I called the next morning, Ted told me what I had been dreading. Charlie's rig was gone.

Chapter Twenty-Five

"I believe that God knows exactly what we're made of, and that this life isn't spent proving anything to him, but to ourselves. We find out how strong we are, just how much we can stand. God knows ahead of time that we'll pull through or he wouldn't give us the trial in the first place. He does it out of love, to show us that yes, we can get through it, that yes, we're stronger than we thought. Most times the overcoming doesn't involve a mountain or a storm or some tragedy. It means just plain getting over ourselves."

Grandma's words came to me that night as I lay in bed thinking. I almost felt her in the room with me, thought I could smell her stale lipstick and Oil of Olay. It wasn't so much that I could see or hear her, it was more that I could feel the same feeling I always had when I was with her.

It had been another trying day. Laura still had not responded to anything. We forced another pill down her, hoping for the best, but we saw no improvement.

Daddy came back over to stay with her and was now sleeping on the couch. I'd sent Josie in to sleep with Benny so Helen could have her room.

I lay there feeling so close to Grandma and her sweet wisdom, missing her more than ever. But like always, I felt stronger simply from her words. Somehow, some way, things would work out the way they should. God is never cruel.

I thought of Mama. She had been ever vigilant with Laura. She'd spent the day reading to her and coaxing food and drink into her. She'd even taken Laura to the bathroom several times. She thought of everything, everything but having faith in God. As she'd sat there with her, I could see her despair, and her anger.

Several times she'd snapped at me or at Daddy, whom she still hadn't forgiven for what he'd said earlier.

"Just move, alright? I can do it. Just…go do something else," she snapped impatiently when I tried to help her get Laura to the bathroom.

And we'd all argued about what should be done with her.

"I just think we should take her in to Pleasant Hills. We don't know what we're dealing with here," Harold had kindly suggested.

"No, I won't have her in that place again!" Mama had shouted, startling all of us. "I can take care of her better than they can! They don't care about her! Look what happened to her last time she was there!" Mama's head shook terribly. "I'll pull her out of it. We just have to be patient."

For the time being, we let her have her way. It was odd, but it always seemed that once Laura was admitted to the mental hospital, for a while she only grew worse. We never knew if it was just a matter of timing, or if that place had a way of bringing out the worst in people. It was almost like those who'd been checked in just gave up once they were surrounded by other crazy people.

And so we waited, and hoped, and some of us prayed.

There was one small miracle that day. It was Helen, who held her tongue.

Harold carried Laura to her bed when the rest of us were exhausted. We all turned in for the night after a hard day, but I doubt any of us slept. Harold was not snoring so I knew he was still awake.

Suddenly, I heard the sound of bare feet walking across the wood floor. I got up and looked out into the hall. It was Laura. She was up and walking!

"Harold! Harold! She's up!" I whispered.

He instantly stood, throwing the covers to the floor. We followed her quietly out into the living room.

Daddy saw her coming and quickly sat up. "Laura?"

She was crying. "Daddy, I had a bad dream. I'm so scared. Can I sleep with you?"

Daddy's arms swung wide and he welcomed her onto his lap where she crawled like a child. He hugged her to him, tears streaming down his cheeks as he rocked her back and forth while she sobbed.

He gently stroked her hair. "What was it about, Lolly?" he asked, using her childhood nickname.

"I don't remember, but I was so scared. Hold me, Daddy."

"Oh, I will. I'll hold you as long as you want, Baby Girl. You're gonna be alright now."

Mama came out into the living room and stood at the end of the hallway watching. I could see she was relieved, but a little hurt as well. After all her hard work and service to Laura, she'd gone to her daddy for comfort.

"Can I get you anything, Laura?" Mama asked.

Laura shook her head before nuzzling up against Daddy's beard.

Mama stood and watched them together a moment, her head still shaking, then turned and walked back down the hall.

Harold and I went back to our room.

"Harold, did she seem okay to you?" I asked.

"Well, she's up and around, not like a zombie anymore."

"I know, but I mean, did she seem like she was…"

"No, Nan. I don't think she's out of the woods yet if that's what you mean."

I sighed. I thought the same thing. At least, though, she'd managed to pull herself out of the nightmare that had kept her trapped for almost two days.

The next morning, I awoke to the pleasant smell of pancakes. Daddy made absolutely the best pancakes in the whole world and I smiled as I snuggled against

Harold under the covers. It was a Saturday, so Harold wouldn't be going to work. We could all be together.

I got up a few minutes later and yawned as I walked into the kitchen.

"Mornin,' Nantucket," Daddy said, looking up from the griddle. "I got some hot and ready for you."

He handed me a plate of steaming golden-brown pancakes. "Syrup's on the stove. You're the first one up, 'sides me anyway."

It was going to be a perfect morning, complete with Daddy's homemade syrup. I even put some butter on my pancakes, not caring about the calories. As I chewed my first sweet mouthful, Laura emerged from the living room.

"Mornin' Laura!" I said thickly, my mouth a little full.

"Hi Nan."

Laura came and sat down at the table. She leaned her chin against a hand and watched me eat.

"Are you hungry?" I asked.

"Yes, but I can't eat."

"Why not?"

Laura's eyes grew very serious. "It'll kill me if I do. I just better not."

Suddenly the pancakes tasted like ashes. Laura wasn't going to be alright. It would not be a perfect day.

"Laura, these are Daddy's Saturday morning special pancakes! You love pancakes!"

"Not anymore," was all she said before she got up. "I just can't eat them today."

Daddy looked desperate for a moment. "Laura, I made these for you. If you want to get better, you have to eat."

"Who says I want to get better? Maybe I like being crazy!" she yelled at him. "Maybe I like everyone being just a little afraid of me! Maybe I like no one knowing what to do with me! You all expect so much out of me, and it's just…it's just crap! I'm crazy, see! I can't do some things! I won't! And I won't eat those damn, stupid pancakes!"

Laura reached out and flung the plate Daddy had been offering her. It shattered on the floor. Suddenly Laura burst into tears.

"I'm sorry, Nan! I'm sorry!" she sobbed, getting down on her knees to pick up the broken pieces of the plate. "I didn't mean to break your pretty plate! I didn't mean it. That was dumb, just dumb, I know. I'm so dumb sometimes!"

I knelt down beside her and tried to stop her from picking up the sharp pieces. "It's OK, Laura, it's OK. It's just a plate. I don't want you to cut yourself.

Don't worry about it."

But Laura continued to pick them up. Suddenly she jumped back as a sharp piece cut into her thumb. She watched in horror as blood began to trickle from the cut. "Oh, I'm bleeding!" she whispered. "I'm bleeding! That means I might die! I might die Nan!" She sounded panicked, but suddenly her voice changed.

"That's OK. Sometimes I wish I was dead anyway."

"You're not going to die, Laura, not from a teenie old cut on your thumb.

Now calm down. Let's get it cleaned up," I said as I helped her off the floor and guided her to the sink.

I held her thumb under the cold water and watched as her blood washed down the drain. The cut was actually quite small once I got a good look at it. "See, that's just a little bitty scratch. Hardly even noticeable. Now, stand here and hold it under the water while I get you a Band-aid."

When I returned, Daddy was standing next to her with his arm around her.

Laura was crying. "I just don't want to be here anymore, Daddy."

"Well, you can come and stay at our house. We'd love to have you."

"No, I just don't want to be HERE anymore. I want to be with Grandma."

"Well, we'd miss you too much, Laura. We need you here." he said, squeezing her shoulder. "Please, Laura, please just try."

"OK," she said then. "I'll eat some pancakes."

For the next few days, we tried everything. We continued to give her the medicine and we took turns staying up at night with her. She seemed unable to sleep. That had all of us worried.

One night when it was my turn, I sat by her on the couch watching an old movie. Laura wasn't inclined to talk much. Every once-in-a-while she'd get up and wander around as if she were looking for something, then she'd sit down again.

"What's on your mind, Laura?" I finally asked.

She fidgeted for a while with the couch cushions before responding. "You told him. I know you did. He's going to leave me, isn't he?"

I'd heard her ask that question before. A lump came to my throat, and at first

I couldn't answer her.

"I don't know if I can stand it, Nancy."

I knew I couldn't, but Laura was stronger than me. "Laura, he just might leave. I don't know, but I do know that you can stand it. You can stand anything!

I swear, you are the strongest girl I know. If he doesn't come for you, well then that's just fine. You'll go on and get a nice job. You have a bachelor's degree, remember? You can do anything!"

"I don't want him to see me like this."

"Well, that's just fine. Don't worry about it. Just work on getting your head straight. Don't worry about anything else."

"You worry enough for both of us, Nan. You worry too much."

"I know. I can't help it. I just want everything to turn out nice, that's all."

"I think maybe you should check me in to the mental hospital. I don't want to feel anything anymore."

"Well Laura, if you're sane enough to think that, maybe you're going to be just fine. I mean, a couple more days, and maybe you'll snap out of it. Isn't there a saying somewhere that says if you think you're going crazy, you're probably not?"

Laura chuckled. It was nice to hear it. "It's when you think everyone else is crazy that you should really be worried."

"That's right," I said, glad to be changing the subject. "Is everyone else in this house crazy?"

Laura suddenly became serious. "A little."

I burst out laughing. "Yeah, I guess I am running a regular nut house lately."

Laura giggled. "Maybe we should put a sign out front."

"Maybe. I could charge admission."

Laura sighed. "I don't want to be a burden to you, Nan. Don't you think you have enough?"

"You're not a burden to me, Laura!"

"Yes I am. I'm a burden to you all the time, even when I'm well. I didn't want to tell you this before, but I've been having horrible thoughts. I'm afraid of what

I might do. I'm afraid of what they're telling me to do all the time."

"What do you mean?"

"Sometimes I think I might hurt someone."

"Are you angry at us?"

"Sometimes."

"Laura, I'm so sorry about that day when the storm came and I thought you'd hurt Marie. I know you wouldn't do that. You think I don't trust you, is that it?"

Laura was quiet. "I don't trust myself, Nan. I mean it. I want you to take me in to the hospital tomorrow."

"No, Laura! You know what happened to you last time you were there!"

Laura's eyes brimmed with tears. "I let that happen, Nan. I let him take advantage of me. I just didn't care at the time. It wasn't 'til later that I…I felt…dirty."

I never wanted to believe that Laura had been raped that last time she was there, but it had always nagged at me. I realized then that it didn't matter if it really happened or not. In Laura's mind it was real, and the emotional repercussions to her and the rest of us who loved her were the same.

"Oh, Laura," I sighed. "I just don't want to take you there. It's like admitting defeat. I feel like you can pull yourself out of this one."

"No, Nan, it's not admitting defeat. It's admitting I can't do it by myself, and you can't do it by yourself. Depression is ugly, Nan. Schizophrenia is ugly, and I don't want you all to have to see it anymore. Let people who don't care about me one way or the other take care of me and clean up my messes."

"Laura, what you're saying doesn't sound crazy to me! It sounds like you're using your head."

"Nancy, I can't turn them off. I'm hearing voices almost all the time, even now, and I want out of here before I do something I can't fix. Please, Nan." As she spoke she clutched a throw pillow tightly.

She sounded desperate, but I could see Laura in there struggling to get out. It seemed like she was so close, and checking her in always meant taking two steps back. They'd heavily drug her at first. Then if she acted out, they'd isolate her. It wasn't a good environment to get better in.

"Just one more day, Laura. I know you can do it. Please, just give us one more day to help you!"

"What does one more day matter? I'm a schizophrenic! I'll always be a schizophrenic! Charlie isn't coming back! I know it. I know things, Nan. Just because I'm crazy doesn't mean I can't know things that are important."

She got up then and started to pace, her footsteps following a distinct pattern on the floor. She began to count. "Four, five, six, seven…that's how I'll get to heaven…nine ten eleven twelve…go too far, I'll go to hell."

"Laura, what are you doing?"

Suddenly she stopped and looked at me. "What?"

"What was that you were saying?"

"I wasn't saying anything. Are you hearing voices too, Nan?"

The following morning, I called my parents together for a meeting in my living room. Harold, I knew, would at least be on my side in what I wanted to say. Laura was in her room with the door closed.

I took a deep breath. "Laura is not improving. I think we all know that, and I think we all know what the next step needs to be."

Mama looked angry. "No, Nancy. If it's too much for you, I'll take her home with me. I'm not going to see her in that place again. Absolutely not! No. I'm putting my foot down. No."

"Mama, it isn't your decision to make."

"Well, just who the hell do you think you are? I didn't raise you to talk to me like that!"

"I think I'm the person here who's willing to see what's right in front of her face! Laura isn't getting better because she doesn't want to."

Mama slapped me across the mouth. Tears sprung into my eyes. Even more than the acute sting on my skin was the embarrassing hurt of being slapped by my mother in front of everyone, including my children. Suddenly I wasn't grown up at all, just a little, ashamed girl.

Harold took a step toward her then stopped himself. He put his arm around me and walked me out of the room, leaving Mama alone with Daddy. Benny and

Josie followed us.

We sat together on the bed and could hear them arguing in the other room.

"Dora, you are out of line this time. I want Laura better just as much as you do, but you're not doing anything to improve the situation. You had no right to slap Nancy in her own house. She's a grown woman Dora, and so is Laura.

Shame on you!"

"Shame on you, George! You want to give up on her and put her in a place we all know isn't safe! You just don't want to face her. You just don't want to deal with her!" Mama's voice was shocked and hurt. Daddy rarely spoke to her this way.

"Dora, you know that isn't true."

"No, I don't! I think you're just too scared! You can't stand to see anyone act a little crazy! You can't stand to be married to me. I know you blame me for

Laura's problems, and that's just fine, but I'm not going to be the one to desert her in there. You hear me! I'm not going to do it!"

Mama broke down sobbing then. "I won't do it. I can't." she kept saying between sobs.

I wondered if Helen could hear us. She hadn't come out of her room. I wished she wasn't in my house right then. I just didn't want anyone to see us like this, at our very worst.

"Dora," I heard Daddy say quietly. "It's time for us to go home. I think we've wore out our welcome for awhile."

Mama continued to sob. "I'll get Laura's things."

"Dora, no you won't. Nancy is right. We're all just fooling ourselves if we think we know what to do with her. We don't."

I came back out and peeked sheepishly into the living room. Mama was glaring at him, then tried to push her way past him to the hallway that led to Laura's room. He stepped in front of her.

"No."

Mama tried again to get around him, but he picked her up bodily and carried her out the front door. She struggled at first, then melted into his arms, sobbing against his chest as he walked out to their car.

"You did the right thing."

I turned to face Helen, who had come up behind me.

"This is a hard thing, Nancy, and you're doing just fine. I want to be able to help. You know, I could drive her there if it's too hard on you."

"Oh, Helen," I sighed. "I'm just so tired."

"Come on now, Honey, sit down. Let me get you something to drink." As she spoke, she steered me to the couch and pushed me gently, but firmly down into it. "Just take a break for a minute and catch your breath. I'll get you something cold."

She returned after a few minutes with a glass of ice water. "You're getting a little low on groceries, I see. I'll have to stop by the Supersaver this afternoon and pick up a few things."

"Helen, you don't have to do that. You've done enough."

Helen sat down heavily next to me. "No, I never can do enough. I'm so sorry,

Nancy, Honey. I feel so awful, and here I am staying with you. 'Course I don't have the slightest idea where else I could go. I never could stand my own sister.

We were never close the way you and Laura are. I just feel like I can't do enough to let you know how much I appreciate you. Goodness knows you can use a hand, so I'm here to give it. The condition of that bathroom alone is enough to inspire divine intervention!"

I looked up at her and could see a sparkle in her eyes. She was teasing me. I didn't know she was capable. Surprising myself, I leaned over and hugged her.

I could tell we both felt a little awkward afterwards. "So, what are your plans for your house?" I asked then, desperate to fill the uncomfortable silence.

"Oh, I just don't know yet. I had homeowner's insurance on it, so I guess I'll file a claim. I had so many pretty things, though, Nancy. Things I can never replace." She shook her head. "But you know what? I don't care near as much as

I think I should. I almost feel giddy. I get to start out fresh, and you know how much I love to shop."

She sighed then, suddenly in a reflective mood. "I do miss Lars, though. I can't excuse what he did, but I miss him. I miss having someone to look after.

Just let me know if I go too far in looking after you. Just kick me right out the door if I get under your skin, OK? Sometimes I just can't help myself."

Something she'd said got into my thoughts and stayed there, forming an idea that was almost frightening. I kept it to myself for the time being, afraid to vocalize what might prove to be a horrible idea. I'd have to think on it some more.

Harold came back out into the living room with the kids. I could tell he'd been doing some explaining to the kids. Josie came and sat next to me.

"Does it hurt, Mommy?" she asked, putting her hand over my mouth.

"It won't if you kiss it better for me," I said, hugging her.

She reached up then and kissed me. "Grandma didn't mean it, Mommy. She's just wore out. That's what Daddy said."

"Yes, I know Sweet Pea. Now, why don't you and Benny go outside and play for a bit. We've got some grown up things to discuss."

After they'd gone out, I knocked softly on Laura's door. She opened the door slowly. I could see she'd been crying.

"What's wrong?" I asked.

"We never took a picture."

"What do you mean?"

"I don't have a picture of Charlie! Could you draw me one?"

My heart had had just about all it could stand in one day. "Laura, I'll try, maybe later. Right now, I want to talk to you. Could you come out here in the living room?"

It was a long drive to Pleasant Hills. Theo came over, and he and Harold stayed to watch the kids while Helen and I took her in. It felt odd to spend a Sunday morning doing that instead of going to church, but I was sure God would understand.

Helen drove. I sat in the passenger seat, and Laura sat quietly in the back, watching the barren field where the pump jacks bobbed up and down, unceasing.

Several times I pulled down my sun visor so I could see her in the mirror. She didn't say anything, just looked out the window.

I ached for her. She was on her way to a place most people would never even see, a place most people would like to deny even existed. Laura knew every room in that place. Depression is ugly, she'd said. Schizophrenia is ugly. It was, but Laura wasn't. She looked more beautiful to me than ever in her confused sadness as we silently drove along the highway, admitting this thing was out of our hands now, and trusting that it was in God's.

Chapter Twenty-Six

"Theo, you didn't mean to kill him, did you?" I finally asked when he joined me out on the porch. I couldn't stand the way we'd become so distant and formal since the funeral, so I decided the best way to get over it was to go right to it.

Theo sat down heavily and sighed. "I don't know, Nan."

"Well, I mean, it wasn't like you sat there thinking, 'I'm gonna kill him' was it?"

"Nancy, I'm sorry you have to know about all that. I've been thinking on it lately. You can't just set something like that aside. Believe me, I've tried. I was thinking maybe I'd turn myself in. You know, as my retirement plan. Room, board, food…it's very tempting, and all on the state of Texas." He was joking, making light of things like he always did, but his eyes were hard.

I put my hand on his arm. "Theo…"

"Listen, Nancy. I wanted him dead. I wanted him dead for years. I'm no dummy. I knew what kind of hell my sister was living in. When I saw him hit her that last time, I just decided it was enough. I made sure it was enough."

"But Theo, I can't believe that you were a cold-blooded killer that night. I just can't believe that. It was self-defense, only you weren't defending yourself. You were defending Grandma because she couldn't."

He put his head in his wrinkled and worn out hands. "That may be, but he's dead because I killed him. Nancy, I'm going to be honest with you. I'm glad he's dead. I've never wished him alive once. I just wish I wasn't the one that did it, that's all. There's a price to pay when you break a law and a commandment. I've been paying it for years but my money's been counterfeit."

"No, it hasn't. You gave Grandma freedom. Freedom had to come at a price, right? No matter how bad you feel, Grandma was better off because of what you did."

Theo rubbed his eyes in an attempt to hide his tears from me. "Nancy, you can't make this thing clean."

"No, it's dirty as hell, but think for a minute. You're old, Theo. What makes you think I want to spend my hard-earned tax money to house some old fart like you who wouldn't hurt a fly anyway?"

Theo chuckled. "You better watch that mouth there, Miss Nasty. I noticed your little potty mouth has been getting worse lately."

"I know. Been hangin' 'round you too long."

We sat together in silence for a while. I sighed. "I miss Laura. Can I just talk to you for a while, Theo, just to get some things off my chest?"

"Hold on a minute. I'll get us some lemonade. It's too damn…dern hot out here to be spilling your guts without a little nourishment."

When he returned, I talked for quite a while, mostly about Charlie.

Finally, I said, "I think Charlie would have killed him. I could see it in his eyes.

It was terrifying. But he didn't. I mentioned Laura, and he backed off."

"He's a good one then, better than me. Alice begged me to stop, but I didn't."

Theo was quiet for a long time before he shocked me with what he said next.

"There are times I do believe that God is in cahoots with the devil."

"Don't let Helen hear you say that. She'd say it was blasphemy!"

"No, just listen once. Now see here, take Adam and Eve for instance. There they were, lollygagging around the Garden of Eden, naked as jaybirds. Then along comes Satan and gets them to take the fruit, and bam! They're kicked out.

Satan laughs. He thinks he really put a wrench in the works. Now some will say that's the fall of man, and at the hands of a woman no less. But I don't see it that way. I don't see that they were doing anybody a bit of good just skipping around there naked and not knowing what's what. Here's what I mean: I don't believe for a minute that God couldn't stop Satan from coming into the garden there.

He let him in, knowing full well what would happen. That was the only way. He let them choose, and guess what? Thousands of years later, here we all are. Satan didn't know it, but he did us a favor."

I nodded, beginning to understand his meaning.

"Now, this Jim fella, or Satan, whatever you want to call him, came in there and made a mess for you, thought he was going to hurt you and Laura and Charlie. He was just mean. But see here, Charlie knows now. Nothing we can do about it. But, thanks to Jim, Charlie will see what kind of a creep would abandon a person when they need him most. In fact, Charlie bashed his nose in! Now think on that, Nancy girl. He'll come around. For the first time since he met her, he's going to be allowed to choose what to do. He won't be any Jim, or Clance either, for that matter."

I thought a moment before asking, "You know what he told me, Theo?" "Who?"

"Charlie. He told me he can't read." "Good. That's good."

"I don't see how that's good. I think it's just awful. It's so sad . . . a grown man with a handicap like that. What do you mean, good?"

"Here's how I see it. Laura is flawed. No way 'round it. Sweet as she is, she's got something wrong with her. Somebody without a handicap of their own would never understand. Don't get me wrong. I think she deserves the best. What I'm saying is, you need to be with someone who will understand you ain't perfect. Sounds to me like Charlie needs to be with someone who would understand that, too."

I sure hoped he was right. "Theo, I love you. You know that, don't you?"

He chuckled. "Course you do. Who couldn't love an old toad like me? I'm so ugly I'm darn near cute."

I took a deep breath and tried to find the words for the idea I'd had a few days ago.

"Theo, how are you making out in that big old house by yourself?"

"I'm gettin' by."

"Are you eating good? Have you cleaned out your toilet any time in the last two weeks?"

"Now hold on a minute. What are you getting at?"

"I just want to know something. Has it even occurred to you to scrub out your toilet?"

Theo eyed me suspiciously. "Is this a trick question?"

"No, I just want to know."

"Well then, no."

"That's what I thought. I was over there yesterday and I could tell. A woman notices things like that."

Theo was watching me. I grew nervous as he scrutinized my face. "You helped take care of Grandma all those years, but in truth she took care of you, too. Am I right?"

He nodded, tears in his eyes.

"So, here's the deal. You can tell me if I'm absolutely crazy if you want to. I was thinking of someone who's wearing out their welcome in my house. Now, mind you, it's cleaner than it has ever been. But still, I want to be in charge of my own place, and Helen's got my canned goods alphabetized for Pete's sake."

Theo was shocked, I could tell.

"Now hear me out first. She's got no place to go. She's got just a ton of money, and yet she still hasn't filed a claim against her property. I don't think she ever wants to go back there. She thinks I need her, Theo, so she's staying. I don't.

But one thing I know for sure—she needs somebody to take care of. It's in her nature. And you need some taking care of. You're getting to be quite the old fart.

I mean it."

Theo threw back the last of his lemonade like he would a shot of whiskey, fortifying himself. "Nancy, that there is one doozie of an idea."

"I know. It's just a thought. Don't answer right away. I haven't said anything to Helen. Just think on it."

It had already been a week since Helen and I had taken Laura in. She'd requested that we not see her for a while. Though I honored her decision, I hated not knowing how she was doing.

The day we arrived I noticed that old "Psycho Joe," as Laura called him, was spending some time there again as well. I took comfort in that for some reason and asked him to watch out for her. He'd been honored that I'd asked him. He saluted me as we left.

Meanwhile, the lake had disappeared. The sun bore down without mercy 'til the expanse of white clay became crazed, broken into a million pieces.

I thought of Laura almost all the time. I felt guilty. It seemed that it was my fault this time. I knew it was her decision to quit taking her medicine, but I realized that I was the one who had brought things to a head.

At first, I couldn't understand why everything had gone so out of control 'til I realized what I really had done. Laura was a person of integrity. She didn't like keeping a secret like that from Charlie. She was waiting for the right moment when she would know everything was going to be OK, like Grandma had said. When I lied to Charlie, I did something she couldn't stomach. It was bad enough to not tell him, but it was unbearable for her to lie to him when she'd come to love him like I knew she did. That's when she realized she had to tell him, and she'd grown afraid. She couldn't face it. She'd rather go crazy than tell him the truth.

"Nancy?" I heard her familiar voice on the other end of the phone. "Laura! How are you?" I asked, relieved to be hearing from her at last. "I'm OK, I guess. Grandma's been coming to see me."

I didn't know what to say. At least a delusion like that wouldn't hurt anybody. Finally, I responded. "What does she say when she comes?"

"She mostly talks about Helen. Isn't that weird?" "That is weird," I said, playing along.

"She keeps saying that she and Helen are the same."

"No, they're not! There never were two more different people!"

"I know, but she just keeps saying it, though. I guess she knows now about

Lars and how he hung himself. I guess maybe she's saying that because of the way

Grandpa died. Only he didn't kill himself. Somebody murdered him."

"Did she say who did it?" I asked, my heart pounding.

"No, she won't tell me that. You know what else she said? She said to tell you about the banty hen."

I got goosebumps. Now that was nonsense! It sounded like complete nonsense, 'til I remembered what she'd said about the hen on the walnuts. I was quiet for a long time as I tried to gather my thoughts. I shivered. Grandma and Helen the same? It didn't make any sense. But then again, Laura very often didn't make any sense.

"Nancy, are you still there?" she asked, sounding agitated.

"Yes, I'm here. Sorry."

"Will you come see me?"

"I would love to! When do you want me to come?"

"Today. Could you bring me some sandals?"

"Sure, why?"

"Somebody here stole mine. I've been barefoot for two days."

As I drove, I thought about what she said. I pictured Helen perched on a nest of walnuts, and I pictured Grandma doing it. The circumstances were different, but both were living a delusion, both trying to make something out of a relation- ship that was as false as believing that walnuts would ever hatch. Grandma had said just before she died, "Tell Helen it isn't worth it."

I'd often wondered what on earth she'd meant by that. Now I was beginning to understand.

Suddenly I realized something else that was the same. Theo. Theo saved Grandma, and now Theo would save Helen! I thought about it for a while, then frowned. Helen didn't need saving, Theo did. They were both hopelessly flawed. They both had a terrible thing behind them that no one else would understand. Theo's words came back to me. "You need to be with someone who will understand you ain't perfect."

I arrived at Pleasant Hills sooner than I expected. I'd been so caught up in my thoughts, the miles had sailed by. I wondered if I had even been watching the road.

I went to the front desk and asked for Laura.

"Sign in here," the nurse said, handing me a clipboard.

"This is new. Guests have to sign in now?"

"Yes, we want to keep track of visitors. We only allow those who are on the list provided by the patient."

"Why?"

"It's to protect our patients." she said, taking the clipboard back. "Laura is in room 107."

I smiled as I walked. I felt better about Laura staying here. Obviously, some changes had been made.

I knocked on her door and waited. No one answered, so I opened it a crack and peeked in. Laura was in a rocking chair gazing out the window. "Laura? It's me. Can I come in?"

Laura turned to me and nodded, then looked out the window again. I sat down on her bed. "How have you been?"

She rocked slowly back and forth before responding. "It's a green rig. I've been watching for it. I saw one that was greenish blue today. It wasn't his, though. He might drive by. I mean, it's a public highway out there. There's a lot of trucks."

I noticed her bare feet as she pushed herself gently in the rocker. "I brought you some shoes, Laura."

Laura looked at me, her eyes hazy. "He might drive by. He doesn't know I'm here, but I'd know it was his truck if he drove by. I'd just watch it, that's all. Just watch it go by."

I knelt down at her feet, slipping the shoes on and trying to work the buckles.

I tried my hardest not to cry. I wanted to cheer her up, not mope right along with her. "Do these fit alright?" I asked, my voice catching.

Laura looked down. "Those aren't my shoes."

"I know. I bought them for you. Do you like them?"

Laura studied her feet. "I guess. I had my other ones worked in, though. These are a little stiff."

"Well, we're just going to have to work them in then. Let's go for a little walk," I said, holding my hand out for her. "Come on."

Laura got up, still looking out the window. "I might miss him, though. I've been watching for two whole days. I didn't think of it before."

"Well, I think a little break wouldn't hurt. I bet he's not on this highway today anyway."

Laura chewed her lip thoughtfully. "OK."

We went out into the hedged courtyard. Others were out there, some with visitors, some alone. Laura walked slowly, like an old woman.

"Laura, do your feet hurt?"

"No, I just have to be careful with these new shoes."

"Why?" I asked, confused.

"I don't know," she said, suddenly brightening. "That's dumb, isn't it?"

"Yep."

Laura burst out laughing then and decided to run. I followed her.

"Look out!" she hollered, laughing. "Crazy woman running! New shoes! Crazy woman running in new shoes!"

She ran around the courtyard twice then stopped, panting. "Boy, I'm tired," she said, collapsing onto a bench.

I sat down next to her. "Did Grandma come to see you today?" I asked.

"Grandma's dead, Nan."

"I know, but you said…"

"Look!" she shouted, interrupting me. "There's my shoes!"

I looked in the direction she was pointing. An older woman, probably in her sixties, was walking along talking to herself, and sure enough, she was wearing

Laura's shoes.

Laura got up and marched right up to her. "Give me back my shoes, Edna! I know you stole 'em."

"I did not! You gave them to me! You want them back? Fine! You're an Indian giver!" she shouted, throwing the shoes back at Laura.

Laura stood there, stunned. "I think I did give them to her. I might've. I can't remember."

Edna stomped off barefooted while Laura stooped to pick up the sandals. "Edna, wait!" she called, running after her. "Look! I've got new shoes. You can have these, OK?"

Edna stopped and eyed Laura mistrustfully. She took a cautious step toward her. Laura held out the shoes for her. Edna swiped them from her like a hungry, shy dog takes a biscuit. She ran to the next bench before sitting to put them back on.

"That woman is crazy," Laura said, watching her walk away, resuming the conversation she was having with herself. "Everyone in here is crazy. Pleasant Hills, my butt. Crazy Hills is more like it."

When we got back to her room, a tray of food was waiting for her.

"When did they start delivering food to your room? Don't you still eat in the cafeteria with everyone else?"

Laura went to sit on the chair and began poking at the food. "No, I'm just special, that's all. I get my lunch brought to me."

"Well, that's nice, I guess," I said, a little confused. We'd passed the cafeteria on the way in, and there were quite a few people there already starting their dinner.

"No, it's not. They just don't want me in there, and they always give me stewed spinach. They know I don't like it!"

"Well, why don't you ask if you can get your own food?"

Laura sighed, then started to laugh. "I wish you could have seen it, Nan."

"Seen what?"

"The food fight I started. Can you imagine? A whole cafeteria full of nuts throwing food around! It was the funniest thing I ever saw!" She fell onto the bed, laughing hysterically. "I mean, peas were flying like bullets, chunks of cottage cheese splatting all over…" She gave herself over to another bout of laughter.

I started to laugh, too. I could just see it.

"They all thought it was so much fun. I started it. I knew they'd like it. It was a good idea, don't you think? This food flies better through the air than it does out your backside. I mean it, Nan. I've never been so constipated in my life."

I burst out laughing then. Laura always made me laugh. She had an odd sense of humor like Theo.

As she laughed, she glanced out the window. Suddenly she stopped. "I missed it! I missed it, Nan!"

I got up and looked out. I could see a truck, but only the trailer, not the cab.

"How do you know? Was it green?"

"I don't know, but I bet it was. I bet it was! I missed it!" She wrung her hands and sat down again.

Just then there was a soft knock at her door. She didn't look up but sat staring out the window again.

I got up and opened the door. It was Joe. "Hi Joe!" I said. "Laura, Joe's here."

"Go away Psycho Joe."

He looked hurt. Tucked under his arm was a small boom box. "But what about our dancing lessons?"

"I don't feel like dancing."

Joe came in and sat down, adjusting his giant glasses. I wondered how old he was—fifty, maybe sixty. It was hard to tell. He had an odd sort of agelessness about him. As he sat there pouting, I thought maybe he was forty. He wore the same dark green robe that had become a part of him in my mind, and his eyes loomed large and sad behind his thick glasses.

"You said, 'Seven o'clock, come dance with me Joe.' That's what you said."

"I did?"

"Yes, you did!" he insisted, adjusting his glasses once again. "And I even brought us some music."

"What did you bring?"

"Glen Miller, best stuff ever made, and a few others."

Laura eyed him a moment, then turned again to the window. "I guess there's no point in me sitting here."

"None that I can see," he responded. "Now, this here's called A String of

Pearls," he said, pushing the play button.

She stood and took his extended hand. It was obvious that Joe was an excellent dancer as they whirled to music that made your feet dance almost by themselves.

Laura began to smile as they danced. I loved the way she looked dancing with him like that. It was such a hopeful smile, such a joyful look in her eyes as she spun in and out of his arms. It was obvious they'd been practicing. They were both out of breath as the song ended. A String of Pearls was followed by jagged, mournful piano music.

"I don't like this one," Laura said then. "It's sad. What's it called?"

"Basin Street Blues, Louis Armstrong."

The irony of it struck me forcefully as I watched the two of them cling to each other, two people at the bottom, together in the bitter basin.

As the song went along, the beat picked up a bit, sounding almost cheerful, almost hopeful, but the couple in front of me danced slower, clung tighter to each other. Laura hugged him the way I'd only seen her hug Daddy, and he didn't pull away. As they turned slowly, their feet moving out of sync with the final drums, I just barely heard her whisper, her voice sounding like a wistful, frightened child, "You won't leave me, will you, Joe?"

Chapter Twenty Seven

I came in to see Laura again a few days later. I went directly to her room. She wasn't there. I saw a pile of crumpled papers on the nightstand by her bed and walked over to them to see what they were.

I picked up the torn page at the bottom of the pile and squinted at it, trying to make out what she'd written. It was a jumble of scratched out lines and smudges. From what I could make out, it was a poem.

Why can't I see you again?

I wanted and loved only you.

How does it feel to love again?

It hurts. I still think about you.

You'd think it would help to forget. I can't seem to manage that one yet. I don't like to regret

The strange day that we met. Should I say "Hi" if we meet? Think of it then, and don't give in, If our eyes and hands meet?

Memory stay–I'll smile, and never give in.

Glance, but not fall into your eyes. Facing the truth, not lies.

Hearts beat apart, tumble and still rise

Singing softer, sweeter, I fly.

After that there was a jumble of scribbled out phrases smudged by what I could only guess were her tears before the final stanza:

It's just nonsense that I spill out on paper Noise is all that sings from metal and wood. An expression is all I get back.

What was it I gave?

I drew a deep and ragged breath, trying my hardest to get a hold on my emotions, trying to quell the bitterness that rose indignantly inside me. Bitterness because she was so sweet and so confused, and it just wasn't fair.

Where was he anyway? I'd allowed myself to hope he wouldn't abandon her, yet we hadn't heard a thing from him. I realized that I never did know where exactly he lived.

I went back out to the front desk to locate her. I asked the nurse where she was.

"Oh, that's right. I'm sorry," the blonde woman behind the desk said then. "I'm so sorry I forgot to tell you."

"What?" I demanded. "What is it?"

"We had to isolate her again. We couldn't get her under control this morning.

It would be best for her, I think, if you didn't try to go and see her right now. I'm sorry you drove all this way."

I turned around and started to walk out. I was furious. Sometimes anger is the only emotion that seems to give any comfort.

"Wait! Mrs. Parley? I've been meaning to ask you something."

"What?" I said, hating the harsh sound of my voice.

"Well, I'm under the strictest orders not to allow anyone in here to see her who isn't on the safe list. I just can't make any exceptions. But there's a man who came in several days ago that wanted to see her. I had to turn him away."

"Who was he?" I asked, my heart suddenly light as a feather.

"I don't know, I can't remember. He told me his name, but I forgot it. I just remember the look on his face when I had to turn him out. Is he a friend of hers?"

"What did he look like?" I demanded, my heart pounding.

"Well, he was tall, and he wore a white Stetson."

I turned and ran out the door, leaving her thinking craziness just might run in the family. I got into my car and pulled out, my tires squealing as I headed for the highway.

The entire drive home I was craning my neck at every semi I passed or that passed me. I got smiled at, stared at, and hollered at by the various truckers I attempted to run down. I almost veered off the road when I realized suddenly that I'd forgotten to tell the receptionist to add him to the list. Sometimes I could strangle myself. I sped all the way home, impatient to get to my phone.

When I got there, Helen was hollering at the kids.

"Now listen, I don't care who did it, you two are going to clean it up!"

I walked into the kitchen and found a horrendous mess. It looked like Benny and Josie had attempted to turn the refrigerator inside out.

"But we were having a picnic!" Benny insisted.

"I don't care what you were doing. You're gonna stop and pick this up! This instant!" she said, stomping her foot.

The children sulkily got up from the floor.

Helen saw me and gave me a withering glance. "You tell them, Nancy! They just won't listen to me!"

I ignored her and headed for the phone. "Anybody call?" I asked.

"Not that I know of, but we were out to the park for a while. Now listen,

Nancy, these two just think they can get away with anything. I mean, you're just gonna have to start putting your foot down. And it's not just this, either. Benny won't flush the toilet, and half the time he misses anyway!"

I noticed there was a blinking red light on the answering machine. I pushed the button, craning my neck to listen over the racket Helen was making.

"Nancy, I mean it! Are you listening to me?" she demanded.

"Shut up Helen! Let the kids have their damn picnic! Just shut up a minute!"

I'd shocked her to silence. Her lips all but disappeared, though her eyes looked like they'd pop out of her head.

I leaned closer, waiting for the message. I thought I could hear static, maybe a rush of wind. I leaned in even closer and heard a familiar sound, the sound of traffic, then nothing. The machine beeped and that was the end of it.

"Aaaaghhhh!" I screamed in frustration. "Why didn't he say something?!!!"

"Who?" Helen demanded as I picked up the phone and dialed Ted's Take a

Break.

I fluttered my hand irritably, trying to get her to be quiet. "Shhhhh!"

Helen threw up her hands and went to the living room.

It seemed like hours passed between each ring. Finally, Ted picked up. "Take a Break," he said brightly.

"Oh, I wish I could, Ted. Listen, this is Nancy. Have you seen Charlie?"

I could just see Ted scratching his half bald head. "Now let me see. Yeah, he was in a few days ago. I gave him the number to the mental hospital where you told me they were keeping Laura. He said he'd tried to call you, but no one was home. I had to look it up in the phone book."

"Bless your heart, Ted!" I said. "Bless your heart!"

In my excitement I didn't realize at first that I'd slammed the phone down and hung up on him. I hit redial. He answered almost immediately.

"Hi, me again. Call me as soon as you see him, will you? I mean, the very minute he walks in that door!"

"Alright," he chuckled. "How is Laura?"

My excitement ebbed. I sighed. "She's not doing too good. It's like she's given up."

"I'm sorry to hear that. We sure miss her around here. Every trucker comes in here wants to know what I did with that cute freckly waitress. You tell her I'm holding this job for her."

"Thank you. Well, let's just hope we can find Charlie."

"I'll call you if I see him," he promised.

My heart was soaring. I felt giddy. I grabbed a bag of multi-colored mini marshmallows and tore them open, flinging them up into the air like confetti.

"What on earth?" I heard Helen exclaim behind me. "Nancy Parley, you feeling alright?"

I whirled around and hugged her. She pushed me back, forcing me to look at her. "Listen, why don't you go lay down for a while," she suggested.

"Maybe I will, but I have to make one more phone call first."

As I sat up that night, unable to sleep, I thought about Charlie. I couldn't get him out of my mind. A little after midnight I heard crying coming from the nursery. I pushed the covers aside and went to get Marie. I sat in the rocking chair in the dark as she nursed. Feeding

Marie always had a calming effect on me. I felt like cobwebs were being cleared from my mind as I rocked back and forth, trying to remember something that I knew was important.

After a while she dozed, spilling the milk out the side of her mouth. I stood and put her back into her crib.

There it was again, that feeling that I was supposed to do something. There was something I was supposed to do. I wandered out into the living room, hoping that being in the right room would help to jiggle the memory loose from my mind. I walked to Laura's room and cracked open her door. I sat down and looked at her bare walls. She never did hang any pictures in there, even though I told her she was welcome to. I guessed she didn't have very many.

There it was! Suddenly I remembered. Laura had said the day she left that she'd never taken a picture of Charlie. She had nothing to remember him by and she'd asked me to draw one for her.

I got up and ran down to the basement. I headed to the farthest corner to an old blue trunk where I stored my art supplies. I hadn't done much of anything since college. It smelled musty as I threw back the lid. I rummaged through the chest, trying to find my sketch pad.

Suddenly I heard footsteps on the stairs. I whirled around, startled. Harold was squinting down at me. "Nancy? What are you doing?"

"Oh hi, Harold. I was just trying to find my sketch pad and some of my pencils."

"What for? It's the middle of the night, Honey. Why don't you come to bed?" "Because I can't sleep anyway. I just have to do this right now."

"It'll wait 'til morning, won't it?" "Absolutely not."

Harold stared at me a minute. "Are you feeling OK?" "I'm fine, why?"

"Well, you're acting strange and Helen said something to me today when I got home from work. You sure you're OK?"

I looked up at him as he walked down the stairs, deep concern in his eyes as he watched me.

"Think I'm going crazy?" I asked.

He walked across the floor to me. "Are you?"

"I don't know. I just might be. I'll tell you in the morning. Now leave me alone. Go on up to bed, will you?"

He stared at me a moment as I turned again and knelt to rummage through the trunk. Finally, I heard him turn and walk back up the stairs.

I found my box of drawing pencils and charcoals, but I had to dig further 'til I finally found my sketch pad, which was at the very bottom. I picked it up and flipped through it, looking at my mediocre renderings of figures and objects. I sighed. This was going to be hard I knew it.

I sat for quite a while just holding the pencil over the paper, staring at it. It felt awkward. I was afraid maybe it had been too long. Plus, I didn't have the object I wanted to draw standing in front of me. Several times I tried to sketch a face, only to tear it out and crumple it up. Finally, I burst into tears at my lost talent and threw the sketch pad across the floor. I put my head down into my hands. I couldn't do it.

I just cried for a while. It had been too much lately. I felt like I was being stretched so thin I was at my breaking point. Laura had to get better. I didn't want Charlie to see her at her worst if he did come back. I had such a feeling of panic, such a feeling of doomed failure as I sat on the cold cement floor. I couldn't see him, so I couldn't draw him, and if Laura couldn't see him, she wouldn't get well. Despair was ugly, too.

I sat for a long time, letting the cold of the cement floor creep up into my body. I felt so alone 'til I heard a voice so distinct it could only have come from inside me.

"We all have our bad times. Sometimes you're a jerk and sometimes you're nice. Sometimes you can do it and sometimes you can't, but that's what families are all about. You take turns, you balance. One of you gives up, one of you digs in. That's how it works."

Grandma had left me another pearl, woven intricately into my being, like the perfect stitches that came together as her hands flew with her knitting.

"One of you digs in," I said quietly.

Laura had given up. That meant I had to dig in. I picked myself up off the floor and walked over to the sketchbook. It was lying open to the very first page where I'd scrawled something a long time ago.

Draw what you know, not what you see, until you understand what you're seeing, and then you can draw it.

I closed my eyes.

Chapter Twenty Eight

I vaguely remembered Harold carrying me to bed sometime during the night. I wondered if I'd gone crazy. I remembered sketching something, something beautiful. I'd become so caught up in it, I felt almost obsessed. I'd felt, for the very first time, like an artist. Someone told me once that the creative process was a form of insanity and I felt like I'd gone through the mill that night. I finally opened my eyes and found myself in my bedroom. So, Harold had come and brought me upstairs. I hadn't dreamed it. Then I remembered the sketch pad. Where was it?

I sat up and swung my legs over the side of the bed, then realized painfully that I had a dreadful headache. I sat still a moment holding my head, then stood. I looked around the room, but it was nowhere to be found.

I must've left it in the basement. I dreaded climbing down the stairs with my head throbbing, but I started down anyway. As I descended, I could see it lying flat on the floor in front of me. I slowed down with each step I got closer. I was almost afraid to look—afraid to see what I'd done in the middle of the night— afraid to see that what I had done came from a diseased mind, not an inspired one.

I stood over it for quite some time then bent slowly, the blood rushing to my head causing it to throb. I picked the pad up and climbed the stairs again. I would look at it in the sunlight.

I went out onto the porch and sat down, cradling it in my lap as I flipped slowly past the first few pages of sketches.

I stared at the drawing for a long time. Finally, not trusting what I saw, I called to Helen. "Helen, could you come out here please?"

She didn't respond. I went inside to look for her. I heard strange sobbing coming from my bathroom. I went in and found her down on her hands and knees scrubbing the floor around the toilet, sobbing uncontrollably. Her large bottom quivered in her efforts as she plunged wholeheartedly into the task. It was both grotesque and pathetic.

"Helen, stop. It's clean enough," I urged, not looking at her.

She reached over and blew her nose into some toilet paper. "No, it's dirty,

Nan. This whole floor is just…well, it's a mess. I can't rest 'til it's clean."

I watched her as she resumed scrubbing. "Are you alright, Helen?"

She responded by dumping more cleanser onto the floor. "Good grief, Nancy!

This floor is j-just the dirtiest I've ever s–seen. Why do you let it g-get like this?"

She'd begun to hiccup between sobs the way Benny did when he was all worked up. "You really ought to be ash-sh-shamed of yourself! How any woman could l-let her floor go like this is just…"

She stopped talking, her whole body wracked with sobs.

I grabbed a sponge and got down beside her. "Well, I guess it is pretty bad," I lied. I began to scrub, too.

"Helen," I said quietly. "It wasn't your fault."

Her chin trembled as new tears poured down her face. She looked at me as if stunned, then bit her lip before tackling the floor once more.

I put a hand on her back. "I appreciate you doing this, Helen. When you're done could you come outside? I need some fresh air. I have a headache."

It was a long time before Helen emerged, wiping her hands on her apron as she stepped out the door, all business and no nonsense once again. "What is it?" she inquired, coming closer. Suddenly she stopped in her tracks and drew a deep breath. "Oh, my…" she said as she came to stand behind me. Several times she started to say something then stopped. Finally she whispered, "I wish someone would look at me like that. Nancy, that gives me goose bumps. It's like he's looking right at me. Is that...yes, it is. It's that man who's been seeing Laura, isn't it?" She sat down next to me and took the sketch pad, studying it closely. Her eyes positively sparkled. "You drew this? I can't believe it. For Pete's sake, Nancy, I think I'm going to cry!" She sniffed for a moment, then asked, "How draw that without even seeing him? Is this what you were doing last night?"

A lump had come to my throat. It was good. In fact, it was beautiful. Somehow, in the dim light of the basement I'd managed to catch the look he had in his eyes the first time I'd realized that he loved her. It was when we were all down there hiding from the storm hearing Laura sing.

"Yeah. That's what I was doing."

"No wonder you have a headache! I can't even imagine having the concentration to do something like this." She stared at it a while longer. "I don't have any talent like you do, Nan. I can clean, though. I'm awful good at that."

"Well, we're just wired different, I guess. I sure wish I was as good a housekeeper as you are."

"I'd trade you in a second," she said, getting up as Theo's truck pulled up into the driveway.

Theo stepped out and walked straight toward Helen. "I've got a proposition for you, Helen."

I smiled. Theo had been considering what I'd said. He stopped about ten feet in front of her and spat, then kicked dirt over the wet spot he'd made on the ground. Helen cringed.

"What is it, Theo?" she said hesitantly.

Suddenly he lost his confidence and reached down into his pockets, his head bent. Finally, he looked up. "I'm 79 years old. My back's been aching me, I can't kick this derned cough, I can't hardly see the morning paper, and I think my prostate is shot."

"You want me to drive you to the doctor?" she asked, eyeing him in confusion.

"Well, it may come to that since my vision is going, but not today anyways.

I've been thinking on it, and I realize I've got a lot to do around that house—a lot that sometimes I even forget to do. Nancy tells me my toilet is shameful. Alice took care of that stuff." Theo cleared his throat. "What I'm saying is, I got a room you could have there at my place, if you want it. I guess I might just need a little help now and then."

I knew it was hard for him to admit it, just like I knew it was hard for him to accept that he wouldn't be able to drive much longer.

Helen's eyes narrowed. "Are you asking me to marry you?"

For a moment I thought Theo's eyes would pop right out of his head. Then he threw his head back and laughed so hard I was just sure he'd pull something.

"Land sakes almighty, woman!" He shouted, clutching his stomach and continuing to laugh. "What do you take me for? I'm old enough to be your daddy!"

"Well, then what on earth do you want from me, 'cause I sure don't need anything from you!" she shouted, angrily. I could see she was mortified. I wondered if her first proposal had sounded something like that. I wouldn't be surprised.

Theo wiped his eyes and tried to suppress his laughter long enough to say, "I was just wondering if you wanted a place to stay."

"I can get my own place to stay, for goodness sakes! I'm not some kind of charity case!" Helen's eyes looked like they might burst into flame any moment as she shoved her glasses higher up her nose. "Besides that, it ain't decent for a woman to just shack up with a man! What would the neighbors say? I am shocked, just shocked! Shame on you Theo!"

Helen stomped into the house, slamming the door. Theo looked at me and shrugged.

"I haven't laughed like that in years!" he said, still chuckling. "That old sour puss thought I wanted to marry her! Lord have mercy on us all if it ever came to that!" he said, between chuckles.

"Well, Theo, if it ever comes to that, you'll have to work on your pitch. I don't believe most women would consider the mention of your prostate and your toilet the height of romance."

Theo shook his head, his eyes sparkling. "That old girl…I could sure get to arguing with her, don't you think? If she were to stay at my place and act like she owned it, we surely would get to butting heads! I'd have myself a good argument once in a while. Hell, we'd argue 'most every day!" Theo's eyes continued to sparkle as he leaned over and spat again. "Nancy, you are one intelligent girl. I haven't had me a good argument since Alice…" He nodded, suddenly silent.

"Yes, Nancy, it will do."

We sat on the porch for a while, Theo nodding occasionally to himself and trying to suppress a chuckle. My head still ached. Finally, Theo asked, "What's that you've got there, Miss Nasty?"

I silently handed him my sketch book. He opened it, flipping through the pages, chuckling at some. "Not a person in here has a stitch of clothes on." He said, eyeing me.

"Well, in school that's the way we drew them. We had to understand the human body," I said, a little embarrassed.

Theo's eyebrows went up as he continued to flip through the pages. I held my breath, waiting for him to find it.

Suddenly he stopped and leaned back away from it, holding it out in front of him. He studied it for a long time. Finally, he raised his eyes to mine. "Miss Purty, I do believe you've become an artist. That there is fine! Mighty fine! You gonna give this to Laura?"

"Yes. I was hoping that maybe if she could see him, she'd try to get better. It's like she's given up."

Theo knit his eyebrows together in concentration, still staring at the drawing. "I didn't want to say anything before, Nancy, but if he doesn't come…this might make it harder on her."

"Oh, I forgot to tell you! I was such a mess yesterday. Guess what? The receptionist over there said a man came by and tried to see her, but they turned him away because he wasn't on her safe list!"

Theo looked up from the drawing. "And you think it was…" "She said he was wearing a white Stetson!"

"There are more Stetsons in the state of Texas than ears of corn in Iowa, Nan."

"I know, but I just know it was him. It had to be. I'm willing to gamble on it." Theo leaned back, still looking at the drawing.

"I'm going to try and see her today. Would you like to come?" I asked.

"Nah, don't believe I will. I'll take one step through those doors and they'll lock me in for sure!"

Later, as I fed Marie, my mind raced. There had to be some way to get hold of Charlie. I just wished I could figure out how. I wished Marie would hurry so I could get going. As I sat fidgeting, Benny and Josie came into the room.

"Mommy," Josie began, "we made something for Aunt Laura. Will you give it to her?"

As she spoke, Benny pulled a paper plate from behind his back. It was loaded with chocolate chip cookies. "Helen helped us," he said proudly, "but I put the chocolate chips in!"

"Oh, my!" I said. "That's just perfect! I'm sure Laura will love them. Thank you, Baby!" I said hugging him. "Come here, Josie girl! Thank you, Sweetie. I'll tell Laura you two made them, alright?"

Josie stood in front of me with her eyebrows knit in concern. "Mommy? How come Aunt Laura is sick?"

I wasn't sure how to answer at first 'til I remembered something Daddy had said once. "You know, Josie, how you get a cold, and things go a little wrong with your body?"

She nodded solemnly. "Like when my nose is runny and I have a fever?" "Exactly. Well, Laura is sick in her brain, not her body. It's kind of like her brain has a cold and isn't feeling too good. She needs to take medicine and be with doctors right now 'til her brain gets better."

Benny was listening intently, too. "How does your brain catch a cold?" "I don't know, Baby."

Before I left, I called Pleasant Hills to make sure I could see Laura. The receptionist didn't think it was a good idea. Laura was out of isolation but wasn't talking to anyone. She just stayed in her room.

I decided to go anyway. I hoped I had the medicine she needed. Just before I stepped out the door, Helen stopped me. "I found this, and I thought it might...well, just give it to her for me." She shoved a small box into my hand and pushed me out the door.

As I drove, I kept careful watch of the semis on the highway around me. I knew I was breaking the speed limit, but I just had to pass each one I came to, hoping to see that green cab. I got there in record time but with no luck finding Charlie.

I struggled to get through the doors, what with a plate of cookies in one hand, and the picture I'd matted of Charlie in the other, along with another surprise that had come in the mail. I signed in, flipping through the list carefully, hoping to find his name, but I didn't. I sighed. He wouldn't just give up, would he? I looked down at the picture I was holding. No, no he wouldn't. I could see it in my charcoal rendering of his eyes.

I found Laura in her room, lying in bed. I put my gifts down on the bedside table and shook her gently.

At first, she didn't respond. Then she slowly rolled over, saw me, and pulled the covers over her head.

"Laura?"

She ignored me.

"Laura, Benny and Josie made you some chocolate chip cookies."

I watched her still form under the covers. It didn't move at first, but then slowly she pulled the covers down. She sat up quickly, tucking her mussed and now frizzy dark hair behind her ears. "Chocolate chip?" she asked.

"Benny put them in all by himself."

She reached out and took one, eating it very slowly. "This is good," she mumbled as she ate. "We hardly ever get cookies in here. Balanced meal, balanced mind..." she quoted.

Laura reached out for another one and spotted the picture I'd leaned against the wall on the table. I'd turned it so it was facing the wall.

"What's that?" she asked, pointing with a cookie.

"I made something for you, too." I hesitated, wanting to say it right. "Remember when you said that you wanted me to draw you a picture...of Charlie?"

As I spoke, I turned the picture around slowly, afraid of her reaction. I just didn't know how she'd take it.

She stared at it. The cookie she held dropped to the bed. As I watched her dark blue eyes, I saw at least ten thousand thoughts crossing them. She looked like she was trying to get the picture in focus, like she didn't believe what she was seeing.

I couldn't stand it, so I asked, "Do you like it?" She nodded, her chin beginning to tremble.

I watched her tears roll down her cheeks unheeded as she stared at it. I thought for a moment that I was breaking her heart again. I hadn't meant to do that.

"Laura, you have to work on getting yourself out of this. You have to try to get better. I drew this so we could put it on your wall in here, so you could see it and try to get better." My voice was shaky, threatening to crack, but I would not let myself cry.

She continued to stare at the picture.

"Laura, he wants to see you. He hasn't left you. He came in here, but they wouldn't let him in. You forgot to put him on your safe list!"

Laura looked stunned. "Is he here?" she whispered.

"No, he's not. I don't know where he is. We have to find him, Laura. But first you have to find yourself."

"I don't want him to see me like this."

"I know you don't. That's why you have to work on getting yourself better.

Have you been taking your medicine?"

She looked guilty. "Sometimes."

"Laura!" I said, exasperated. "You have to take it all the time!"

She bowed her head then, looking ashamed. "I'm sorry, Nancy. That was dumb, wasn't it?" She sighed. "Sometimes I'm really dumb."

"Well, when you're sick, not taking your medicine is pretty dumb." I hated the sound of my voice, but I continued. "Do you want to be sick? Do you like living in a nuthouse?"

She'd begun to cry again, but she shook her head, sniffing. I reached for a tissue and handed it to her. "Here, blow your nose."

She did. Then she looked around, not sure where to dispose of the used tissue.

I took in from her and shoved it in my pocket without thinking.

"Listen, Laura. You're sick, and you always will be unless somebody finds some miracle cure. In the meantime, you have to take whatever medicine you can get for it." I cupped my hand under her chin. "You are stronger than you know.

You can get better. Trust your doctors, take your medicine, and say your prayers, you hear?"

I remembered my other surprise and pulled it out of the bag. "Laura, I want you to see what you did. That's your name on there. You did that, you hear me?" I handed her the diploma that had come in the mail that morning.

Laura was looking at me intently, like she was devouring every word. I don't even think she blinked, so I continued. I picked up a small plastic dish that sat on her table. "See this? It's a basin, right? It has a top, and a bottom, with smooth sides, see?" I took a cookie and let it slide down the side to the bottom. "This is you. You slipped and fell in. You're stuck down here at the bottom, and guess what?" I took another cookie and held it over the edge as if it were peering down at the other. "This one's Charlie. He can't come down into the basin with you. You don't want him to, right? You have to get up and get yourself out."

Laura nodded and climbed out of bed. She propped her diploma against the wall then walked across the room and shut the door. She knelt down by her bed. "Will you pray with me, Nan?"

As I stood, something fell out of my purse that I'd perched on my lap. It was the box from Helen. "Wait, I forgot to give you this."

I stood over her as she opened it. It was a small brass plaque. Laura's face began to glow as she read it. I peeked down over her shoulder. In beautiful swirly letters it said:

Faith:

God never would send the darkness

If he felt we could bear the light.

But we would not cling to his guiding hand

If the way were always bright;

And we would not care to walk by faith,

Could we always walk by sight.

Anonymous

Laura nodded slowly as she read it. She clasped it tightly between her hands and held it in her lap. I'd never been more proud to call Helen family.

I got down beside her on the cold tile floor and bowed my head, listening to her talk directly with God. I had the familiar warm, peaceful feeling again of being certain that He was listening.

Chapter Twenty-Nine

For the first time since Laura had checked in, Mama called. I'd been too afraid to call her. I knew she didn't think I'd done the right thing.

"Nancy?"

"Hi, Mama. How are you?"

"Oh, I'm alright, I guess."

She sounded sort of distracted and distant. During a long and quiet pause, it seemed that we were both holding our breath.

"Nancy?" she asked then.

"Yes, Mama?"

"I'm sorry I slapped you. I didn't mean it."

I struggled for a moment to find something to say. "I know you didn't. It was a hard day for all of us. It's OK, Mama."

Though she didn't talk again for a while, I knew she was crying. I could tell by her staggered breaths.

"Mama?"

"I just wanted to protect her. I just wanted to do what was best for her. She's my child, and I wanted her close to me. When you girls were little and one of you got hurt, I just held you to me. I stroked your hair and kissed your hurts. After a while, you were fine and wanted to go play again." She paused to get hold of her emotions. "I guess I don't like to admit that what she needs is for someone else to take care of her."

"Have you gone to see her?"

"I did yesterday. That's a beautiful picture you drew, Nan. Laura showed it to me. She seems…she seems better."

I hadn't gone to see her for the last couple of days. I'd been so busy with the kids that I hardly had time to think. "What do you mean?" I asked, curious.

"Well, she was pretty upset about a pair of sandals. We got her calmed down about that, but she doesn't seem to be so distracted now. She said a lot of things that made sense. I can tell she's trying."

I was relieved. I felt that if she could just stay on her medicine and see the counselors there for a while longer, we'd have Laura back home with us.

"That's wonderful. I can't wait to go see her again. You take care, Mama. Tell her if you see her before I do that we'll have a party for her when she gets back."

"Have you heard from Charlie?" she asked then. "No, I haven't."

"Well, let's give him some time, I guess. You take care too, Honey. Bye bye."

I called Ted several times over the next few days, but he assured me that Charlie had not been around, and that he would have called me if he had.

I didn't quite understand. If he had come once, why wouldn't he try to come again or call us? Did he think Laura didn't want to see him? Had he given up, or was he just sorting things out? I said silent prayers daily while I did the dishes or folded laundry, or whenever it struck me, asking God to bring him back to us, to let him know he was welcome.

At lunchtime Theo showed up wearing the wrinkliest pair of plaid pants I'd ever seen. They looked like he'd got the legs wet and then tied them in knots before hanging them up to dry.

"Well, hi there, Theo. What's new with you?" I asked, trying not to stare at his pants.

"Oh, not a whole lot," he responded nonchalantly.

I looked into his eyes and saw the familiar mischievous sparkle I'd come to miss. He most definitely had something up his sleeve. I noticed, speaking of his sleeve, that his shirt had several stains on it and was missing two buttons.

"Where's that old girl?" he asked.

"Oh, you'll find her out back hanging my sheets on the line. She washed every last one of them in my linen cabinet. She said they needed some air. Honestly,

Theo, she's got this place in complete order. I think she's getting hard up for something to do. She's even trained Benny to flush the toilet."

Before he headed into my backyard, I caught him raking a hand through his white hair, to make it stand on end.

I chuckled. He did look a mess. I realized then what his strategy was. Soon Helen would stay up nights, horrified that there was a man out there wearing wrinkly plaid pants, living in filth, and eating who knows what. Theo was playing his cards perfectly.

I walked out to join them. Helen was busy trying to pretend he wasn't standing there. He regarded her for a moment. "Now, Helen," he began, "you know about cleaning solutions and such and I was just wondering something."

She peeked warily around a sheet. "What?" she asked crossly.

Theo cleared his throat. "Well, I ran out of dish soap, so I used some of Alice's moisturizing shampoo to wash the dishes, and derned if my glasses don't shine like they used to. They got this film on 'em I just can't seem to get rid of. Now, should I soak 'em in vinegar or bleach?"

Helen's eyes bulged. She had strict rules about the proper use of cleaning solutions, and she never, never crossed over, not even to use the shower cleaner for the toilet. Theo had struck a nerve.

"Shampoo?" Helen was obviously having a hard time digesting this heresy.

She cleared her throat. "Well, I've never had that particular difficulty, but I suggest you try the vinegar first."

Theo nodded then stepped into the house, not looking back. If he had, he'd have seen her watching after him, horror and pity battling to take hold on her face.

I smiled. Theo had things in hand. It wouldn't be too long before I could once again, have my house back. As I thought of that, though, I realized how much

Helen had actually done for me, and I hadn't really thanked her properly. She was doing her best to make her amends and doing it the only way she knew how.

Sometimes when I'd get up at night to use the restroom, I could hear her in

Laura's room, sobbing quietly. I supposed she had loved Lars after all, in her own way. I decided to do something nice for her that I was sure she'd never do herself.

"Helen, come on inside and let's have some lunch. I invited Theo over because I caught him eating cold beans straight out of the can for breakfast yesterday when I stopped by." I figured it wouldn't hurt to put my two cents into his campaign.

Helen clicked her tongue as we walked through the back door and into the kitchen.

As I tossed the salad, Helen set about making the sandwiches, and Theo set the table. I smiled as I watched him. One thing that Helen harped about endlessly was the proper way to set a table, even for a casual lunch. She hadn't noticed yet that Theo had rummaged through my cupboards to find the most mismatched of my tableware. He set out mugs to drink lemonade from and used salad plates, which would hardly be big enough to hold both a sandwich and a salad. He put out knives, forks, and spoons, and simply piled them atop the plates. For napkins he grabbed my roll of paper towels from the dispenser and set it in the center of the table.

"I got the table set," he announced. "You girls got the food ready?" Helen turned and flinched when she saw the table.

I called the kids in and set about cutting the sandwiches in half for them. "Hey, I want a whole one!" Benny protested.

"Well, you eat that one first, then I'll give you another half." Benny folded his arms quickly in protest. "I want a whole one!"

While I argued with Benny, Theo was busy spearing his sandwich with a steak knife. Suddenly he stood and walked over to Benny. "Now, boy, here's a "hole" sandwich for you!"

He set the plate down in front of Benny. He'd cut a round hole out of its center. Benny stared at it a moment then held it up, peering through the hole. "Cool!" he exclaimed as Theo took Benny's half sandwich and sat back down.

Josie decided it wouldn't do to have half a sandwich, either, so Theo set to carving another "hole" sandwich.

"You're spoiling them, Theo," Helen warned. "A child should learn to appreciate what's put before him." She shot a glance at Benny, who ignored her.

Theo, meanwhile, had begun dumping half a bottle of blue cheese dressing onto his pile of salad. Helen was quick to notice that as well. "Theo, you sure you need all that dressing? A man your age ought to be concerned with his cholesterol intake. Honestly, have you no respect for your arteries?"

Theo merely grinned as he forked his drenched salad, dribbling some of the dressing onto his shirt. He bent, holding his already stained shirt up to his mouth, and licked the dressing off.

Helen was sent into a sudden coughing fit. For a moment, I thought I'd have to perform the Heimlich maneuver on her, but she got it under control. I shot a warning glance at Theo so he wouldn't overdo it. He smiled, his eyes sparkling.

When She Walked on White Lake

Chapter Thirty

"So, what would you like to see?" I asked Helen as we stood looking up at the cinema marquis.

"Well, I have no idea. I can't say I know a thing about any one of these. It looks like there's two that start at four thirty."

We settled on the romantic comedy. As we stood in line for popcorn Helen fidgeted. "Are you sure the kids will be alright with Theo?"

"Helen, they'll be fine. I'm sure the house will be trashed, but don't let that spoil our date, OK? Harold will be home at five thirty, so really Theo's only going to be in charge for an hour. Besides, we've earned a break, wouldn't you say?"

Helen didn't look convinced and continued to fidget in her purse. We'd already had a huge showdown over who should pay for the tickets. She wanted to pay even though it was my idea.

When we got up to the counter she stepped in front of me and held out a twenty as she ordered a bucket of popcorn and a box of Dots. "You want something to drink, Nancy?"

I ordered a root beer. Helen insisted on carrying the bucket of popcorn into the theater but nearly dropped it when she saw the various discarded lollipops and soda cups scattered all over the floor. She stopped in her tracks. "Nan, are you sure this is a good idea? We might catch some sort of disease in here."

I assured her we would be fine. "I need to use the restroom. I'll be right back." "Please, for Pete's sake, don't sit down in there, Nancy! I mean it! I knew a woman once who swore she got a yeast infection from a toilet seat at Walmart."

When I returned, I noticed she'd gotten herself settled, but she looked sorely out of place. Fortunately, the lights dimmed, and we were immersed in darkness and soon drawn into the latest Meg Ryan film.

As the movie played, I could see Helen really was enjoying herself. It was a good idea. I was glad I'd thought of it.

When the credits began climbing the canvas, we stood and stretched before heading for the exit signs. Helen absolutely refused to throw the leftover popcorn away. She toted it half full out to her car. "We'll bring it home for the kids. Waste not, want not," she quoted. "Besides this thing cost five dollars!"

As we drove out of the parking lot Helen asked, "How do you think my hair would look if I had it done the way hers was?"

"Meg Ryan's? I think it would be cute. Kind of spunky."

"Well, it was certainly cute on her, but I wonder if it would suit me. I'm a lot older, you know."

"Well, that shouldn't..."

I stopped talking suddenly, not believing what I was seeing as we approached the freeway bridge. I squinted. No, my eyes weren't fooling me. That was most definitely Charlie's rig.

"Helen! Get on the freeway! Get on the freeway!"

"What are you talking about Nancy? I never drive on the freeway!"

As she spoke, I took control of the wheel, forcing her car onto the spiral on-ramp.

"Nancy! What on earth is the matter with you?" she demanded, then looked forward again at the on ramp, which we were already committed to. Several cars pulled in behind us, honking. "Nancy! I can't drive on the freeway!"

I thought my brain was going to explode. Already a whole line of cars had come between us and the small white square that was the back of Charlie's trailer.

"Helen, you have to get up to speed! You can't merge going 25 miles an hour!"

I could see Helen was going into shock and that she truly was afraid. "Helen, listen to me. See that semi up there? It's Charlie! We have to catch it! This may be our only chance!"

Helen revved it up to 35. Her knuckles were white.

"Listen, if you don't get up to speed we will most definitely crash. The speed limit is 65, Helen. Everyone else is going at least that fast. Get her going!"

"I can't! I can't!" She wailed.

I stepped on her foot just as we merged and got the needle a hair over fifty. We barely made it as cars zoomed by us.

"Helen, look! You're driving on the freeway! You're doing it! Now give her some more—that's it. See if you can get her up to sixty-five."

"Heaven have mercy!" she exclaimed as beads of sweat began to form on her forehead.

"Heaven is on our side today, Helen, but we're going to need a miracle unless you speed up. The Lord helps those who help themselves, remember? We have to catch him!"

I could just barely see the semi now, and wasn't sure which was his, as there were now three more semis ahead of us.

"Lord, give this Caddy wings," I prayed out loud.

"Amen," said Helen as the speedometer reached 75 miles per hour and Helen passed her first car in her entire driving record.

"That's it Helen!" I cheered. "Pedal to the metal, you speed racer!"

Helen laughed nervously and gave it a little more. We were doing eighty and beginning to close in. Charlie's rig was only three cars up. Just as we passed them and were moving alongside his trailer, I noticed bright red and blue lights flashing in my side mirror. I opted not to tell Helen, who was leaning forward in concentration. I glanced at the speedometer again. Eighty-two. I adjusted the rear view mirror so that it only showed the bucket of popcorn in the back seat.

"Get her moving, Helen! Get us up there!" I urged, trying not to look back over my shoulder.

Unfortunately, the car in the lane ahead of us decided not to go any faster—making it impossible to draw even with Charlie's cab. "Helen, pass him on the right! Pass him on the right! Get over!"

"Just how many traffic laws would you like me to break today, Nancy? For

Pete's sake!" she protested as she swerved quickly to the right. I was watching the rear view mirror as the bucket of popcorn toppled, spilling all over her leather seats.

She heard it and turned to look at the mess. "Oh no!" she wailed, losing her nerve. "Oh no!" she screamed again. "There's a cop behind us!"

"Don't you dare pull over Helen! I'll pay for this ticket myself if I have to!

Catch him, Helen!"

As she drove, she began praying out loud. I prayed with her. Suddenly the white trailer disappeared beside us, replaced by a shiny green rig. We'd done it.

"Wave your arm out the window! You have to make him see you, Helen!"

"That's just it, Nancy! I will not, not at this speed! You want us to crash?" she demanded.

"Honk then!"

Helen pressed down on the horn. Finally, Charlie looked over at us. He only saw Helen and had no idea who she was. He squinted at her then turned again to watch the road.

"Roll down your window!" I commanded.

She did, and the sound of sirens blared in at us, drowning out Helen's voice as she hollered at him. He stared at her, not knowing what to think of this old woman in a Cadillac screaming at him. I unrolled my window and sat on the ledge of the open window. I held on with one hand as the wind whipped viciously at my hair, blowing it into my face. I waved. He saw me, but I knew my hair was getting in the way. I turned my face into the wind and suddenly his eyebrows shot up as he recognized me. I motioned for him to pull over.

When I got back down into the seat, Helen was hyperventilating. I was running on sheer adrenaline myself. "Easy now, Helen. Take it easy. Slow down and pull onto the shoulder there. That's it. Don't brake too much! We don't want to get rear ended!"

Finally, after what seemed like forever, we rolled to a stop. Just as Helen put it in park, she passed out cold.

Charlie brought his rig to a stop in front of us just as the cop got out of his squad car and ran to us, holding his gun. When he bent his square face down to the window, I instantly recognized him. "Oh, no," I thought. "Here we go again." It was the deputy sheriff who had been bursting with self-righteous law enforcement when he'd pulled me over several months ago.

He tapped on the glass. I pushed the button on her side to roll down the window. His face was purple.

"Now just what in Hell do you think you're…"

He trailed off when he realized the driver was unconscious and he looked at me. "What's been going on here?"

I gulped and prepared myself for another bald-faced lie. "I think she was having a stroke. Thank goodness you're here!"

He reached in and took her pulse. "She's alive," he assured me. "Is that why you were hanging out the window?"

"Yes! I panicked. I just didn't know what to do!" I thought for a moment that

I would burn in hell for the lies I'd been telling, but I decided to worry about it later. I could see Charlie walking toward us. "I need some air!" I exclaimed, and opened the door.

"I'll call an ambulance," he said, raising his CB. "Walk around a bit," he suggested. "Helps keep you from going into shock."

I nodded and walked toward Charlie.

"Nancy?" Charlie exclaimed, breaking into a run. "You could have gotten yourself killed! Good grief!"

I was panting as he reached me.

"Are you alright?" he asked, looking down at me with concern in his eyes.

I was feeling a little light-headed. "Charlie, thank goodness. I've been looking all over for you! Where on earth have you been hiding?"

I don't remember what he said, but I do remember his arms around me as I heard a loud buzzing in my ears and had the sensation of spiraling down a black tube.

Chapter Thirty-One

"Have you lost your mind?"

I squinted, trying to get the familiar voice into focus. At first it just swirled about in front of me, a disembodied voice without a face.

"Harold?" I whispered.

He didn't answer. I could tell he was furious. I wondered why he was so mad at me. Then, like a rush of hot air through an open window on the highway, it all came back. I'd been hanging half my body out a car window while Helen was speeding at over eighty miles an hour and a cop was behind us. Yes, I supposed, I most definitely had lost my mind. It sickened me to think of how dangerous and how crazy it had all been. I could see now why Harold was so angry. I'd finally done it—done what he'd been dreading—and gone crazy myself. It ran in the family, after all.

I remembered all of it then—the way the ambulance had arrived, only to find two women perfectly conscious, who'd only passed out from shock. How the cop had a livid, purple face as he wrote out two more tickets: one to Helen for speeding, and one for me for recklessness on the highway.

And I remembered Charlie, whom we'd followed once it was all over to Ted's.

He had left his truck there and drove us back home in Helen's Caddy.

He'd been angry too. He reminded us several times on the way that we could have just as easily been arrested if it hadn't been for the other call that had come through on the cop's CB.

It was funny, though. Helen didn't scold a bit. Of all people, I was sure she'd have been the most angry. I'd forced her into it, after all, but she was silent as we drove home. I didn't know if she was still in shock or saving up her wrath the way she saved coupons, waiting for the right moment to go in for the kill.

I went to bed as soon as we got home. Harold wasn't off work yet. I was absolutely exhausted and didn't want to think anymore. I told Charlie to sleep on the couch, but Theo had insisted he come over to his place and stay with him.

Harold wasn't home then, as we'd planned, he'd had to stay at the lumberyard late and must have arrived after I'd gone to sleep. Obviously, Helen had given him a briefing before he'd come into our room.

He came into focus as he stood over me. I didn't like the way he was looking at me. Harold had always been a little more serious, but until this moment, I'd honestly thought he got a kick out of me sometimes, despite himself.

There was no amusement in his eyes this time. I couldn't even see in them that he liked me at all. I cringed.

"What on earth did you think you were doing?" he demanded. "Trying to get yourself killed?"

Shame bit into my chest with each word he said in that calm voice that had a dangerous quiver around the edges. He was trying his hardest not to explode.

I had no idea what I was going to say. There was no explanation. It was like Theo had said—there's all kinds of crazy. I'd jumped right into the murky water to save my drowning sister. I wasn't killed though, not like those two sweet girls who'd become legend in White Lake. I wasn't afraid of the alkali anymore. I was fine and Laura was fine–everything would go back to normal. I suddenly remembered what the doctors had said so long ago about Laura and I going back to normal. Me after losing my baby, and her after losing her mind. Why do people say the word "back" anyway. Wouldn't that mean we'd been there before? I sighed.

"I did it for Laura." I said quietly. My voice sounded more calm than I expected it to. It even sounded triumphant. I liked the sound of it, so I repeated, "I did it for Laura."

Harold sat down heavily on the corner of the bed. He put his head into his hands, his elbows resting on his thighs. "And what, exactly, did you think you were doing for her?" he asked wearily.

"Throwing her a lifeline."

Harold looked up suddenly, squinting at me as if I were something peculiar he'd found wiggling under a rock. He'd obviously decided I was nuts. I almost wanted to laugh, but I couldn't because he was making me so mad.

"Charlie!" I blurted. "Charlie is her lifeline! Don't you understand, Harold?

She was drowning without anything to hold on to! It's been that way her whole life. She's been drowning with nothing to hold on to, and I almost let her drown!

I left it up to Helen last time because I was too chicken to go out onto the alkali after her. Laura was never as lucky as me! She never had a husband sitting at the corner of her bed, angry as hell and thinking he knows everything while his wife is nuts!"

I burst into tears and then lay down again, pulling the covers over my head. I could feel the warm weight of his body on the bed. He sat there a long time in silence. I wondered if he was looking at me, but decided he probably wasn't. I'd become repulsive to him. No one would want to look at a crazy wife. I decided then what Harold's problem was. He was too perfect, too absolutely normal. I wondered if that was why I'd married him. There wasn't an ounce of crazy anywhere in him. Even Helen turned out to be more interesting.

I understood also, why Harold had never liked Theo. Theo was crazy like the rest of us, only his showed a little more since he had no desire to hide it.

In a desperate moment of insight, I realized that Harold had been fooling himself. He'd been trying for a long time to believe there was nothing wrong with his wife, and then I realized my folly: I'd been trying to prove it to him as well.

I wondered if our marriage was doomed to failure now that things were out in the open like they were. I did love him. I loved his kindness and his seriousness. Between the two of us we'd struck a delicate balance, and I thought maybe I'd disturbed the scales enough to cause the other side to jerk violently in another direction.

I was wrong, though and glad of it when he lay down next to me, pulling my body against his, infusing me with his warmth. He stroked my hair, then parted it and kissed my neck. "I'm sorry," he whispered.

I thought back to the way we'd met. The big misunderstanding we'd had because he'd unknowingly insulted a piece of my artwork—a piece of me— because he didn't understand it. And he'd said he was sorry. I forgave him again.

Chapter Thirty Two

"You're going to kill those hollyhocks?" Helen demanded, stunned.

"Well, yes. I figure I ought to just put them out of their misery. They've been dying slowly since Alice left, and I just can't stand to watch," Theo replied, ready with a shovel.

Grandma Alice's hollyhocks were legendary in our neighborhood. Sometimes they grew almost as tall as her house. She'd always managed to keep them standing up straight, not all bent over like they were now.

"Well, have you been watering them?" she wanted to know.

"Every day. The dern things miss her, I guess."

Helen got out of the car and strode over to Theo, taking away the shovel. She surveyed the ground and poked the shovel in. "Now see here! You're over-watering them! They can't stand up straight cause their roots are in a puddle. Good grief, Theo! Everyone knows hollies need firm ground if they're to stand!"

I watched, amused, from the passenger seat of Helen's car. We had driven over because I wanted to see Charlie and talk with him, and Helen, seeing I was going to Theo's, said she'd thrown together a little something for him to keep in his freezer.

"I can't stand by as a Christian woman and let that man live on cold beans from a can," she said, following me out the door. "It's just not sensible, anyway, to eat like that." She plopped several disposable casserole dishes into the back seat, then pulled out. I noticed she drove almost thirty miles an hour the whole way over.

I got out of the car and walked past them as they argued about the proper way to water. Theo was no amateur when it came to gardening, but he managed to sound like a doddering old fool while Helen lectured him.

I found Charlie seated on Grandma's davenport. He was watching news footage of a mudslide that had taken several beautiful homes clear down the side of a mountain.

I didn't know what to say, even though I'd been up all night thinking about it. But I had to say something, so I sat down and ventured a comment.

"Why on earth would a person buy a home when they know full well it's in a high-risk area?" I asked, shaking my head in disbelief as the news announcer stated that one man in particular had rebuilt his home twice on the same spot.

Charlie looked at me sharply. "Well," he began hesitantly, re-crossing his booted ankles, "Some go into it blind, and set up in a house with no idea what they're getting into–and they're the first ones to leave when it's pulled out from under them." He cleared his throat. "Can't blame 'em, I guess, but you should always know what kind of ground you set up on."

His eyes were strange, piercing, as he continued. "Some are desperate, with no other place to go, and they just buy up house insurance and keep their fingers crossed, or else pretend they don't know what the risks are."

I was beginning to understand what he was actually saying.

"And some understand the risks and build a home anyway, because they're not going to let fear ruin their enjoyment of where they want to be."

I swallowed. "Which kind do you think you are?"

"Oh, I reckon I've been all of them at one time or another."

I was absolutely amazed at his insight. He could have been a poet.

"I was coming back," he said flatly. "You didn't need to go hanging out of a car, risking your life, you know. I was coming back."

I didn't know what to say. I felt pretty dumb, actually.

"I tried it out—not being with her, I mean. I was angry, and I felt tricked. I drove around for days, not going anywhere in particular, missing her, wasting gas and time, trying to sort things out."

"And did you figure anything out?" I asked.

"Yes, I did. I figured out that life without Laura sucks, and it cost me four hundred dollars in gas."

So much for the poet in him, but his feelings were genuine. I chuckled, delighted with him.

He smiled back at me, suddenly sheepish again. "I hope you don't mind too much, Nan, that I'm head over heels for your sister."

I was a little nervous as I drove him to Pleasant Hills. I didn't call Laura first. I wanted to surprise her, but I was still hesitant. I could see Charlie was, too. He sat there biting his nails to the point where I was sure he'd draw blood any minute. I reached over and pulled his hand away from his mouth. "It's going to be fine. She'll love them!" I assured him, and myself.

We passed a sign. "Fifteen more miles," I said. "Almost there." I looked over at him. "Are you OK?"

"I just hope she doesn't hold it against me for leaving. I mean, what kind of a person just ditches somebody like that?"

"The kind you punched in the face and tried to choke." I smiled at Charlie. "Sounds like you gave yourself a good kick in the butt while you were at it, and here you are. Remember, Charlie, she left you first. Fair's fair."

Charlie took his hat off before I knocked on Laura's door. He held it in one hand and a box in the other.

I opened the door and peeked in. She was sitting in her chair crying, looking out the window at the highway.

"Laura?"

She looked over at me and wiped her eyes. "Hi Nan," she said sadly. "I'm still a mess, I guess. I'm trying to get better, but I still get confused. Somebody stole my shoes."

I noticed her feet were bare again. I figured some other woman had them on.

Laura was always a giving person. I was sure she'd simply given them away again and forgotten. I was glad Mama had told me.

"I don't mind, though," she sighed. "Guess I won't be going anywhere for a while." She turned back to the window. "I get so mad sometimes. Most of all I'm scared, though. What if he doesn't…"

Charlie stepped into the room then. "Come back?" he finished in a thick voice.

Laura clung to the arms of her chair. She was too stunned to move. I think he was afraid to move, too. Finally, Laura turned toward him. They were frozen as they stared at one another, but when she finally tried to get up, he strode toward her, clearing the floor in just two steps. He scooped her out of the chair and held her to him, carelessly throwing his hat and his box aside.

I felt like I was intruding. I closed the door and went to get a drink and find a tissue. I was crying, but I didn't care if anyone saw. Joe did, though, and walked toward me.

"Why are you crying?" he asked, his caring eyes huge behind his glasses.

I hugged him. "Just because, Joe. Just because." I knew I didn't have to explain—not in this place anyway. He patted my back.

"Sometimes I get to cryin,' but then I usually can't remember what I'm crying about after I get into it. Makes it easier to stop," he said.

I pulled away and smiled at him. "I forgot already."

When I opened her door again, I found Charlie on his knees in front of her. My heart stopped 'til I realized he was simply strapping on the new pair of sandals he'd bought for her. She was looking down at the top of his head. She reached out to touch him as if she didn't believe he was real.

He looked up at her and smiled. "Shall we break these in?"

I watched from a bench as he walked her around the small garden. She clung tightly to his shirt with one hand, but after a while, he took that hand and put it in his as he bent to kiss the top of her head.

From that day on, I understood what God had in His mind all along, since the horrible day He reached down and took Laura's.

After time, Mama forgave Him, too, and sheepishly stepped into church one

Sunday morning and sat down next to Daddy. He put his arm around her, careful not to make too much of it for her sake, and they shared a hymnal for the first time in months.

Occasionally, I'd get to sorting through my worry box when money got tight or the mortgage was due. Seemed like I didn't look through it as much as I used to, though. So many things just found their way to the back of the box, and never made it to the front. God saw to that. He shuffled those cards better than any dealer in Reno could've done.

Laura quit her job at Ted's and got hired as a peer counselor in a group home for the mentally disabled. They all loved her. Her job was to take them to their appointments, take them shopping, listen to them, and take them out to the movies. Of all the counselors there, Laura was the most beloved. She had been there, and she of all people, could understand.

Meanwhile, I turned thirty and survived the surprise party Helen threw for me, and the endless jokes about me getting old. I bought the whole line of Oil of Olay and started worrying about wrinkles.

One day Laura came home absolutely beaming. I could tell she was just bursting to tell me something.

"It was the weirdest, most satisfying thing…" she began.

"What?"

"Well, I took Carrie—you know, the one who's on Clozaril too—anyway, I took her to the clinic to have her blood drawn and that awful nurse came out and said, 'Carrie, where is your peer counselor? You know you're not supposed to be here without your counselor.'"

Laura was beaming. "She looked right at me, assuming I was next in line for a draw. So, I stood up, and said, 'That would be me.'"

Laura burst into laughter and I joined her. "I wish I could have seen that old bat's face!"

Laura imitated it for me, sending me into another bout of giggles.

"Were you on your way out?" she asked.

"Yes, I found some of Helen's things she left here, so I was going to take them over to her. Will you watch the kids for me?"

As I drove, I thought about what I'd seen the evening before. I knew it wasn't meant for my eyes, but I was glad I saw it all the same. I was doing the dishes, watching Laura and Charlie standing on the back porch as the sun set over the dry lake. It was dry as a bone—bitter, crazed alkali, but the slant of sunlight turned it gold as he got down on one knee and asked, "You wouldn't mind being married to an illiterate trucker, would you? I just want you to be there for me when I come home…to take care of me." His eyes were pleading as he looked up at her.

"What if I get sick again?" she asked softly, her head bowed.

He stood and hugged her, kissing the top of her head. "Then I'll take care of you."

I was still smiling when I pulled into Theo's driveway. The hollyhocks were blooming again and stood as straight as they ever did for Grandma. I still missed her terrible. I got out of the car, carrying Helen's things, and started to walk to the back door but stopped when I passed the kitchen window.

"Damn and Hell, woman!" I heard Theo roar. I had to duck just as several biscuits shot out the window and bounced onto the pavement.

For resources regarding mental illness, please visit The National Alliance for Mental Illness, known as NAMI, at **nami.org.**

www.ingramcontent.com/pod-product-compliance
Lightning Source LLC
LaVergne TN
LVHW021757060526
838201LV00058B/3129